WITHDRAWN

| DATE DUE | | |
|----------|----------|---|
| SE 21 '94 | JA 18 | |
| NO 17 '94 | | |
| DE 14 '94 | | |
| JA 13 '95 | | |
| MY 8 '95 | | |
| JY 2 '97 | | |
| SE 24 '97 | | |
| AP 25 '98 | | |
| JY 8 '98 | | |
| AG 6 '98 | | |
| 4 '99 | | |
| FE 15 '99 | | |
| MR 10 '99 | | |
| SE 17 05 | | |
| MY 18 05 | | |
| MY 18 05 | | |
| MY 02 07 | | |

Demco, Inc. 38-293

# The Lost Kingdom

# CLINT KELLY

A
JANET
THOMA
BOOK

## THOMAS NELSON PUBLISHERS
Nashville

Published in Nashville, Tennessee, by Janet Thoma Books, a Division of Thomas Nelson Inc., Publishers, and distributed in Canada by Word Communications, Ltd., Richmond, British Columbia, and in the United Kingdom by Word (UK), Ltd., Milton Keynes, England.

Unless otherwise noted all Scripture quotations are from THE NEW KING JAMES VERSION. Copyright © 1979, 1980, 1982, Thomas Nelson, Inc., Publishers.

Map by Dale Kegley

**Library of Congress Cataloging-in-Publication Data**

Kelly, Clint.
    The lost kingdom / by Clint Kelly.
        p.    cm.
    ISBN 0-8407-7822-8
    1. Rain forests—Africa—Fiction. 2. Dinosaurs—Africa—Fiction. I. Title.
PS3561.E3929L67    1994
813'.54—dc20                                                                    93-34195
                                                                                  CIP

Printed in the United States of America

1 2 3 4 5 6 — 99 98 97 96 95 94

*For the brave men and women of the*
*International Society of Cryptozoology*
*who aren't afraid to ask "What if?" and "Why not?"*
*Their fire helps keep the God-given spirit*
*of adventure alive and kicking.*

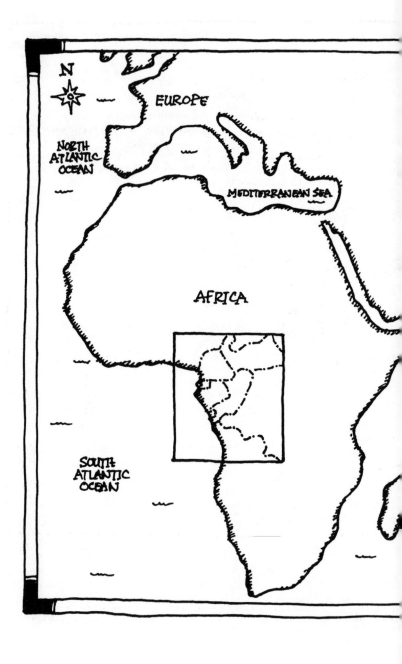

CENTRAL AFRICAN REPUBLIC

CAMEROON

UBANGI RIVER

Lagoon

Ologu Encampment

Sangha Mercy Mission

CONGO RIVER

Epuluville

LiKouala
Swamp
"The lost
Kingdom"

REPUBLIC OF
ZAIRE

BON REPUBLIC

CONGO RIVER

PEOPLE'S REPUBLIC
OF THE CONGO
Brazzaville

Kinshasa

CABINDA

ATLANTIC
OCEAN

ANGOLA

-LEGEND-
MOKELE-MBEMBE ATTACKS

**R**eg Danson stepped into the room, and she smiled up at him. Suddenly he erupted into laughter, the music of it hopscotching across the polished linoleum like kids at play. He was staring at the brand new T-shirt she was wearing for the occasion. At the top, against a powder blue sky, an artist's rendering of Noah's Ark jutted from the side of Mount Ararat. Below that, in brilliant yellow capital letters, was the inscription: ARK-eologists Love Any Old Thing.

He swept forward, laid the carnations on the afghan, and still laughing, gathered the frail old woman in his arms. She smelled of Emeraude and Roses talc; but somehow his mind registered Jergens Mild hand soap and White King D laundry detergent, and he was a child again.

They hugged; she "honeyed" him. Then he held her at arm's length and eyed her reprovingly. "What's this I hear? You've been charged with assault and battery?"

His mother sniffed, a twinkle in her rheumy eyes. "Wasn't any battery about it. Whacked the old guy a couple of times in the noggin, that's all. He had it comin'. I took the bid. Thinks he can break trump before I do, he's got another thing comin'!" She nervously patted the ringlets of her strawberry blonde wig. Ernestine, her hairdresser, paid attention to details. Carrie liked that. Age could steal your hair, but Ernie knew where to find more. "Slap this wiggy on there, Carrie Ann, and I'll make you a new woman," Ernie had said. Carrie had started going to the pinochle tournament after that. Funny how some new siding on the old homestead could make all the difference.

Reg shook a finger in mock sternness. "Is that conduct becoming of a saint?"

Carrie buried her nose in the carnations and shrugged her shoulders. "Well, bub, all I know is the old guy asked me to the rummage sale this Saturday. The sodas are dutch treat, but he promised he'd buy me that butterfly brooch I've had my eye on all week." Her smile was sweet innocence. Reg chuckled and shook his head.

"Carrie Ann Danson," he scolded, patting the dear old hands with their knotted, arthritic joints, "you are *some* case!"

"And just what do you expect?" she retorted, beaming mischievously. "My great-great-great-grandfather was a Methodist circuit rider, a one-man crusade to unstuff the stuffed shirts in the church. Drove him crazy the way some folks would be on the constant lookout for borderline infractions. Out of earshot, he used to say legalists like that objected to fornication only because it might lead to dancing!"

"*Mother!*" Reg exclaimed. "Mind your manners!"

She dismissed his disapproval with the wave of a hand. "Listen, sonny, I still know how to use a knife and fork, so don't get on your high horse with me. Grandpa Thomas would not approve!"

Before he could reply, Reg's mother turned and spoke loudly across the room. "Gussie, this here's my sassy son, Reggie. You might have heard of him. Been in every newspaper and magazine in the country!"

Reg hadn't realized someone else was in the room. In a corner chair by the window was a tiny African-American woman sewing a quilt. She was wrapped to the neck in a beige terry cloth robe that looked two sizes too big. Her hair was as white and fine as spun cotton, and her small brown hands were swift and sure at joining dark cloth swatches of blues and greens and mahoganies with lighter ones of yellow and orange and red. Gussie's lips moved, and her eyes were intent upon the work as if it were a living thing, as if she could speak the quilt into being.

"Hello, Gussie. That's certainly a beautiful quilt you're stitching," Reg proffered, but the woman did not deviate from the work or acknowledge him. Carrie touched his arm and made a face. She tapped her temple knowingly and rolled her eyes. "Not always here, if you know what I mean," she said in a coarse whisper twice as loud as anything else she had said.

The patchwork pieces yielding to Gussie's sure touch were uneven and unmatched, a "crazy quilt" in the African tradition, quite unlike the repetitious predictability of the western European style. African quilts told a story, often a family saga, and were as individual and unpredictable as life is. Those made by slave women of the South might contain bits of sacking, overalls, a dead husband's old bandanna, or a fragment of a pocket torn off a sold child's worn pants. Memory patches they were, a cloth diary of earth's travail. Often they were tear-stained from times of trial and some even contained bloodsoaked bits of cloth torn from the shirt of a loved one whose back had been laid open by the master's whip. A runaway, perhaps, dogged to death, made to pay.

Sometimes the slaves had the last laugh on their owners. Those who served as maids and cooks in the plantation mansion would take what mites of wool, silk, gabardine, stocking, and dress material they could find in their daily duties; secret them inside their aprons; and whisk them out to the slave cabins under cover of darkness. Many a plantation mistress slept with a slave quilt brushing her delicate milky skin that, unbeknownst to her, had been fashioned from pieces of her own life. The old black woman's grandma, Elsie Mary Taylor, said it went to prove plantation masters couldn't "read" neither.

"So, bigshot Danson, you're too famous to visit your old ma?" The love and concern in Carrie's face eased it some, but Reg still felt a twinge of guilt. He'd only seen her once since the Noah's Ark expedition, and now he was going to say good-bye again.

The publicity—no, *pandemonium*—since he and his son, Tony, along with a band of international scientists, Turkish military personnel, and a Moslem cleric, had rediscovered the Ark had been nothing less than frantic. Interviews, speaking engagements, book offers, movie rights, even commercial endorsement contracts had flooded in. He was almost glad to have another assignment so soon, disturbing as this one was.

"Sorry, dear heart, but all the hucksters and curiosity seekers from here to Katmandu have demanded equal time. I know I shouldn't neglect you, but it's your fault I am what I am, you know." He gave her a wink.

His mother sniffed again. "I gave you a sense of adventure, young man, but you took it to extremes." She looked over at her roommate again. "My Reggie's one of those newfangled crypto-whatchamacallits!" she shouted. Gussie continued quilting without pause.

"Cryptoanalyst," supplied Reg, amused. "Hunter and unraveler of earth's unsolved mysteries."

Carrie made a face. "Crypto blipto. I'm still the one who changed your diapers, buddy boy, and don't you forget it!"

There were tears in her eyes. Would she live to see her boy come back from Africa? Why did he have to go into such dangerous places? But she would never voice these questions to him.

Reg smiled crookedly and stroked the back of the hands that had whacked him, caressed him, steered him, and applauded him all the days of his life. "Hey, Ma, why the sad face? Doctor says you're a fighter. What's a little diabetes, a little—"

"Save it, Puddin'," she stopped him. "Everything I've got's in revolt, including my spleen. I haven't lived long enough to find out what a spleen does, but mine doesn't care to do it anymore."

Reg looked away, a lump in his throat. His mother was indispensable.

She'd promised herself they would not get on to her ailments. But here they were, and she'd have to bluff her way out. "In the old days, when a person was angry and melancholy, we'd say he was showing lots of spleen," she said, noticeably brightening. "Now you tell those folks in the Congo that you have a spleeny mother. That's one who is peevish and irritable with hypochondriactic inclinations."

When Gussie heard the word *Congo,* her fingers halted, the needle poised in midair. She turned to the Dansons for the first time and gave them a wide, toothless grin. A joyous, ululating chortle rippled from deep in her chest and came out her mouth with explosive force. She threw her hands high in the air, tipped her head far back, and began to jerk her upper torso in convulsive spasms. Over and over the eerie chortle rose and fell in rhythm with the jerking motion as Gussie swayed to a beat only she could hear.

The hair rose on the back of Reg's neck. His mother looked disgusted and jabbed the nurse call light at the side of her bed.

In seconds, a young woman in a crisp white nurse's uniform answered the summons and made a beeline for the ecstatic woman in the corner. "There, there Gussie, enough of your singing now. These people are trying to have a visit. Why don't you just go back to quilting quietly and save your voice for Brother Williams and the Sunday morning hymnsing? That's a girl. My, that's a nice panel you're sewing now. Is that a giraffe you've got there?"

Gussie said nothing in reply but returned to her sewing as quickly as she had stopped. Her mouth continued its silent conversation with an unseen audience.

"Hmphf!" grumped Carrie. "Oddest body I ever saw. Good thing I've got a boyfriend, or I'd have to talk to myself same as her." Then she leaned close and gave a conspiratorial wink. "Truth is," she said in a low voice, "a lot of it's just for effect. Gets all kinds of attention on slow days. It can get pretty entertaining. But she can be sharp as a tack when she wants to be."

Carrie lay back against the pillows and peered up at her son. "You remarried yet?"

Reg sighed, then chuckled in amused exasperation. His mother and father had been married for forty-one years, and she had been solidly devoted to her family. Conway Danson, an aerospace engineer with The Boeing Company in Seattle, had died of stomach cancer. The six-foot-two-inch, 250-pound giant of a man had been reduced to 110 pounds in four months. For the last month, Carrie had nursed him at home, and Con had died in her arms five minutes into St. Patrick's Day.

Carrie was not about to go on without an answer to her question. She knew there was probably no one else on earth with whom her son could find the partnership he'd had with his wife, Barbara, who had died three years ago. But at thirty-nine, he was as handsome and capable as always. And when he returned from Turkey to worldwide acclaim, some of the mail waiting contained bold offers of marriage from women in France, Germany, Spain, and Switzerland, not to mention just about every state in the U.S.A. Maybe. . . .

She looked at Reg, "out with it" written all over her face.

"What are you looking at?" he said in mock offense. He knew she was only concerned for his welfare. "I am married to my work, and I'll thank you to let it go at that."

"Oh, Reggie, Reggie," she crooned, using the name she'd been calling him all his life. "You really are a stubborn boy. You must remember Al Einstein's admonition on the subject—"

"*Al* Einstein?" Reg interrupted. "You knew him *that* well?"

"Don't be fresh," she scolded. "I knew him well enough, and he said that he did not care to teach in a coed school because the boys never paid attention to their math and physics. Always gawking at the girls, you know. Well, his friends chided him about that, saying, 'Now, Al, you know very well the boys would rather listen to what you have to say.' I remember his answer clearly. 'Such boys,' he said with that understated way of his, 'are not worth teaching.'

"If you haven't room in your life for love, Reggie, you'll become unteachable!"

"Not to worry, Mother. God's in control. I'll trust His judgment." Then he leaned forward and patted her shoulder. "That grandson of yours promised me he'd fly out and visit you next school break. That's only six weeks away. You'll like what you see, Mom. He's strong, tan, muscled, and as opinionated as his grandma."

"Visit!?" Carrie scoffed. "More likely he'll rent a motorcycle and want me to buzz down to the Oregon coast with him. I'll not do it, Reggie. Tony is a good boy and a deep thinker, but he never could keep a bike on the trail. If he'd only let me drive, but oh, no, he's much too macho for that. Of course, anymore with these eyes I can't tell a stoplight from a tomato."

Reg did not laugh this time. He looked at the woman who had given him birth and almost wished he was ten again when she'd gotten him to eat his lettuce by dipping it in the sugar bowl. How he would miss her and these lively visits of theirs.

"What's the job this time, son?" On the phone from Istanbul all he had told her was that he was being sent to Africa to map the habitat of a near extinct animal species. She supposed it was in conjunction with the work he had been doing with an animal breeding bank, just before he'd been rushed to Turkey to seize the Ark.

She tried to read his face now like she had when he was a little boy, but she could see better then and he had been a youth as transparent as a spring-fed pool. She would have to sift his voice for the truth today.

"This one's pretty farfetched," Reg began, wondering how he was going to tell her enough without telling her too much. He could not bear to think of her lying there, maybe dying, worrying about him. "I'm being sent to the Ubangi-Congo river basin about a thousand miles north of Brazzaville. Many natives, especially pygmies and various offshoots of the Bantu people, have reported numerous sightings of a curious water beast that supposedly inhabits the riverbends. Most likely a variety of hippo. They are said to grow quite large in that region, and what with the hocus-pocus those people put their faith in, you end up with something three parts imagination and one part reality. Several pygmy hunters have drowned, capsizing their canoes out of fright. I wouldn't be at all surprised if it was superstition that has stunted the pygmies' growth all these years."

His little attempt at humor was not fooling his mother. She could read the tightness in his voice and the increased pressure of his hand on hers. He was troubled.

She patted his hands briskly and tried to keep her response light. "Such a fascinating part of the world. Tropical rain forests are just teeming with life, some of which I've heard we have yet to catalog."

"Yes," said Reg, glad to have a neutral topic for discussion. "Truly one of the last untouched regions on earth. Better take my insect repellent. There are literally tens of thousands of insect species and many thousands more of plants and animals. Vines eight hundred feet long. Three hundred inches of rain. Eight-ounce monkeys and gorillas with eight-foot arm spans . . ."

Carrie jumped at that revelation, and Reg realized he was painting a fearsome landscape. He changed tack.

"Oh, Mom, I just hope we can make a difference to the last unspoiled garden on God's earth. Richard Bascomb says that sixty-eight percent of the Congolese rain forest is slated for clearing. If we can demonstrate that this forest is a gold mine of yet unnamed cures for disease, undiscovered animal life, and a rich source of global oxygen, maybe we can save it. If I find what I'm looking for, Bascomb says he will compensate the Congolese government over the next ten years whatever revenue they would derive from cutting the forest." Richard Bascomb was Reg's benefactor, owner of the world's largest heavy equipment company and director of the Enigma Society. He had sent Reg to find Noah's Ark. He was now sending Reg to find something else, something beyond belief.

Reg was about to enter Likouala Swamp, fifty-five thousand square miles of largely uncharted marsh and dense jungle rain forest, one of the most remote, disease-filled, and dangerous regions on the face of the earth. He was looking for *Mokele-mbembe*, the "monster animal" that made "the river run backward" whenever it surfaced and flattened a six and a half foot wide swath of vegetation whenever it dragged its tail through the jungle.

Reg Danson was hunting living dinosaurs.

"Well, you had just better be sure your maps are better than what the gas station gives. I suppose galoshes are of little use?" She was joshing him, and it felt good to have her treat him like a kid again. He wouldn't have that much longer. How could he tell her, anyway, that the maps of the region were almost all white, empty, and stamped "insufficient data to delineate terrain"?

He couldn't.

"Mom?"

"Yes, dear."

"You need to know how much I rely on your prayers when I'm out like this. It's a great comfort to know that Carrie Ann Danson is rattling the gates of heaven on my behalf!"

She raised up and kissed him on the forehead. "You've got it, kid. And remember, honey, what Helen Keller said. 'No pessimist ever discovered the secrets of the stars, or sailed to an uncharted land, or opened a new heaven to the human spirit.' You stay positive out there, or you'll have me to answer to!"

Reg bent over and kissed his mother's cheek, whispering, "I love you, Mom. Please don't whack anyone while I'm gone. And by the way, you look absolutely gorgeous today!"

She punched him playfully in the arm. "Sure you don't want another run at being a banker?" his mother teased, a sly smile playing at the corners of her mouth. She reached up and scratched under her wig. "Your Uncle Louis still has contacts at Chase Manhattan."

Reg returned the smile. "Sure you don't want to be camp cook? Monkey prepared your favorite way!"

"Ha!" she retorted. "Only if I get to water ski behind a dugout canoe. I hear those pygmy boatmen can pour on the steam."

After the man left Room 218 in the Powell Valley Convalescent Center and the old woman in the bed by the door drifted off to sleep, Gussie Jackson stared at the quilt panel she had just joined to the others. She shuddered despite the warm terry cloth robe. She was uncomfortable with remembering, like when the painful settling in her joints meant she couldn't sit still much longer.

When the quilt was at last finished one day, the history of her family would all be there, from the golden days of the Kongo Kingdom under Chief Mani Kongo to the hellish days of slavery in Georgia to the second class citizenship of the twentieth century; it would all be there to be read and wept over by generations to come.

She wished she were dancing with her mother in Moses Pierce's slave cabin on a winter night. Outside, icicle drools hung like silver strands from the mule's muzzle. Inside, all warm and sweaty, what a sight Mam had made! Dancing and dancing with a toddy of beer on her head and not a drop spilt. Abraham Hunter playing the bones; LeonJoe sawin' on the gourd fiddle with the horsehair strings. When Mam began to stagger from exhaustion, they threw a quilt 'round Jefferson, the handsomest black boy God ever made, wound him up like a cocoon, and every lady there gave him a good kiss. Mam would save hers for the end, and its length and intensity would always draw hoots and hollers from the men and protests from the other girls.

But now Gussie's hands shook so, and she was not at all certain when she would be able to pick up her quilting again. She'd shuddered because the swamp green flannel before her depicted not a giraffe as the silly nurse had so offhandedly guessed. White folks sure 'nuff could *not* read.

The long snaky neck, the thick leathery body, the small head with the vacant, staring eyes, the long jaws that could kill an elephant or chew a man in two—this was the terrible dragon that inhabited the waters of Gussie's ancient homeland.

The beast could drink the river dry and shatter trees with its mighty tail.

She would have shown it to the man if his mother weren't so impatient and the nurse equally so. Surely this was the water creature he was after.

But he would be good and sorry when he found it.

**T**he *Colonel Lokele* rounded the riverbend, wheezing and shuddering in the last stages of mechanical emphysema. The rusty barge negotiated the turn with the delicacy of an elephant performing CPR. Grime-encrusted smokestacks belched their foul contents and the *clang-thud-whump* of the engines announced the barge's arrival long before the emasculated horn croaked the official word.

He'd been three weeks negotiating the seven hundred miles from Kinshasa, Zaire, above the terrible cataracts of the Congo. Twenty-one days packed in a tin can with hundreds of other sardines, every one of them full of fight and wiggle. The barge was a tumult of color, a cacophony of sound, a confusion of smells, and a menagerie of wide variety. P. T. Barnum would have loved the place. The cramped, floating jamboree had provided a crash course in jungle community.

The passengers were mostly tradesmen, entrepreneurs, street vendors of the most vigorous sort, with the occasional adventurer and, on this particular journey, the headman of Epuluville—their destination—thrown in for good measure. The women wore bright skirts of the most brilliant blues, reds, and lavenders. The men wore bright green, yellow, or orange shirts. Giant butterfly prints and dark tribal symbols decorated the clothing of both sexes. The multicolored assembly transformed the barge into a giant carnival of man's rummage and nature's bounty. Tiny stalls tucked into every stairwell and landing sold all manner of soaps, cloth, hooks, beads, baskets, amulets, skins, horns, machetes, rope, belts, and sandals. Hunters and their women handled a stomach-turning array of fresh and smoked kill, bleeding carcasses of crocodile, antelope, bongos, duikers, wild hogs, boa constrictor, fruit bats, eels, and a hundred appalling varieties of fish yanked spiky and unidentifiable from the dark river's depths. A never ending torrent of water and blood and fish slime slickened the steel decks, coating them in a glossy oil and rendering walking treacherous.

Stowaways were constantly pursued about the tight quarters by the barge police. Those freeloaders caught had their heads shaved and were clapped in a makeshift cell where they could sit but not lie down. Two taverns in the hold did a brisk business in "Zaire whiskey," a potent yellowish liquid brewed from corn and guaranteed to send the eyeballs spinning. It was the subject of great debate whether a man would find more fire in the whiskey or in a bottle of amoeba-laden river water. Reg drank only bottled water, but he once made the mistake of getting too close to an open bottle of Zaire whiskey. The smell alone sent him to the rail.

He gave tetracycline to a young prostitute of fourteen with a mild case of gonorrhea. She was selling herself for ten cents to help her impoverished parents. Reg had ransomed her for twenty dollars and set her ashore at her village. He told her that only God could set her free forever and made her promise to seek guidance from Jigs Wiggins at Sangha Mercy Mission. She promised, and he left her in the embrace of father and mother, their thanks lost in the grinding resumption of the *Colonel Lokele*'s headway.

One thousand perspiring bodies clung to the tottering railings and crowded the flaking red roof for a first glimpse of Epuluville, the trading hub of the Ubangi-Congo Basin, the last civilized stop before the unexplored vastness of Likouala Swamp. Not that anyone who knew better was going there. *Last chance gas* thought Reg Danson sardonically. *Next rest stop, Tripoli on the Mediterranean Sea—two thousand miles.* He was crammed between an elderly man, unlucky at gambling, dropping playing cards one by one into the gray steel waters, and a buxom woman laughing and waving a slimy Congo catfish in triumphant semaphore to young girls crying welcome from the shore.

Danson felt strangely unelated. At last he was going to meet the man who would take him where he was not at all certain he wanted to go. There still existed a "deepest, darkest Africa," and this was it. Behind that thick jungle wall of vines and trees reaching twenty stories into the sky was a place at once incredibly beautiful and savagely lethal. Species without name and seemingly without number and dangers equally uncountable. The birthplace of the delicate African violet was thought to be the breeding ground for AIDS. Contagion thrived where bananas, oranges, mangoes, and papaya grew like weeds. It was eerie how the brilliant sunlight that captured the river's every watery ripple in its unmerciful glare left the forest sealed in mysterious, primeval shadow.

He stared hard at the seemingly impenetrable forest, the brooding curtain of relentless green. There was far too much he did not know.

The lean, tan face broke into a rueful grin. *Next assignment, Reggie boy, we're going someplace cooler. Deal?*

The barge slowed, engines protesting. Its chipped and jagged bow, looking like the upturned beak of an ancient snapping turtle, aimed for Epuluville Landing. Three teenage Bantu boys dove naked off the rickety fantail into the purling waters of the Ubangi River. They gladly exchanged the sticky, humid fetidness of the *Colonel Lokele* for the only slightly cooler but infinitely more delicious wetness of the main tributary of the mighty Congo River, "the river that swallows all rivers." For one mad, exquisite moment, Reg entertained the thought of doffing his clothes and joining them. They laughed and shouted their delight, wrestling and dunking one another, silver droplets of water clinging like diamonds to their hair and washing their faces a shiny nut-brown.

Now the bow of the phlegmatic barge touched bottom and a surge of humanity washed over the side. Coming up to meet it was a countersurge of Epuluvillians, hands full of all manner of fruits and vegetables. "*Mbote! Mbote!* Hello! Hello!" they cried in their native Lingala. "*Sango nini!?* What's new!?"

A gigantic exchange of news occurred on the spot. Danson stood mesmerized, trying to gain his land legs, while the streams of excited babble and commerce swirled about him. The barge had been expected for the last six days, give or take sandbar groundings, engine failures, hippo chases, and unscheduled stops at what seemed like every bend in the river where someone flagged the barge to a halt to inquire about a rumor, sell a product, or request newspapers or medicine. They had passed only one village without stopping. A cholera outbreak had rendered the place deathly silent. Crossing to the far shore, they had chugged past the ghostly palm thatched huts without hearing a voice or seeing a soul. An uneasy hush settled over the entire barge until the village of death at last slid from view. Cholera, malaria, typhoid, and yellow fever were not uncommon in this river world.

River barges were nothing to count on. The chances of Wiggins of the Sangha Mission being there to meet him were slim to none. The man had to come from twenty miles upriver in a dugout canoe. Wiggins would come when the jungle telegraph said come.

An odorous bundle landed with a heavy thump on the dock next to Reg. Two more bundles landed in quick succession, reeking of charred fur and singed skin. Reg looked into the frozen screams of ten dead white-faced monkeys, smoked to keep them from spoiling. Two more thumps and a wiry pygmy landed, cut the cords holding the monkey bales, and began to sell his wares. Barefoot shoppers flocked to the monkey man and carried their purchases off by tails wrapped around the necks of the deceased to form handles for easy transportation. Like a clearance rack of seared handbags, the dead monkeys disappeared at bargain prices, destined for the supper pots of Epuluville.

The gamy taste of his last monkey came readily to Danson's mind. He'd purchased a bowl of monkey stew from the soup vendor on the barge and found the meat stringy and strong-flavored like that of rabbit. Not all the fur been removed in preparation.

Reg ran a hand through his fine sandy hair shot with premature gray. Stretching his six-foot frame, he flexed the kinks from his strong shoulders and back. His eyes were a warm caramel brown, full of adventuresome intensity, easily engaged by the many dark eyes of the nationals. He moved with the grace and confidence of one much accustomed to hanging his hat and stowing his duffel wherever the winds of good fortune took him. His lithe body was an exclamation mark, and few met him who did not themselves stand a little straighter in his presence.

The loose-fitting khaki pants and shirt were dark-stained with sweat and badly in need of pressing. Barbara had always seen to his explorer's wardrobe, and he didn't feel nearly as swashbuckling without her. Some of the character lines at the corners of his eyes were modified lines of grief, etched at the time of her drowning in Loch Ness. Other lines his headstrong son, Tony, had added, and several new ones had come courtesy of Mount Ararat, the mother of all mountains and tomb of Noah's Ark. The unsuccessful expedition to retrieve the Ark had taught him a great deal about God's will and human folly, especially his own.

"*Ah-loo-rookok, ah-loo-rookok . . .* " A lovely melody sung by merchant and customer alike swelled above the clamorous din. It was so infectious that Reg took up the chant, not knowing what it meant but wanting to blend with the sheer joy of it. "The barge is in! *Colonel Lokele* has bravely made the journey of great danger!" sang a loud, raspy Westerner's bass. The sound came from somewhere beyond Reg's line of vision. "Aren't we blessed to have friends and family back, and so bountiful a load of goods! Such pretty cloth! Such fine meat! Such good sweets! So many favorites to make my tears flow in gratitude to the Mighty One, the Giver of Life! *Ah-loo-rookok, ah-loo-rookok, ahhhhh . . .* "

The crowds parted, and a white man with a thatch of red hair and a voluminous red beard strode commandingly into the circle that had opened between him and Danson. He was a head shorter than Reg yet so clearly in command of the street, the village, the jungle. All the body language in Epuluville, including that of the headman's, deferred to the leather-skinned redhead.

The lovely, melodic cadence stopped as if by order, and the stocky man crossed the clearing and planted himself toe-to-toe with Reg, wearing the fiery gaze of a sawdust evangelist zeroing in on a fresh convert. "*Mbote,* Reg Danson," he boomed. "Jigs Wiggins's the name. Epuluville is more complete with your coming! Cup your hands now and receive my welcome!"

Reg smiled quizzically and cupped his hands. Wiggins grabbed them in his rough, meaty paws, and lifted them to his lips. His brown cotton shirt was sleeveless, like a vest, and one muscular bicep sported a tattoo of a black serpent entwining a dagger dripping blood and the words *Kill or be killed.* The man's steady, knowing gaze never left his guest's. Wiggins smiled warmly and spat into Reg's palms.

The smile froze on Reg's moist face and he stiffened. Time stood still in the village gouged in the bank of the River Ubangi. A dog barked halfheartedly in the distance. The *Colonel Lokele* creaked and sloshed at its moorings. The sea of ebony faces did not move, nor did they seem to breathe. Reg stared woozily at the flecks of spittle clinging to the tangled thicket of red beard. A thin-lipped mouth cut a deep channel between a mountain of nose and the heavily forested foothills of chin below. The feathery creases at the boundaries of the pale green eyes looked like an aerial view of the Ubangi-Congo watershed.

Wiggins released Danson's hands and with a grand flourish produced a soiled handkerchief from the pocket of his coarse cotton trousers. He bowed low, handed the handkerchief to Reg, and announced to all: "Reg Danson and Epuluville are one!"

Instantly, the haunting melody resumed more vigorously than ever, oddly complementing the clamor of commerce. Barge day was clearly a thing of great moment in the lives of these people. Wiggins leaned close to Reg. "Sorry, Danson, but it's an old custom I picked up from the Rendeille nomads. They only spit on the ones they accept. The people like it. Gotta give them a little magic with their religion or, like the gum, it will lose its flavor on the bedpost overnight."

Without waiting for a response, Wiggins turned and again added his rude bass to the ebb and flow of song. "*Ah-loo-rookok, ah-loo-rookok, ah-looooo-rookok!*" Danson caught his arm and returned the handkerchief. "Pleased to meet you, Wiggins. What do the words of the song mean?" he asked, feeling lighthearted despite the strange welcome.

Wiggins hooted. "Roughly translated, they are equivalent to our 'fa-la-la-la-la, la-la-la-la' or 'shoo-be-do-be-do.' It's how people around here deck their halls!"

Danson's host led the way down an avenue of impromptu sales stalls, pointing out the exotic delicacies and handcrafts of a resourceful and creative people. Merchants lustily touted the selling points of their wares, and children moved among the milling customers with sample trays of sometimes startling contents.

One little girl in a bright red smock approached the men with a chipped porcelain bowl of what at first looked to Reg like large, orangy-pink prawns. "Fresh palm grubs!" cried Wiggins gustily, patting the girl on the head and tossing a fat grub into his mouth. Seeing Reg's face blanch, he motioned him over to a low wooden table upon which sat plastic, porcelain, and aluminum tubs filled with all manner of green, black, and white caterpillars, grubs, termites, butterfly and moth larvae—a gourmand's cornucopia of protein.

"Get used to it," said Wiggins perfunctorily. "Insect flesh is nearly as nutritional as red meat or poultry and a whole lot more available in this country. Male hunters sometimes return with only a fraction of what they wound, and if it weren't for insects to supplement their diet, the women and children would perish. Bee pupae is especially important upriver where we're going. When dried, it consists of more than ninety percent protein and eight percent fat. These people are protein and calorie poor without them. That makes bugs a better food buy than lobster or crab. You'd have to eat seven pounds of shrimp versus just one pound of winged termites to meet your daily caloric needs."

Wiggins motioned to a cheerful woman sitting behind a little makeshift stove of hot coals on which a fry pan sizzled with cooking oil. Then he motioned to Reg and pantomimed nausea by rubbing his stomach and making a sickly face. She laughed heartily, scooped up a handful of fat caterpillars, rolled them in a mixture of manioc flour and breadcrumbs, and sprinkled them into the fry pan. They snapped and popped and writhed before settling down to a simmer. Cooking them to a golden brown, the woman removed them from the grease with a wire ladle, wrapped them in a banana leaf, and handed the package to Wiggins with a grin and some rapid words in Lingala.

He handed her some coins and turned to Reg. In a low mutter he said, "Take at least two and make a big deal about how good they taste. Look disgusted and she will be offended." He unrolled the fast food caterpillars, and Danson said his prayers. Reg threw two of the insects into his mouth and chewed.

Though he tried to imagine every T-bone steak and juicy double burger he'd ever consumed, Reg made the mistake of looking across the avenue at a rack of dead flying squirrels and a half dozen limp porcupines. He squeezed his eyes shut and emitted a low moan that the cook took for a sign of barely contained pleasure. She chattered excitedly and pointed Reg out to her neighbors. They too pointed and giggled and clapped their hands at another convert to the delights of insect cookery.

Reg was pleasantly astonished to find that the contents of his mouth crunched and tasted much like corn chips. As clearly and steadily as he possibly could, he said, "Could I please have another?"

Jigs threw his head back and cackled his delight. "More!?" he proclaimed with a roar that caused two captive chimps to screech their disapproval. "By heaven, give the man some more!" Danson was game, and Wiggins liked that.

When Reg had polished off another three or four caterpillars, Wiggins tilted his head and winked at the new arrival. "Once you've had a little more time to adjust, I'll treat you to toasted dung beetle sautéed with herbs. Has the flavor of raw potato."

Reg made a little gurgling sound in his throat, but Wiggins was obviously enjoying his role as master of the jungle. "Much of the world's population eats insects to one degree or another," he said. "Entomologist Franz Bodenheimer believes the manna the Israelite children dined on in the wilderness was actually a crystalized secretion of surplus sugar from a species of scale insect that is native to the Sinai Peninsula. And it was certainly no accident John the Baptist survived quite well on locusts and wild honey. An excellent, nutritious combination!"

The two men left the commercial stalls and wandered back to the barge landing. Away from the buying and selling, apart from the crowds for whom he was a Pied Piper of sorts, Wiggins seemed less jovial, less expansive. In fact, he might have clammed up altogether had Reg not broken the silence.

"Water?" He proffered a small plastic bottle of treated water. Wiggins, lost in thought, shook his head. Reg sat on a crate and looked at the little pile of his belongings being hoisted to the shoulders of pygmy carriers for transfer to a dugout canoe. Behind him, the oppressive mystery of the jungle, its rank, steamy interior as seemingly impenetrable as any fortress, lay thick and poisonous. Away from the singing, babbling throng, the dense forest threatened like a predator. To enter its rotting cavity, where each living thing sought to choke and devour every other living thing, suddenly appeared most unattractive.

Wiggins began to pace, then stopped and turned his face toward the sun. He squinted the right eye almost shut. The left eye lay hidden in the missionary's bristly, whiskery auburn undergrowth, backlit by a descending sun.

"You've come," stated Wiggins, his voice flat and without any of its recent conviviality. "Can't say as I'm pleased."

Reg blinked. Would Bascomb ever send him where he would be welcome? The Kurds hadn't been keen on his efforts to find Noah's Ark, and now Wiggins—it was plain the missionary had been playing to an audience back at the market.

"Odd thing for a man of God to say," Danson replied evenly.

Wiggins locked his hands behind his back and rocked up on the heels of his boots. The serpent on his bicep lengthened. "Not so odd when you consider the devil's had his way with these people for centuries," answered Wiggins. "And in the history of Africa, the people have had less to fear from tsetse flies, drought, and famine than they have from the whites. Whole regions were depopulated by the slavers, *still* depopulated to this day! Ten million people were killed or taken captive in the central African holocaust. Packed five and six hundred into a single large ship, confined to a space the cubic capacity of just ten double cabins on the Queen Elizabeth II.

"No, Danson, the salvation of Africa is not in the discovery of its hidden wealth but in its isolation. Let the world forget about Africa. Remembrance brings exploitation, and these people have had enough. They don't want you here; they're just too polite to say so."

"I have no intention of exploiting these people. Why was I sent? Why did you come to meet me?" An unpleasant gnawing was building in Reg's gullet. He hoped it wasn't the caterpillars coming to life.

Wiggins stopped rocking and fixed Danson with a disgusted glare. "Because my mission board says there's a sizable contribution coming our way from Bascomb to build a school and hire two teachers. Do you know what that would mean to these people? They would give up food for a school. They would kill for a school. Have you ever seen little children sit in an empty school room day after day so as not to miss a teacher that will never come? I've seen it. Teacher salaries in this region are less than a beggar can make in a good year at the Brazzaville train depot. And if they do show up for class, there are no books, no papers, no chalk.

"Never mind turning water into wine. Turn the old Boundji coffee processing plant into a school, and these people would become Christians out of sheer gratitude. A fully funded school and two teachers? These people would think Christ had come a second time."

"Then why are you against my coming?" Reg asked, genuinely puzzled.

"Because I don't like coercion, and under every good Western intention hides a bandit who will steal your jewels and leave you to the vultures. I remember when the Zambian government installed a water pump in a village, thinking they were helping the overworked women save time and energy by not having to walk all the way to the river. The women ignored the pump. Why? Because they exchanged all the news with neighboring tribes-women at the river. Only there over their common need for water could they express views on children, crops, lazy husbands, and weighty matters of household importance.

"You're no more sensitive than the Zambian officials. You come in here looking for some prehistoric curiosity, open the area to worldwide media scrutiny, and pretty soon the place is crawling with foreigners with all manner of projects to modernize Africa. No sir, not while Jigs Wiggins is on the job. I've spent many years in Africa helping people, living among them, loving them, and teaching them about God. Better that they should remain academically ignorant than to open the door to technological plague."

Maybe it was the sun or a stomach in revolt or twenty-one days living cheek-by-jowl on the *Colonel Lokele*, but Reg Danson was not going to sit on a crate in the middle of nowhere and be berated and accused of a desire for heartless conquest. "Stop right there, Mr. Wiggins. You—"

"*Reverend* Wiggins, sir!"

"Reverend!?" Reg hadn't meant for it to sound so derisive, but fatigue and a short fuse were conspiring against civility. "You are every bit as arrogant and self-serving as you accuse me of being! You don't even know me."

"I know of your kind."

"My kind!? My *kind!?* I'm not some alien from outer space, Wiggins. I am a fellow Christian, a legitimate researcher, a man who cares very deeply for the future of Africa or any other place. You, sir, possess the arrogance of the aesthete. Because you have lived the simple, unencumbered life of the bush dweller, you think you can pass judgment on me. Forget it! I can hire my own boatmen and guides, and you don't have to bother yourself another minute!"

Reg grabbed two five-gallon plastic water jugs and started after Wiggins's carriers. He would thank the men, pay them for their time, and set off in search of his own crew. Jigs Wiggins could toss his acid at some other target.

"You can't." The way the missionary said it stopped Danson in his tracks. It was said calmly, matter-of-factly, and without any hint of retreat whatsoever.

Reg turned and looked at Wiggins. Carrie Danson would have whacked this "old red coot" across the noggin and challenged him to a game of cutthroat pinochle. Reg wished he had her negotiating skills.

"You can't," said Wiggins again, more forcefully this time. "The jungle pygmies won't talk to you or cooperate with you in any way apart from me. They believe you will eat their children.

A holdover from slave days." He looked amused at Reg's disbelief. "Don't blame me. They came by that wisdom hundreds of years before I ever got here."

"And it doesn't appear as if you have done anything to allay their fears," Reg snapped. Then he caught himself and sighed. He set the water bottles down. "Look, Reverend Wiggins, I'm sorry. But I have the permission of the People's Republic of the Congo to be here. I have been inoculated against every disease known to man. I have searched for arks, sea serpents, sasquatches, and the answers to all sorts of other riddles.

"I believe that wonderful cures and unknown species of flora and fauna that might benefit mankind in a hundred different ways are out there in the rain forest, and if *Mokele-mbembe* has survived for thousands of years, who knows what else may be out there? The Ubangi-Congo basin has not undergone climatic or geophysical change since the Flood. No glaciers. No new volcanoes. No earthquakes or other cataclysmic upheaval to alter or disrupt the continuity of plant and animal life. If prehistoric crocodiles continue to thrive, what better place for there to be remnants of the big beasts that once roamed this continent?"

Danson looked at Wiggins, but the missionary said nothing. "Gorillas weren't even 'discovered' until the mid-1800s, man!" Reg paced as he spoke. "The horselike okapi were not known until 1900. The hooded pitohui bird was not found until 1992! You could hide herds of dinosaurs in the unexplored jungle swamplands of the Congo. And you know as well as I do that the rain forest is slated for clearing by land developers. Where will your pygmies be then? Maybe we can stop them, Wiggins, together! If we find the water monster, the world community will bring incredible pressure to bear that will result in the wholesale preservation and study of the forest instead of its destruction." Danson stopped and looked defiantly at Wiggins; yet he asked himself, *If I am so convinced, why do I feel so uneasy about what lies beyond the dark, fearful wall of green?* Wiggins named the dread. "I, too, am sorry," Wiggins said. "But there is an evil out there that you do not understand; neither do I. Witchdoctors and demons abound, a darkness of heart so terrible that I have made little headway against it in seventeen years among the pygmy."

"Surely you're not suggesting it is a darkness beyond the reach of Christ's light?" asked Reg softly.

"Oh, the Light is here," said Wiggins resignedly, "but I fear there are a good many shadows in the Likouala Swamp."

Reg made a feeble attempt to lighten the moment. "I've heard that cannibalism has been eradicated, that the pygmies' poisoned arrows are now used only in the hunt for food, and I have antivenin for six different vipers. What else could possibly go wrong?"

Wiggins was silent for a long while. His pale green eyes flickered over the forest green, and a shiver rose along Danson's spine. *What is he searching for?*

"Christianity is a crutch for the weak," murmured Wiggins.

Reg could not believe it. It wasn't bad enough that Wiggins neither wanted him there nor seemed to care about the future of the Congo. He also paraded himself as a minister of the gospel as he sported a serpent and dagger on his arm and a contempt for Christianity in his heart. Bascomb could sure pick them!

"Oh, great!" Danson said. "The *Reverend* Wiggins and Karl Marx share the same definition of faith!"

Wiggins spat on the ground, and Reg involuntarily wiped his hands on his pants. "That's what I mean about you," Wiggins said, loud and angry. "You have your mind made up about everything. What I've read of you tells me you like to throw your weight around and call the shots. Well, you'll not do that here whether I take you or you barge off on your own. Either way, that attitude will lose you your darn fool head!"

They glared at each other a moment, then Wiggins went on. "When I say Christianity is for the crippled and the weak, I mean that I am too feeble in my own strength. Only Christ can lift me and keep me from my old ways. Only the crutch of Christ has kept me here, and only the crutch of Christ holds me up.

You come in here with your North American swagger and you'll be neck deep in quicksand before sundown. And won't you be surprised when I turn my back and let you sink!"

With that, Wiggins stormed off in the direction of the canoe. Reg kicked at the water jugs, mad at himself. "You've shot yourself in the foot so many times, it's a wonder you can stand," he muttered to himself.

Wiggins or no Wiggins, Reg was not going to back out now. He opened the top of his duffel and removed a tightly wrapped parcel about the size of a large paperback book. It had been waiting en route for him in London. The only instructions had been a hastily scribbled note from Richard Bascomb:

> Reg, lad, welcome to bonnie old England and the official start of your journey. Perhaps one of these days we shall undertake a pilgrimage of truth together. At any rate, Godspeed.
>
> I commend to you one Edward "Jigs" Wiggins, with Sangha Mercy Mission upriver from Epuluville. He knows the jungle and the jungle dwellers as well as any Westerner. Should you get stuck for any reason, all you'll need for a successful mission is contained in this package.
>
> No need to open this until safely inside Africa. You've enough on your mind. Remember, should you find the quarry, and I pray you shall, hit it with the elephant tranquilizers. A close examination and recording (in writing and on tape) is essential. Mark the location well and then leave. Do not under any circumstances kill or attempt to remove one of these beasts. God willing, we can return with a fully mounted expedition at a later date.
>
> Remember what Dr. Luke had to say: "What is impossible with men is possible with God."
>
> *Bascomb*

Reg hated to admit he was stuck one hour after arriving in Epuluville, but this was no time for wounded pride. Danson pulled out a penknife and slit the ends of the package, which was tightly wound with an abundance of strapping tape. There was enough daylight to study any detailed maps of the region before he would have to seek shelter for the night. He knew Bascomb would not leave him without a plan B.

But there were no "insider's" maps contained in the parcel. Just a plastic-bound Bible and one bookmark.

His breath coming faster, Reg tore at the wrapping, studying it inside and out for something more in writing—a clue, anything. He checked the inside covers of the Bible for a message, a folded set of instructions, a ticket home.

Nothing. Just the Bible and the bookmark.

Reg laid the Bible on the pack and put his head in his hands. He had to get a normal job someday. Bascomb never gave him straight answers.

# 3

It was midnight still in Room 218 of the Powell Valley Convalescent Center. Carrie Danson had stayed awake long beyond her customary bedtime. Thoughts of Reg, an unnamed anxiousness, kept her praying fervently, and she had skipped Saturday night pinochle. Medications she couldn't skip, but no sooner had she gulped the eight small pills and the two horse pills than she was back to praying for Reg's safety and whatever problem he was facing right then.

At last she drifted off to sleep in the small circle of light from the reading lamp. A nurse came and switched off the light, pulling Carrie's favorite afghan up over her thin shoulders.

Gussie Jackson watched the nurse attend to Mrs. Danson. The nurse knew better than to bother with Gussie's light. The last time someone had turned it off too early, Gussie had set up a shriek to wake the dead. They had to sedate her to get her to stop. Since then they let her sleep with it on—not that she slept much.

"Uhm-m-m-m-m, yo-o-o-o," Gussie hummed to herself. It was a tune she had crooned to her grandbabies. Easter Jackson had been her favorite, so plump, her skin the color of ginger cake. "Uhm-m-m-m-m, yo-o-o-o, uhm-m-m-m-m . . . "

She sewed straight through the night sometimes. Her grand-mammy had had to sew by moonglow as no light was allowed by the master. Grandmammy quilted right through three night's sleep once so that Gussie's granddaddy Big John could have quilted underbreeches for winter.

A family of fifteen they'd had. Gussie supposed she must have sixty or seventy nieces and nephews and who knew how many cousins. Good thing she didn't know where—or who—they all were or she'd quilt herself to death.

She was adding a panel now of bright yellow in memory of her graduation from high school, the first Jackson so privileged. There was a little white gabardine diploma in the middle, and the whole was joined to the deep purple swatch depicting Grand-pap's preaching stick carved with holy stories. He would turn the stick until he found a story worth telling, and off he'd go like a pony stung in the rump. She "whooped" the yellow to the pur-ple, hot to cool, cool to hot like the African-American field yo-del or "whoop."

"*Ah-loo-rookok, ah-loo-rookok . . .*" She switched uncon-sciously from the lullabies of the New World to the ancient chant of her forebears. It was a light and airy thing, and she liked rolling the *r*'s. In Africa, people could read other people's status from a distance along a road. By the color of their clothing, they could be offered proper greeting.

Pain and loss. Triumph and tragedy. It was all there in Gus-sie's quilt. An aroma, a song, a taste, a prayer that would materi-alize each time the quilt was handled. When her mam died, Cousin Odessa and Cousin Peculia swept the quilt over the open grave, and old, old 'Lijah Pierce played the comb, the only per-son she knew who could make a body weep playing the comb.

But for as many patches as brought a calm and a smile to her mouth—like the big grinning teeth and lips on the blue jonquil panel in memory of "Cussie Gussie" who'd only been cured when Pap had made her gargle with kerosene—there was always the one large patch of misery in the center. *Mokele-mbembe,* the dragon. The center was where it belonged, trapped by a circle of brightly colored happiness.

"*Ah-loo-rookok*," crooned Gussie. "Uhm-m-m-m-m, yo-o-o-o. Keep the beast from my hut. Give it no babies to eat. Make it go back to its cave so that it does not crush my tiny Kongo home." She looked at the bed by the door, and her eyes grew moist. She threw her head back, and a piercing cry tore from her throat. "Ei-e-e-e-e-e-e-e-e! Ei-e-e-e-e-e-e-e-e . . ."

Nurses and orderlies ran to Room 218 to put a stop to the high-pitched wail of mourning that shredded the midnight calm.

Carrie Danson was dead.

Reg found Wiggins in the stern of the dugout fiddling with the outboard motor. A streak of oil smudged his forehead, and he looked as angry as the serpent patrolling his bunched bicep. The pygmy carriers sat smoking and watched the two white men warily.

"Reverend Wiggins," Reg began, then stopped, hating the formality in his voice. He could accomplish nothing without this man, and he knew it. "Jigs, I'm sorry for acting so pigheaded back there. This is your home, and I am your guest. Please forgive my attitude. See?" He walked up and down in front of Wiggins. "No swagger." He smiled, but Wiggins wasn't easily softened. "I need your help, man. This expedition has me uneasy. And you're absolutely right, this is not Loch Ness or Istanbul. I'd be useless out there without someone of your expertise and knowledge of the swamp and the people. Maybe I won't get anywhere. But I promise you I won't stay any longer than necessary either. Win or lose, you get the school *and* the teachers *and* the supplies. What can it hurt?"

Wiggins stopped adjusting the motor and sat staring at it. Several minutes passed before he spoke. Without looking up, he said, "Ndoki! Ndokanda!" The two men reclining with their smokes rose to their feet and approached. Wiggins looked at them without smiling and jerked his head in Reg's direction. "Mr. Danson will be joining us after all. Danson, I am pleased to introduce Ndoki and Ndokanda, pygmy brothers, two of the finest converts to our Lord this misbegotten jungle has ever produced. They take their palm wine in moderate amounts and no longer use hallucinogens. They are one with the forest and may be all that stand between us and some nasty unpleasantness."

Reg slid his right hand forward hesitatingly, not certain what welcoming rituals pygmies might employ. To his surprise, they took his hand surely in their smaller ones and shook firmly and solemnly, the sinew and muscle of their long forearms displaying the strength of their fight for survival. They each stood a little under five feet tall, weighed probably eighty to eighty-five pounds each, and wore bright blue basketball shoes and olive green shorts. Their bare upper torsos were a rich coffee-and-cream color, lean and powerfully muscled. The brothers allowed their handsome, strong-jawed faces to reveal nothing save an intense scrutiny of Reg that made him uncomfortable.

They jerked ramrod straight and cried proudly in unison, "*Efe'eni!*"

Reg looked to Wiggins for interpretation. "They say they are pygmy of the Efe nation, master archers of the rain forest. A remarkable people, my copper kinsmen." Wiggins stopped, his eyes troubled, as if unsure of telling Danson anything more about these secluded people. Then he stood and stepped from the burned out log-turned-canoe.

He fixed Danson with a look that was chillingly direct. "Every time I tell an outsider of my forest friends, the Efe are diminished. But, as you say, their doom may be sure and swift if the forests are logged. I just don't want the media doing eye surgery with a machete. These are a gentle, peaceable people, and they deserve our respect."

He whirled, stepped back into the canoe, and made for the bow of the twenty-foot vessel. The brothers motioned for Reg to follow, and he made his way over food and supplies to a low plank seat behind Wiggins. The pygmies hopped lithely aboard, cast off, and started the engine in one deft sequence. Epuluville swiftly grew smaller in size and sound in the gathering dusk.

The little outboard cut diagonally across the current and fought its way upstream like an angry hornet. The rapidly shrinking village with its happy clamor and caterpillar café suddenly seemed to Reg a most civilized and comfortable place to be. Never had he felt so hastily torn from life as he knew it. Jungle jaws were gaping wide, and he was tumbling down a dreadful hole. Would anything in this dream world be the least bit familiar?

Wiggins shouted over his shoulder at Reg. "Maybe two hundred thousand pygmy descendants left, but there are only fifteen thousand pure-blooded ones in a forest of twenty thousand square miles. Hunter-gatherers for the most part, most with nets, a few like the Efe with bow and poisoned arrow. They're a quiet people who've been put down by the taller African Negroes. For nutrition's sake, the pygmies are forced to trade with the agricultural Negroes on the forest fringe." He pointed to the mounds of garden vegetables, rough tuberous roots, and leaf tobacco in the bottom of the canoe. A small clutch of metal-tipped arrows lay beside the produce.

"The townsmen treat the pygmy like slightly intelligent animals," Wiggins continued, turning a little to face Danson. "They like the wild game and honey the pygmies bring in trade but scoff at the hunter's prowess as a sign the pygmy are on a par with the beasts they slay. True, the Ologus we're going to find are the most primitive of the pygmy, but surely even they could learn to love God and live a life of praise. But would the townsmen give them a chance? No. Prejudice is not a Western monopoly."

Reg found it difficult to tear his eyes away from Wiggins's tattoo which looked eerily alive in the half light. Both men were sweating in the torrid heat, and the rivulets of perspiration sliding down the shaft of the painted dagger gave the drops of crimson blood a glistening life of their own.

It was perhaps a quarter mile to the opposite bank, and as they neared shore, the jungle wall charged down the incline to meet them. Inky black with coming night, the expanse of tree and vine snaked along the water's edge. A million insects ticked and whirred in the darkness, and a howler monkey blasted the pests' arrival with a vigorous bawling out.

Ndoki tapped Reg on the shoulder. "*Tala nsima na yo, na okomona na moliei ya yo,*" he said, pointing back across the river to the night fires of Epuluville.

"He says, 'Look behind you and you will see your shadow,'" said Wiggins as the brothers cut the engine, and they made ready to land. "He means that Epuluville is the last shred of your modern ways. From now on, you belong to the womb of the baboon. It's their way of welcoming you to their world."

Reg smiled faintly at Ndoki, whose expression did not change.

The slender wedge of the canoe's bow slid softly to a halt four or five feet up the bank. The four men leapt out and pulled the canoe securely up for the night. Ndoki and Ndokanda immediately removed their pants and shoes and packed them away for the next trip to town. Meager dun-colored loincloths draped them fore and aft, the two pieces of material joined by a single waist string. With that simple change in apparel, they transformed from a couple of friendly village youths into wilderness men. They moved with a fluid and earthy grace to establish the night's resting place.

"Incredible, aren't they?" asked Wiggins. "Did you know that for thousands of years, the pygmy have practiced a lofty monotheistic religion akin to our own? They have their own accounts of Adam and Eve, the Garden of Eden, the giving of the commandments, and the second coming of the pygmy messiah."

As soon as Ndoki and Ndokanda had a fire started and thatched sleeping mats elevated on a platform of saplings four feet off the ground, they ran to two *anjuafa* trees and climbed, gripping the rough bark with their bare legs and feet. Reg marveled at the toughness of their skin.

About twenty feet up, Ndokanda tied a kind of hide thong around the tree and around his waist, securing himself to the trunk like a phone company lineman. Next, he removed a net he had slung over his shoulder and cast one end expertly over to Ndoki, who was likewise secured to his tree. They fastened the top of the net, then climbed down ten feet and secured the bottom, leaving a kind of loose, baby diaper bulge on the downriver side.

When the men dropped softly to the ground, Wiggins clapped his hands. "Ah, bats for breakfast!" he exclaimed heartily. He saw Danson's disbelief and gave a short laugh. "Bat trap, old boy. Fruit bats. They eat the fruit, and we get all the vitamins. Surely you're not against the food chain? We'll cook a few up before we break camp in the morning."

Wiggins wandered over to a grassy knoll and sat down. He stared at the remains of a red-gold sunset and removed a pipe from a breast pocket. Apparently it still possessed its last load, for he lit the contents of the bowl without freshening it and blew a stream of smoke heavenward.

"Don't tell the home office about this," Wiggins chuckled, pointing to the pipe. "They don't approve of such bodily contaminants. Exposure to elephantiasis and dengue fever is perfectly acceptable, but for goodness' sake, don't light up!" He slapped at a mosquito, and Reg flicked away a multilegged insect that dropped onto his sleeve from the canopy above. A light rain of insects fell from the upper and understories far overhead, plopping and slapping against leaves and ground before scuttling away. Thousands of plants and animals and millions of crawling things made their homes far above the forest floor. Ferns and peppers, orchids and strangler figs, ants and beetles by the carload inhabited the heights. Reg wasn't surprised by the diverse population. On a collecting expedition in the Costa Rican rain forest, using a biodegradable fog insecticide, he had recorded as many as two thousand species of insects from a single tree.

Night clamped down upon them with a dramatic finality. The only sky visible was a river-wide ribbon of blue-black about a half mile from end to end, or from river bend to river bend. It was the only visible sign—that and the flickering lights across the water—that there was life beyond this tiny open sore of a clearing. The pygmy kept clear of vegetation so they would not have to stay overnight in a town where they were social pariahs. Useful traders by day, despised outcasts by night.

An occasional snatch of laughter carried over to the little camp from the quieting village, but the forest noises changed in pitch only as the night creatures took over. The pygmy squatted by a small basin of coals cooking Congo catfish cured onboard the *Colonel Lokele*. The smoky gray flesh was of indeterminate age but mostly free of worms. To Reg, the heavy darkness felt thick and malignant. Even the moon seemed unable to penetrate the fortress of roots and fronds that stretched crooked fingers and bony legs across the paths of the innocent.

"Tired?"

Reg jumped.

"Sorry," said Wiggins affably. "Seventeen years out here, and I still get spooked from time to time." He called over to the brothers, who were murmuring over the fine aromas wafting from their cookpot, "Sing!" whereupon the brothers began a very spirited humming as backup to the missionary's lively "Battle Hymn of the Republic." When he realized that Reg had not joined in, Wiggins stopped.

"If I tell you about the tattoo, will that help?"

Reg coughed, embarrassed. "Was I that obvious?"

"There's a Ugandan proverb that says never insult a crocodile until after you've crossed the swamp. Well, you weren't in town half an hour before you'd offended this croc. You're too concerned with appearances, my friend. The food, the customs, even the expressions of faith have you passing sentence faster than a hangin' judge from Santa Fe. Relax. Plenty more shocks where we're headed."

"Guilty," said Reg, joining Wiggins on the knoll. He sat down and sighed heavily. "I've got a job to do, and I don't like it when plans get changed midstream."

"Get used to it," Wiggins responded, blowing smoke at three huge winged insects descending like paratroopers strung from gossamer chutes. They reversed engines and flapped full throttle in the opposite direction. "I could have the tattoo removed or keep it covered, but God's against it."

Reg glanced over at him quizzically. "How's that?"

"The Lord does not look at the things man looks at. Man looks at the outward appearance, but the Lord looks at the heart. God told Samuel that so he would choose David, the youngest and least likely of Jesse's sons, to be king of Israel." Wiggins pointed the stem of his pipe at Danson and peered down at his arm. "This tattoo is a testimony to the power of God. It's a constant reminder to me of what I've been delivered from, and it causes other people no end of agitation wondering just where I'm coming from!" He arched his eyebrows at Reg and slid the pipe stem once more into hiding somewhere inside the great expanse of red beard.

Reg smiled in surrender, and Wiggins continued. "I gave you a bad time back at Epuluville, but you had it coming. And you'll find you need some sort of edge to your personality, or likely as not you'll find yourself impaled on an *okoume* tree. Some people are full of guile; others, full of hot air. Me, I'm full of irritants, and like antifreeze back home in Minnesota, it keeps me thawed and gets me started in the mornings."

The brothers brought the steamy hot fish on plates of *mongongo* leaf and plastic mugs of hot, thick bush coffee. Reg surprised himself with how quickly he wolfed down the tasty morsels. Perhaps his belly was getting used to its recent exotic diet.

## THE LOST KINGDOM

Wiggins finished the fish, tossed the leaf aside, and wiped his mouth on the same soiled handkerchief he had lent Reg back at the market. He gulped the scorching coffee. "Seventeen years at home, six in prison, thirty years in Africa," he said. "I got the tattoo in prison."

Reg said nothing. His mind raced, but he held his tongue.

"My daddy said I'd end up there. 'Course, when he first laid eyes on me, all wriggly, red, and wet, he didn't know whether I was a son or something to bait his hook with. My mother birthed me in the pantry. She was reaching up high for the pickles, and I decided it was time. Daddy was a merchant seaman and only put in an appearance a couple times a year. He said by the time I was five I had a beard. I don't know about that, but by the time I was twelve, I was thieving pretty steady, and Momma was fit to be tied. I spent my seventeenth birthday in a cell for shooting a man in self-defense. They said it was manslaughter, but he came at me with a sledgehammer and I was cornered.

"Best thing that ever happened to me." Wiggins restoked his pipe and looked upriver as if the memories flowed down from there. Some night animal snorted beyond the firelight, and Reg's head snapped up. "Probably a wild hog rooting for grubs," Wiggins said, the calm in his voice welcome and soothing. "I thank God for prison, Danson."

Reg saw a challenge in the older man's eyes, daring him to contradict the assertion. He nodded and waited for Jigs to continue.

"A man headed for death row told me no matter what I'd done, Jesus had done the time for it and an eternal pardon was mine if I wanted it. Boy did I want it! I fell down on my knees by my cot, six feet from a cockroach-infested toilet, and surrendered the whole works to the Lord. Well, I'll tell you, I never had it any better than that. Where else can you work for the Lord twenty-four hours a day at government expense? I told guys night and day about the power of Christ to set them free, regardless of their crimes. Some jeered at me, a couple beat me up, but a good number enlisted in God's army. I have never been freer than as a locked-up Christian. I'm sure not that free now." The ex-con's jaw tightened, and his eyes moistened.

"I don't know if you can understand, Danson. I had a captive audience behind bars. Many of those guys were at the end of their ropes. God had softened their hearts, and all I had to do was come along and scoop them up. Out here in this godforsaken wilderness, I'm lucky if they stop gambling and fornicating long enough for me to say grace at meals." The note of bitterness that tinged his voice caused Ndoki and Ndokanda to glance up with a look of concern.

"Sometimes I hate this place!" Wiggins jumped up, spilling coffee, fists clenched. He fought for control. "I've been hunting with the pygmy at times when I swear I could smell the entrance to hell. And when they scar themselves and mutilate their children for cosmetic reasons, and the blood runs red down their legs, I want to kill them *all!*"

He paced and glared at the brothers. They cowered at the edge of the firelight, making as if to bed down but painfully aware that Wiggins's anger was directed at their people. This was clearly not the first time he had lost his temper in their presence.

"They worship the power of the forest because it provides their livelihood," Wiggins railed on. "They're animists, pure and simple. They go on and on about the underworld and the kingdom of the dead. They are full of incantations and exaggerations, and they deform the truth at every opportunity . . . " He pointed accusingly at the brothers, as if they were the incarnation of pygmy belief. "They love palaver and even have certain designated palaver trees where they love to listen to themselves talk—"

Ndoki had heard all he could stand. He jumped down from his sleeping mat, planted his fists on his hips, and let loose with a string of rapid speech every bit as hot as what Wiggins was dishing out. Even in the weak firelight, Jigs visibly colored. His fists clenched and unclenched. His arms shook.

"What—" Reg began, alarmed at the vehemence of the debate.

"Smart-mouthed little gnome!" shouted Wiggins. "The fool has the nerve to fling my own words back in my face after all I've done to doctor and educate his people. I've got half a mind to pack up and retire from this business. The slave trade is not dead, Danson. Only now the missionaries are the slaves, and the depraved people they spend themselves on are the masters. When you've seen the sin parades I've seen, you wonder at your own sanity for staying another minute in this unholy stink pit!"

Reg spoke low and evenly, hoping to ease the tension. "What did he say that has you so steamed?"

Wiggins jammed the unlit pipe between clenched teeth and bit hard. That seemed to relieve the strain and redirect his adrenaline. At last his shoulders slumped wearily, but he kept the pipe in place, speaking around it. "Once when I'd had my fill of their magical mumbo jumbo, I took Ndoki aside and blasted him for the people's pagan stubbornness. I quoted the Arabic scholar Babu Conde, and he just now quoted him back at me."

He stopped for a moment and eyed Reg defensively. "You'll laugh," he said self-consciously. "You may even think I got my just desserts for that little fit of temper. I might even agree with you." He stopped again, and Reg gave him an insulting little grin. "Oh, all right, you may as well hear it. Conde, through Ndoki, said, 'To talk without saying anything is the mark of a baby learning to walk, the jealous woman, and the madman. But not the mark of a man.'"

Wiggins glowered at Reg, daring him to laugh. Reg obliged. Soon the brothers were having a hoot. Wiggins, despite himself, joined them. "You can't tell a pygmy anything you don't want to hear again," he sputtered. "Their oral and retentive acuity are remarkably high." Wiggins removed the coffee bucket from the fire and took the brothers a peace offering.

Soon the pygmies knelt for prayer, then they drifted quickly off to sleep. Wiggins went for a constitutional. Reg felt a restlessness he could not shake and returned to his seat on the knoll to swat a new squadron of mosquitoes. Fifteen minutes later, Wiggins returned and sat down, his back to a tree. The pipe was back and freshly stoked.

"Taking your chloroquine?" he asked.

Reg flattened another mosquito on his pants leg. "You bet," he said, fishing a mosquito out of his coffee. He swatted his neck. His hand came away spotted scarlet. "Thick, aren't they?"

"'Bout normal," Wiggins grunted.

Reg envied the pygmies, practically naked, no tent, yet seemingly unbothered by the attack. From the corner of his eye, he watched a bright green and red frog bound into the circle of light. It hopped within inches of Reg's boot, and he bent to pick it up.

"Don't!" Wiggins barked. "Poison dart frog. Produces a lethal chemical in its skin that some pygmies use on the tips of their blowgun darts. High toxicity, low survival. The frog parents carry their tadpoles on the tops of the trees where they grow up in the water-filled leaves of bromeliad plants." Jigs rose, wrapped a hand in the indispensable handkerchief, snatched up the frog, and deposited it in a little cloth bag. He tossed it near the sleeping men. The handkerchief returned to his pocket, and Reg made a mental note to decline any offer of it in the future.

"Such incredible contrasts, Africa," Wiggins noted, resuming his seat as unconcerned as if he'd just deposited the trash. "So incredibly rich with natural resources, so incredibly destitute with poverty and ignorance. Diamonds and gold, famine and pestilence. The International Suffering Index says three of the five most miserable nations on earth are in Africa. People on top of people—some 143,000 people per square mile in Lagos, Nigeria, compared to only 11,500 per square mile in New York City. AIDS threatens to destroy entire generations of Africans. I've traveled through large areas in Uganda where only the very young and the very old are left alive. But it wasn't always so.

"Once upon a time Africa could have developed a civilization to rival that of Europe! The Kongo Kingdom was one of several great Iron Age civilizations that flourished on the African continent before white men arrived. Chief Mani Kongo ruled justly over five million subjects, and what slaves he kept were criminals or prisoners of war who were allowed to earn back their freedom. But you add white explorers and traders, firearms and liquor, the transatlantic slave trade, and the Moroccan invasion, and you've got a recipe for disaster."

Despondency furrowed Wiggins's forehead. "Tribal wars were encouraged by white men, and African brother was pitted against African brother, blood feuds that last to this day! Millions were led away as slaves on forced marches to the sea for transport to Arabia, Spain, South America, and the New World. Belgian King Leopold was so bent on conquest that when Africans fought back, his agents were told to bring severed hands as proof they had not frivolously wasted their government-issue bullets on animals. Soon they were bringing the hands of men, women, and children by the basketful, many of them hacked off the arms of the living since corpses were not required proof. Some Belgians bought their way out of military service with a payment of hands.

"I tell you this, Danson, so you will know what breeds some of the resentment and the darkness of heart that we will encounter up there." He nodded upriver, a region rapidly becoming a place of festering evil in Reg's mind.

A three-toed sloth shifted on a branch above them and emitted a soft, snuffling sound. Everything except the pygmies seemed to have trouble sleeping this night.

Wiggins took a drag on the pipe of such duration that Reg thought the missionary would choke. Wreaths of smoke rising from his beard like spotfires in the bush, Wiggins continued. "The Congo River's the second greatest in volume in the world. Drains almost a million square miles of rain forest. It could by itself produce thirteen percent of the world's hydroelectricity. But these countries are too poor to do anything about it. And in contrast to the great rivers of Europe and the Americas, none of this continent's five great rivers are navigable inland for much distance. Add to that the fact that a third of Africa is desert and half the population's under the age of fourteen, and you've got a geographical and cultural nightmare in the making.

"We've got France to thank for plundering the natural resources of this part of the Ubangi-Congo Basin. Not the least of which was the people. The construction of the Congo-Ocean Railroad from Brazzaville to the sea cost twenty thousand lives. Entire villages were drafted to build the thing. I helped mine gold and diamonds along the Kouilou River in the Mayombe Mountains, iron ore in Zanaga, and copper in Mindouli. I worked for years in the tuna processing cannery in Pointe-Noire, the deep water port at the railroad's ocean terminus. I even spent six months in a state-run cassava farm near Matoumbon producing cassava pellets and starch.

"Part of me wanted to atone for white men's excesses of the past, part of me wanted to work shoulder to shoulder with my African brothers before I proclaimed the gospel among them. I grew to love them very deeply."

Danson believed him. His passion for these people was now bright in his tone. "But why didn't you stay in the towns and cities? Why come to the most remote spot on the map where the people are so scattered and, as you say, so primitive in belief? Wouldn't you make better headway among the more educated in places where they knew you?"

Wiggins scowled and left the knoll with the urgency of a suddenly remembered appointment. He shifted the coffee bucket off the coals, but it was obviously make-work. Something Danson had said disturbed him a great deal, and Wiggins did not answer the question.

Suddenly, a mighty rush of wings swept across the little camp clearing—hundreds of fruit bats on their night rounds in pursuit of a meal. In ten seconds the bat cloud was hundreds of yards downriver but a good two dozen bats short. The stragglers were hopelessly caught in the net of Ndoki and Ndokanda. A high-pitched squeaking filled the air but, like the mosquitoes and the frog, the sound barely concerned the pygmies.

Reg shuddered. Bat bodies beat against their prison walls but there was no escape. Wiggins walked to the tent the pygmies had erected, paused at the doorway, and declared, "Breakfast!" before plunging inside and closing the bug screen.

Danson stood alone for a time, thinking. He recalled that the Chinese character for *crisis* carried the symbol for danger above, for opportunity below. However lonely, frightening, and puzzling this all was, God could use it for good. When he at last crawled in next to the snoring form of Jigs Wiggins, Reg prayed, *You are the God of order, and you are the God of truth. I place my complete faith in you. Please, Lord, help my unbelief.*

It was a long while before he could sleep. The cry of the trapped bats sounded at times like the plea of drowning kittens. But it was more than that. Not once in their conversation that night had Wiggins made any mention whatsoever of *Mokelembembe.* Did it mean nothing, or was he avoiding the issue? When at last Reg did drift off to sleep, it was to dream of lost worlds populated by giant spitting frogs and catfish kings.

Upriver from the clearing where four men slept, in a slow and brackish bend of the swamp tributary known as the Gamboma, a pair of yellow-green parrots shifted their feet nervously on the branches of the ebony tree, smelling the night wind. In the flooded forest, a bush cat snarled irritably over a poor day's hunt, and something moved in the depths.

The humus overlaying the waters formed a mat of decaying air roots, leaves, and straw. The movement below made the mat undulate. The nearer the thing came to the surface, the more wild the dance of the humus.

There in the phosphorescent night, a slick black thing parted the waters and rose high above the swamp in a sinewy arc. Water dripped from it, and pieces of decayed vegetation slid off it and smacked the surface of the swamp.

But the thing itself made no sound at all.

# CHAPTER

# 4

"Y our grandmother was a dear lady," the nurse said kindly, patting Tony Danson on the shoulder. "She was queen of the day room. No one could touch her at pinochle."

Tony's shoulders rose and fell in a long sigh. "I know," he said and looked up. "She taught me how to play." Tears streaked his handsome face. *He looks so much like his father,* thought the nurse appreciatively.

Tony had wanted to surprise his Grandma Carrie. He was taking a minimum of archaeology credits this semester—for rest and recuperation—and was able to double up on his classes a couple of days. Doing so freed him for a long weekend, and he hadn't seen his grandmother since before the Ark expedition. Seeing her now was better than waiting for Christmas break. He had so much to tell her, his heart was full to bursting. At least it had been until he reached the nursing station and was told that Carrie Danson had died in the night.

"Do you know how we might reach your father?" the nurse asked gently. "Arrangements have to be made."

Tony shook his head. "No, I don't think that's possible. He's out of the country. I'll phone the American consulate in Kinshasa, Zaire, but to get a message to him could take some time. He's on another expedition . . . " He trailed off, the thought of losing his wonderful old grandmother more than he could bear.

The nurse squeezed his arm, and he winced. The bullet wound was healing nicely, but the bone had been badly bruised. He would not be rappelling any time soon. Still, it had been a small price to pay for what he'd found on Ararat—Noah's Ark and his father's love. And one thing more—a faith in God more powerful than fear or resentment, more powerful even than a youthful passion for total nuclear disarmament. At least heaven would be a nuclear-free zone, he was certain of that.

He desperately needed to find and touch some trace of his grandmother. "Would it be all right to visit her room for a little while?"

The nurse felt a flood of compassion for the strapping young man grieving for the slight, frail woman who had obviously meant so much in his life. "Sure, you go ahead. 218. Down the hall that way on your right. The bed closest to the door. We'll gather up her things later and keep them until you or your father are able to pick them up. As for your grandma, we'll notify the funeral home of the delay. They will await your instructions as soon as you've contacted your father."

Tony made his way down the hall, but in his mind it was the ragged path leading up to the sagging front porch of a frumpy little cottage. The silver maples held their leafy umbrellas protectively over the house and garden, creating a shimmery entrance to another place and time. The robins hopped from rusty coffee can to rusty coffee can, full of self-importance. How he had loved to give them a drink from the dark green hose, filling the cans until they overflowed with sparkling refreshment. Tubby bumble bees buzzed in and out of their woodshed aerodrome, and he would follow them past the root cellar as far as the ancient cesspool, a mysterious cavern wherein frightening creatures lay, covered by a weathered old discarded barn door. Little boys had to be especially careful not to let the toes of their black hightop basketball shoes ever brush against any part of the wooden door. To do that would have disturbed the creatures and unleashed an awful mess of banshees.

But Anthony Lucas Danson had to go that way. It was the only path to Grandma Danson's raspberry patch.

Grandma Danson's. Sugar cookies and Donald Duck grapefruit wedges sweet as sweet could be. Wood cooking stove and musty compost heap. Bulge in the kitchen ceiling from the leaky roof. Reading his dad's collection of Bob Hope comic books on the floor by the toasty hot oil furnace that was lit by dropping a flaming piece of tissue down inside. Dancing the grasshopper jig on the porch, his face pressed against her floury apron. No cares a slice of her lemon meringue pie couldn't cure. Seven-Up floats before bedtime and a safety ring of antique dining room chairs to save a little boy from falling off the sofa in the night. Grandma Danson's. Heaven.

He stood now by the bed where she had drawn her final breath. The bed had been changed and freshly made up, the smell of hospital-clean strong upon the sheets. He tearfully fingered a little pile of her possessions—purse and hairbrush and greeting cards. The faint aroma of Emeraude cologne drifted up and wreathed his head. He closed his eyes and smiled a little, remembering. Dad chopping kindling on the back porch, releasing the scent of Christmas fir into the frisky air. Thick-sliced bacon snapping and spitting in the cast iron skillet. Drawing up the cellar door and descending into the musty earth, a culinary tomb for jars upon jars of canned cherries, pears, and "lazy housewife" pickles. The cloying cachet of mothballs in her immense walk-in closet, the exquisite hiding place of old dresses, hat boxes, and a fox fur piece complete with beady black eyes and tickly whiskers.

*Thank you, Lord, for my grandma and her constant faith in you. Get her to make you some of those raspberry thumbprint cookies she entered in the Pillsbury Bake-Off that time. You won't be sorry.* Tony sighed and sniffed, a fist of lead in his stomach. Carrie Danson was dead, and the earth was one jewel short.

"Miss your grams?"

The voice startled Tony. He hadn't expected anyone else to be in the room. He whirled and looked in the corner by the window from where the question had come. There, bundled in an oversized beige robe, was one of the tiniest women he'd ever seen—not so much her height as her features. Nose, ears, mouth, everything in miniature. She peered bright-eyed and quizzical from the neck of the robe as if to see if the coast were clear and she could climb out of there.

"Yes—yes." Tony stuttered. "She—my grandmother—was a grand lady, and I didn't get a chance to say good-bye." His face crumpled, and he bit his lower lip to keep from crying.

The little woman shifted the quilt she was working on and fixed the young man with a penetrating stare. "You're too young for good-byes," she said in a high, sing-songish voice. "You get older, and you'll be saying good-bye every time you turn around."

He thought that was a queer comment.

"Your gram thought I was a crazy quilt," said the woman with a mirthless chuckle. "But she gave me the chocolate candies she didn't want. Jelly-filled ones mostly. Some had a bite out of 'em, but I didn't care."

Tony smiled warmly. That was for sure his grandma. He walked over to the woman and stuck his hand out. "My name's Tony. Tony Danson."

She let his hand hang there, her hands continuing to race over the stitching without pause. The woman's hands were small but swift and sturdy as she pinched and tucked panel to panel. The stitches were long and loose and not so uniform. That was the slave way. No time for intricate, tight stitching. Had to be in the fields at dawn. No time.

Then, completing the bold orange swatch she was on, she reached inside her robe and removed a lopsided triangle of denim and began to join it to a niche between the orange piece and a canary yellow one.

There'd been a few things she'd meant to tell this young man's grandmother. But between the nurses poking pills into the roommates' mouths and Carrie's frequent flirtations with the pinochle man, opportunity hadn't presented itself. She decided to tell this generation. "My mam used to say every time you break pattern, it's a rebirth of ancestor power inside you. You become possessed by that ancestor. When you sleep under that quilt, that long-ago loved one is lying on top of you, protectin' you. I don't suppose you bein' a Christian, you believe that, do you?"

"I haven't always been a Christian, and there's a whole lot I don't know," Tony replied hesitantly, amazed at her clear-mindedness. "I've often been comforted by memories of my grandma and the things we used to do when I was a kid. Those memories feel warm as a blanket, and safe too."

For the first time since she'd arrived at Powell Valley Convalescent Center, Gussie Jackson deliberately stopped quilting for another human being. She fixed the young man before her with a penetrating look that seemed capable of reading the very blueprint of his soul. Then she said quietly, "Do you believe in the beat?"

Tony didn't think he'd heard correctly. "Excuse me?"

"The beat of life. Do you believe in it?"

"I—I'm not sure I understand." What an odd little woman.

"Africans believe there's a vibration down deep, in here . . . " She paused, tapping herself on the chest. "A voice from the depths of the soul, they call it. Western folks have lost touch with it, but a true African is open to the call of that voice. It's in the blues, in the jazz." She spread the quilt out more and pointed to the multicolored patches. "Blue against red, orange against green—we call that dark to bright to dark again 'hittin' the quilt,' same as what the jazzman does when he shouts to the band, 'Hit it!' and they take off like a hound on the scent."

Tony smiled at her, and to his surprise she placed her deep brown, birdlike hands over his big white ones. Their heat transmitted a strength to his, well beyond their diminutive size. The snowy white head bobbed, as if to some inner rhythm, and she stared hard at a place beyond the mauve walls of the room, beyond even the ends of the earth.

"Uhm-m-m-m-m, yo-o-o-o," she hummed quietly, taking up the needle again without missing a stitch. "My mam believed quilting was her callin'—a divine act. She took delight in the unplannedness of it. But she sure thought God was a-guidin' every stitch of the cloth diary, and when I'd ask her if she could make another quilt just that same way, she'd laugh. 'Laws no, chile.'" Gussie mimicked the deep throatiness of her mother. "'Every one's like a new recipe, a deep breath o' fresh air, but if you liked that one so much, you gonna like this new one every bit as much or more!' I knew the even, sunny bits she sewed was the calm times, and the crookedy, dark ones meant Mam was nursin' some hurt or other.

"Well, sir, whatever my mam had I got too, and it's up to me to hold the hand of the generation before. Life goes on in the quilt. I'd as soon stop breathing as to stop quilting."

Tony Danson let his eyes wander over the woman's labor, the humble symbols of a life, the personal glimpses that perhaps only she was left on earth to read. All the panels, irregular and individual as they were, seemed to radiate from a single dark green oval of felt at the center, for the most part folded under the portion she was currently stitching. He wondered if he dared touch the quilt; he wanted to see what it was that formed the heart of the family tree.

He reached for the quilt. With the lightning-quick reflexes of a coiled cobra, Gussie's left hand shot forward and stayed Tony's hand with a vise grip about the wrist. She probed his soul a second time with a look so fierce it made him afraid. He had skydived off cliffs and bungee jumped off bridges, but few of those plunges were scarier than that look.

Without a word, she relinquished his hand, unfolding the quilt in her lap. With a start, he instantly recognized the creature, as unsophisticated a rendering as it was, very nearly a likeness of a figure in the rock paintings found in a cave at Nachikufu in Northern Rhodesia. His father had shown him a photograph of the drawings—three four-legged creatures with long necks, tails, and bodies. Two could possibly be explained away as crocodilian in nature, except for large, distinct heads clearly separated from thick necks. But the third was dragonlike, a dinosaur so much in rendering like a sauropod, it could have been a rough illustration for a science textbook.

And here it was again. An elephantlike body; four thick, powerful legs; a long, heavy tail tapering to a whippish end; a wide, serpentine neck ending in a small, hard-plated head. *Where did this woman—*

"Uhm-m-m-m-m, yo-o-o-o, uhm-m-m-m-m, yo-o-o-o," she hummed again, eyes transfixed by the creature before her. "Do not overturn my canoe," she sang, the notes rolling up and down, up and down, like an ocean swell. "Do not step on my sleeping one's head . . . uhm-m-m-m-m, yo-o-o-o, yo—" she broke off abruptly, locking eyes with Tony Danson, an untamed light illuminating her features.

Then, to his horror, her eyes rolled up into her head, and her upper body began a convulsive, jerking motion. Her hands flew high in the air and little flecks of spittle formed at the corners of her mouth. He reached for the nurse call light, but the old African woman cried, "NO!" He stopped, and she spoke in an eerie, far away half-whimper, half-groan. "Your father is in very grave danger . . . he has gone where he cannot go . . . to seek the dragon that will not be found . . . STOP HIM . . . bloody death . . . beware the witch's lizard . . . love him . . . save him . . . stinking fire breath must be stopped . . . grab the babies or they will be eaten . . . my home, my home is gone . . . everywhere the brains of brave men have been scattered by the tail like the trunk of a tree . . . will kill your father if you don't hold him . . . runfromthebeastorliveindarkestdespair . . . Ei-e-e-e-e!"

Tony stumbled back from the old woman, covering his ears, his heart banging against its rib cage. Her powerful convulsions rocked the chair back on two legs. Suddenly, she pitched forward and began savagely jamming the needle into the quilted creature, never ceasing the piercing wail of death. Blood stained her robe and quilt crimson black where the needle went through both and into her flesh. Tony tried to stop her, but the force within Gussie Jackson seemed a different entity from the body that contained it. With great slicing arcs, she stabbed at the image of the beast as if to obliterate it. Every ounce of her tiny body was joined in battle, a battle to the death.

The nurses and orderlies rushed past Tony to restrain the last resident of Room 218. She was carried kicking and biting and wailing from the room, but long after her shrieks died behind padded doors, Tony stood numb with what he had witnessed.

One thing he was now convinced of. His father did not know what he was getting into. Tony had to warn him, to stop him if he could. He ran from the room where his grandmother had died, back down the hall, the path away from the cottage of his youth.

The robins scattered before the reckless teenager running pell-mell for his car. He tripped once, the toe of one black high-top basketball shoe catching the corner of the cesspool cover in his grandmother's backyard. It opened just a crack, but it was enough. The creatures stirred within.

Morning on the Ubangi River awakened steamy and rank. The female river horse shifted painfully in the mud wallow, shedding the afterbirth with a groan of fatigue. Beads of pink sweat lubricated the rough hide against the remorseless equatorial sun.

Normally, dawn would not have caught her exposed on a river bar, but the hippo had spent the night in a bed of trampled reeds and just before first light gave birth to a sixty-five-pound male calf. She nudged her baby to its feet, and five minutes after birth it was sniffing and exploring the perimeter of the birthing bed. It stood near her now.

The male with whom she had mated was submerged up-river with the rest of the school. He had gained supremacy over the oldest male by breaking the opponent's foreleg in a roaring, slashing river fight that lasted nearly an hour. The broken limb made it impossible for the four-ton hippo to walk on land and therefore impossible for it to eat. At last, too weak to rise up for air, it had slipped back into the river and drowned.

But the younger male's lordship was short lived. A hippo school is a matriarchy, and when in their reed beds, the males must defer to the females. When the object of his courtship arises, he must lie down. Not until she lies down again can he get up. Should he not observe the rules, he will be attacked by the entire herd of females and forced to leave the school.

The younger male had paid attention to details and was that morning still paying proper homage to the other females before setting out to the feeding grounds along an exclusive path marked with his own dung.

The new mother would rest a while before undertaking the careful training of her young. The calf would have to learn where to walk and where to swim in reference to its mother so that she could keep a watchful eye on it.

Something watched her this morning through feral, slitted eyes. Submerged in the deep, slow pool of the river's bend, hood and eyes just above the surface, it did not like this invasion of its feeding grounds. Just beyond the birthing bed over against the bank was a luxuriant tangle of *malombo* vines, resplendent with beautiful white flowers and an abundance of nutty fruit with a milky white sap that was sweet and very agreeable. The creature fed on great quantities of swamp reeds and grasses, but it would kill for fruit.

The mother hippo stretched in the warm mud, certain she should return to the safety of the herd but not wanting to yet. She nuzzled her baby tenderly and allowed a white egret to alight on her armored rump. Flies swarmed about, crawling in and out of her ears and snout, but she seemed not to care.

With a mighty rush, the watching creature rose from the depths, throwing the river from its back, and crossed the river bar with a speed that belied its size. The female hippo felt the pounding approach of the great beast through the ground. She barely had time to stand and plant herself between her baby and the attack, huge mouth gaping wide, a roar of mother defiance putting the egret to hasty flight. Grasses dangled from the hippo's nose and chin hairs, and the oyster cream-and-gray of the soft interior of her mouth and throat reflected the searing sun. The charging creature aimed for the flashing mouth, despite a wicked display of three-foot canine tusks.

The beast's incredible bulk slammed into the hippo, knocking over the six thousand-pound mother with ease and crushing the newborn beneath. The mother struggled to wriggle free but was pinned fast. With one immense effort, she managed to carve a deep gash in the attacker's right foreleg before the creature's neck bent almost double and it fastened jaws of iron about the hippo's neck. The river horse tried to bellow once more, but with a terrible wrench, the creature from the pool silenced the thick throat forever.

Hummingbirds drank from the white *malombo* flowers and the sun rose higher in the bleached sky. The creature looked at the inviting fruit and dropped its gory mouthful to the sand. It was time to feed.

Reg Danson managed to beg off the spit-roasted bat that morning. The charred little carcasses did not appear to contain much meat anyway, and he'd made it a rule never to eat anything that squeaked. Wiggins seemed peeved for a time, but he gradually loosened up.

It was hotter than the day before and not yet noon. But at least heading upstream in a dugout canoe powered by an outboard motor kicked up a breeze, however limp. Twenty miles upstream lay the mission compound and hopefully a few more amenities than those afforded by a galvanized cooking bucket and a two-man tent. He was curious to see how Wiggins lived and to meet an entire village of pygmies.

But it was to be a short-lived respite. After one day of resorting and packing, they would be off to the interior in search of the elusive Ologus.

"Are you certain you want to go through with this, Danson?" piped Wiggins from the bow of the boat. "They say the Bangombe pygmies kill their visitors and festoon the trees about their camp with the dismembered body parts of their victims. The Ologus are their close relatives, you know."

He grinned, and Reg smiled cheerfully. "Well, Wiggins, I figure if they've let you live for seventeen years, there's hope for me." It was easy to be flippant in the bright Congo sun. Jigs nodded good-naturedly, licked an index finger, and put one point on an imaginary tote board in Reg's favor.

The miles clicked steadily off, and the feelings of isolation mounted. Dozens of little tributaries and side swamps slid past, and it suddenly occurred to Danson how utterly dependent he would soon be on Jigs Wiggins and his auspices. Ndoki and Ndokanda seemed to have minds of their own. Now they lounged in the stern, each spelling the other at the tiller. With one arm draped casually over the tiller, the other blocking the sun from his eyes, Ndoki looked as if he'd caught the red eye from Boston to New York and had time for a brief snooze before an eight o'clock breakfast meeting. Except for needing a shave and forgetting his vest, he might even hold his own among the primitives of Wall Street.

Reg said as much to Wiggins. He agreed. "I believe it was Twain who observed, 'There are many humorous things in this world; among them the white man's notion that he is less savage than other savages.'" Jigs removed his Chicago Cubs baseball cap and wet it in the river. "Phew! She's a corker today! Hard to believe that almost due east of here lie the Mountains of the Moon, at seventeen thousand feet the highest range in Africa. They're crowned by snow and only thirty miles north of the equator. Do you ski?"

Reg laughed. "No, but I think when I'm done with this one, a week in Aspen will be just what the doctor ordered!"

A few moments of silence passed, and then Reg said, "I've got a kid who skis—and flies, dives, jumps, runs, and climbs over, into, and off of anything you put in front of him. You have family, Wiggins?"

Jigs looked at first as if he would not answer.

"I may have," he said slowly. "Had a couple of kids before jail, but they weren't there when I got out. I can barely remember what they looked like then. Gone. Pffssst!" The sound and an upward thrust of his hand made it clear that his family and he no longer communicated.

Reg said no more. There was a great deal bottled up inside Jigs Wiggins, and if it poured out at all, it would be because Jigs chose to pour.

The miles slid lazily past, a relentless and nearly unbroken march of trees and vines painting the world a brilliant green. Brown, blond, and auburn monkeys chased one another about their gigantic jungle gym, occasionally soaring out over the water like kids on a rope swing. Loud, brassy parrots splashed dabs of clown red and orange and blue among the leaves, darting in and out of the dense jungle curtain like harlequins teasing the audience just before showtime.

Wiggins began to hum in his raspy bass a snatch of a spiritual somewhat familiar to Reg. Then he began to beat out the rhythm against the port side of the canoe. "'Follow the drinkin' gourd! Follow the drinkin' gourd, for the old man is a-wait-in' for to carry you to freedom if you follow the drinkin' gourd. When the sun comes back and the first quail calls, follow the drinkin' gourd, for the old man is a-wait-in' for to carry you to freedom if you follow the drinkin' gourd.'

"I love those old escape songs the slaves used to sing in the fields so the masters and their overseers wouldn't know they were communicating. The drinking gourd was their name for the Big Dipper and the message was, 'Escape's on for tonight. Keep coming in the direction of the Big Dipper, and you'll find the conductor for the Underground Railroad waiting to take you to freedom.' I used to sing 'em in prison, wishful thinking for all the good it did me." He smiled a little, remembering.

"'Steal Away to Jesus'; 'Oh, Sinner, You'd Better Get Ready'; even 'Swing Low, Sweet Chariot' alerted the slaves that an escape plot was hatching. Harriet Tubman, 'the black Moses,' told them to 'Wade in the Water' to throw the bloodhounds off the scent. You can just taste the yearning for freedom in every word. They're so full of bounce and spring! I think Beethoven would have loved to sink his teeth into a good Negro spiritual!"

"Hallelujah, brother!" shouted Reg helpfully. Breathing was easier whenever Wiggins climbed out of his taciturn moods.

The missionary nodded appreciatively and continued. "I can just imagine those slaves, bowed from work and whip and wickedness, closing their eyes for just a second and seeing golden chariots driven by a band of angels galloping across the skies, coming to take them to heaven. Can't you see it, Danson? I close my eyes sometimes and see a long, sleek limousine, sent by my rich Friend, fully equipped, coming for me. Pulls up with a whisper, door pops open with that expensive *schlunk,* the sound a well-made thing makes. A man dressed in soft gray, all bathed in golden light, comes around and holds the door for me and as I climb in, he doffs his hat and says, 'Very good, sir!' gets in the driver's seat, and asks me over an intercom if I am comfortable and if everything is to my liking. It is, Danson. It is the only place where everything is very much to my liking. Very much indeed." He closed his eyes, and he was seeing that limousine. He tilted his head to the sun and wet his lips as if he could taste the divine extravagance that would send a private car for him. He rocked and hummed while the river slipped endlessly by.

The canoe skimmed sideways into a wide turn in the river, and Ndoki increased the throttle on the outboard. The current was stronger here, and he steered toward a large river bar to the right where the water flow would be less insistent.

There was a prickling along the nape of Ndoki's neck. His skin crawled. The jungle here was silent. Where were the Evil Ones, the crocodiles that could always be found in such calm backwater? And what of the hippos that should surely lay claim to such a natural mud wallow and plenty of surrounding marsh? There was something at the far end of the bar, but it was too still, too misshapen to be a . . . He shook Ndokanda awake.

The brothers shrieked in alarm, first pointing in horror, then shrinking as far back as the stern would allow without their going overboard. They let loose with a string of terrified Bantu, their eyes bugging from their sockets. Ndoki grabbed the tiller in both hands and flung it as far forward as he could reach. The canoe cut sharply left, the bow nearly going under the surging current. Reg fell half into the water before catching himself, a stab of pain in his right shin from where it ground against the thwart. Wiggins lunged for his pack in the bottom of the canoe and struggled with the fastenings. The canoe straightened out, and Ndoki gave it full throttle downriver and back the way they'd come.

Wiggins grunted with the exertion of bracing himself in the pirogue but found what he was looking for. He whipped his arm into the air, and a pistol shattered the jungle silence. Again. A third time. The brothers covered their heads and cowered. Wiggins scrambled to the abandoned tiller, roughly shouldering his carriers aside. He eased the tiller about and brought the canoe around so that it again faced upriver.

Reg looked at him questioningly, but Wiggins's stormy countenance supplied few answers. "You don't survive long in the diamond mines without a gun," he explained. Reg drew a deep breath and let it out slowly. Monkey stew. Fast food caterpillars. A gun-toting missionary ex-con.

Jigs cut into the shallows at the near end of the river bar and scanned the muddy sand. They followed the *ngubu,* hippo tracks—six inches across, four stumpy toes ending in hooflike nails—for about fifty feet before Wiggins throttled back. Tight-lipped and grim, he pointed to the water's edge.

There, dissecting the path of the hippo, was a larger set of tracks, as big and broad as an elephant's. The tracks were scuffed and elongated as if the beast had been running, dragging the tips of its feet as it plunged forward, but the depth of the prints spoke of the creature's enormous weight. Deep, narrow indentations sharply indicated three claws on each foot. Even more prominent was the channel dug between the prints. Something obviously thick and heavy had been drug behind the beast. A tail as big as a tree.

Ndoki and Ndokanda practically lay in the bottom of the canoe, whimpering and refusing to look at the tracks in the sand. The childlike fear of these jungle hunters unsettled Reg. "Poor beggars saw a brother hunter who'd been killed by this thing not too long ago," said Wiggins in a strained voice.

Reg had no sooner taken in the prints than Wiggins emitted a sharp "Fffftt!" and Reg looked ahead to see one of the saddest sights of his career. A mother hippo lay in a huge, dark ring of blood, most of which had been absorbed by the sand; but some had coagulated thick and gelatinous at the place where the animal's throat should have been. Instead, there was a tremendous gaping wound between jaw and chest. Literally pounds of flesh had been ripped away, nearly severing the head from the torso. Oddly, it was the only fresh wound on the animal, its old scars from past battles with hippo-kind long since healed over. Odder still, the great slab of flesh that had been chewed from the hippo's neck—the pink wound was ragged, not surgically precise—lay by its forehead as if spat there by the killer who did not find the taste to its liking. Ants busily rushed about the carcass, cutting and hauling exposed flesh fast as they could before the bonanza was discovered by nature's larger undertakers.

Beneath the mother, its perfect little features frozen forever in infancy, lay a dead baby hippo. Reg had read of an overprotective female hippo in a zoo that kept smothering its babies, but it seemed unlikely in the wild. Somehow the mother had accidentally fallen on her newborn. Instead of being full of the sweet nourishment of mother's milk, the baby's mouth and snout were clogged with sand.

Wiggins turned, brandished the pistol at the cowering pygmies, spat out a warning in Bantu, and leapt lightly ashore. He motioned Danson to follow.

They stood together surveying nature's wreckage, not believing their eyes. A black and yellow hornbill watched them from a nearby bush, its banana-colored bill and bizarre helmet of honeycombed bone giving it a top-heavy appearance. It made no sound nor did it move, seemingly stunned by recent events.

"Probably eight or ten feet at the hip, maybe sixteen, eighteen tons overall," mumbled Wiggins shakily. "Then, here, look here—" He strode back to the bush line, running from spot to spot pointing at the freshly torn vegetation and the trampled ground. "It shredded these *malombo* vines, stripped the fruit, then turned here—" he indicated a wide patch of sand where a large body had reversed directions, sweeping the ground flat and rubbing it smooth, except for the broad, stumpy indentations where its clawed feet had stood, "and came down here and reentered the water," he concluded, walking sideways, one foot over the other along the edge of the tail swath, then wading partway into the river as if he might dive after the thing and follow it to its submarine lair.

Jigs stood there shin-deep, gun pointed at the water, daring the creature to surface. Reg looked from Wiggins to the dead hippos to the tracks and back to Wiggins again. "You mean the monster did this? It was here? This morning? *Mokele-mbembe* was *here?*" He felt like shouting out loud.

At the mention of the creature's name, Ndoki and Ndokanda screamed and grabbed for the rope starter on the outboard. Wiggins whirled and fired. A burst of splinters tore from the seat under Ndoki's left thigh, and immediately the two men dropped back down and resumed their frightened whimpering.

Wiggins stormed over and placed his mouth about three inches from Reg's ear. "Do not mention that name anywhere near these people!" he snarled, but only loud enough for Danson to hear. "Why do you think I haven't said a word about this thing since you arrived? Their parents and grandparents have told them that to even speak of the creature is to die. Evil is in its loins, and a demon lives in its brain. These two may believe in Jesus, but they are not too quick to discount the wisdom of the elders."

Reg grabbed Jigs by the upper arms. "And you, man?! What do you believe?" he said, barely able to contain himself. "Surely you don't think that *any* creature is greater than the Creator?" Wiggins looked away and did not speak. A slight tremor in his arms betrayed his misgivings.

Reg resumed. "Jigs, listen. No one's been more ambivalent than I about coming here. I've felt very uneasy about the whole thing, and again my employer, Richard Bascomb, has presented me with a bagful of questions and a thimbleful of answers."

He paused a moment as if unable—or unwilling—to say what he was thinking now. "And, yes, if I'm honest, I had more than a little skepticism. Dinosaurs that still roam the earth? But this, this—" he swept an arm about the carnage on the river bar—"what's here cannot be denied! Let's camp across the river. We can set up a blind in that overhanging tree and keep a watch until it returns."

Wiggins fixed Reg with soulful eyes. "It won't be back anytime soon. All the *malombo* fruit is gone, and it's not a carnivore. It kills, but it does not eat flesh. Because there are no other tracks or sign, this one was probably traveling past in search of more plentiful forage. But there are others. They'd have to be eating machines, devouring vast tonnage of vegetation to maintain their massive size. Deforestation, drought, and the encroachment of man further upriver may be driving them south, but I have never known one to come this far down."

"Maybe," Reg responded. "But what you're describing is an ectothermic herbivore. They require much smaller amounts of food for production of body heat than, say, an endothermic carnivore, like the lion, that needs to eat its body weight in prey every eight days. The ectotherm? Every sixty to sixty-five days or so. Probably only three to five percent of the ancient dinosaurs were actually meat-eaters."

Wiggins shook free of Danson and shoved the barrel of the pistol into his waistband. "I don't know about that. But I do know I resent Bascomb's intrusion along the Ubangi. This thing could easily backfire. In the end, I assented to your coming only because I have an interest in reaching the peoples further north of the mission. They—they've never been successfully evangelized—" and here he looked away again and dropped his voice to a barely audible whisper— "rumors of pagan practices . . . awful sacrifices. That's how it is with rumors, the wilder the better. No, I wouldn't attempt it without another Westerner along. All I have at the mission station are natives, and they lack the detachment necessary to evaluate the situation. Everything's incantations and hidden meanings with them. They wouldn't know out-and-out shysterism if they fell over it. It does appear that the northern people are starving for some unknown reason . . . strange, that portion of the jungle has always been rich in game and honey . . . . Now, I don't know what's happening." He looked at Danson, shaking his head as if shaking off the thought of having to go north.

Suddenly, the black pipe was in his bearded mouth, unlit, patrolling the perimeter of thin lips like a watchful doberman. "They say there is a *griot* among the Ologus of the BaMbuti who knows the creature, who even—" he snorted derisively—"has an understanding with the creature. It's probably just the *iboga* talking. Common as chewing gum, the *iboga* plant. Keeps 'em awake and 'prophetic' for days."

Reg arched his eyebrows. "The *griot?*" he inquired.

"Soothsayer, guardian of the word, custodian of civilization, oral historian without peer, preserver of myth and magic," Jigs said grandly. "This guy's witchdoctor, lawyer, priest, and king all rolled into one.

"It's even been said that when an old *griot* dies, a library burns. The black continent is an oral continent, Danson. A *griot* was actually assigned to each royal house, and all the customs, culture, and folk wisdom of today were passed on by these oracles. It is with him that we have our best hope of understanding and observing what you have come after."

Wiggins removed a red and orange Blackhorn's Best tobacco pouch from his breast pocket and dug near the surface for a bowlful. He held the pouch with an odd gentleness as if the contents were fragile and he dare not spill a single shred. *Tobacco must come dear in the jungle,* thought Reg.

Wiggins carefully replaced the tobacco pouch, half turning as if he didn't want Danson to see. But Reg noticed the curious movement of the fingers. Before Wiggins slipped the Blackhorn's Best back into its pocket, he felt the bottom of the pouch. *He couldn't be checking the level; he's just scooped some off the top because the bag was full. What's he feeling for?*

Jigs looked at the ruined hippos again and sighed heavily. "You're young still, Danson. Go back to the Smithsonian where they ship you a couple of bones of a long-dead something-or-other and all you've got to do is fill in the rest with modeling clay and a vivid imagination. Nobody gets hurt that way."

"Except the truth," Reg said, annoyed. "Truth always gets butchered when the academics and the theorists are given license to fabricate the history of the world from a hank of hair and a piece of bone. I want to hand them a living sauropod and say, 'Well, now, what do you make of this?'" He slapped his hands together, rubbing them in anticipation. "I saw with my own eyes. Jigs, I'm telling you, there was room enough in the Ark for dinosaurs and then some! The evolutionists aren't going to win this one!"

"Neither are the Ologus," said Wiggins under his breath.

"Excuse me?"

"Nothing. Let's get back on the water. The station will think I've eloped with the princess of Zaire. Shame to waste all this meat, but the villagers won't eat it once they know how it died." He retrieved a machete from the pirogue and hacked into the large hippo's haunch until he had a couple of good-sized slabs of meat. "Lunch for the two of us," he explained, wrapping the hippo steaks in a burlap sack. "If we avoid food poisoning, it'll go a long way in convincing them of the difference between truth and nonsense."

Reg sincerely prayed he would live to see the inside of a supermarket once more before he saw the other side of glory. Wiggins managed a little grin. "Next stop, Sangha Mercy Mission. Take the tiller, Danson, while I remind the brothers grim that perfect love casts out fear."

**F**rom a half mile off, Sangha Mission seemed to consist of one colossal *baobab* tree, bristling above the swamp like a fantastic conning tower.

"What good's a river if it doesn't lead to a village?" asked Jig Wiggins, pronouncing the old Congo saying under his breath.

As the mission compound at the tree's base materialized from the surrounding quagmire, the *baobab* grew wider and thicker and all-protective, a massive mother of a tree. Its witchly branches reached for the sky, misshapen and barren. The tree looked deathly dry, its thick trunk jutting from the earth as if the whole thing had fallen from the sky and punctured the ground, a rough and splintery javelin of the gods. Frayed buildings and sheds of the mission huddled resignedly in the lee of its knobby arms, looking needful of its protection but hardly grateful.

"Took ten years to convince my entourage they should build at the base of old Broom Hilda," said Wiggins, indicating the hefty tree. "For generations it had been a place of taboo, a vent pipe to the kingdom of the dead. Apparently, some two hundred years ago, a chief was buried under the tree along with several of his less than eager wives. His face, of course, was turned toward the rising sun to indicate strength; theirs were turned toward the setting sun to indicate feminine weakness. About the only deity the sick had to turn to was *mbori,* the king of the ghosts. It rarely did any good, though, because he more often listened to his brother ghosts and pulled the plug on the dying. The ghosts below needed another spirit more than the world above needed another mouth to feed.

"So, the legend developed that the *baobab* had been planted upside down and those are its awful dried roots that you see sticking out of the ground. Evil spirits were said to inhabit its crooks and knotholes; it was the dwelling place of coiled cobras hungry for human blood. They would tell this story to their children at night and make the boys sleep beneath the tree as a rite of manhood. It's a wonder any of them could string two sane words together when I got here."

Ndoki was back at the tiller, sullen and uncommunicative but mindful of cutting a straight course for Sangha. Ndokanda had mumbled a few words of apology and seemed suitably impressed that though Wiggins and Danson had consumed the hippo steaks for lunch, the two men were still very much among the living. The only face Reg had made was over the toughness of the meat and its strong, gamy flavor.

A bulging burlap sack lay ahead of Ndokanda's bare feet. It contained the head of the hippo and the torn flesh surrounding the gaping throat wound. It warranted closer examination. Reg was hoping to find tooth marks, which in animals could be every bit as revealing as human fingerprints.

They had encountered no further sign of *Mokele-mbembe,* but Reg kept watching the green purling waters. Thinking of the creature submerged beneath them drove all thought of drowsing from his mind. He suppressed a shudder. Were these the dragons of legend? The Chinese used their bones in medicine. "Dragon bones" were reported found at Wucheng in the southern Qinling Mountains during the Jin Dynasty, third century. Sauropod fossils were located at thirteen thousand feet in Tibet. Babylon's King Nebuchadnezzar commissioned the Ishtar Gate, and the artist made renderings of lion and bulls and "sirrush," the dragon. And long before that, somewhere around 1500 B.C., Job gave an eye-witness account of a behemoth that could only be a sauropod: "tail like a cedar . . . his bones like beams of bronze . . . he lies . . . in the covert of reeds and marshes [jungle swamps] . . . " Sightings and descriptions of the fierce creatures for thousands of years since had been commonly reported over wide regions.

The outboard droned its incessant growl, and the nearer they came to Sangha, the larger the *baobab* grew.

Jigs pulled at his beard as if it were ill-fitting. "Never grow one of these things, Danson," he admonished. "The pygmies wear 'em, but they are blasted nasty on a hot day!"

They were still a good thirty yards from shore, but the commanding tree claimed even the river in its smothering reach. He pointed up into the branches that now overhung the River Ubangi. Gourd-shaped fruit hung down, looking like coconut-sized kiwi fruits with a dusting of yellow fuzz. "The irony of these people! They very nearly starved to death before I proved to them the fruit is edible," said Wiggins pensively. "The leaves, when there are any, make a passable soup, and you can roast the seeds or make a drink out of them. *Baobab* wood ash contains sufficient chlorides to substitute for salt. Out on the savannah, I've heard of thirsty hunters who don't believe the ghost tales tapping the trunk where great quantities of water are stored.

"It is highly unusual to see one of these in this flooded region where the swamp fans out. River leaks like a sieve along here, and *baobabs* seem to thrive best where water's least. But this old girl climbed up on this point of land and said, 'I'm taking over!'"

Indeed she had. The clearing beneath the spreading *baobab* was as smooth and hard as a Spanish plaza. Banana-leaf huts with three-foot high entrances circled the outer boundary of the clearing, and little fire pits for cooking smouldered here and there. A rough log house with thatched roof and a slumping porch commandeered the area immediately above and to the right of the canoe landing. A couple of storage sheds and a high wooden rack of blackened strips of flesh over a trench of smoking coals completed the mission's accoutrements. The aroma of roasting meat with slightly fishy overtones wafted out to the canoe and its occupants. A child wailed, and several others chased one another about the clearing, hooting their delight. A toughened woman of indeterminant age shouldered a six-foot piece of firewood. She walked nimbly along the bank and gave Jigs a little wave and somber greeting. Two old men sat on logs notching arrows. They too looked up and waved. The children wore nothing. The men wore shirts and shorts, and the woman with the wood wore a dark purple loincloth that extended almost to her knees.

Women and girls attended the fires, one or two of which held shriveled little carcasses of unidentifiable origin roasting on a spit. "Game's getting scarce," said Wiggins, a sour note of worry in his voice. "Especially in the north hunting grounds where we're headed. The young men are gone almost constantly now, trying to find anything they can to feed their families. Nutrition's a constant battle. I get multivitamins into them when I can, but tablets are a poor substitute for fresh meat. Thank God for the fish in the river."

Ndoki cut the motor, and the canoe slid noiselessly onto the shore. Wiggins leaped out and held the bow steady for the others. Reg reached toward one of his packs, but Jigs shook his head no. "First things first," was all he said.

Wiggins turned and shouted a greeting in Bantu. The children shouted a mellifluous response, and the old men added their scratchy hellos, leaving their arrows. Children spilled out of the little huts and carried the elders along in their tide. The wave of chattering humanity washed up at the base of the baobab, hopping about on first one dusty foot then the other. Wiggins leaned back into the canoe and fished up an oil-stained paper sack. With a wink at Danson, he tucked the bag into his belt and waded into the brown stream of humanity. It rose about him in excited anticipation, ever widening as tributaries of little ones and female teenagers and an occasional old man or woman joined the main stream.

Reg was struck with the enthusiasm and the handsomeness of the people, all less than five feet tall. Pretty adolescent girls wrapped from breast to knee in a single threadbare length of cloth flashed large black eyes coyly at Danson. Little boys, bellies distended slightly by early malnourishment, scratched various itches, cuffed one another playfully, or jostled for position as befit the brotherhood of boys. A young mother, bare from the waist up, held an infant on her hip in the manner of mothers everywhere. She cooed fondly at her boy, shyly avoiding Reg's gaze. The boy reached with tiny fingers for one of his mother's long, flattened breasts, but was denied, surely but kindly. His fingers closed instead on the blue and white beaded necklace about her neck. In contrast to the black, close-cropped hair of his neighbors, the boy's was brown on top and bright orange around the sides from undernourishment. The pygmies lived on the edge of existence, despite the benevolent hand of the mission.

"Have you been without other Westerners long?" asked Reg. Jigs snorted derisively. "Only the productive missions get fresh troops. Two conversions a year don't amount to revival stats. They don't consider that these people have been spiritually dead for thousands of years. It's all about numbers, Danson, and we don't rate a blip on the screen."

The woman who had carried the firewood walked up to Wiggins. It was clear from her rough skin, knobby joints, and thick, blocky limbs that she was old, shaped and misshapen by a life of demanding physical labor reserved for pygmy women. The men were the providers of food, sport, and legend. They bore the dangers of the jungle and felt it fair trade to leave the heavy domestic work to the women.

The woman's face was tattooed in a spider web pattern, lines emanating from her mouth and eyes as if she had wept black tears. Her chest was similarly festooned as was the area between her shoulders.

She proffered Wiggins the half-charred leg bone of some animal, the joint at the end hacked open to expose the nutritious marrow within. The missionary nodded with dignity and raised the joint to his lips. With a noisy sucking, he withdrew a tiny portion of the precious marrow. He nodded to the woman again and handed the bone to Danson. "Make a convincing slurp," he said from the corner of his mouth. "Ceremonial. The poor beggars can't afford to give away what little nourishment they have." Reg ordered his stomach to behave, made his bow, and touched the bone to his lips. The sound he made, though a distant second to Wiggins's, was sufficient to bring a ghost of a smile to the old woman's sagging face.

"*Mbote!* Hello! *Sango nini?* What's new?" asked Wiggins.

"*Sango te.* Nothing," the woman replied.

"Her husband, a *griot,* died last year," said Wiggins to Reg, his eyes not leaving the old woman's. "Something of a legend in his own right. He was known far and wide as a tough negotiator, an uncompromising master of the story. People traveled for days to sit at his feet and hear the fairy mumbo jumbo he could spout. But Isese was just a two-tattoo man when it came to swaying public opinion. His wife here, Kakese, is a three-tattoo woman and a force to be reckoned with. They came out of the jungle together, but he died without confessing the Lord while she became a new creature in Christ. She's the real glue of the mission and a genuine drawing card. Plus—" Wiggins's eyes danced with a merry light—"no one dares leave Sangha to return to the nomadic life of the jungle far from the light of God. Not while Kakese's on duty!"

She smiled broadly at the twice mention of her name, and there was much nodding of appreciation at the warmth in Wiggins's voice when he spoke of the woman. One of the old men, as if having followed the conversation, pointed at Kakese and croaked, "*Azali mwasi matata!*"

There was melodic laughter at that, the little knot of villagers in obvious agreement. Wiggins grinned broadly and clapped the old man on the shoulder. Kakese frowned in mock disapproval, and Reg raised his eyebrows questioningly. Wiggins laughed. "Old Joe here says Kakese's one tough woman!"

Jigs led the way to the spot where the ancient *baobab* disappeared into the ground. *How like a pied piper he is,* thought Reg, marveling at the cranky but benevolent red-haired giant towering over his charges. The children clung to his pant legs and bounced around him like unruly puppies. But once they arrived at the tree trunk of meeting, the pygmies fell silent. They assembled in neat little rows before him and bowed their heads respectfully. Even the little ones stopped their fidgeting after a fashion and squeezed their eyes tight shut.

Wiggins lifted his head to the white hot heavens and raised his arms imploringly. First in Bantu, then in English, he cried, "'I came to testify to the truth,' said Jesus. 'I am the truth,' said Jesus. 'You shall know the truth and the truth shall set you free,' said Jesus. 'He who knows the Son shall be free indeed!' said Jesus. He is the divine *griot,* as One with the Father, the source of all life!"

Jigs turned his back and clapped skyward. Loud and vigorous applause rose from the assembly, reaching for the heavens with a hand offering for God. Reg joined in their clapping and singsong repetition of the name, "Jesus! Jesus! Jesus!" They swayed slightly in the torpid heat, all thought of fire and food far from them.

Ndoki and Ndokanda were most vigorous in their declaration of the Name, all fear of the unknown monsters of the night unable to penetrate the hallowed circle at the foot of the *baobab.* The cathedral of crooked branches sheltered the worshipers beneath, and life without end welled up from the scrawny patch of earth.

The people began a low humming. "Great God of our needs," Wiggins spoke again, "thank you for safety upon the river. We do not know what tomorrow brings, but we are grateful for today. Thank you for watching over these your children and your children in the jungle who hunt the game you provide. The game dwindles, Father, but grant that our faith may not shrink with it. You, who can make bread from stones and rain food from heaven, know our needs, and it grieves you when we hurt. Thank you for providing food from downriver and for the people across the oceans who gave the money to buy it. May they be warmed and filled even as they have warmed and filled us."

The humming increased in volume, a tender melody, familiar yet flavored with the swell and syncopation of African rhythm. "Keep us from the evils of the night, the darkness of our souls, the terrors of the swamp . . . " Wiggins prayed with growing intensity, fingers outstretched as if straining to touch the fingers of God. There was an unmistakable tremor now that had not been there at first. " . . . lead us not into temptation and deliver us from evil that some men seek, a thing of curiosity and disgust, child of perdition, spawn of Satan!" The last three words exploded from Wiggins. He whirled back and fixed Danson with a fierce and frightening look. He stood there for a long minute, chest heaving from the exertion of his own soul, words paralyzed deep in his throat. He shook his head, as if recovering, and spoke again, directing his words at Reg, but speaking so all could hear.

"Consider the dung beetle, how it hides its eggs inside little balls of excrement. Life from waste. Offspring from offal. These people are my hatchlings, but I have snatched a few of them from the sewage of unbelief. Those have breathed the fresh, clean air of understanding. But the people to whom we go choose to smear themselves in the excrement of hatred, treachery, and idolatry. May their sins not be visited upon these my kinsmen!" The people murmured anxiously at the distress on their friend's face and in his speech.

The tension released when Jigs again threw his arms out to heaven. "Great God of the ages, hear our prayer and heal our land." As if from nowhere, a light misting rain fell in benediction, and the people again lifted arms and hands in applause. The sky clouded over with startling speed, and the rain descended in sheets. The people evaporated, disappearing inside the tiny huts about the circle, and Danson ran with Jigs to the shelter of the mission station porch. The water beat madly against the tin above them and became noisy falls where the roof buckled and slouched. The difference between the clearing and the river became much less defined. In the torrential downpour, it almost felt as if the station house were adrift in a flotilla of leaf igloos riding out a tropical ocean storm.

"I suppose you think it strange we haven't erected a chapel complete with spire and cross?" shouted Wiggins above the downpour. He blew the rain from the beard beneath his lip, and water bombed the weathered porch flooring with a shake of his hoary head. The words were more of a challenge than a question.

"Not at all," Reg replied. The rain stopped as suddenly as it had come, the sun blazing again and turning the compound into a sea of thick mist. "Outdoor churches are all the rage in California." The attempt to lighten the suddenly oppressive atmosphere was a lame one. "I thought you said you'd had little results among these people. I didn't see anyone skipping church."

Wiggins looked irritable. "Don't be deceived. They'll hum hymns while carving a fresh idol. Few there be with true faith."

The piercing shriek like that of a woman being murdered nearly gave Reg cardiac arrest. Jigs looked unperturbed, pointing to the west end of the house. Reg followed the finger and the sudden beating of wings. Inside an enclosure of about one hundred-fifty square feet were four beautiful pheasants with bright green heads, small scarlet crests, white and black ruffs, green breasts and mantles, blue wings, yellow backs, red rumps, and very long white tails barred in black with orange feathers at the base. Two more males emerged from little wooden shelters at the rear of the pen followed by two drab females.

"A little indulgence of mine," said Wiggins offhandedly. "That and a drag on the pipe now and then." He sighed despondently at the precious few indulgences he was allowed. "Lady

Amherst's pheasants. *Chrysolophus amherstiae.* Lovely to the eye and a constant reminder of the Creator's handiwork. These people have so little. A splash of color, a thing of barter, a Christmas feast. Only these won't make it to Christmas. They'll have to be butchered this evening. The little kids have suffered long enough."

Reg nodded sympathetically. "Beautiful birds. I believe the Chinese ringnecked pheasant is South Dakota's state bird?"

"Ah, yes. *Phasianus toequatus.* But believe it or not, no species of pheasant is native to North America. All came from Asia. These simple people have such difficulty with that. They think I invented the silly birds from a few spare parts I had laying about the shop. Asia might as well be on the moon. I'd like to take that skeptic Ndoki to the States for a weekend. But they are so primitive, so rudimentary, what on earth would they do with Western civilization? When I brought the outboard in, they would have built a shrine to it if I'd let them.

"It does them some good to live on the edge like this, though. I hate to see the little ones crying in pain, but if they have to wonder where their next meal's coming from, it sharpens their reliance on God the Provider. What I've brought in the canoe today they see as an answer to prayer, and so it is. There's still some fruit in the jungle, less every day, but the monkeys and the wild hogs are disappearing. Far to the south and east of us, the natives aren't experiencing these kinds of shortages." He lowered his voice as the people began to pour forth from the little entrances to their huts. "They think it is the fault of *Mokele-mbembe,* that he is a devil beast. The brothers will accompany us only because they hope we can somehow reverse the scourge and convince the monsters to leave. Then, they believe, the little forest animals will return and pygmy bellies will again be full. Of course, the mission agency would never allow them to die of starvation, but we are small and donations few."

"What is causing the food shortages?"

Jigs shrugged. "Probably a combination of pollution, poachers, and progress. Animals know when their world is closing in on them, and people from Epuluville and beyond strip the jungle of its resources to make a buck in trade and put nothing back. The government does not want to appear retarded in development, so they bring in heavy equipment, cut down the trees, and put in roads to nowhere. The animals flee to the interior, and that makes the competition for the available food greater. They die out. The rains come, wash out the roads, and the people make new ones. They'd rather wear Western clothes, drive Western machinery, and get a paycheck like a Westerner than be seen as a bunch of ignorant bush dwellers. Of course, they're simply trading one kind of bondage for another, but you can't show them that."

"Are Bascomb earthmovers part of the destruction?" The question needed to be asked, but Reg didn't like asking it.

"Now you're catching on," Jigs said with surprisingly little anymosity. "But, hey, if it's the only way to get a school, you make allowances. Don't look so glum. If Richard Bascomb is prepared to halt the roads in the name of rain forest preservation, he can't be entirely profit-hungry."

Wiggins called to the people, and they ran to the area in front of the porch railing. The big man withdrew the paper sack from his belt, reached in, and pulled out multicolored jelly beans. He tossed them to the crowd like a whiskery clown at a parade, and they scrambled for them as eagerly as children anywhere. He paused and looked out upon the forest tangle pressing in upon the mission outbuildings. The worry in his eyes was palpable.

"They ought to freeze this," he said incongruously, waving a hand over the encroaching green. "There's a Professor Senforth or Renforth—Benford, that's it. Professor Gregory A. Benford of the University of California says we ought to fan out into the rain forests of the world right now and gather samples of every living thing and freeze 'em. Just get out there and grab one of everything before it's too late. He calls it a 'library of life.'

"Makes sense to me. I mean, when you think there's more than fourteen hundred species of tropical rain forest plants alone thought to have anticancer properties, not to mention those species that fight malaria, high blood pressure, and mental illness. Why, some have even shown promise in the war against AIDS. And here we're letting people mow down the tropical forests at fifty to a hundred acres *a minute* to graze cattle and grow carrots!" He left off with an exasperated wave of his hand.

"I've heard of Professor Benford's work," said Danson, nodding in agreement. "He maintains that with five thousand species of tropical rain forest plants and animals going extinct *every year,* we must deep-freeze them in liquid nitrogen immediately. Whether science can revive them later or not isn't the issue. What's important is to preserve the genetic blueprints of extinct species for examination by the researchers of tomorrow."

"Do you buy it?" asked Wiggins without looking at Reg. Danson stared hard at the jungle beyond. The rain had stopped, but the continued runoff of reservoirs of rain, captured by great leaves and plants deliberately cupped to hold water, barely slowed. The massive transpiration from the ground and the plants that dwelt there lent the distinct impression that it was actually raining up.

"I do buy it," Reg replied at last, the line of his jaw set hard and unyielding, "and by the grace of God, before this expedition is over, we will have genetic proof of *Mokele-mbembe* and the origins of Eden!"

He'd said it quietly so that the villagers wouldn't hear, but a boy of seven who'd scrambled under the porch after a rolling red jelly bean heard the horrible name. The boy believed that there was holiness in Wiggins and undoubtedly great strength in so mighty a beard as wreathed the missionary's face, but this visitor had spoken the unspeakable. What protection did he have?

Not nearly enough, decided the boy, cramming the errant bean in his mouth and wiggling his tongue in rare delight at the dissolving sugar. He had once found the remains of a man who had vowed to kill the creature. It had ripped open his belly and back in its jaws and flung the limp body to earth with as much disregard as the boy had for his sister's reed doll. Then it had stepped on the man's head, grinding it to an unrecognizable pulp in the mud of the riverbank. As long as the boy lived, he would not forget the gruesome mangle above the man's neck. It made him sick now, and he spat out the remains of the precious candy.

Tony Danson threw his hands in the air in disgust. The Kinshasa taxi driver would have made Billy the Kid look benevolent. He was demanding extortion prices to take the American to the embassy. When Tony explained he hadn't had time to cash his traveler's checks but that he desperately needed to see the consulate general before the embassy closed, the skinny driver folded his arms, puffed out his cheeks, and feigned no comprehension of English.

The "taxi" was a battered blue moped that looked as if it had been assembled by Dr. Frankenstein on a bad day from dubious remains in motor vehicle graveyards. The front fender had been removed and attached upside-down to the front handlebars to serve as a rack for the driver's lunch. The rear passenger's platform, full of holes, revealed a threadbare tire which hadn't seen tread in five or six seasons. Tony started to yell at the driver, who calmly reached over and tooted his horn in time to the American's angry grievances.

Tony was about to let the air out of the man's tires *and* cheeks, when he caught himself. *Ugly American,* he remonstrated. *Get a grip. You're a pray-er now, not a fighter. Please, Lord, I can't hope to find Dad without your help. Give me a breakthrough here or I'm just plain stuck. Thank you.*

With a great air of dignity, the driver gave one last long toot on the horn, then dusted off the seat with an oily rag from a pouch in the moped's saddlebags. Tony sighed thankfully at the man's change of heart and started to climb aboard. The driver stopped him with an outstretched arm and moved him gently but firmly back to where he'd been standing. Then, with an exaggerated bow, the driver made way for a Zairian in a shabby suit, clutching an emaciated chicken under each arm. The man straddled the platform seat and cinched up his chickens a little tighter, giving the disbelieving American a deferential nod. Then he was gone in a sputtering blue haze of pollution and chicken feathers.

Tony blinked, hands on his hips, mouth ajar. Traffic screeched and snorted in both directions, and the little moped melted without hesitation into a line of trucks that might have been a military convoy. The drivers laid on their horns, and Tony could just make out the moped's shrill but defiant reply.

He tried to think of something to yell, but nothing suitable came to mind.

"Excuse me, sir. Can I be of service?" Tony looked into the boyish face of an American nicely dressed in a three-piece suit. The eyes twinkled with resolve above a faint five o'clock shadow and a lopsided mouth used to laughter.

"Sure," Tony said, searching the distance again in the hopes the taxi would return and they'd all have a good laugh at the gullible American, perfect foil for the keen Zairian sense of humor. "Know how I can get to the American embassy before four o'clock?"

The boyish man coughed apologetically. "Sorry to say, the embassy has already closed. It closes early on Saturdays." Tony's shoulders slumped dejectedly. "Oh, Dad, Dad, forgive me. I'm trying . . ."

"Excuse me?" said the man, eyes lit with interest.

"Oh, sorry," said Tony, noticing the man again. "It's just that my father is . . . I need to get word to my father because . . . My dad could be in some danger, and I think I need to warn him . . . " He trailed off weakly, unsure exactly why he had come.

The man studied him for a moment in genuine interest. "Your father wouldn't happen to be Reg Danson?" He smiled inquisitively.

Tony stared at him wide-eyed. "Yes, that's my dad. Do you know him? Have you word of the expedition? Is he all right?"

"Whoa, whoa . . . just a minute! It's Tony, isn't it? Tony Danson?"

Tony nodded eagerly.

"Well, Tony, surely with a father like yours who travels the world and explores in some, uh, unusual places in the hope of finding some, uh, unusual specimens, you must be quite used to the kinds of danger he exposes himself to. And if I'm any judge of character, from what the proud father says about his son, you're no stranger to danger yourself. So, why all the, uh, anxiety over *this* expedition?"

Tony took a deep breath and let it out slowly. "I don't know. Call it premonition. Call it God's prompting. Call it anything you like, but I'm afraid for Dad. He's never gone anywhere this remote. He didn't have a lot of preparation time for this trip what with wrapping up the Noah's Ark expedition and all. I'm afraid some loose end is going to trip him up. I should have gone with him! College could have waited . . . "

The man smiled warmly and gave Tony a pat on the back. "Your father has chosen to go to what they're calling the last Eden on earth. The country is forbidding to the uninitiated, but the people of the Congo are largely peaceable and, I believe, helpful. They and their ancestors have crisscrossed this region for thousands of years. Communications aren't the best, and we've heard nothing since he left twelve days ago; but that is hardly surprising with the excruciatingly slow speed of the river barges. The Ubangi River country isn't the most hospitable, but then neither are parts of Chicago. I've heard it said there are perhaps as many as five hundred serial killers now at work in the United States. To my knowledge, there are none in the Congo!"

The man's attempt at levity was having little soothing effect on the agitated teenager in front of him. "Look, if you know my father, help me to get to him." Tony's mother and grandmother were dead. His dad was the only real family he had left. He was determined to find him. "Do you know where I could find the consulate general of the American embassy at this hour?"

The man smiled delightedly and stuck out a hand. "I can do better than that," he exclaimed with relish. "Perhaps I should introduce myself. I am William Fulgate, U.S. ambassador to Zaire. My car is just over there. Hungry?"

Tony Danson was positively famished.

Reg Danson dumped the hippo head onto the table with a grunt. The fetid flesh was crawling with flies and other insect undertakers that worked even faster than the heat to break down and dispose of the dead. Reg worked with a cloth dipped in rosewater covering his nose and mouth and a pair of plastic goggles strapped to his head.

He was in an anteroom off the main station house, furnished sparsely with a long metal table and two rusty cabinets housing some basic treatments for colds and malaria, one or two antibiotics, and a couple of antivenins. Should the snake in question be neither a black mamba nor an African cobra, the victim would have a difficult time using this, the meagerest of apothecaries.

In the main office quarters adjacent, Wiggins directed the unloading, unpacking, and repacking of every single item intended for the expedition. The pygmy brothers assisted, and curious onlookers crowded the porch to piece together the clues that would tell them the purpose of the secret mission. What they did know was that the two white men and the pygmy carriers "who do nothing for the village because they do not hunt but wait upon Friend Wiggins" were setting out for the north to the land of terrors. Would it mean good or ill for Sangha? They did not know.

Danson's plastic-gloved fingers probed the pulverized flesh of the throat area where a sizable chunk of meat had been bitten off. The wound could easily have been made by the inch-and-a-half peglike mock incisors at the front of the mouth common to aquatic browsers. Lacking giant molars, the aquatic dinosaurs nipped off the buds, fruit, twigs, and leaves necessary for their survival. While their teeth were not meant for mastication—they probably swallowed their food whole—the teeth did make excellent clamps, and the tremendous strength of the jaws and neck could wrench the throat out of a lesser animal with ease.

Who might have guessed that a plant-eater would display such aggressive behavior against another animal? It was certainly consistent with native stories of overturned canoes and even attacks on humans—whole villages terrorized by creatures looking for . . . what? Food? It seemed unlikely. Pretty energy-efficient, the plant eaters. An American Museum expedition to Mongolia had found evidence that herbivorous dinosaurs aided the digestion of whole, fibrous vegetable matter by swallowing multiple stones. One set of dinosaur remains included 112 of these polished "gastroliths" in the gizzard cavity. Food was ground against the rocks by the agitation of the gizzard wall, literally pounding the matter to bits like a giant abrasion chamber.

Danson nearly missed it in his haste to be rid of the loathsome head. The bulging, sightless eyes sat on a flat plane ending in a muzzle of slitlike nostrils and sparse bristles. He did a cursory examination of the putrifying mouth cavity, marvelling in morbid fascination over the jagged teeth and yellowed, rapacious tusks. A long, shiny brown millipede wriggled up out of the darkness of the throat and crawled over the coarse, blubbery tissue. And there it was, something caught on the broken ridge of one tusk, a gouge of flesh foreign to this mouth. Reg swabbed it onto his right index finger and took it over to the window for closer examination.

In the half light pushing through the crusted windowpane, the pink-gray blob quivered on Danson's unsteady finger. Dinosaur flesh! It had to be. The hippo must have inflicted some damage of its own before it went down. *Gutsy old girl!* Its baby was everything in the hour of death. Danson pinched the specimen with a pair of tongs and lowered the flesh into a cylinder of liquid nitrogen. He'd take it back to the U.S. for proper analysis by the scientific community.

What they'd make of it was anyone's guess. Reg had embarrassed the Smithsonian clique more than once. Then he'd discovered Noah's Ark, and they had tried to hire him back at twice his old salary. He had made it quite clear that he didn't fit in with test tube jockeys who thought they were still evolving—the same guys, and three or four women, who had pooh-poohed the "Black Eve" theory of human origin postulated by biochemists Allan Wilson and Thomas Kocher. The genetic record of mankind, so the theory went, was much more reliable than the fossil record with its highly publicized missing links, questionable dating methods, and interpretive subjectivity. On the other hand, by tracking the consistencies and mutations of mitochondrial DNA over time, a family tree can be constructed, the branches of which led back to a common mother who supposedly lived in Africa two hundred thousand years ago.

While Reg did not agree with all of Wilson and Kocher's postulations, he felt far more comfortable pursuing that line of research to its logical conclusion than relying on subjective prehistoric bone reconstruction. He'd seen enough "artist's renderings" of Homo erectus and other theoretical humanoid species to last him a lifetime.

Africans could well represent the oldest population of mankind. Even the oldest traces of man among the bone boys were found in South Africa. When Adam and Eve were driven from the Garden of Eden, they could have settled in Africa and walked with the dinosaurs in a veritable greenhouse of vapor mist. The very lushness and variety of life in today's dwindling tropical rain forests argue forcefully that much of the entire earth may once have been a tropical paradise. Rain and sun, temperature and humidity, all climatic conditions in divine balance. Scientists believe that atmospheric pressure was greater then, and oxygen in more plentiful supply, thereby increasing the health and vitality of all life. Animals were more abundant, vegetation contained more nutrients, and man, more robust and virile than today's feeble relations, lived longer in the land.

Reg returned the gory head to the burlap sack. He had dug a pit behind the station to receive the remains of the postmortem. Dumping the head in the river would invite crocodiles; in the forest, lions; anywhere that the people could see, demon hordes. The setting sun and the soreness in his back and neck reminded him it had been a long, eventful day. He peeled off the gloves and threw them in with the carcass. A cup of strong, hot tea was just what the doctor ordered.

Shouts of alarm and confusion sounded from across the compound. Reg strode to the window and saw that ten hunters had returned home from the killing grounds. All carried quivers over their arms, some empty, some with but a few arrows left. Two of the muscular men had small, cloven-hoofed animals slung about their necks, but they received no notice from the clamorous villagers. Instead, it was the limp body of the bleeding man six of them carried in by the arm and legs that caused the commotion.

Danson rushed into the other room just as the front door was thrown wide with a bang and the panting, blood-smeared lot burst through. Jigs cleared the table he was working on with a mighty sweep of one arm. The men stumbled across the floor and heaved their load onto the empty surface with the dull slap of dead meat hitting the butcher's block.

The sight was one Reg hoped never to see again. The mortally wounded pygmy was a teenager of seventeen or eighteen, tall for his race, once handsome in every regard—like Tony. But now blood gushed from his riven side, laid open from armpit to hip, much of the flesh gone. Entrails spilled slick and dripping from the chasm. The right arm was missing altogether, the shredded stump of bone glistening stark white through a sticky brick-colored paste of blood and dirt. Two of his stricken bearers, bathed in their comrade's blood, fell to their knees, yelping their grief. The others backed wet and trembling against the wall, barely able to stand upright themselves.

Jigs tore the curtains from the window and jammed them into the awful hole in the boy. The yellow cloth turned instantly crimson with the gushing blood, and it was too obvious there was nothing to be done to save this life. Far too much was missing to put him back together again.

Wiggins demanded of the men what had happened. They all seemed too dazed to answer except for one with a long, narrow face, bleeding from a gash in his own leg. "*Mabaya sana! Mabaya sana!*" he groaned again and again.

"I can see it's very bad!" Jigs yelled impatiently. "What *happened,* man?"

"*Mabaya sana! Mabaya sana!*" the man shouted back, undeterred.

Jigs Wiggins hurried over to the man and slapped him hard across one cheek and then the other. The man shook his head as if to clear it and began to weep. He looked up into Wiggins's eyes, and the whole room seemed to fill with the sorrow of that gaze. "*Mo—Mo—Moke—Mokele m—mm—mbem—be!*" he choked out.

Then, with a ferocious groan, he ran from the room scattering children and screaming, "*Hatari! Hatari! Hatari!*"

Danson squeezed his eyes tight shut, but fountains of blood seemed to fill his brain, and he had to open them again. "What's the fool saying now?!" he yelled in shocked exasperation.

Wiggins placed one hand gently beneath the dying man's head and the other over the blood-spattered forehead, closing the stunned eyes. "He's crying, 'Danger!'" The big man sobbed. "Danger! Run for your lives!" he shouted to the room, but no one moved.

Wiggins bent and kissed the forehead. "Our Father, who art in heaven, hallowed be thy name. Receive thy servant Sangono into thy hands . . . "

He could not finish the prayer. Instead, in a choking whisper, he wept, "Sangono, my brother," and fell to his knees.

# 6

**N**ight surrendered to the dawn with arrogant dignity. Though captured by light for a time, darkness would soon rule again.

The great green lungs of the forest canopy lay shrouded in a dense swirl of mist, billions of gallons of last night's rain rising like hot vapors from the throat of a volcano. Every limb an arboretum, the trees suckled 28,000 species of plants that would never lay a root on the forest floor. Brilliant butterflies and hummingbirds spattered the deep verdure of emerging day with neon reds, blues, yellows, and greens, absurd in their intensity. The fuschia, coral pink, and lemon yellow blossoms that they probed had been licked clean of nectar in the night by bandit bats. The morning's winged creatures would need to fly empty a bit longer.

Slowly, the sky lightened to reveal a breathtaking treescape of exploding vegetation. Spreading fungi, fast-growing molds, and decay from baking sun and high humidity produced commingled rot and rebirth. Through the cloaking mist, what at first must be a towering species of palm would, upon closer inspection, transmutate into a ridiculous fern from a land of giants by Jules Verne. Hundreds of feet of liana vines entwined their host trees like elevators of death rising relentlessly in quest of the sun, strangling their hosts in the process. The lianas emerged in the upper world with a burst of crimson-flowered triumph while their hosts rotted from within, the now hollow liana casings the only proof they'd ever lived.

A jungle cat rose stiffly from its bed, sidestepping a river of leaf cutter ants coming off the graveyard shift. They scurried past, hoisting their sections of leaf for the nest so that they looked like a flotilla of green sailboats. A nearby family of forest hyraxes called to each other, their cries beginning with a mew and ending in a piercing scream. That noise triggered a band of colobus monkeys who were sitting at the tops of the trees in reverence, gazing skyward in silent meditation. Glossy black with long white tail plumes, the monkeys now screeched irritably before beginning a day of promiscuous mating and foraging for their favorite coarse leaves. Today demanded extra caution. Chimpanzees had been spotted the day before, and they were known to eat their slighter cousins.

The forest began to swell with sound, the clickings and whirrings and ratchets of legs and throats and beaks.

On millions of similar mornings, ninety percent of the world's species greeted the dawn in the startling lushness of a tropical rain forest. Twenty percent of the world's fossil fuels and seventy percent of the world's prescription drugs existed here, in nature's hope chest.

Into this vast breathing, drinking, eating organism of the rain forest swamp slid a slender pirogue and four occupants. They paddled in a long, slow rhythm, digging deep with each stroke. An outboard would have frightened wildlife and wild men alike.

Each man was silent, locked in his own thoughts, dumbstruck by the otherworld of vine and vapor. It was a dark and moody fantasyland where God in His inventiveness had exercised creative free fall. Every leaf a clue. Every blossom a turn in the divine trail. Every sound an echo of God's footstep.

And every twist in the watery channel they followed could bring them face to face with the beast.

Wiggins spoke hesitantly, as if to bring a little reality to the alien surroundings. "As the old cartographers used to write at the edges of their maps of the known world, 'Here be monsters!'"

At first it didn't seem that anyone would respond. Ndoki and Ndokanda were rigid, their features stonelike, eyes darting rapidly about for the slightest indication of danger. Reg didn't want to speak. He had populated the reedy shores of his mind with herds of diplodocus and brachiosaurs, long snaky necks craning across the channel to pluck a succulent branch from the opposite shore. The little canoe passed soundlessly by, four stories beneath the creature's ruminating jaws. The nostrils on top of the small head opened and closed, eminently suited for browsing among the tasty marsh weeds in the swamp shallows. Where the fifty-foot long tail joined the spinal column, a second brain operated, a reflex mechanism for controlling the massive hindquarters, much like the rear steering unit attached to extra-long vehicles.

The brief glimpses of sky in Danson's vision were thick with swooping pterodactyls, their wing membranes filtering the sun through a latticework of spindly veins. All bony framework, the giant birds looked as if they must creak and groan when they moved, like wooden sailing ships at anchor.

"Dragon caves!" breathed Danson giddily, feeling the old exploratory surge, a potent tide of adrenaline and an accelerated heartbeat. "There, in that bend where the channel takes a sixty degree sweep to the west. Look how wide it is, and deep. Look how the bank is scooped and scoured by floodwaters, and the exposed roots form a little parking garage for our canoe. Let's put in there. We'll be relatively hidden and able to scan nearly one hundred and twenty degrees of river and jungle."

They were in the Maya Maya, a slow tributary of the Ubangi, about five miles inside Likouala Swamp. The Ologus were last rumored to be somewhere ahead. If and when they showed, there was a sack of manioc and some dried vegetables that would make a welcome addition to their meager diet. The exploration party carried sacks of rice and manioc flour which they would supplement with forest fruit, fish, and whatever generosity of meat and honey the Ologus might be predisposed to share. The explorers also carried carefully concealed bags of strawberry candies that even the pygmy brothers did not know were aboard. Sweets were an international language of their own.

"Aye," grunted Wiggins, filling his pipe. The thick, heavy fingers with their little tufts of red hair around the knuckles again traced the contours of the bottom of the pouch, relaxing only when every familiar bump in the terrain had been accounted for. "As likely a dragon's lair as any." He shuddered again at the memory of Sangono's split body and the look of stunned disbelief in the dying eyes.

Yesterday, Wiggins had permitted the pygmies their ancient funeral rite, smearing themselves head to foot with white clay, wearing the stiff straw skirts of mourning, and pasting wide leaves over their mouths to contain their grief. But he had not permitted the dance of death. The mourners gathered instead at the base of the *baobab* tree and listened to the missionary's impassioned declaration of life after death in Christ Jesus. Sangono was a believer and would one day wear a robe of righteousness at the foot of the Savior's throne. "Had Djeke the unbeliever died"—and here Wiggins and every mud-smeared one of his congregation turned to stare hard at the pygmy named Djeke, a most determined pagan—"then you could dance yourselves ten feet underground for all I care. Nothing can save him from his worthless gods and their lust for obedience, none but the very Son of God."

Then they had sung the chorus to "Higher Ground," sung it straight at Djeke who stood as impassive as a dead branch. These people of flood and swamp understood the need to climb up onto heaven's tableland, dry and secure above the chaos below. A few had found a higher plane, and their feet were firmly planted there. The mud and the straw skirts were for them now only a sign of respect for the dead and a link with the familiar as reassuring as covered dish casseroles and coffee at funeral receptions on another continent.

Now a flash of teal and jade turned Wiggins's gaze upward to a pocket of fruit, growing in startling profusion from a huddle of six great trees. The calls and whistles and vivid feather flashes of several different bird species erupted from the tangle, and as the explorers drew closer, they were treated to a busy village aviary.

Birds of rich tropical hues flitted busily about while others dressed in black with snowy white "shawls" across their wings drank from the pools of rainwater trapped in bowls formed at the joints of leaves and stems. The black birds darted among their bright turquoise and amber cousins, trailing incredibly long tails that forked into two pencil-thin sections ending in a wide fan of iridescent feathers. The collection of multicolored birds liked to flock together where much edible fruit grew. Besides satisfying hunger, the fruit provided camouflage against forest predators. Orchids grew here in extravagance, adorning the vivid aviary with what seemed an excess of color. Small ones of white and yellow with purple spots framed bouquets of larger ones of pale violets and pinks, their fragile, erect blossoms resembling the rotor blades on a helicopter. Most produced sweet perfume, a few the stench of carrion.

"Drink it in; you won't see many of these wild fruit stands," said Jigs forlornly, motioning to the pygmies to paddle beneath the root overhang. "The last couple of years, even fruit has gotten scarcer and scarcer in these parts of the swamp—like the wild game. Pardon my pessimism, but I don't think you timed your expedition real well."

Reg drank in the beauty of the grotto and turned to Jigs with a scowl. "Look on the positive side. Lack of food has made our quarry bolder and our chances of success greater. I know Sangono was a dear friend," he said softly, seeing the anguish in Wiggins's expression, "but you said he was a brave, compassionate boy. Now we must be brave and press on in the courage of

Sangono. You know what Steinbeck said about sorrow: 'A sad soul can kill you quicker, far quicker, than a germ.'"

Wiggins did not look at him. "You won't die from too much of me," he said without expression.

Reg sighed. He was no one to talk. When Barbara died, no one could get near him for months. Grieving took time. Wiggins had been buried in the bush for many years. That little band of pygmies were his wife and children. There had been a death in the family, and Reg must be sensitive to the loss.

The canoe slipped beneath the matted tangle of earth and roots as neatly and silently as a yacht into the marina. The earth smelled old and stagnant. The roots formed a spidery curtain between them and the deep pool.

Reg reached out a hand to steady the canoe by grabbing fast to a shadowy knot of roots. The "roots" sprang at his touch and elongated into a mottled brown python. The heavy snake, sluggish in its morning slumber, thudded half against Danson and half against the canoe. Before it could recover, Ndoki and Ndokanda beat it with their paddles, and it submerged in a swirl of water.

"What the devil?!" exclaimed Reg, his fingers tingling from their encounter with the raw muscle of the coiled serpent.

"Not quite a devil," commented Jigs with a wry smile. "That was a fairly small one. The rock python's known to get up to thirty-two feet. Then you know you've seen a snake! A small Malay boy of fourteen is said to have been eaten by a python, but you know how these stories can grow. But gazelles, impalas, and bushbucks, for sure. Saw the remains of one poor old viper that had swallowed a porcupine and six or eight quills had punctured right through the stomach wall. From a distance, looked like he'd been shot by a band of pygmy bow hunters."

"Is it true all their teeth point backward so once the prey is in, it can't back out?" Reg asked, using the conversation to help calm his nerves.

"Yep," Jigs replied. "First they ram their victims with their heads to stun them, then get them in a body squeeze that cuts off their air. Strangest case recorded is a 1608 account of a python jumping onto an elephant, digging its eyes out, and beating it breathless with whips of python tail. That must have been one sluggish pachyderm. I've seen elephants stomp pythons flat but never the other way around." He reached up into the recesses of the rootwork and pulled down the python's shed skin casing. It was faded white and transparent thin, the diamond pattern sparkly and rough like the side of a beaded purse. "We'll take this along for effect. It's proof we've consorted with serpents and lived to tell about it!"

Wiggins pulled on the remaining casing, and it kept coming like the magician's handkerchief. When the end emerged at last, he threw the skin carelessly into the bottom of the canoe, and Reg shuddered. It was fifteen feet if it was an inch. Wiggins laughed at Reg's uneasiness. "That's nothing," he said. "I understand a one hundred ten-pound kimodo lizard has been observed swallowing a sixty-eight-pound pig in seventeen minutes flat. Ahh, the food chain! You can't beat it for sheer excitement. Aren't you glad we're at the top?"

All Reg could think of was the illustration from a nineteenth century edition of *Swiss Family Robinson* showing a dreadful snake swallowing a hapless donkey whole.

"What a place," said Wiggins expansively, peering intently between the hanging roots. "Fish that eat fruit. Bats that eat fish. Spiders that eat birds. Insects that look like flowers and flowers that look like insects. Hummingbirds small as bumblebees and slugs big as rabbits. Monkeys that may live their entire lives without ever touching the ground. A continuous symphony of creaks and croaks, chirps and cries, squawks, scrapings, buzzings, whistles, and hums—"

"Were you ever happily married?" Reg interrupted. He didn't know why he said it—then, or at all. It was apropos of nothing, or everything. It was certainly none of his business. But a strong remembrance of Barbara had come over him then. The bouquet of multicolored birds and orchids would have pleased her so much. "For you, sweetheart," he would have said with an extravagant bow, as if he'd planned it.

Oddly, Wiggins took no offense at the abrupt change of subject. He drew hard on the pipe and sent two jets of smoke out his nose. "Kay was as bonnie a girl as ever there was. Kneldrith was her full name, like something out of a medieval legend. She could handle anything—horses, hurricanes, hard knocks of any sort. What she almost couldn't handle was a husband with a past who wasn't yet ready to get on with life. She bore with me through my prison time, kept the kids mindful they had a father who loved them. But she saw the panic in me as I neared release. I had ended a man's life, and though Jesus had washed me clean, I'd never been a normal teenager. I married at sixteen, went to prison at seventeen, and emerged at twenty-three, an ex-con. I'd never even mowed a lawn or been to a high school football game. Now I was supposed to find a job, support a wife and two kids I barely knew. Well, I couldn't."

Jigs's voice had grown softer and softer until the word *couldn't* was little more than a puff of air. He looked at Reg with red-rimmed eyes. "Desertion," he said flatly. "Desertion, plain and simple."

For a minute, he said no more. The sweet scent of the pipe smoke hung pleasantly suspended in the still pocket of air beneath the curled lip of the bank. The pygmy brothers dozed, the forest lightened, and the placid waters of the big river bend showed not a ripple.

It was becoming hot and sticky beneath the earthen overhang. An ant dropped from the ceiling down the back of Reg's shirt and delivered a stinging bite that hit like a mule's kick.

"Yow!" he yelped, leaping up, banging his head and bringing a shower of dirt down upon them. Reg ripped off the shirt, trying frantically to see the damage to his lower back. He saw the ant scurrying over the floor of the canoe and ground it into the wood with his boot. Wiggins put out a steadying arm and administered a foul-smelling salve that cooled the sting instantly.

The words *secret recipe* were printed across a dirty strip of once-white adhesive taped to the lid of the salve can. "You've got a welt the size of Texas, but at least your skin won't fall off," Wiggins offered. Reg scrambled back into his shirt before another ant blaster decided to dine. Wiggins flicked the skin of his ruddy, weathered forearm. "Hide," he said. "Over time you get hide and the insects lose interest."

"Sorry," said Reg, hoping to right the tipped cart of their previous conversation. "You were saying something about, uh, desertion." It sounded especially awful in the small, cramped space beneath the roots, but it was the word Jigs had used.

"We deserted each other," Wiggins said. He drummed his fingers on the salve can lid. "I went down in the diamond mines to become a man, and she hocked her diamond ring to make a home for our kids. I've sent money every month, however meager my earnings."

"Never remarried?" Reg probed as gently as he knew how.

"Never divorced. At least, I never did. The statute of limitations ran out long ago, and she's probably found someone else. Couldn't blame her.

"But I love that woman, Danson. We prayed together, and she helped disciple those guys in the pen. We called them our baby converts and made sure there was someone there when they got out. But she loved me too much to be there when I got out. I'd have crumbled under the weight of measuring up to manhood, let alone fatherhood and being a husband. I know you probably find that hard to understand. You think I'm a shirker and no keeper of Christian duty."

"You mean that in all these thirty years you haven't sent for her? Your children are grown. Why isn't she here with you now?"

Wiggins squeezed the salve can viciously. "Don't you think I've wanted her by my side? What a godsend she would be with the pygmies, especially the women and children."

"Then why, man, why haven't you sent for her?"

"Because the Congo is no place for a woman. There is too much darkness, too much sin. How many pygmies do you think I've buried since I first came? More than five hundred, Danson. Their life expectancy is half yours or mine. Infant and child mortality is high. Malaria, typhoid, measles, tuberculosis, and influenza are just some of the killers that float on the swamp. Many of the disease-carrying insects inhabit the upper story of the forest, but when trees are heavily logged as they are north of here and south of Epuluville, insects fly nearer the ground and infect human beings.

"We're not immune either. Sure, we've got diethylcarbamazine along for parasitical intestinal and filarial infections, but don't kid yourself. There's a hundred virulent bacterial maladies that could have us retching our guts out in minutes. We can boil the meat we eat and fry it in palm oil, but just one little wiggly gets past the gate somehow, and you've got a fever that'll unhinge your brain for weeks, months—you may never recover. You can carefully collect only rainwater for drinking and treat it with Halazone and still come down with cramps that'll cut you in two.

"Even if God is gracious not to visit one of those attention-getters upon us, I can get complacent and go out one morning for a constitutional, forget the toilet paper, reach for a leaf, and set my hindquarters on fire with a rash straight from Hades. That's the reality of the swamp, and I haven't even mentioned the unmentionable." He arched his eyebrows in the direction of the drowsing brothers and jerked his head at the river.

"No, I wouldn't bring a wife here. I've told her that in a letter. I said that neither could I return home to Minnesota. I had grown up at last and could not run out on my pygmy brothers as I had my own family. If I were to leave, the pygmies would be destroyed. The ones at Sangha are under my protection, and as long as some remain, I remain. A few are genuine Christian brothers and sisters who have had a change of heart. Because they no longer worship the jungle, they are no longer in tune with it, and it does not feed them as it once did. The rest tolerate them or pretend to be Christians themselves to get the farm food hand-outs, but if I were out of the way permanently, they would force the others to recant or die. I told her all that, and Kay replied to it. It's the one and only letter from her in all this time. She said she understood, that if I was engaged in the Lord's work among the heathen, her mind would rest easy. Meanwhile, I've a flock to shepherd and now this new danger from below"—he stared hard at the pool, and there was hatred in his eyes—"leaves me no choice but to fight for my people."

For another hour they waited and watched, but the only change was more dissipation of the mist, a brief rainburst, and increasing light. Danson and Wiggins were by now soaking wet from the humidity. Water poured down their faces in the closed quarters of the embankment, yet the naked pygmies seemed little bothered. "Evaporation is low in this atmosphere and sweating is not the efficient cooling system it is on a windswept mountain in the Colorado Rockies," Jigs explained. "The brothers have a lower metabolic rate and generate less heat than we do. Plus the fact they are shorter and smaller means a large surface area compared to their overall bulk. They can shed heat from their bodies more quickly. They sweat less and need less water intake than we do. What can I say? They're built for the tropics."

At last, Reg called a halt to their vigil. Except for a dragon-fly the size of a model airplane, the pool remained unruffled. "Let's move on," he said, heaving his body up onto a seat and trying to work the kinks out of his neck and shoulders.

Wiggins nodded in agreement and picked up a paddle. The brothers made no effort to hide the fact that they were glad to leave. Inactivity here in the swamp seemed to unnerve them, but their loyalty to Wiggins was plain and at times touching. Despite the chewing out Ndoki had delivered around the campfire two nights ago, his eyes seldom fell on the missionary without some flicker of solicitude.

"What's your theory about dragons, Danson?" Wiggins asked as they exited the rootbound hideaway. "Word has it they were dinosaurs with a three-chamber stomach: one for rapid digestion of sugar-rich foods for quick energy; a second large storage chamber for digestion of woody materials, which was made possible only through prolonged fermentation; and a third for storing the copious amounts of methane gas produced in the second. To snort fire, friend dragon had only to burp the methane, click its teeth, and the resulting pyrotechnics is the stuff of legend."

Reg chuckled, digging in a paddle, glad to be free of the bank. "Sounds like the birth of the butane lighter to me. But the bombadier beetle can shoot out super-heated gases in self-defense. And in the Bible, the Lord Himself talks about leviathan, how firebrands stream from his nostrils and smoke pours from his nose.

"I don't know. But I do know many dinosaur nasal cavities were quite spacious and the sinus passages fairly intricate. Big as they were, they needed heavy duty air conditioning. Those big bodies absorbed lots of heat, and all organs close to the surface, especially their brains, were in danger of overheating. With big nasal airways, they could gulp great quantities of air through those pipes and cool down much quicker."

None of them saw the leopard crouched on the overhanging limb they had to duck to slide under. Eight feet from nose to tip of tail, the cat was one hundred fifty pounds of spring steel. Tawny yellow with small black spots, it blended with the mottled shadings of the forest and the play of shadows in the mist. When the smaller forest creatures had become scarce, the leopard had developed a taste for human flesh. The scent of it was in the air. When the prey moved, the cat moved with it.

As the leopard sprang down upon the canoe, the waters below geysered upward. The bow of the canoe stood nearly perpendicular to the surface, spilling men and loose supplies into the churning Maya Maya.

The murky depths of the swamp stream were yellow brown from the tanic acid of rotting vegetation. But up through the faint half light, the black thing distinguished from among the wild splashings the spotted coat of the disoriented leopard. The thing's long slick neck propelled the head upward, the jaws gaped, and the leopard gave a last strangled growl of fright.

Reg heard the backbone snap and saw the cat disappear in a mighty foaming surge of slick, leathery black, and dark water. The dark mahogany backs of the sea serpents he'd seen in Loch Ness flashed through his mind. Barbara falling overboard in an accidental collision of observation boats. The frantic, lung-bursting search in those other murky waters. The leaden realization that his wife, his love, was forever gone. He fought the awful memories and quickly swam to a struggling, gasping Ndokanda and saw that Wiggins had Ndoki securely in hand. They reached the muddy shallows at about the same time, each heaving a man far up on the sand until they could get to their feet and scramble out of reach of the still agitated waters. Wiggins and Danson stumbled after them, pushing the brothers further into the dense shelter of the forest.

"Incredible! Did you get a good look at it?" cried Wiggins, shouting in his excitement. His hand closed on the precious tobacco pouch. He did not check to see if the contents had gotten wet, only that it was there and his pocket still buttoned down. Everything was apparently in order. He breathed a long sigh of relief. "Was it a croc?"

Reg shook his head no and crouched low behind a log. The brothers, nonswimmers, had swallowed a great deal of water. Ndokanda bent over, heaving the swamp water from his stomach. Ndoki was either unable or unwilling to vomit. Wiggins rushed to his side and grabbed him in a firm headlock. Ndoki put up a furious struggle. "Make . . . him . . . lose it!" Wiggins gasped. Danson rushed over, grasped the pygmy's jaws and forced the mouth wide. He jabbed two fingers down the back of the man's throat and leapt aside. A fountain of amber water gushed onto the ground. They let go of Ndoki, and he fell to his knees and released the remaining water on his own.

While Jigs put a comforting arm about Ndoki's heaving shoulders and gently explained in quiet Bantu why he needed to get rid of the swamp water, Reg stared out at the pool. The canoe was upside down in the center of the river bend and going nowhere. Why wasn't it moving with the current? The main packs with their precious cargo of medicines, some food, Bibles, and the tranquilizer gun had been securely jammed beneath the seats of the canoe and would be under there still, though the manioc and dried vegetables were likely lost. Without the canoe, they were in desperate trouble. There was no way to bring it in from the bank.

Reg had to go back in.

His companions tied a liana vine about his waist and prayed with him. "Oh God, my God, how excellent is your name in all the earth!" he cried. "Go before me, oh Lord, and shut the jaws of leviathan. Into your hands, I commend my spirit!"

And then he waded quietly in with as little motion as possible, his companions playing out the vine, nerves taut, ready to yank him back at the slightest sign of the creature's return.

Reg stepped down and fell, his foot giving way on a loose stone. His companions hauled back on the line, thinking he was under attack. Reg twisted around to face the three frantic men, grabbed the vine, and gave a furious yank. In their haste, they took that to mean Danson was being pulled into the water by the unknown menace, and they hauled all the faster. Reg slipped and skidded up the bank in the ridiculous tug-of-war but was no match for the three on the opposite team. When at last he stood nose-to-nose and looked into Wiggins's florid face and beard full of bits of leaf and dirt, he smiled ruefully. "I tripped on a rock," he said. "Can I go now?"

The three looked genuinely disappointed at the false alarm and watched sheepishly as the vine with Danson on the end again unreeled to the water's edge.

Hot as it was, Danson felt chilling cold inside. With one last prayer for protection, he submerged and frog-kicked toward the canoe.

He had never before experienced the sensation of being observed from below, but the feeling was strong upon him now. There must be an underwater lair here where the creature could hide, perhaps even an airspace where it might breathe without revealing itself. Was it satisfied with the leopard, or did it want more?

Reg reached the canoe and felt under the thwarts for the packs. Just as he'd surmised, they were snuggly stowed and all there.

"My gun? The pistol, is it there?" insisted Wiggins. Reg felt in the top of the bow pack. "It's here!"

He dove underwater to look for what anchored the canoe and discovered the bowline taut as a bowstring, caught on something further down in the murky depths. Obviously, it had trailed loose and snagged on a sunken tree. Pulling with all his might, he could not free the line. Lungs bursting, he kicked for the surface.

Reg broke through to air and sucked it in in great gasps. But the muggy heaviness of it relieved the pain in his lungs only a little. "Bowline's snagged on something!" he called to the anxious three on shore. "I'm going down as far as I can and cut it loose." Before they could protest, he was gone.

He almost collided with the twisted body of the dead leopard. Fur matted and chewed, nose trailing blood, mouth frozen in a frightened snarl, it drifted slowly past like a ghoulish museum piece. The powerful hindquarters dragged behind at an unnatural angle, mute testimony to the killer's crushing strength.

Hand-over-hand, Reg followed the nylon line deeper into the watery darkness. He had to save as much of the line as possible. It was the only synthetic rope they had, and every strand was precious. He drew his hunting knife and continued the descent.

Something slid across his face like a thin film of cellophane wrap. He stabbed at it in revulsion and saw the discarded gossamer python skin twirl and drift away in the current like a strand of transparent ocean kelp.

Just another four or five feet and he'd be where the snagged end of the yellow rope disappeared into the blackness. He reached and cut the rope free.

The blackness moved.

Too late for Reg, the shadows took on form and rammed his chest with improbable force, flattening his lungs and driving from them the little air that remained. *The eyes . . . the eyes . . . like a shark's . . . wild . . . cold . . . no mercy . . . no mercy . . .*

It was his last conscious thought before everything went black.

Gussie Jackson sat alone in solitary observation at Western State Hospital for the mentally ill. They'd taken her quilt, her needles, and her clothes, put her in a hospital smock, and left her alone on a bare cot. The scabby puncture wounds on her upper legs were the reason she was in solitary. A danger to herself. A blamed nuisance to others. She was a candidate for certified crazy, but no one in administration had yet been able to locate next of kin to sign the papers. And it was sometimes easier to assume insanity than prove it.

She kept quilting. They couldn't stop her. Her hands went patiently and painstakingly through the motions, imaginary needles flying over imaginary patches of life, here a pattern called Parson Jordan's Choice, there a swatch of Essie Sanderson's Pride. Each stitch a prayer.

If they tied her hands, she'd quilt with her mind, joining the orangy black African buzzard to a black John the Baptist baptizing a black Jesus in a blazing blue Jordan.

Right now it was November 1833 in her mind, the night the sky caught fire. Her great-gram Angelia and six hundred other slaves were lying flat on the ground, groaning, clutching the backs of their heads, or raising their hands to heaven begging God to save the world. Meteor storm, said the people down at the newspaper, but when you are pinned to the ground between two and six in the morning with ten thousand stars streaking through space, you know there's more to it than that. Versie tried so hard to cover her baby with her own body so it wouldn't get hit by a falling star that she smothered it to death. Ella Moses gave birth six weeks early right there in the field under the brilliant night sky, and little Joshua Moses born with dirt sod up his nose became the prettiest singer of cotton songs on ten plantations. And it had been a sign that Gram's son, 'Lijah, and his son after him and so on, was to take up preachering with no more sass about it.

Stop quilting, stop being. You didn't need some high-priced psychiatrist to figure that out. Life, the story of life, was in the quilt.

Gussie Sweet Pone Jackson better not stop quilting. With Carrie Danson dead, her boy Reg had no mama to pray for him. Gussie had to pray for him for her.

God knew he needed it.

# 7

Tony Danson anxiously shifted his weight from one foot to the other. *What's keeping him so long?* he wondered. Ambassador Fulgate had been huddled up with the chargé d'affaires for Brazzaville and the local commissioner for the Epuluville region for more than an hour now, and the day was getting away from them. Occasionally loud and heated words drifted through the closed door, and it was obvious someone was treading on someone else's toes.

The news from upriver was not good. A man had been brutally killed by the monster known as *Mokele-mbembe,* and it was the second death in as many months. The creatures had long been rumored to be far back in the uncharted swamps, but now frequent reports from villages along the Ubangi indicated the monsters were becoming more aggressive. Though game was becoming increasingly scarce for the malnourished villagers, they were more reticent than ever to make the several-day hunts deep into the Likouala. At least there was still fish in the Ubangi.

There was only death in the swamp.

Tony had met William Fulgate only the day before, and already they were in Epuluville. A Missionary Aviation Fellowship pilot squeezed them into his Cessna between a crate of pheasant chicks bound for the Sangha Mission and two grinning village boys with casts on opposite arms who'd just experienced the wonders of Brazzaville General Hospital. Twins, and quite used to doing everything together, they'd held hands and jumped off the roof of the café in imitation of the soaring MAF plane. Had they known getting an actual ride in the plane was as easy as breaking an arm, they would have done it long ago; they were even then planning what to break next to earn a return flight.

The plane had taxied up to the riverboat landing on gleaming pontoons, and the passengers, mail, pheasants, and supplies were deposited on the spot where days before a fascinated Reg Danson had watched the stacking of monkey carcasses.

At last, the door of the office opened abruptly, and the three men strode out, grim-faced. Even the kindly William Fulgate looked angry. The other two men left the building, but Fulgate walked over to Tony. "I did what I could, but they will not allow us to fly into Sangha. The people there are very frightened over the latest attack by what they say is *Mokele-mbembe* and by the scarcity of game. To land a plane in there right now, they believe, would cause even the fish to disappear, and the people would starve or have to be evacuated at government expense.

"Between you and me, I don't think the People's Republic of the Congo would spend the money on the pygmies. Survival of the fittest, they'd say, has been the law of the jungle since the beginning of time. Leaving the pygmies to their fate would be of no more significance than the thinning of the herd, a process that is cyclical in nature among pretty nearly all species. Among the more sophisticated Bantu, the pygmies are something of an embarrassment and are considered to be little more than animals anyway. The more powerful Bantu have enslaved the pygmies in an odd sort of way, making them dependent upon Bantu agriculture to supplement their sparse diet. The Bantu fear the forest, cutting it down and clearing the land to eliminate the shadows of the unknown. The pygmies fear the villages and feel exposed in the open land and the demands of a faster-paced way of life.

THE LOST KINGDOM

"At any rate, the pygmies at Sangha Mission are in a real stew over your father taking off with their 'father,' Jigs Wiggins. They hope he will somehow convince *Mokele-mbembe* to stop these random attacks, yet they are scared to death Wiggins may become the next victim. The best I could do is to get a police motor launch that unfortunately is a day and a half upriver from here tracking elephant poachers near Bafwasende. They have the men in custody and are on their way back. The river barge is due in a couple of days, and they will stow the miscreants in the brig to stand trial in Brazzaville. Only then can they spare the launch for Sangha."

Frustration welled up in Tony. Maybe he was more like his father than he'd thought. Both of them wanted action, and delays like this one were difficult to stomach. "We'll pay one of the villagers to take us in a dugout," he said desperately. "We can't just wait around . . . "

Fulgate laid a firm hand on Tony's shoulder. "I don't think so, son. I've already gone out on a thin limb. We can't simply pick someone at random and expose them to the dangers upriver. If anything were to happen, I could kiss the foreign service goodbye, and your father would not be welcome anywhere in Africa. We need the more powerful motor launch and the two police that go with it. They've got some firepower, and we may need a little muscle where we're going."

Tony shuddered. He kept playing the awful scene at the nursing home over and over in his mind. The old woman's eyes rolled back in her head like a zombie's, convulsing in her chair, going on about "the witch's lizard," the creature that would "kill your father if you don't hold him . . . "

He hoped he had a couple of days. His dad would joke that he couldn't possibly die before the last college payment was met. *I love you, Dad. I'm doing everything that can be done . . . hang on, just hang on a little longer . . .*

▼

The shifting patterns were thick and indistinct at first, and there was a drumming at the bottom of a well . . . *Rum pum pum pum . . . I am a poor boy too . . . pa-rum pum pum pum . . . no gift to bring . . . to give the king . . . pa-rum pum pum pum, rum pum pum pum, rum pum pum pum . . .*

The patterns gradually sharpened, then all at once snapped into focus. Reg Danson had a sudden, violent urge to vomit everything he'd ever eaten in the last twenty years. He proceeded to try.

Jigs Wiggins held Reg's head while the younger man regurgitated swamp water until the pain in his belly nearly shouted down the ache in his chest. He wiped a sleeve across his mouth and fell back with a groan. "Did someone please get the license number of that bus?"

Wiggins smiled a little and unbuttoned Danson's shirt. He pulled it aside and laid a cool hand gently alongside the rib cage. He pressed and Danson yelled. Reg gritted his teeth during the rest of the inspection. No broken bones, some bruising, and one beauty of a welt encircling the torso just beneath the ribs where the vine had been tied.

"You never saw three men reel in so fast in your life," said Wiggins, daubing "secret recipe" on the welt. "You'd a thought we were trolling for pike the way that monster came boiling along behind you. Then, in an instant, it was gone in a deep dive that turned the whole river bend into a whirlpool bath."

"You are to be commended for your quick reflexes," said Reg, panting. He was unable to take deep breaths. "Could you make out anything, anything at all?"

"Nothing. Just a hulking black shadow beneath the surface like a manta ray skimming the surface of the ocean—only bigger, much bigger. And a long projecting shadow out front, like a neck. What got you, Danson? Did *you* see anything, man?"

"Eyes, that's all. Staring, cold as ice, no emotion whatsoever, like it was going through some incredible instinctual motions. Shark eyes, uncaring . . . automatic." Danson shivered despite the heat. "Where are the brothers?"

"Down retrieving the canoe. It got pushed downstream in the melee, but they're coming along with it now."

Reg sat up as best he could, rubbing his ribs gingerly. His clothes felt clammy and had a rank smell. He would never again complain about having to do his own laundry. He rested on his elbows, squeezed his eyes shut, and put his head back.

The brothers warily pulled the canoe along the bank. Ndokanda checked the trees for leopards while Ndoki looked intently at the river for any sign of the thing's return. Ndoki looked up at Wiggins to say something, but the words froze on his lips.

"Danson." The one word Wiggins spoke was a warning, and Reg snapped his head forward. There, not three feet from his face, was the business end of a wooden arrow, the tip honed to needle sharpness, the shank of the tip notched like the ruffles on the outstretched neck of an agitated rooster.

"Poison." Wiggins spoke the word low out one side of his mouth. Reg didn't dare breathe. There, behind the arrow and the curved bow stretched taut, was the fiercest face he'd ever seen. Framed by a bristling fur headdress, it was painted bright red with a white mouth that curved down in a grotesque frown extending to the Adam's apple. The nose was wide and flat, gleaming with a wet brownish-red that made it look mangled and bloody. The eyelids were white with narrow darts shooting out to the ears. Beneath and above the eyes were painted more eyes, that in the shaded darkness of the bushes gave the eerie illusion of three archers in one. But what turned Danson's insides to water was that he recognized those same, pitiless eyes.

They belonged to the creature in the pool.

Without a perceptible move, the bowman released the arrow. So great was the speed of it, Danson flinched to the left *after* it passed. But it was not a miss. The stranger had not intended the arrow for Reg. It stuck fast in a moss-covered *ato* tree just over his right shoulder. Danson's cheek prickled with the memory of its passing.

Wiggins slowly and deliberately reached out a hand and pried the arrow loose from the tree. He looked at it, then handed it to Danson. The missionary spoke in the same low, measured speech. "*Adani*. Arrow message. Says we are property of Ngomba, *griot* of the Ologus."

Reg handled the arrow carefully, avoiding any contact with the tip. The notches glistened with poison. His face deadpan, his entire body prickling now with how numbingly close it had come to paralysis and death, Reg examined the shaft. A pattern of designs and symbols was carefully and intricately etched halfway along its length. Some resembled Roman numerals.

"His *property?*" said Danson, shakily. "What is he getting at?"

"They not only communicate with these things, they divine with them," said Wiggins grimly. "What the Greeks called *belomancy.*"

A second arrow streaked out of the forest behind them and buried itself in the *ato* tree. Wiggins pried it loose. "Two days' journey," he read. "Begin now." When he looked at Reg, there was both fear and defiance in his eyes. He spoke under his breath. "We have, I think, little choice at the moment. This band knows more of the swamp than anyone. You wanted *Mokelembembe*. I think you've found it."

Nine pygmies, identically painted as the first and bare except for little girdles of shiny leaves in front, sprang from the forest brandishing drawn arrows. Each wicked tip glistened with the same deadly liquid. They crouched and circled the exploration party. Two of them motioned with their bows for the brothers to pull the canoe up on the bank. The brothers hesitated, looking to Wiggins for a sign of what they should do. Before he could respond, one of the bowmen kicked Ndokanda in the stomach, knocking him back over the bow. Ndoki made a move toward his brother, but before he had taken two steps he received a savage blow to the base of his spine. He went down on his face with a yelp. Jigs lunged to their defense, but Reg grabbed his leg and wrenched him to the ground. Quickly he crawled up to Wiggins's head and hissed in his ear, "Don't be stupid! These guys hold the winning hand!"

Wiggins saw the sense in that and went limp.

The bowmen continued to circle the party.

"MMMMMMM . . . MMMMMMM . . . MMMMMMM . . . " The alien thrum originated in the strangers' throats, but it seemed to circle the captives above their heads and independent of anyone—as if they were able to throw their voices. The unearthly cadence rose and fell in hypnotic waves, and Danson prayed it would stop.

"MMMMMMM . . . MMMOOOO . . . KAAALAAAY . . . MMMMMM . . . MMMBEMMM . . . BAAAY!" They began to whirl like dervishes, releasing a hail of arrows that crisscrossed the clearing with deadly abandon. The explorers hit the ground and covered their heads with their hands. Each felt the foot of a pygmy warrior grind into the small of his back and looked up to find a new arrow pointing between his eyes.

"My Redeemer lives . . . my Redeemer lives . . . MY REDEEMER LIVES!" Reg sang at the top of his lungs, wanting to drown out the demon chant and to fill at least his own ears with the blessed truth.

"At *His* name every knee shall bow!" intoned Wiggins in vigorous antiphonal response. "AT HIS NAME EVERY—"

The two stopped abruptly. They were suddenly the only ones making a sound.

"Look at their eyes," Wiggins said. The eyes of the warriors had a dreamy quality, glazing in and out of reality. "They're high on *iboga* leaves and as lethal as a spurned bull elephant. Some say the dinosaurs vanished because they became *iboga*-dependent. These guys are on about a three-day toot or I miss my guess. Powerful stimulant. Keeps them awake the whole time without fatigue. In large doses, their visions have visions. Probably drank to it with fermented *raffia*. It would appear we are the only game they've been lucky with."

Two of the archers shook their heads to clear them, then shoved the brothers into place by the dugout. The four of them hoisted the pirogue clear of the river and threw the packs onto the ground. The bowmen pointed at the packs and motioned for food. "Give them the jerky," said Wiggins. The dried meat was on top, the rest of the food in the bottom of the packs. Perhaps the bowmen would look no further.

The archers tossed the bags of jerky to their fellows, and it was quickly devoured with little chewing. They flung some of the spare clothing about, one of them drunkenly slipping into a pair of Reg's boxer shorts—over his head. But they soon tired of this sport and went no further.

It was clear that the prisoners were to carry their own gear. Jigs, Reg, and the brothers hoisted the packs onto their backs, positioned the tumplines around their foreheads—instantly transferring the weight from their backs to their necks and shoulders—and each with a pygmy bowman ahead and behind, plunged into the forest after the tallest of the archers, who seemed the leader of the band.

The pace was swift and the terrain very unfamiliar. Even the sure-footed brothers, unaccustomed to the region, had trouble keeping up, sometimes tripping and falling, earning a sharp shove from behind for their trouble. Before long their bare feet were lacerated and bloody.

Soon the trek settled into a monotony of heat and insects conspiring to drive Reg mad. The misery he suffered from a battered chest and ribs cut him like a knife. And he could imagine the dreaded bacterial diseases the flies and ticks were pumping into his bloodstream even as they extracted nourishment for themselves. But if he dared to swat at them, his pace would slow; sometimes he dropped the pack, earning quick and painful retribution.

Wiggins was behind Danson, and it did not sound as if he suffered any less. Once when they both fell over a hidden log in the trail, he called out to Reg in as cheery a voice as he could muster: "C. S. Lewis said pain is the megaphone of God. Well, brother, He's got my attention!" At once, both the pygmy in front of Jigs and the one behind rained vicious kicks and blows down upon the missionary's head and back. One grabbed a handful of red beard and wrenched so hard, Reg thought sure half the man's face would come away with it. The bushman held up his prize and added the bloody patch to his fur headdress.

Wiggins felt dizzy and prayed that the pistol was still serviceable. He'd placed it in a watertight bag with silicon lining. More than that, he had to find a way to get to it without drawing attention. It and the elephant tranquilizer gun, also in watertight packing, were the only real weapons they had.

The green wall of the jungle towered all about them. Beneath their feet, the thin soil supplied little of the nutrients necessary for survival, the forest needing instead to feed upon itself. This vegetable cannibalism was so efficient that every rotting leaf and branch became a meal of decay in the hothouse of the rain forest. Upon the death of a plant or tree, the roots and creepers and gnawing insects rushed in and ate their fill, breaking and dividing the corpse until every bit of it had been sucked up and absorbed by the living.

Despite his misery, Reg could sense the wonder of this land that time forgot. To travel through such a vast, uncharted region so utterly untouched by modern man was both exhilarating and frightening. Who could possibly know where they were? Who could find them? To leave the river, that albeit thin tributary tie to all that was human and warm and familiar, and plunge into this nearly trackless wilderness quagmire stripped him of both physical and psychological bearings. To be in the hands of these drug-stupefied, decidedly unfriendly people could spell catastrophe for both the expedition and their lives.

Suddenly, the fourteen men dropped down a steep embankment and were quickly up to their waists in swamp muck. Danson's view, his head bowed from the weight and bulk of the pack, changed from the lean, muscular brown thighs and buttocks of the tall pygmy ahead to the tight, bunchy muscles of the man's narrow shoulders and back. On and on they traveled like this, all sense of time and place rapidly eroding. The temperature was well in excess of ninety degrees, and there wasn't the slightest movement of air. The swamp stank, every step sending great sickening bubbles of methane and hydrogen sulfide popping to the surface. Insects, voracious enough in the forest, were unceasingly ravenous and of greater variety here in the swamp. Jigs's and Reg's fair skin swelled and tightened from countless stings. The soothing, merciful "secret recipe" in the pack on Wiggins's back might as well have been light years away.

The sweat poured from the white men, and Reg started to feel sick from the loss of water and salt. He almost hoped he would fall into a sinkhole. Underwater in this cesspool had to be preferable to the hellish torture just above its surface. He'd gladly risk another beating if it meant he could bathe in a liquid other than his own sweat.

Just when he knew he must sink or die, the land rose under his feet, and they were soon on higher ground, momentarily free of the muck. The lead pygmy called a halt and motioned for the four to drop their packs. Reg could have hugged him but knew that neither would survive the ordeal. The pack off, Reg felt as if he could float up and out of the swamp, and it didn't sound like a bad idea. Instead, he fell to the ground against the duffel and made drinking motions with his hands. The leader snorted haughtily but waved a hand of permission.

Reg removed two canteens from his pack, handing one to Wiggins and the other to the brothers. The gratitude in the brothers' eyes let him know that they hadn't suffered a great deal less than he even though they had spent all their lives in the rain forest. Poor Wiggins looked pale, and the torn skin on his chin and cheek was crawling with bugs. Reg cleansed the wound with hydrogen peroxide, daubed it dry, and applied the "secret recipe." They both slathered their necks and faces with the salve, and Reg sincerely hoped there was another tin or two of it in Wiggins's stores.

They were up against an enormous stand of bamboo, a hundred feet across and twenty feet high. Herons and cormorants browsed nearby as did a family of ducks. The pygmy leader, whom Danson decided to call Bigshot, stood sentinel and sniffed the air. Then, with a sharp "Thwit!" he bent over and ran along the bamboo stand to a vantage point where the hummock again dipped into the swamp. He silently drew another arrow from its quiver and strung it in place on the bow.

The blue duiker would normally be found only in dense vegetation where it could hide from the eagles and pythons and tribesmen who enjoyed its flesh. But the tiny antelope, only sixteen inches tall and weighing thirteen pounds fully grown, was itself hungry. The buds and tender shoots it preferred were scarce today, less and less bountiful as the days wore on. Perhaps the duiker could find a mouse or a baby duck along the fringes of the bamboo and that would satisfy for now.

Stepping forward timidly, the streamlined little animal flicked its tail nervously, lifting first one hind foot, then the other, testing, always testing the air, the sounds, ready to bolt at the slightest hint of danger. It chose to travel alone, not in herds like other antelope. Single animals did not generate the telltale odors and tramplings that attracted notice. The little duiker had a mate to which it was devoted for life, but even they did not stay together except to breed for fear of doubling their chances of discovery. The duiker placed one tentative hoof forward.

Without a sound, the poison arrow pierced the duiker in midstep, stopping its heart instantly. The antelope sat down as if bewildered over this latest turn of events, then fell over and was still.

The voracious archers pounced upon the dead antelope like lions on a waterbuck. They widened the arrow wound, sucked the residual poison from the point of entry, spat it out, then ripped the soft, pretty hide from the carcass. Grabbing the four limbs, they wrenched and cracked the joints and tore the body into four gory sections separate from the head. Then they fed on the raw meat. In less than five minutes, all trace of the duiker had vanished except for the hide, the tips of the hooves, the skull, and a few lengths of mangled bone too tough to swallow.

The four captives viewed the feeding frenzy with disgust and were not at all certain they could have eaten had they been invited to dinner. Obviously, they had taken nourishment more recently than the archers, and it did not surprise them to be offered not a single hair of the kill.

What made Reg more nauseous were the eyes, the hated, vacant, staring eyes of death he had looked into in the murky depths of the Maya Maya. They followed him everywhere now, painted on each bushman, blurring with every toss of their heads into a monster freak show. The antelope blood smearing their mouths and hands, the bits of raw flesh clinging to their fingers and lips, could have been his blood and his flesh in the jaws of *Mokele-mbembe.*

The captives were afraid to expose any of their own carefully rationed food for fear the bowmen would confiscate it all.

Their fingers still covered in sticky blood and animal grease, Bigshot and his lieutenant, "Littleshot," grabbed their prisoners by the necks and hauled them roughly to their feet. The march began again. Ndoki was limping.

It was good to be back in the forest and when the rains came in midafternoon, their driving force washed the swamp slime and stink from the men. Bigshot actually brought the party to a halt at one point and allowed Reg and Jigs to remove their clothing for an impromptu shower. It was perhaps the oddest moment in Danson's life. To stand exposed in a circle of painted wildmen, scrubbing his armpits in the stream spilling from a banana leaf twice as tall and broad as he, was a strange experience.

Sensing less hostility now that they were well away from the Maya Maya, Ndoki chanced a grin and pointed at Reg. The pygmy said something rapidly and laughed. "He says, 'Why do you think we wear no clothes? We were clean as soon as the rains began!'" Wiggins interpreted.

Reg glanced furtively at Bigshot and saw that he was in a meditative trance, rocking slowly up and down on the balls of his feet. Reg quickly stuck his tongue out at Ndoki and several of the men, including captors, laughed. "Tell mister fashion plate that while I concede a person's birthday suit is most wash and wear, I do not intend to entertain any bug bites where the sun does not normally shine and will continue to cover up, thank you very much!" Wiggins puzzled a moment over the translation, then spoke in half the words Reg had used but with the aid of a couple of graphic hand gestures. The boisterous laughter that followed brought Bigshot to his senses; and with a few clear hand gestures of his own, including a sharp blow to Littleshot's right ear, he indicated the comedians could dress again immediately.

The rains stopped abruptly as if with the turning of a spigot. Bigshot shoved Ndoki to the front of the line, nearly throwing him to the ground. Ndoki stumbled over the rough, uneven path, went to his knees, and cried out. Bigshot clasped his two hands together and raised them to strike.

Wiggins fought his way forward and bent over his fallen friend, taking the savage blow meant for Ndoki. The missionary put out a hand to steady himself and shouted at Bigshot, then at Reg. "Danson, this man needs medical attention. He's got five or six nasty footworms burrowing under the skin. Probably picked them up in the swamp. If we don't get them out now, they'll fester. As soon as they figure out he's not the pig or the gorilla they like to inhabit, they'll die in there and cause a bacterial infection that's the devil to fix. Come give me a hand."

While Bigshot fumed at the delay, Danson upended Ndoki and exposed the wide, flat sole and thick, splayed toes of the right foot. A dozen cuts oozed blood and dirt. With one boot on Ndoki's belly to keep him from rising up to look, Reg stretched out the pygmy's leg and held the ankle tight.

Jigs sterilized the blade of a penknife in the flame of his lighter. As soon as the flame came to life, the bowmen shrank back with a gasp and then began an excited chatter, pointing and making sharp, guttural exclamations. Wiggins quickly snapped off the lighter, stuffed it back into his breast pocket, and set to probing the wormholes with the knife.

To his credit, Ndoki screamed only once. But with a liberal coating of "secret recipe" and a cloth binding that Wiggins hoped together would keep out the germs until they got wherever they were going, the pygmy seemed relieved and limped less.

They had gone another two or three miles when they entered a huge stand of *rofo* trees, covering the forest floor in a blizzard of snowy white blossoms. The brilliant white against the deep greens of the jungle hurt the eyes. Bigshot stopped, extracted a thin piece of wood from his quiver, and blew on it. A harsh, high-pitched whistle sliced the jungle calm, and monkeys and parrots noisily agreed that it hurt their ears.

"Honey flute," said Jigs.

The men descended into a lovely, blossom-filled amphitheater of the forest floor and were immediately swathed in the buzz and hum of thousands of bees hustling between flower and hive.

The bowmen relaxed, even closing their eyes and swaying ever so slightly to the droning symphony of the bees. Smiles came over their lurid faces and their whole aspect became carefree and, if not outright friendly, at least benign. The captives seemed temporarily forgotten in the beauty of the bees.

"Bushmen are never happier than when the honey flows," said Wiggins, coming alongside Danson. They and the pygmy brothers stood watching their captors wander about the amphitheater like shoppers in the perfume section—tilting their faces upward, sniffing the air, expelling their breath in satisfied *ahhs*. Reg couldn't help thinking they had stayed a bit too long at the makeup counter.

The bowmen darted about the *rofo* glen, kicking up blossoms and searching the canopy overhead. Suddenly, Littleshot shouted and pointed to a crotch high in an *anjuafa* tree where bees could just be detected entering and exiting a hole the size of a coffee cup. Bigshot played a victory trill on the flute, and then the bushmen scattered in pursuit of other hives, marking each hive tree with an arrow.

From behind Danson and Wiggins came a low, short whistle. They turned to see Ndoki motioning to them with the pistol. He'd fished it from the pack and was holding it by the barrel. Jigs slowly reached a hand forward and took it from him. They spoke animatedly to one another, and there was much flinging of arms and hands in the direction from which they'd come and the way they'd been heading. Finally, Ndoki threw his arms up in disgust and said, "*Py wapi?* Wiggins, *py wapi?*"

Jigs looked at Reg and sighed. "Decision time. Ndoki wants to know which way we're headed. He thinks we should hightail it back without further ado. Says these crazies are too unpredictable and we'd be better off without them. I'm inclined to agree. They're weird even by pygmy standards. Much more aggressive and violent than any I've ever seen. Who knows what this Ngomba's like? Judging by his messenger boys, he probably took first prize in the Idi Amin lookalike contest. We'd best cut our losses. By the time they come back for us, we could be well down the trail and maybe between the Lord, the gun, and the *iboga* weed, we can keep in front. Leave the packs; they'd only slow us down."

Reg shook his head. "What are our chances with Ndoki limping like that? These guys rip through the forest like Olympic sprinters. They could pick us off with those arrows before we even figured out what's shadows and what's them. And what if they took us back alive after escaping? Can you imagine the welcome then?"

"We can't trust these guys," Jigs insisted. "They're painted for war, and God has just granted us a stay of execution. Let's not question it."

"This is a big swamp, Wiggins. We need help. If they wanted us dead, they would've killed us back at the canoe," Reg argued. "This Ngomba, whoever he is, wants us alive. If he can take us to the thing we're after, then he's our man."

Wiggins looked back at Ndoki and shook his head. Ndoki rolled his eyes and snorted in disgust.

The snapping of saplings indicated the bushmen continued to busily locate and mark the hives, seemingly oblivious to their prisoners' quandary whether to stay or bolt.

"Jigs, let's ask the Lord what to do," Reg said. "Let's talk to Him separately, then compare notes."

"Agreed," Wiggins replied, "but nothing windy. It will dawn on our hosts before too long that they've gotten separated from the tour they were leading."

Reg leaned back against a tree he first inspected for ants and peered up into the canopy. "God of the jungle," he prayed, "give us your wisdom."

Wiggins knelt among the fallen blossoms, his chin on his chest. "You love these people, Lord," he whispered. "Help us do no less."

A couple of minutes passed in which Ndokanda gestured imploringly to his brother to leave. These Ologus had a terrible reputation: they might even eat their own; they certainly would eat their enemies. It was said that they spoke the language of the snake-necked monster. Some were even convinced that the Ologus were the offspring of the terrible dragons and that beneath their human skin was the flesh and organs of the lizard beast.

Ndoki was torn between his black and white brothers. Trust in God and the shed blood of Jesus the Risen One, Jigs had told him again and again. When Ndoki's wife and infant son lay dying, Wiggins lay with them, cradling the baby in the warmth of his red furry chest while Ndoki caressed his wife and wiped away the fever droplets from her brow. She had died then, but the baby lived five years before dying of dysentery. Wiggins buried the baby and very nearly Ndoki when two days later the grieving pygmy missed while cutting palm fronds with the machete and the blade sank deep into his calf. Infection left him a raving madman, but Wiggins stayed with him four nights soaking the wound, holding Ndoki when the thrashing was worst, and praying with him for deliverance. Deliverance came and Ndoki believed.

Ndokanda still believed the first man was created by the moon at God's orders. Wrapping some skin around a bit of earth and pouring blood into the skin, the moon angel punched holes in the skin for all the essential orifices and stuffed the insides with organs, vital and otherwise. The angel breathed into the earthen figure, and Efe the god, the father of all human beings, was born.

God told Efe the god to be fruitful and multiply and populate the forest. As long as they obeyed God and stayed away from the forbidden *tahu* tree, his offspring would live forever. But while Efe was away in heaven, a woman convinced her husband to pick the fruit of the *tahu*. He did, gave his wife to eat, and tried to hide the peelings under a pile of leaves. He ate some of the fruit as did all the pygmies, but the moon angel saw and told God. He was angry and said that for their disobedience, the people he had made must one day die. The disobedient woman was bedeviled by a dragon and later gave birth to Efe the son incarnate of Efe the god.

It was close enough to the Christian account of original sin and the birth of a savior to satisfy Ndokanda. After that, pygmy legends became very complicated and fanciful. The simple, pure teachings of Jesus the Christ were better. And if Jesus Himself claimed to be the Son of God and worked miracles and conquered the land of the dead, then Ndokanda would be His follower.

But the Ologus were another matter. The reason the painted drinkers of blood hadn't killed their captives yet was plain for all to see. The Ologus were returning to camp from the hunt empty-handed. The only thing they would have to show for their time in the forest was some honey and the four prisoners. What Ngomba would do with four more mouths to feed was anyone's guess.

Wiggins rose from the ground and returned slowly to Reg. He stood sideways to the adventurer, not looking him in the eye. "You first," he said.

Reg folded his arms over his chest. "God is dealing with this bull head," he replied, flashing an apologetic smile. "I must learn my lesson from Mount Ararat." Sadness for the lives lost in search of Noah's Ark still weighed on him. "I was too hasty at Loch Ness, and it cost me my wife. I barged ahead on Ararat, and people died. Risking my own life is one thing; risking yours and the brothers' is quite another. If you sense the danger is too great, then I must not argue." There was disappointment in his voice but no compromise. He got up from the tree and motioned for the brothers to head back along the trail.

"Wait!" Jigs fumbled nervously with his shirt pocket, first extracting his pipe, then returning it unlit. "I believe it's time for a miracle." Habitually, he felt the contours of the tobacco pouch. "In seventeen years in the rain forest, I have prayed for a miracle, a spiritual breakthrough for these, my people. The Ologus may be thugs, but you're after the monster that overturns their canoes. I've been tracking the monster that darkens their hearts. If we turn back now, the monsters win. I want to find this Ngomba and tell him of God's love and Christ's redemption for the Ologu people. And I trust God for a miracle. If He can change the Ologus, then stand back! There will be revival in equatorial Africa!"

Jigs's eyes blazed. He'd not had the gumption to search out the hidden forest dwellers on his own. The coming of Reg Danson was a sign—and a kick—from God.

Reg grinned and took Jigs by the shoulders and squeezed. "You fuzzy old fig!" he said with genuine affection. "Two sorrier looking dragon slayers I've never seen, but what the hey? Christ's disciples weren't much to look at either!"

They did not see the grim worry on the faces of Ndoki and Ndokanda. Wiggins and Danson knew nothing of the evil ahead.

A sharp whistle sounded from across the amphitheater. Littleshot motioned to them to come. They followed him to the base of the *anjuafa* tree where the first hive was spotted. Rapidly fashioning two rough baskets of *mongongo* leaves, Littleshot filled one with damp leaves and humus from the forest floor and pantomimed fire and smoke. Then he gathered together some dry tinder and pointed to the lighter in Wiggins's pocket. He remembered the flame it had produced when the white man had dealt with Ndoki's foot infections. Wiggins obliged and the pile of tinder burst into vigorous flame. Littleshot leapt back and ran a safe distance off until the lighter had been put away. Then he returned, made a little nest in the center of the leaf basket, and placed the pile of burning tinder inside. Covered with the moist vegetation, the jungle smokepot was soon puffing acridly.

Littleshot pulled down some thick vines, rapidly braided them into a single thick cord, and tied it and the two baskets about his waist.

Because the crotch of limbs fifty feet up the *anjuafa* tree offered the first branches, Littleshot was forced to scramble up a smaller tree beside it. At the crown of that tree, he began to sway back and forth until he could grab the lowermost branch of the hive tree. He tied the two trees together and crossed over to the *anjuafa.*

Ignoring the agitated bees, Littleshot held the smoldering basket beneath the hive hole until the occupants became sluggish from the billowing smoke. Then he reached in and withdrew a huge chunk of sparkling honeycomb dripping its sweet treasure. Without hesitation, he crammed honey, beeswax, a couple of bees, larvae, pollen, and all into his mouth. He chewed with wholehearted abandon, snorting and slurping, smearing the sticky bronze all over his face and chest. Again and again he reached inside the tree and wolfed down the contents, some pieces gorged with honey, others white with bee larvae. It seemed as if nothing would ever be placed inside the gathering basket.

Another twenty minutes and Littleshot at last seemed sated. He placed the last three pieces of honeycomb inside the basket and began to make his way down to the ground. "Mr. Generosity will take that back to his family," muttered Wiggins. "Two pounds in his belly, six ounces for the wife and kids."

Littleshot belched loudly and was answered in kind by Bigshot and several of the other archers returning to the amphitheater. Between them, they had spared enough for one basketful of honeycomb for an entire village.

Then, their stomachs as fat and round as melons, the honeymen proceeded to lick the excess honey from each other's faces and shoulders. "Waste not, want not," muttered Wiggins, earning another sharp rebuke from Bigshot.

Ndoki licked his lips hungrily, remembering the sweet ambrosia of past honey hunts he'd been on. Bigshot saw the intense longing in Ndoki's expression and held out a piece of comb oozing with nectar. Ndoki looked uncertain, sensing a trap. But a flood of hunger swept away all caution, and he lunged at the honey like a starving dog. Bigshot was quicker and let the comb fall to the ground. Ndoki dropped to all fours and would have snatched the prize except that Bigshot's foot found it first. With a leer, he ground and smeared the delicate liquid chambers into the rot and decay of the forest soil. Before Ndoki could rise, Bigshot pinned the captive pygmy's neck to the ground with his filthy, honey-smeared foot. The leader of the archers barked a command and released his foot. Ndoki sprang forward and swept the astonished Bigshot off his feet. But before Ndoki could press the advantage, nine poison arrows were drawn and aimed inches from his face. Were anyone to blink an eye, Ndoki would die.

Bigshot jumped back to his feet, hatred twisting his face into a gargoyle. He put his foot back on Ndoki's neck and rammed the helpless man's head against the ground. Nine arrows followed every move.

Reg started forward, but Wiggins held him back. To fight was suicide. Again Bigshot barked the order, and this time Ndoki did not resist. He opened his mouth and licked up the bits and pieces of honey thick with twigs and blossoms and dirt. He coughed and choked, but everything he spit out, Bigshot made him lick up again.

When he'd finished to Bigshot's satisfaction, Ndoki rose up on his knees and looked at the face of his tormentor. Bigshot smiled triumphantly and raised the encrusted foot to his victim's lips. Ndoki felt faint, recovered, and cleaned Bigshot's foot with his tongue.

When the foot was clean of debris and honey, Bigshot planted it on Ndoki's mouth and shoved him over backward. The Ologus laughed raucously.

This sport completed, the head bowman pushed the other men toward the packs, and the fourteen resumed their march to Ngomba, *griot* of the Ologus.

Reg Danson bit his lip. Why hadn't they run when they had the chance? *Rum pum pum pum . . . martyrdom dumb . . . run, run, me and my drum . . .*

**L**ooks like it'd be a cornucopia of edibles, doesn't it?"

Tony Danson looked at the wild green rampart of the rain forest with a growing resentment. William Fulgate could kill time by viewing the jungle with studious detachment, but Tony could not. It had his father, and while they stood about on the porch of the commissioner's office doing nothing . . .

Fulgate gave Tony's neck a friendly squeeze. "The Africans have a proverb. It says that salt comes from the north, gold from the south, but the word of God and wisdom and beautiful tales are found only in Timbuktu. Perhaps this is your father's Timbuktu, and only here can he find the truth of what he seeks."

Tony turned and looked at Fulgate, worry souring his good looks. "Dad's Timbuktu I could handle. It's his Waterloo I'm concerned about. It's—it's like he's no good without Mom or me. She's gone and I should be with him, not standing around drinking tea and waiting for the mail."

Fulgate stared straight ahead. "Have you asked anything in His name?"

Tony looked at the ambassador curiously. "What?"

"Christ said to ask anything in His name and He would do it. Have you asked?"

"Yes."

"Then you can drink tea until the boat gets here; until Christ returns for that matter. Running to and fro, all in a sweat, doing your manly best out of your own strength is really the lesser choice. Mint or Earl Grey?"

Tony's shoulders sagged in resignation, and he joined Fulgate at a small table set for tea. He hadn't had tea since his mother had made him drink it with lemon and honey for a sore throat. "Mint, please," he said, and Fulgate poured.

"Excellent choice," said the ambassador expansively. "The mint's from Malawi."

They sipped in silence for a time, the nearby drone and squeal of the rain forest performing a percussion ensemble that had been laying for thousands of years.

Fulgate eyed the young Danson over the rim of his steaming cup.

"Do you think black is beautiful?" It was said without expression, the steam off the tea alternately clouding and clearing the man's eyeglasses as he blew and sipped the hot contents of the cup.

Tony hadn't expected such a question. "I—I think so. I haven't had all that much contact with African-Americans. Martin Luther King had a powerful and righteous message, but Malcolm X had too sharp an edge for my liking. I remember as a kid seeing Ethel Waters, and when she sang 'His Eye Is on the Sparrow,' I cried like a baby. Mrs. Hall, my kindergarten teacher, was a black woman with a heart so big that for a long time, I thought maybe that's where heaven was. Is that what you mean?"

Fulgate just blew and sipped. "Do you think Jesus was white?"

"No, He was Semitic."

"Moses?"

"No, he was a Hebrew.

"Adam?"

"Well, no, I suppose not. Doesn't his name translate 'red man' or something like that?"

"Close. It sounds like and may be a derivation of the Hebrew word *adamah,* their word for 'ground.' He was most probably dark reddish-brown to black like the soil he came from."

Tony looked perplexed.

"I know what's going through your mind. Every flannelgraph Sunday school lesson you've ever had and every Hollywood epic you've ever seen depict a western European muscleman rising up from the ground and wandering about the Garden. How long do you think a naked, fair-skinned man like that could last in a hot, tropical environment like this? He'd look like a broiled lobster in no time. Add to that the fact most of the world's people are medium to dark-colored and that leaves us whites, the bleached-out ones, definitely in the minority!"

Fulgate could see that Tony was struggling with a set of notions long ingrained. "Ethiopians, Egyptians, Libyans, even Arabs and Filipinos are all members of the black race if you read the anthropologists I read. Noah's sons would be black, and the name of one of them, Ham, literally means dark skin; Abraham's concubine Hagar, was black; Moses's wife, Zipporah, was black; Joseph and Solomon married black women. If the Canaanites were a black race as many suppose, then Rahab, the prostitute, one of only four women mentioned in Christ's genealogy, was black. Sure there was diversity of skin tone and features, not all were Negroid, and probably few were as blue-black as Central Africans can be, but you just have to look at the amazing array of people in Africa today to see that black comes in a wide variety of shades. Many of the pygmy people are copper-colored or golden-skinned.

"But whites cannot produce dark-skinned people on their own, agreed? So if, as the Bible says, from one blood all nations came, and man was created in the tropics where the indigenous people are of darker skin, then I would say the truth is our forefathers—yours and mine—were black men!"

Tony refilled Fulgate's cup and gave him a dubious look. "Sounds to me like maybe black historians are working overtime to turn the tables on their white oppressors."

Fulgate smiled agreeably. "Revisionism would certainly be a strong temptation given the turbulent history of the two races together. For whatever reason, whites have had ascendency over blacks in much of the last two millennia. But we have confused that with forcing the black man to divorce his own culture and take up ours in order to be Christian, as if they have no Christian roots of their own.

"The African Judeo-Christian tradition is well established. The Ethiopian Christians date back to the fourth century A.D. while the Ethiopian Jews date back several hundred years B.C. Jewish Egyptians were present at Pentecost and undoubtedly began preaching Christianity upon their return home. Luke mentions Apollos, a Jew of Alexandria, who 'had been instructed in the way of the Lord.' The emperor Hadrian in the second century wrote of 'those who call themselves the bishops of Christ' in Egypt.

"Even Antony, the father of Christian monasticism, was born in Egypt to Coptic Christian parents. He preached to the persecuted Christians in the mines and prisons of Alexandria. My only point is that all this 'dark continent' rhetoric from the Tarzan films is no more true of Africa than of America. Dark hearts are not to be confused with dark skin."

Tony set down his teacup and stared worriedly at the impenetrable face of the jungle. "I know it's not all Simba, Bwana, and Cheetah out there. But if Dad escapes all the physical dangers of snakebite and malaria only to fall into the hands of those whose own misconceptions are of ruthless white men with big whips and even bigger egos, then all the preaching in Alexandria isn't going to help him, is it?"

Fulgate got up from the table and walked to the porch railing, hands on his hips. Distractedly, he picked at the sticky shirt adhering to his body. Dark perspiration stains left large circles under both arms and a wide damp streak down his back. Wet coils of black hair lay plastered against his skull. His gaze bored a hole in the profuse green, wanting to X-ray the contents of the jungle and expose Reg Danson. Almost under his breath, he replied, "I wouldn't be so sure of that, son. I just wouldn't be so sure."

The rains beat in rivers against the huts of the Ologus. The work had stopped; man and jungle animals had taken cover. The gods were busy, and they wanted everyone's—and every-thing's—attention.

Ngomba seethed at the evil of the new day. Both hunting parties were overdue.

His favorite wife had announced her pregnancy even though her newly married daughter had not yet conceived. It was taboo for a mother to overstep her daughter in pregnancy. It was so from the time of the girl's puberty to her first conception. Ngomba would be shamed, and the wife would have to die.

Worse, the keeper of the fire had fallen into a drunken stu-por in the night from too much *iboga* and palm wine and had slept right through a demon rain. While the entire camp of twenty huts had nearly washed off the land rise, the precious fire coals, lit from some original fire long ago and carried from fresh hunting ground to fresh hunting ground carefully wrapped in thick leaves, had been left exposed to drown. At first light, the coals were dead and cold, the life in them gone.

The Ologus did not know matches or flint. The dying of the fire meant bloodshed.

But not the blood of the offender. The useless dung of a man who had killed the coals must be punished, but by a fate worse than death. He would be taken from his young wife and made to sleep with the barren widow. She was so old and clumsy it was rumored that she hadn't been born at all but slipped on a cloud in heaven and fell to earth. Her fall was broken by the up-per canopy where she lived for many years. When she finally got on the nerves of the animals, she was tripped by monkeys and pushed from the high trees, then landed on the roof of an Ologu hut. Vile-tempered and hard of hearing, she was once said to have swallowed a live viper so that the wiggling in her stomach would make others think she was with child.

A boy of five years came from behind a hut where he'd gone to play. One look at the chief's raging countenance and the child fled with a shrill cry of alarm.

As soon as the hunters returned, they must prepare for war. They would attack the Bwambati and take their fire. The Strong One of the forest would protect them, and then there would be much dancing and drinking and abundant *iboga*. Always *iboga*. It was sacred medicine.

They would succeed because Ngomba their holy *griot* and mighty sorceror would gain full power for battle by lying with his own married daughter. The people of the forest knew that incest and witchcraft were linked, and no one should engage in it except the sorceror, and only then under extreme circumstances.

To be without fire was extreme. Ngomba knew of other ways to gain fire, but he would not let his people know. Done correctly, this way would increase his hold over them. Renewing the fire by war called for the most powerful witchcraft. He and he alone would bring back the fire for cooking and making grateful sacrifice to the Strong One.

The rain stopped, and within minutes the clouds dissolved. The sun beat madly down, angry that its golden splendor had been so brashly interrupted. The forest steamed, and as if telling one another the storm was over by talking all at once, the insects and animals of the Congo spilled forth in noisy song.

Ngomba stepped through the hot rising fog of the pygmy fairyland and walked among the huts, playing a five-stringed *ndomu,* or bow harp. Its vegetable fiber strings thrummed an invitation to emerge from the huts as babies from the womb. Young adolescent girls and boys were first out, moving slowly from the confines of the palm-leaf dwellings in order to conserve energy. Meat—nourishment and strength—was in short supply and not to be wasted on the young not old enough to feed the camp. Next came the little ones, among them those who had recently learned to walk. On their heels came the mothers and grandmothers and old men who had long lasted on little. A couple of mothers bore baskets containing tiny infants. The babies cried at the sudden bright light but were left to cry.

The Ologu mothers were careful not to touch their children except for the most necessary functions. Ngomba had decreed it. Meat was becoming so scarce that most of the children now died of either malnutrition or disease. Mother's milk, and mother's love, were critically low. The mothers were told not to bond with their children but to steel themselves against the day when the children would surely die.

Ngomba himself did not suffer. The people brought him the firstfruits of their hunting and gathering, which in most cases was most of what they could find. The *griot* was the most important person among them, the hunters second. They would gladly starve that he might thrive. Neither was he to expend energy on the hunt himself. He had the much more important task of keeping spirit and community together, especially in lean times. He knew the language of the Strong One. The least they could do was to feed him and give him their adoration. They needed him more than ever now that the forest kept its bounty from them. Ngomba was their oracle, and he must never know hunger.

Suddenly, a shout went up from the edge of camp. The hunters had returned!

The ten archers and their four captives—torn, bug-bitten, and beaten, bowed almost double from lack of rest and the weight of the packs, their clothes in tatters—filed into the clearing. The Ologus shrank back from the white men, covering their faces and making little gagging sounds in their throats as if tear gas had been lobbed in their midst. Ngomba clicked sharply with his tongue, and the people immediately quieted and dropped their hands.

Reg Danson was at the end of his stamina. He threw down the pack, not caring if it earned him a kick or not, and straightened his breaking back. Wiping the sweat from his eyes, he took in the strangest tableau he'd ever seen.

They were in a pretty, sun–dappled clearing beneath a ring of immense *kombokombo* trees. The undergrowth had been hacked away and the branches and saplings used by the women to make the framework for the earthen–floor igloos of leaves in which each family or family group lived. The original layers of *raffia* leaf roofing, looking like thick-skinned tobacco leaves, were a khaki brown. Here and there, the ceilings and walls were patched with fresh *raffia,* giant green patches to stop a leak or keep out the sun. Several dead campfires rendered much of the clearing a soggy outdoor mess hall. On a small wooden platform near the largest cooking fire ring, as sodden and cold as the rest, were the partially butchered carcasses of two extremely thin dogs. Used for hunting, they were now more valuable as food.

The fifty or sixty Ologus were obviously suffering from lack of food. They looked thin and pained from going without, yet they were some of the most beautiful people Reg had ever seen. They were the color of burnished bronze. A few were olive-skinned, others a yellowish tan. Some looked almost Spanish or Italian. Several of the women's faces and heads were intricately painted with complex geometric patterns. All were pygmies—short legs, long arms, long torsos, large heads.

Though all were naked except for the slightest of waist coverings, the elders carried themselves with a particular dignity. Though they suffered, they weren't broken. Yet something was not right, a strange agitation that was present before the white men showed up. It was in the furtive darting of the eyes, the quaking deference shown to the astonishing man who stood in their midst.

He was an incredible human being, fully seven feet tall, towering over the pygmies as if they all were children. Ebony and gleaming, he might have been chiseled from a great block of shiny basaltic rock, so perfect was the mighty physique: huge feet; powerfully muscled calves and thighs; hard, flat stomach; broad shoulders and chest; brawny, thickly veined arms and massive hands; thick neck; wide, handsome face and dark, probing eyes; bald and completely naked except for a single gold ring in his left ear. The giant's bearing was regal as a king's and as alert as the palace guard's, but a streak of guile wreathed his lips and there was a shrewd cast to his jaws.

And the eyes were the eyes of the creature from the river— only these eyes were full of intelligence and cunning. Danson was seeing a life form more dangerous even than *Mokele-mbembe*. He felt icy cold inside despite the wilting heat. *God, my God, were Goliath's eyes anything like this?*

The hunters laid a basket of honey and a young, fifty-pound okapi at Ngomba's feet, a fortunate find just before last light the previous evening. It was, they believed, a special animal constructed by God of the best parts of many animals: the neck of a giraffe, the legs of a zebra, the body of a waterbuck, the cloven hooves of a cow. It was sacred food to the pygmies and found only in the Congo rain forest.

It was also very small for sixty or more people.

The night before, the captives had been forced to dig a pit with flat, spade-like stones in a side animal trail where there was fresh sign of use. The pit was overlaid with leaves and branches, and just before nightfall, the okapi took its fatal last step.

The bowmen had sprung upon the imprisoned animal and clubbed it to death. The reddish velvet of its coat hadn't been marred and would be used for making quivers. He who hunted with an okapi quiver was a man of high status.

Now the hunters knelt before the giant one and kissed his feet. Wiggins seized the distraction and whispered, trying not to move his lips. "I know this one." He jerked his head at the chief. "He is Ngomba, a Nubian of Kordofan, in the hills south and west of Khartoum in the Sudan. I'd heard the rumors of an immense man from the north who supposedly fled for some terrible deed and ended up in the far back of the Congo. The Nubians used to do a brisk trade in gold, cattle, ivory, and Central African slaves. Then the Nubians themselves, because of their size and strength, became the number one choice of the North American slave trade." The hunters rose from the ground, and Wiggins went silent.

Again without speaking, Ngomba made the clicking in his throat, and four women grasped the okapi by each of its legs. They lifted the kill onto the table with the butchered dogs, took up knives, and began to skin the carcass. A fifth woman divided the honey into two baskets and placed one at the entrance to the largest of the huts. The other was nearly ripped to pieces as the women and children rushed to grab a meager bit of amber succulence. It was gone in a moment, but it brought no pleasure. The babies squalled and several of the older children fought back tears. The poor little smears of sweetness on their hands and lips were worse than no honey at all. A promise of goodness and no more.

"What's to become of the other basket?" Reg whispered under his breath, hunger gnawing at his own belly. They'd had nothing but water for more than forty-eight hours and had marched nearly to exhaustion.

"It's for the big guy," Wiggins muttered. "You don't maintain a body like that on leaves and twigs."

Reg looked at Wiggins in shock. "They keep him going at their own expense?!"

Wiggins nodded. "I told you this was no Disneyland."

A clap like a rifle shot startled the captives to attention. Ngomba lifted his huge hands a second time and brought them together in a sharp, explosive slap. The rest of the camp took up the gesture, creating loud repeating ricochets off the *kombokombo* trees as the people began to circle the four newcomers. A drummer began a hollow, resounding beat with a stick against a log. *I played my best for him . . . pum pum pum . . . when we come . . . it's a good-bye drum . . .*

The many eyes of the hunters narrowed to a ravenous glint, like carnivores before pulling down prey.

"I don't like the looks of this," Danson said.

"With good reason," Wiggins responded.

The hunters bobbed their heads toward their victims and back like cobras, a stuporous leer twisting their humanity into something grossly inhuman. The patch of skin and beard so unceremoniously ripped from Wiggins's chin flopped free of Bigshot's headdress and landed in the dirt. It was quickly ground from sight beneath the pounding of naked feet.

The pounding and clapping resonated in Reg's heart and head with a terrible throbbing. How long ago had it been since Reg had joked with his mother about waterskiing behind a canoe? A decade ago? A lifetime? *Pray for me, Carrie Danson, like you've never prayed before.* Reg squeezed his eyes shut and clenched his fists tightly at his sides. *Lord God, keeper of your word in all times past, have I done that which seemed right in my sight by coming here when it was not your will that I do so? No! I come in your name. There is a way of life and a way of death. You have overcome the way of death in me, now may I show the way of life to these who have embraced death.*

The pounding and clapping intensified. The people whirled about the clearing, each in the grip of some private trance. "MMMMMMM . . . MMMMMMM . . . " the awful thrum began. "MMMMMMM . . . MMMOOOO . . . KAAALAAAY . . . MMMMMMM . . . MMMBEMMM . . . BAAAY!!" The voices came from the ground, the trees, the swamp, anywhere but from the throats of the people. Young and old were throwing their voices like malevolent ventriloquists, and the terrible invocation rained down upon their victims like voices of doom.

Without warning, Ngomba vaulted forward, an incredible standing leap of ten feet, landing in front of his captives as lightly as a jungle cat. He crouched and circled the quarry tigerlike, muscles rippling along his back and thighs. His ears flattened against his head. A snarl began deep in the ebony chest, vibrating against the sound chamber, entering the throat with a feline growl, and bursting from the gaping mouth in a roar much like a lion's. Ngomba's front teeth were ground and polished to sharp points, and as the people whirled closer and closer, sharp-toothed grins appeared in abundance.

Again the clicking rose from Ngomba's throat, this time in a noticeably different pattern. Ngomba leaped in front of his archers and snarled at a young man who looked as terrified as if he were anticipating his own beheading. Three of the archers seized the keeper of the fire and shoved him into the circle with the captives. An ancient man no more than four feet tall, face narrow and sunken, eyes swollen nearly shut, stopped in front of the frightened younger man and spoke rapidly in a high, strangled voice. The drumming, the whirling, and the clapping came to an abrupt halt.

"What's going on?" Reg whispered.

"Seems the young guy let the fire go out. They don't know how to make more fire and will now have to steal it from the neighbors. They're going to war, and the offender is sentenced to life with the village shrew." A severely wrinkled old woman with the grossly inflated legs of elephantiasis stumped into the clearing, chattering hysterically, and tied a rope leash around the young man's neck. Then, cackling with glee, she led him off on all fours.

"Poor beggar," Jigs said, desperately needing to scratch an itch on his upper lip but not daring to move.

When the old woman and her new pet departed for her hut, the crowd erupted in wild, excited exclamations, refilling the hunters' quivers with a fresh supply of killing arrows, petting and fawning over the warriors, undoubtedly admonishing them to keep their eyes open for anything in the next camp that could be used as food. The warriors flexed and preened and tried to suck in their distended bellies, casting knowing glances at the younger females and uttering bloody imprecations against the enemy.

Littleshot looked knowingly at the missionary's shirt pocket where the magic fire maker was kept, but when he tried to speak to the *griot,* he was silenced with a glare.

"Stupid waste," mumbled Wiggins, relaxing a little now that the crowd's attentions were directed elsewhere and Littleshot was unable to gain an audience with Ngomba.

"What?" Reg asked, feeling free at last to take a few deep breaths to calm his own racing heart.

"This fire business," Jigs answered, digging at his lip while the Ologus had their backs turned. "Totally unnecessary. Ngomba knows how to make fire. Unless I miss my guess, he's worn a suit once or twice."

Reg looked at Wiggins in utter amazement. "You don't mean—"

"The guy's a con man from way back. Look at him. He's got sixty people waiting on him hand and foot. Got them thinking he's part god, part animal, part wizard. Part used car salesman, I'd say, with a little mafioso and politician mixed in. If he comes up with the creature we're after, I think we'd better check for smoke and mirrors."

Danson's eyes narrowed, and his jaw muscles worked overtime.

"Give me your lighter!" he commanded.

Jigs didn't comprehend. "What—what are you—"

"Don't argue with me, man. Give me the lighter!"

Wiggins fished in his pocket and handed it over.

"Thanks," Reg said. Then he did the unthinkable.

Springing forward, he grabbed his duffel, unsnapped the top, and grabbed Bascomb's Bible. Before the Ologus reacted, he tore out several end pages, swept up a handful of wood shavings from beneath the butcher table, and dashed to the closest fire ring. Kneeling, he wadded together the thin pages and the dry shavings and set them afire with the lighter. Piling on some dry twigs and leaves, he built a strong blaze that crackled up between him and the astounded Ologus.

THE LOST KINGDOM

A howl of fury tore across the clearing. Ngomba picked Reg up by the throat and hurled him against a hut. It caved in partway but held. The headman grabbed a poison arrow and lunged. Reg rolled and Ngomba fell onto the hut, flattening it as if it were made of paper. Ngomba dropped the arrow and wrenched a skinning knife from a woman's hand. His eyes flashed murderously, and he plunged after Danson.

*Lord God, I need you! Help me!*

Ngomba snatched up a chunk of wood and smashed it between Reg's shoulder blades. Reg went down, then was wrenched to his feet by the giant Nubian. He whipped Danson around to face him and jerked him forward at the same time that he brought his broad forehead down hard. The crack of their colliding skulls made Wiggins wince.

Ngomba forced his long, thick fingers into Reg's mouth and with both hands pried his jaws wide apart. The Nubian's strength was enormous. Fight as he might, Danson felt as if his jaws would crack and his face split in two. He gagged, tongue flapping uselessly.

Wiggins and the pygmy brothers started forward almost at the same instant. They were stopped by a wall of archers, bows drawn.

Ngomba dug his fingers deeper into the soft flesh at the back of Danson's throat. All air was gone. Reg began to lose consciousness. *God, my God . . .*

A shout went up. Ngomba looked and saw his people tending the fire that sprang from the bearded one's pocket. It licked hungrily at the wood they fed it. Ngomba flung Danson aside like a defective doll. His people had made a decision of their own.

A terrible moment of uncertainty passed between the *griot* and the pygmies. They knew he held their life and death in his hands, yet had not the gods sent fire the very morning theirs had died? Could even the great and invincible Ngomba deny the favorable signs?

Ngomba weighed the moment. He could claim to have brought the white men for just such a crisis as this. He could spare the white man choking on the ground and still attack the neighboring encampment. The people would enjoy playing with the white pets, making slaves of those whose ancestors made slaves of the black fathers. Credit would be his for new fire, for showing mercy, for ravaging the enemy, *and* for allowing the four newcomers to be kept as beasts of burden.

But the white man had challenged him. The four would have to be fed and there was little enough food as it was. And where had the captives come from? Would someone not search for them? Better to eliminate all trace.

Ngomba, *griot* of the fiercesome Ologus, must not appear weak. The Strong One would not favor a coward. He thrust out his chest and bellowed his verdict.

The white men must die.

Ndoki and Ndokanda were held so that they could not interfere. Jigs and Reg were dragged to the center of the clearing and each tied spread-eagle to four stakes pounded into the ground. They lay flat against the earth, barely able to move.

The drum in the hollow log beat a slow, funereal rhythm to which the Ologus performed a kind of hypnotic swaying. Four pygmy bowmen were chosen to climb a *kombokombo* tree to a log platform twenty feet in the air. As they climbed, the banshee humming started again, at first a mesmerizing lullaby, then quickly changing with the increasing beat to a raucous and disorienting bedlam. Again, it was as if the voices flying about the clearing did not belong to the dancers but to the spirits of the air.

"You fool!" Wiggins shouted above the din. "Do you give that much thought to everything you do? It's bad medicine to interfere with affairs of state, and fire is one of the most delicate matters of diplomacy."

Reg snickered despite their predicament. "Sorry, Wiggins," he said tightly, feeling as if his jaw had been dislocated. "I didn't think about jungle protocol. But you said yourself this guy's a lunatic. What kind of scam's he running here? These aren't the gentle pygmies back at Sangha."

"He's brainwashed them somehow," Jigs said, squirming against the bonds that held him fast. "No doubt convinced them he's some black giant from above." Jigs stopped straining against the ties. He closed his eyes and prayed loudly, "*Tore! Tore!*" He looked over at Reg. "It means 'God the Father.' Say it!"

Together they shouted, "*Tore! Tore!*" The dancers began to whirl and twirl closer and closer to the men tied to the ground and were soon leaping between their legs and about their heads, coming within inches, but nimbly spinning away, their places taken always by those next in line.

"They're all on *iboga!*" shouted Wiggins. "It dulls the pain of starvation. *Tore! Tore! Tore!*"

Faster and faster the dancers spun, looping low to the ground, then springing high into the air in a wild African variation of Muslim dervishes. The insanity filled the forest with the sound of deranged men, and the animals fled.

All but the human vultures. They continued to circle.

Out of the corner of one eye, Reg spotted a cute boy of no more than five or six crouched low, just out of range of his whirling elders, watching the white men intently. He balanced up on his toes, little arms encircling his knees, hugging them tightly. His look was one of concern and curiosity.

He cared.

From the platform above, Bigshot, the first to bury his arrow in the okapi, was rewarded for such marksmanship with the privilege of firing the first arrow at the condemned men below. "*Eti mune mai oro!*" the archer shouted. "Give me my arrow!" Littleshot presented it to him with a flourish.

"MMMMMMM . . . MMMMMMM . . . " the dancers droned.

The arrow struck the ground six inches from Reg's left eye, and the *thwang!* of its hitting would be with him forever.

"I told you they don't miss!" yelled Wiggins, straining, lifting his head. "They're toying with us before they finish us off!" They strained against their bonds, but the ties strangled their wrists with a brutal finality.

One of the youngest warriors kicked dirt in Jigs's face as he passed and snatched the baseball cap from the missionary's head. He flung it high into the air, and four arrows pierced it in the blink of an eye. It fell to the earth to disappear among the dancers.

Reg and Jigs were pinned to the spot, helpless as mounted butterflies, powerless to save themselves or even to wipe the stinging sweat from their eyes.

Several more arrows sank home in the soft earth about the men's bodies, and each arrow was a simulated death. Would the next strike the heart? Tears streamed down Reg's face. "God, please look after Tony." He was ready to die. "Death, where is *your* victory? The Lord is *my* shepherd!"

Ngomba stepped to the edge of the platform, took up his bow, and positioned an arrow. Reg's last image before squeezing his eyes tightly shut was of a magnificent colossus of a man sharply etched against the sunstruck canopy. Supple muscles stiffening, the executioner took careful aim and stretched the bowstring taut.

The drum went silent. The dancers faltered, several falling into each other, their concentration broken. There was a commotion at the far end of the clearing. The people parted, and in raced eight new warriors breathless with excitement, unable to calm down long enough to tell the news. It was the second band of hunters returned.

They didn't need to talk. Three of them were covered in blood, and the people acted as if they knew exactly what that meant. For the first time since Reg laid eyes on them, the people's faces burst into smiles as if they'd received a new lease on life.

Passionately, they telegraphed the news about the clearing until everyone was talking and gesticulating at once.

"Wiggins," Reg croaked, surprised he could speak at all. "You need to interpret faster. My heart can't take many more of your delayed broadcasts!"

"Sorry, Danson," Jigs gasped, fighting to bring his own heart under control. "Seems our little sharpshooters hit pay dirt. They've killed a forest elephant down at the Maya Maya, not a mile from here. Food for a week at least. There will be one hearty party tonight."

Despite the good news, the white prisoners were not about to be spared so easily.

Ngomba loomed into Reg's vision and planted one giant leg on either side of Danson's rib cage, fury in every twitching muscle. From that angle, the Nubian stretched impossibly tall, his smooth head brushing the tree crowns. Reg felt as if his skin would soon blister and peel from the scorching hatred and frustration in the Nubian's eyes. Ngomba raised his bow and drew back the arrow.

From behind, a warrior grabbed Danson's hair and wrenched his head back. He pried Reg's mouth open. Ngomba bent and inserted the head of the arrow, poison bright upon its tip, into Reg's mouth.

Danson went rigid, sweat streaming into his eyes and ears, every muscle screaming its distress. *The Lord is my shepherd.* The harder he tried to hold perfectly still, the more his head and neck shook with the strain. He couldn't hold his tormented jaws open another second. There was nothing left but to clamp his teeth on the shaft of death and go to meet God. His tongue, thick and swollen, threatened to rise up and taste certain death. To swallow, to spit, to sob—anything—would have been paradise. He couldn't hold it any longer. *Jesus, I come . . .*

And then he was seized by the oddest thought. His predicament seemed familiar somehow. Then he remembered. *This is a lot like going to the dentist.*

A change came over Ngomba. Somewhere deep within his reason, the *iboga* drug took a sharp right turn and short-term memory failed him. The loathing in his eyes metamorphosed into a quizzical bewilderment. He blinked to clear the confusion, then straightened. The arrow rose with him, shedding a single sparkling drop that fell harmlessly onto Reg's shirt pocket. Reg half expected it to fry a hole right through him, but nothing happened.

The giant clicked a command, and Littleshot cut the captives free. Ngomba stared at his prisoners suspiciously but had difficulty accessing all the information necessary to carry out the kill. He needed time to think.

Danson and Wiggins sat up and rubbed the circulation back into their wrists. Reg cautiously brought his lips together and swallowed. Lips numb. Throat dry. Face tingly. Jaws in pain. *All finished, Mr. Danson. Good oral hygiene is a must for the prevention of cavities. Floss regularly, now, and we'll see you again in six months.*

The people clamored about the newest camp arrivals, eagerly pumping them for every detail of the hunt. A few wiped their hands over the bodies of the bloodied bowmen and smeared the sticky redness over their own bodies in sheer delight at the prospect of full stomachs. Ngomba strode into the mob and silenced them with a look. His presence elicited a formal report from the hunt leader. Every so often, a pygmy would steal a glance back at the white men with a look not unlike respect.

"Unless I miss my guess," said Wiggins in a choked whisper, as if he too had to speak around a mouthful of dry dental cotton wads, "our tall friend is caught in a vise. The people link our arrival to the killing of the elephant. We essentially brought them food. You and me, brother, are good omens. Ngomba's kingship is in check."

Reg began laughing at the sheer lightness of being. Every adrenaline-gorged cell released at once, and for one sensational moment he felt he could float above the ground. Then his eyes fell on the single dark stain on the shirt pocket flap, and his smile faded.

Reg was about to try his legs when he looked again into the face of the cute little boy who'd watched the dance of death with such interest and concern. They were close enough to touch, and the compassion that filled the boy's eyes warmed the shaky explorer deep inside. *My Tony. How's school, bud? I sure could use a hug . . .*

The boy slowly stretched out an arm and handed Reg the Chicago Cubs baseball cap. It was ragged with arrow holes and dirty brown from its trampling beneath the dancers' feet, but it said hot dogs and Cracker Jack and homeruns and curve balls and Sunday afternoons throwing grounders with Tony. Reg wadded the cap desperately against his chest. A single tear slid down one cheek.

The boy smiled kindly. His teeth were filed sharp as daggers. Odd, whitish raised scars were randomly scattered across his stomach and ribs. Reg reached in a pocket and withdrew a sticky, mangled jelly bean, pinkish red, half dissolved, and linty. The boy hesitantly reached for the bright candy, casting a wary eye in Ngomba's direction. But the chief and the rest of the camp were too intent on the tale of the elephant hunt to notice.

Reg squeezed the little fingers tightly in his own. *Thank you, little fella.* The boy looked momentarily startled. Reg smiled warmly and nodded. He opened his hand again. The boy took the jelly bean and cautiously touched it to his tongue. In awestruck delight, he quickly popped it into his mouth and chewed dreamily before scurrying away.

Reg sat for a long time wishing the boy would return. He looked up and thanked God for the sign. It had come in a split second. Just before taking the jelly bean from Reg's hand, the little boy had done one other remarkable thing.

Little fingers still touching the stranger's, the pygmy youngster had squeezed back.

**D**arkness, cruel and crushing, commandeered the jungle. The sun had no time to set before being brutally extinguished by the forces of darkness. The vast canopy stood guard, branch to branch in close rank, thick leaves as shields, blocking the night light as surely as a concrete bunker. It was as if they were ten stories below ground in a subterranean vault. In the close, heavy air, the lid to the vault must be mere inches above Danson's head. Coffin lid. Buried alive.

With the coming of night came new terrors. The people gashed the darkness with a great bonfire, feeding the ravenous orange throat of it more and more fuel. The flames licked the heavy, oppressive air with writhing tongues, seeming to suck away what little oxygen there was to go around. The frail huts were aflame with the reflection of fire, shadows, and shapes leaping up and over the thin leaf walls like devilish escapees from the inferno. Slabs and haunches of elephant meat smoked over a smoldering cooking fire, some pieces having the hide still intact. A thick cloud of roasting smoke drifted about, catching at last beneath the canopy where it hung like a ghostly shroud. Insects rained down out of the stuporous smoke. The children ran about collecting them in baskets, surreptitiously slipping a few into their mouths when the adults were preoccupied with other things.

The night creatures chorused from a distance as if they preferred to give the fiery clearing a wide berth.

The Ologus smoked *iboga* until, even in their weakened state, they began to charge about the clearing in a kind of frantic physical revival. One of the adolescent boys who could not hold his *iboga* kept squaring off with a tree, charging it with a roar and colliding head first with the trunk. Five and six times he rammed the tree until his head streamed blood. He staggered near where Jigs and Reg were being guarded and fell face first into the ground.

With a wary glance at the half-drugged guards, Wiggins went to the boy, dragged him to the edge of the clearing, and bandaged his head.

Soon Ngomba emerged from his hut, and the people formed a chanting circle about their living god. First clockwise, then counterclockwise, they danced, knees bent, arms akimbo in a grotesque Egyptian parody. Slowly, methodically, the circle moved ever closer to the one great fire.

When at last the circle came to a stop before the fire and in full view of the prisoners, the people sprang back and fell to their knees. Ngomba was in the center, crouched in a ball, balanced on his toes, head to knees, mighty arms wrapped around his body so that the fingertips of both hands nearly touched at his spine.

Without warning he catapulted into the air and landed before his captives, fully exposed, arms and legs stretched at forty-five degree angles to the powerful body. From head to toe, dozens of pitiless, prehistoric eyes were painted bright red and white as if bloodshot from sleepless, ceaseless hunting for white men too foolish to stay in their safe, comfortable homes.

He began to move in a fantastic dance, jerking and flexing his limbs and muscles and giving dreadful life to the eyes.

Reg was in the pool again. The creature came for him. The eyes stared and probed, now blurring, now clear, now predatory.

Ngomba ran back, but the eyes never left their prey. Then the eyes locked on their victim and raced forward for the kill.

Reg groaned and threw his hands up to fend off the monster. Ngomba flung the hands aside and laughed in Danson's face. The breath stank, and the noise was brutish and guttural. If the creature could laugh, that would be its sound.

Ngomba leapt high in the air and came down on his back like a high jumper clearing the bar. The moment he hit the dirt, the seven-foot man began to convulse, massive shudders contorting his body. Every sinew elongated in a rigid paralysis until his face froze in a horrible rictus of death. The people gasped, then performed the vocal equivalent of a drum roll.

A voice that must have come from Ngomba sounded as if it came up out of the earth. It was deep, and the hair rose on Danson's neck the way it had in his mother's room at the nursing home when Carrie's odd little roommate had uttered her eerie cry.

"He wants our names," said Wiggins hoarsely. "Give him a fake one."

"No!" replied Reg, tersely. "If he gets the best of us now, we're history. If he's the master of deception, then we must be bearers of the truth. Tell him exactly who we are and who we represent."

Jigs looked dubious, then spoke loudly.

Whatever he said, incredibly, put grins on a few faces.

"What did you say, Wiggins? I heard our names in there, but what else did you say? What's so amusing?"

"Told him what you told me to tell him. I said, 'I'm Jigs Wiggins, director of Sangha Mercy Mission on the River Ubangi. And this is Reg Danson, my able but slightly deranged assistant whose ego is as big around as a hippo's gut. Loosely translated, of course."

Reg gave Jigs a scathing look. "Very funny, Wiggins. Now tell—"

The dreadful voice stopped him mid-sentence. "White Danson and white Wiggins have trespassed on the ground of the Strong One," said the voice in crisp, sharply enunciated English. "While they have brought with them the elephant for food, they must not think that they have appeased the mighty creature that makes the river run backward. He is angered that they have come to disturb and to examine and to KILL!"

Ngomba leapt to his feet at the same time that the exploration party's packs were unceremoniously dumped on the ground. "Hey!" Reg started forward in protest, but Wiggins pulled him back.

"This guy speaks English!" said Reg, outraged. "He understands everything we've said!"

"I told you he's no country bumpkin," Jigs said. "He's street smart, and these people are as gullible as suckers at a carnival. He keeps their bodies hooked on *iboga* and on the edge of starvation and fills their minds with superstition."

Four pygmies ran to the packs, snapped them open, and shook the contents into the dirt. Ngomba snatched up the pistol, pointed it at Ndokanda, and pulled the trigger.

The gunshot exploded like a landmine in the tense atmosphere. The bullet sliced through the right side of Ndokanda's neck. With an astonished cry, he fell against his brother's shoulder, then into his lap, smearing Ndoki's skin with a trail of blood.

Ndoki laid his brother on the ground, then turned on Ngomba and charged. He caught the butt of the pistol across the forehead. He fell to the ground unconscious.

Wiggins staunched the wound in Ndokanda's neck and saw that the bullet had missed everything vital. He might get away with little more than a stiff neck from a few damaged nerves if infection didn't set in. Ndoki would get off with a bad headache.

"This is the fruit of bringing your iron death into the Strong One's kingdom!" roared Ngomba. Reg at first thought Ngomba would shoot all the captives, but instead he flung the pistol as hard as he could into the forest tangle. At a contemptuous wave of his hand, the people converged on the packs and carted off the contents faster than shoppers at a half price sale. The candy, even the dry goods, disappeared within seconds into starved mouths. The people coughed and gagged, but choked everything down. Journals, maps, testing equipment, clothing—he took it all. Ngomba salvaged three items as if he'd had his eye on them: the medicines, the elephant tranquilizer gun, and Bascomb's Bible. The last he looked at with some recognition before flinging it at Reg in scorn.

Then he clicked a command and a woman screamed.

She was carried into the clearing above the heads of six hunters. They threw her at Ngomba's feet, which she embraced imploringly. He kicked her loose and stood apart, the disgust for her plain upon his curled lips. "You have allowed yourself to be with child even though your own daughter"—here he motioned to a young girl still quite obviously in her teens—"has not yet conceived. For this act of selfishness, you must die. The Strong One will be pleased, for this night he will receive two sacrifices in the one—you and the forbidden child within you!"

The woman screamed again, half in anguish, half in defiance. Ngomba snatched her off the ground as easily as a cornered rabbit. He held her aloft, and although she squirmed and fought for her freedom, she could not escape the grip of the huge hands.

Ngomba ran with the struggling, hysterical burden, circling the fire and displaying the sacrifice to the bloodthirsty crowd. They were relieved that it was not any one of them and cried their enthusiasm at the particular worthiness of this victim. A wife of the *griot*, his royal seed in her, would truly appease the Strong One, and they could be safe upon the waters once more. It was no life of ease living with the mightiest of all *griots*, but he spoke the language of the Strong One. To be near him was to know the most powerful of all creatures. To defy him was certain death. Their destiny and his were one. They were his people.

The drum began, and the Ologus voiced an infernal drone to its beat. In their drugged state, they became quickly mesmer-

ized by it. "MMMMMMM . . . MMMMMMM . . . " Ngomba
ran faster and faster about the clearing, bearing his wife high aloft,
seemingly oblivious to her screams and whimpers. Every time he
passed the captives, the legions of eyes on his body blurred into
one pair like some illusion from hell.

Abruptly, he stopped in front of the prisoners, and the drum
ceased. For ten breathless seconds no one spoke. Even the incessant jungle song seemed momentarily muted, and the woman's
cries were weakening. Ngomba's strong chest rose and fell, the
myriad painted eyes swelling and contracting with each breath.

The drum resumed, slowly at first, then rapidly increasing in
rhythm and volume. The people's voices matched each beat with
a kind of "Nawh, nawh, nawh, nawh, nawh . . . " until all was at
a fever pitch. The woman felt her husband's body shift ever so
slightly forward, and she screamed with all she had, a last blood-
curdling shriek.

Ngomba pitched forward to hurl his burden into the fire
but suddenly found Reg Danson between him and the flames.

"STOP!" Reg shouted, holding Bascomb's Bible aloft. "In
the name of God the Creator, you must not harm this woman!"

"Dear God," breathed Wiggins. "Oh, dear God!"

"Move, white Danson," snarled Ngomba. "I too have word
from God High, and it says that He accepts human sacrifice!"

"No, he does not, Ngomba. You have a false word. His
people, the Israelites, were told to destroy the Canaanites who
practiced child sacrifice. You are offering strange fire before God
in disobedience to His will. When Aaron's sons offered strange
fire, they were destroyed. If you do this thing, you will be destroyed!"

Ngomba threw back his head and roared in laughter. "Who
is this Aaron? I have heard that white God teachers contradict
themselves, but you are the first evidence. Years ago, teachers
came to the forest and worked with the Ologus to find a way to
record the word of the High God in the tongue of the forest
people. Then the white God teachers died of the fever. But the

word did not die. It is there still in my *baraza,* the meeting place. You *muzungus* make me laugh!"

With a click of command, Ngomba dispatched Littleshot to the main hut of the *griot* king. The entire time Littleshot was absent, Ngomba held his wife above his head, his bulging arms never betraying the least fatigue. Reg had a sinking feeling that anytime he'd wanted to, Ngomba could have tossed the woman over Reg's head into the fire as easily as an empty sack.

Littleshot raced back to the clearing with a thin sheaf of yellowed papers and thrust them at Wiggins. "It's the Bible translation of Billings and Langley!" Wiggins shouted. "We never knew if they contacted the Ologus, and their bodies were never found. Near as I can tell, it's much of Genesis and a small portion of the Gospel of John." He handed the badly typed but still readable sheets to Reg.

"Is that the entire work?" Reg demanded of Ngomba.

Ngomba nodded, an amused smirk on his face. "As I told you, High God men accomplished their work and died."

Danson and Wiggins looked at each other with a start. "Abraham and Isaac!" they said at the same time.

Ngomba looked annoyed, then laughed again, finding the whole thing immensely entertaining. "Yes, white Wiggins and white Danson. High God was pleased that Abraham would sacrifice his son on the altar to High God. I, too, will please High God with this woman and child. Move, white Danson, or three people will be sacrificed today."

"Wait!" yelled Reg, putting up a hand. The humor drained from Ngomba's countenance. He was finished with delays. "Ngomba, listen. You are much too clever a man not to understand that this is not the whole counsel of High God. This is only as far as the white God teachers went before they died. There is much, much more. Look, look at how thick my Bible is. It is the whole counsel of High God. It contains the words of Genesis and the story of Abraham just like your papers, but it also tells of the coming of the Law of you shall *not* kill, of the coming of the only

Son of High God, and how we have been reconciled in love with the High *and* Holy God through that only Son. It tells us again many words later that Abraham found favor with High God because he was willing to sacrifice his son *if* High God demanded it, but it was not required of him nor was it ever required of anyone in the history of earth." Reg slapped the cover of Bascomb's Bible with the sheaf of translation to show that the two agreed. "There are so many more wonderful things that you have not heard, Ngomba. We will stay with you and tell you what they are," Danson pleaded.

Ngomba's real eyes narrowed a moment, then came a look of potent cunning. He flung the woman in his hands into the crowd of bystanders. They broke her fall. She pulled free, looking to her husband in astonishment. He smiled contemptuously at her, and with a cry, she fled from what was to have been her funeral pyre.

"Oh, yes, you *will* stay!" said the *griot* to the captives. There was no mistaking the menace in his voice. He looked after the fleeing woman. "Sometimes to live is worse than death. She will lose the child and that will be her punishment." He turned to go.

Reg thrust the whole Bible forward. It was open to 1 Samuel 15. "'Has the High God as great delight in burnt offerings and sacrifices, as in obeying the voice of the High God?'" he read. "'To obey is better than sacrifice, and to heed than the fat of rams.' Ngomba has done a better thing. Ngomba has obeyed!"

The magnificent Nubian fixed Reg Danson with a look so knowing, so worldly wise, that for some odd reason the American didn't understand, Reg felt acutely embarrassed.

"I do not obey because a white God teacher tells me that I obey." Ngomba seasoned each word with venom. "I obey because the Strong One lives in the land and allows us to stay and feeds us when it is his good pleasure to do so. The High God made Strong One to rule the forest, and it is the Strong One I serve!"

The people murmured, impressed with their leader. That Ngomba, their holy one, could speak fluently in the white tongue was further proof of his supremacy.

Reg held the Bible tightly, squeezing its pages as if to wring it of its truth. "'I will cry out to God Most High . . . '" he recited the words before him from David's fifty-seventh psalm, "' . . . He shall send from heaven and save me; He reproaches those who would swallow me up . . . ' It is only High God that Ngomba or I or anyone should serve, not this Strong One!"

Ngomba laughed derisively, baring a mouthful of fangs.

"' . . . My soul is among lions,'" Reg continued, shaking as he did so. "'I lie among the sons of men who are set on fire, whose teeth are spears and arrows, and their tongue a sharp sword . . . My heart is steadfast, O God . . . I will praise you, O Lord, among the peoples . . .'"

Ngomba came close to Reg, saying nothing, a solid, powerful wall of a man. Reg did not look up but clutched the Bible and breathed hard. Close like this, the *griot's* physical power was awesome and frightening, deadly force in every lean, hard muscle. The thick, ropy veins of his neck and arms pulsed with a latent power as difficult to gauge as that of a wounded rhino. At eye level was the deep, brawny chest, swollen with an unimaginable strength, the pectorals as rigid and unyielding as iron plate.

Goliath.

Reg forced himself to meet Ngomba's gaze. How incredibly regal was this naked man who moments before was willing to ruthlessly murder a woman with child—his wife, his tiny son or daughter. The gold ring in his left ear flashed with the intensity of sunlight, adorning the handsome, burnished skin with all the majesty and honor of a jeweled crown and princely raiment. What he saw in the chief's look unsettled Reg as surely as had the *griot's* crazed actions. It was a totally unexpected expression— not quite admiration but bordering on deference. But it seemed to come and go, alternating with the drug daze that seemed every few minutes to seize and release him. Was he more dangerous lucid or stoned?

The Nubian's rich baritone reverberated in the air. "The whites have so long defecated on Africa that I find little advantage in their presence. You come at a bad season of little food and less patience. Because white men are takers only, why would we welcome you? Even the white God teachers wanted our souls. You cannot win or lose a man's soul, barter or trade in a man's spiritual affections. Our songs, our stories, our land, our allegiances are shared wealth, white Danson. If our souls were ours to give, you would take them back with you, out of Africa, and write down their numbers in a record book, along with the souls of other peoples you have taken, and claim them aloud as proof of your personal triumph. It is then our souls become your property, and for generations they would be your currency and a measure of your stature among other white God teachers.

"No, you are not here to share. You and white Wiggins are here to own. Did God Most High send you to take and own? If strange fire is disobedience to God Most High, then you too have offered strange fire!"

They were sobering words. Reg had come to find *Mokele-mbembe,* to take back irrefutable proof of its existence. That he had to come to Africa to do it was incidental. He would have gone—would have *preferred* to go, actually—to Florida or the Yukon if that was where reports of the creature had surfaced. Africa mattered only in-so-far as that's where the quarry lived. He'd wanted to find the Ologus only because it was said they could lead him to the zoological find of a lifetime. Did he care about these needy people or just the job he was sent to do? More acclaim, more magazine covers. Reg Danson, discoverer of Noah's Ark. Reg Danson, king of dinosaur hunters. Reg Danson the Invincible.

"What are *you* here for, Ngomba?" challenged Wiggins. "What would entice a proud Nubian of the ancient land of Kush to forsake the wonders of the Nile to live among the lowly forest pygmies in hunger and deprivation?" The missionary's irritants were showing. The bearded jaw jutted defiantly.

"Easy, Jigs . . . "

"Easy yourself, Danson. I want to know what an educated, highly intelligent guy like this is doing in the middle of nowhere pretending to be the *griot* of a people who aren't his own."

Reg thought Ngomba might fly into a rage at being directly accused of fraud, but to his amazement, the chief dismissed the people, who went muttering back to their huts. He seemed no longer interested in an adoring audience.

Ngomba looked at Danson and Wiggins and sneered. He stuck his chest out arrogantly. "I am from Abu Zabad near Khartoum in what once was the southern region of ancient Egypt. Many centuries ago, my people ruled Egypt for eighty years. Later, our legend says that we gave sanctuary to the Messiah when He fled with His mother and father from King Herod the Bloody. But not for another five centuries did my people become followers of the Christ. All of Nubia converted, and it is said we had peace of spirit for eight hundred years until Arabian invaders forced us to practice Islam. Then came the slavers, and we learned the bitter lesson that religion and exploitation are bastard twins born of the lust to possess!"

Ngomba went to his haunches, and the white men did the same. The forest was strangely and eerily muted as if silenced by the sheer weight of the *griot's* cynicism. The snapping of the fire and occasional subdued voices were the only noises where the din of madness had so recently resounded. The people ate or sat swaying under the numbing influence of *iboga*. Children slept or crept among their drugged elders looking for unguarded treasure—pickpockets on a night run.

The smells and smoke of seared elephant flesh wafted over the clearing, forcing pungent entry into every hut and nostril. Reg was shocked by the force of his hunger and saddened by the cutting bitterness in Ngomba's voice.

"Nubian males are famed as wrestlers," the Nubian said without joy. "My father, Napatu, was champion for thirteen years. He was strong as six men and could throw two hundred pounds twenty feet. He used to carry me on his shoulders, and when I would rub his head, he would make the great muscles of his neck and shoulders bulge and dance under my legs. I would laugh very much, and he would throw me high into the air and catch me at the last possible moment!" But instead of showing pride in the telling, Ngomba's face was rigid with harsh memories.

"When I became a man of sixteen years, I was half a head taller than my father but only half as strong. We would bathe together in the River Nile and he would throw me back over his head like a catapult. I could stand on his shoulders and see all the way to the river barge landing at Shendi. I would ride on his back, and with my arms wrapped around his great chest, down we would dive, deep and happy, skimming the bottom of the river like fish. Then, with a kick of his legs strong as crocodiles, we would burst the surface with great force!"

It was as if Jigs and Reg had ceased to exist. Ngomba and his father frolicked in the river together, but the joy of it was swallowed up in a dark and violent pain. Hurt curled Ngomba's lips in hatred.

"My father's hearing failed long before his body. No matter. He did not hear the train. When at last he felt its coming, he turned and met it head-on. It took him too long to move because he thought he was stronger than any man or any product of man." The muscles of Ngomba's jaws hardened in the firelight.

"With a dead father like that, I vowed to become the finest wrestler who ever lived. Not only did I grow taller than any man, I built muscle and bone until I was stronger even than my father had been. I fought every match in anger and took every prize in revenge for my father's death. It held no pleasure but was a thing of necessity. I stopped loving, stopped feeling. I stopped just short of injuring my opponents, but I wanted to choke them, to drain them of their blood, to toss their lifeless bodies on the tracks to be crushed as my dear father was crushed. Then, one day, I went too far and—"

Ngomba slammed a hand as big as a salad plate into the dirt, trying to erase one last memory. A brief, stricken expression came over the handsome features but was as quickly replaced with a look of cruelty and contempt. He stood abruptly to his feet. "The Strong One, unlike bringers of religion, neither judges the past nor promises a golden future," he said. Without another word, the big man left them, his great, graceful strides swiftly taking him beyond their sight.

Reg sighed heavily. "Well, I'd say we've discovered the cancer. I say we check on the brothers and have ourselves a prayer meeting."

Wiggins nodded. "He's got some king-sized skeleton in his closet to drive him to this. We need to know his plans for us and soon. You can bet your bottom dollar the Strong One is *Mokelembembe*. God knows how we're going to make his acquaintance, but could he be any more unpredictable than this guy?"

Reg tried his best to give a reassuring shrug. "I doubt it. When you're at the mercy of the Nubian national wrestling champion, you've probably hit bottom." A miserable little grin accompanied the statement, but it was the best he could do. He'd been in the pool and looked into the vacant eyes of the dragon. It was a long way down.

They rejoined Ndoki and Ndokanda and bathed the brothers' wounds from a little wooden basin of water that mysteriously appeared nearby. The brothers murmured their gratitude, but it was plain they regretted ever leaving home.

The four men prayed quietly together, asking for God's help and wisdom to sort out their next move. Reg prayed for Tony, asking the Lord to help his son at college, to keep him oblivious to his father's peril. His voice broke just once at the memory of Tony in hip waders trying to hook a package of Twinkies he'd accidentally kicked off the dock. God willing, they'd fish again and when they did, they'd stuff themselves with Twinkies.

"Lord, thank you for delivering us from evil this day," he prayed. "Keep us the rest of the night, and God, please show us more of the heart of Ngomba. Show us a way to help him, to help his people. You planted a seed years ago in this place, and they've not burned your word in all this time. But they've distorted it and turned it into false teaching. Help us to speak the truth and help Ngomba to believe it. Let us help him get past the grief he still carries for his father and show him a better way."

Wiggins took up the prayer. "Lord of love, Lord of all the earth, reveal to us the unconfessed burden that Ngomba bears. What does he know, Lord, that we don't? Where is he most vulnerable, and what must we do to break the chains that Satan has put around these people? Cast out our fear, Father. Put starch back in our spines and show us that in your strength no harm will befall us. Forgive us our sins, our too small faith."

"Amen." It was a chorus of two. The brothers were kneeling, hands prayerfully clasped. Ndokanda, a bloody patch of cloth stuck to his injured neck, looked to the impenetrable canopy above. In simple faith, he pierced the canopy, his eyes locked on realms beyond. "Christ—save—us!" he rasped in the few words of English he knew. He raised arms to the night sky, cupped his hands, and applauded, slowly, reverently, growing conviction in every clap. Ndoki joined in, and soon all four were cheering heaven's help.

Ngomba watched them from the entrance to his hut. Tomorrow the Ologus would break camp and head deeper into the forest. They were too easy to find. The pygmy brothers from the edge of the swamp would become Ologu slaves.

White Wiggins and white Danson would be of no use. They had come for the Strong One, and Ngomba would grant their wish.

▼

Emotionally and physically exhausted, the explorers from Sangha slept fitfully on the ground. Tent, sleeping mats, everything necessary for even a little comfort had been stolen from them. They wanted to take turns keeping an eye open for further intrusions, and at first the jungle cooperated. Flat and exposed on the ground, they were easy prey for every winged and biting thing that happened by or that dropped from above. Sometime in the night, their mysterious benefactor brought elephant meat in a basket and left it near the water bowl, again without being detected. It was both comforting to know they were looked after and terrifying to know they were sitting ducks.

Before long, the insects ceased their rounds and that for Wiggins was most disturbing of all. It was far too still for the rain forest, which in many respects was usually more alive by night than by day. For a time nothing stirred—not people, not vermin, not even the very air. It was as if all nature itself had stopped breathing.

The pygmy brothers fell into a fitfull half slumber, their grating snores eventually converging into one loud sawing. Though Wiggins was up on one elbow, he settled for a light drowse that included mumbling about drinking gourds and seven-foot crocodile wrestlers. Combine that noise with the fact that they were in a direct line with the entrance to Ngomba's hut and the feeling that they were under surveillance, and Reg finally gave up. He stood stiffly and spied a little patch of barren ground some fifty yards off that seemed slightly less subject to direct bug drops from above, should they resume.

He lay down again, finding a contour between two arthritic tree roots that was surprisingly soothing. He started to dream of Barbara and Tony at the beach, splashing and laughing in the surf, cracking kelp weed whips, having crab races with the winner's purse an entire bag of cheese puffs. He could feel the delight of Tony's little hand in his big one as together they amassed a fortune in sand dollars and agates.

The little hand gripped his harder . . . the grit of the sand . . . the fine boy fingers squeezing the rough man thumb . . . Reg's eyes flew open with a start. He was holding a small human hand in his own.

The small boy fingers gripped his thumb, and when Reg wiggled it, the pressure increased. Reg raised his head. Stretched along the ground at arm's length from him, sound asleep, was the handsome young Ologu who had returned Jigs's baseball cap. *So that's our good Samaritan. Wonder what the penalty is for fraternizing with white God men . . .*

Danson did not want to break contact with this their only human link to sanity, but his leg was asleep and he had to move. Besides, if Ngomba or one of his henchmen saw the boy's kindness, he might be ripe for sacrifice.

Danson sat up and the boy awoke. He let go of Reg's thumb, rubbed the sleep from his eyes, and grinned so broadly that his tiny pointed teeth shone even in the heavy night. And then to Reg's amazement, the boy held out the pistol that Ngomba had pitched into the forest. Reg took it and checked the chamber. Four bullets still in place. He could have kissed the kid.

The boy pointed to his bare stomach. "Keem-boo-kee," he said softly, drawing out the syllables as if teaching a toddler. "Kimboki." Then he shyly poked Danson in the belly and raised thin little eyebrows questioningly.

Reg wondered again at the odd, totally random array of scars that marked the boy's torso. Two of them seemed recent, still pinkish and weeping. Burns? Danson smiled and pointed at himself. "Re-edge," he said, exaggerating the sounds. "Reg." Then he poked the boy's belly and said, "Kimboki!"

The little boy laughed so happily—and loudly—that Reg quickly put a finger to his lips and shushed Kimboki. The boy covered his mouth, but the mirth leaked out the sides and he squirmed in uninhibited delight. Casting an anxious glance into the main clearing, Reg could not help but laugh back. Despite the risk of discovery, it was an ice age since he'd met someone this merry.

The boy gained some control, poked Reg back, and said what sounded like *ridge*.

"No, no—Redge," Danson whispered furiously, and they both got the giggles. Reg rolled toward the boy, grabbing him in a gentle headlock, roughing his hair. The boy tussled with him a moment, then plopped his bare buttocks squarely in Reg's lap.

"Oof!" Reg exclaimed, more surprised than injured. "How'd a friendly guy like you end up in a dump like this?" The boy looked puzzled, then covered a mischievous face with both hands, peeking impishly between his fingers. He was playing.

*Tony peeking out the bars of his crib, light years past bedtime, daring Dad to ignore him . . . can't . . . "Hey, Tony boy, know what a motorboat says? I'm gonna buzz your belly! Brrrummmm!!" . . . "Reg, honey, don't wake Tony . . . come back to bed now, you know he'll be cranky in the morning." . . . "Right away, sweet cakes, soon's I tuck the little monster back in . . . and close the door . . . okay, Tiger, just one more belly buzz, but don't tell your mom or I let the air out of your mattress, got it? Brrrummmm!! . . . Yes, dear, I was just on my way back."
. . .*

The ache in Reg's heart was too deep for one man. He hugged Kimboki tightly, and the boy snuggled against him. A minute passed, and Reg wondered if the boy had fallen asleep. He looked down and discovered the little fellow's ear pressed to Reg's chest, his big, trusting eyes wide with excitement.

He was listening to Reg's heartbeat. *Oh, little friend, can you hear the knock of dread inside?*

A little sob of grief made Reg and the child look up. Twenty feet away stood Wiggins and a young woman watching man and boy embrace. Even at that distance, Danson felt the sorrow. Her thin body contorted in a spasm of anguish, and she held out mother's arms to her son.

Kimboki slipped from Reg's lap and would have flung himself into the waiting woman's arms, but she quickly withdrew them and wrapped them instead about her misery. The child stopped halfway, little body slumping in rejection. The woman's silent wail crumpled the tender face, and she fell to her knees, sobbing quietly.

Reg laid a reassuring hand on Kimboki's shoulder and squeezed. But the boy did not respond, the magic between them broken. The woman's eyes were tight shut, as if not seeing her son would stop the torment.

Wiggins's face was a fury. "She came looking for her boy, all she has since her husband died of fever. Says Ngomba forbids affection between parent and child. Infant mortality is so high, he's made the God-given bond between mother and child a criminal offense! Mourning the death of a son or daughter wastes energy. If the Strong One demands the lives of babies, then he must not be provoked by intimate displays of caring. But Kimboki is such a handful and wants his mother so desperately. She— she has to slap him and burn him with hot embers to keep him away!" Jigs shook an angry fist in the direction of the huge leader's *huvala*. "Yonder lies no man, but a beast, a godforsaken beast! Ngomba's father is dead, and no one else shall ever know the love of father or mother as long as Ngomba lives! You'd better take your hands off the boy, Danson, or the both of you will be murdered for the capital offense of kindness!"

Crestfallen, Reg dropped his hand and stepped away from Kimboki. In that one terrible instant, he turned icy cold to the core. A hatred so virulent he could taste its bile filled the deepest recesses of his being. Had Ngomba appeared at that moment, Reg would have gunned him down without the slightest hesitation. "Kimboki." The boy straightened but did not look at Danson. His chin quivered at first. Then, as if by force of will, the child set his jaw in a grim line and a dread, innocence-stealing look of indifference flooded the handsome features. He too became cold as ice.

He was being remade in Ngomba's image.

"The boy found the gun," said Reg, betraying no emotion. "Four bullets left."

The grizzled missionary studied Danson. Neither spoke aloud, but their eyes communicated volumes. Reg cocked the pistol. A silent agreement was forged. Reg started toward Ngomba's hut.

Before his foot hit the ground, the jungle screamed. It was as if every primate and bird ever given voice let loose at once. Shrieks and howls of alarm sounded from every quarter, unleashing a terrifying barrage of distress. Out of the huts burst a chattering stream of humanity, all gesticulating and talking at once. Men raced about the clearing for every available stick of wood and frantically piled them on the fading fire.

The sharp report of a tree cracking in two made Danson whirl around to face the forest. In the mounting firelight, he could just make out the distant crown of a tree falling out of line, crashing to earth. Then another, closer, cracked like rifle shot before collapsing to the forest floor. Trees adjacent to the fallen ones shuddered and swayed, their tops shaken by a colossal, unseen force.

A force that was coming their way.

Danson felt vibration in the ground, the shock a pile driver makes with every blow. The weapon in his hand was a noisome popgun against the oncoming force. If he did waste precious bullets, the effect would be no more harmful than firing caps on the Fourth of July unless he could hit the eye, the most vulnerable part of a sauropod.

Reg grabbed Kimboki and fled with Wiggins and the boy's mother behind a screen of tall reeds. Danson tried to stop them, but woman and child vanished into the frantic crowd.

What happened next looked as if it had been choreographed. Ngomba, wearing a fur headdress adorned with brilliant green and yellow feathers, loomed above his people with a fierce fire in his eyes. With a forward thrust of his mighty right arm, every man, woman, and child hit the dirt, prostrating themselves in the direction of the coming juggernaut.

Ngomba strode to the front of his prone subjects, planted his feet like the Colossus of Rhodes, and folded his arms across his chest. Immovable.

A third tree fell, and an immense shadow moved beyond the firelight. Ngomba stretched his arms before him and brought the massive hands together in a loud clap. Immediately a drum began its incessant beat, and up from the dirt rose sixty very sincere voices.

"MMMMMMM . . . MMMMMMM . . . MMMMMMM . . . MMMOOOO . . . KAAALAAAY . . . MMMMMMM . . . MMMBEMM . . . BAAAY!"

Over and over the awful chant rose and fell, rose and fell, ahead and behind, above and beside.

Above it all was Ngomba's resonant baritone pronouncing the mystical name, setting the cadence—without ever moving his lips.

The forest calmed, and the force halted. How much time passed in the limbo of uncertainty, Reg did not know.

Then the pile driver blows to the earth began again, and the people's voices swelled in volume. But this time each blow was more distant than the last, and within seconds the unseen threat was gone.

"Back to the river's my guess," said a shaky Wiggins under his breath. Then he marched up to the *griot* with a singleness of purpose in every move. *He's forgotten the gun . . .*

"*Eoto mongo!*" cried Jigs. With great feeling, he said again, "*Eoto mongo!*"

With that, Jigs returned to Danson's side.

"Did you tell him how we feel?" inquired Reg, heart hammering wildly.

"I did," Wiggins replied emotionally, sweat pouring off his forehead. "I told the miserable beast exactly how we feel."

Wiggins stared off into the forest, beyond the circle of light, to the place where the shadows moved and the earth shook.

"Jigs," said Reg tightly, fighting the urge to yell the tension from his body. "What'd you tell him?"

With a catch in his voice, Jigs Wiggins spoke barely above a whisper. "I told him thank you."

# 10

ony Danson fought the maddening urge to fling himself into the River Ubangi and swim for Sangha Mission. As early in the morning as it was, heat and headache conspired to push him over the edge. He'd stripped to just shorts and boots, and a ridiculously oversized pith helmet that gave him the appearance of a mushroom cap on a tall, white stem. Sweaty, sticky, and shaken at the interminable delay, he was ready to bribe anything that moved to take him upriver, ambassador or no ambassador.

William Fulgate sympathized with Tony's impatience and tried now to divert his attention with small talk. "Ever been fishing in New Zealand? Best sport trout on the globe. I went there once with the head of internal investigations for the Secret Service. Bless my soul if he didn't catch his limit in seventy minutes flat. He smeared the hook with some awful smelling concoction he said attracted fish. Must have. I couldn't stand to be near the stuff, and it took me three and a half hours to limit out.

"Ever been rock climbing in Pago Pago? Spent a week there with . . . "

Two girls hopped about the riverboat landing near the one fuming and the other talkative American, tossing pebbles to one another and catching them in little wooden cups. They stole shy glances at Tony and rolled their eyes at one another over the strange white one with the big lid for a hat.

*"Njam'et a Bo-lum-ku, yak'en do; Bo-lum-bu, yak'en do . . . "* The rhythmic canoe chant floated to him from the opposite shore where two canoes, three boys each, raced in the shallows along the bank. One boy in each canoe beat the rhythm with a stick on the side of the boat. The longer canoe on the outside began to force the other into the bank. Both boats rammed into the soft mud, the boys of the stricken vessel falling into the other canoe and tipping the whole lot into the river. Shouting and sputtering their indignation, the boys chased one another to shore and ended in a giggling, writhing tangle of arms and legs.

"Let me call Bolombu, come down here; Bolombu, come down here . . . " sang an ancient, scratchy voice that seemed to well up from the ground behind Tony. He jumped, but it was only a thin, toothless elder he'd seen around the commissioner's office watching the diplomatic comings and goings with great interest. "They play and we ponder," the man said in English, pointing a bony finger at the children, his English heavily accented but easily understood. "Your heart is rolling from side to side, isn't it, my young American friend?"

Tony flipped the helmet back and immediately winced at the unscreened brightness. "Hello, again," was all he said. *Where is that police motor launch?*

The old man scratched beneath his red and blue bandanna. "You are undecided. The best course of action escapes you. What will it take to be in the town of the men of the tribe of God instead of standing in empty Epuluville? You are laughed to sadness of heart by the Bad One. Old Jackal knows of what he speaks. God is silent, is He not?"

Fulgate looked hard at the man as if he'd been eavesdropping on state secrets.

Tony jerked the helmet off his hot head and slammed it to the ground. "God's not silent, but He's not chosen to speak to me today." Tony strode to the water's edge and stared upriver. He bit his lip.

The old man followed and placed a hand rough as elephant hide on Tony's bare arm. "Have you chosen to speak to Him?"

Tony's shoulders shook. "No—no, I did what I've always done. Clam up, stomp off . . . "

"Clam?" the elder said.

"Yeah, you know, a little edible shellfish—never mind."

Jackal placed his hands together in prayer and raised them to the sky. "God, your young white man's liver is vexed. His back feels heavy with the thought of the Bad One coming up behind. If you are the One who put things in order through your Christ, please bring order to this boy's life. Before the sun sleeps again, show his father the size of your hand."

Tony's shoulders stopped shaking. Almost simultaneously, the girls at the landing and the boys splashing about on the opposite bank stopped what they were doing and gave an excited shout. Coming toward them from upriver, growing bigger by the second, sped the black and white police motor launch of the People's Republic of the Congo.

At the same moment, a plane sounded overhead, and the men looked up. A Cessna float plane banked north, its white underbelly sliding upriver like a fish to spawn. It banked again to the west, then came full circle, gradually descending to a gentle touchdown a hundred yards upstream. It buzzed determinedly toward the landing, cut its engine, and floated neatly up to a dilapidated wooden dock, little more than three logs lashed side-by-side and anchored by a rusted cable to a ramshackle gas house. The makeshift pier tilted precipitously downward when the pilot jumped onto it from the aircraft's tiny cockpit. He immediately turned and offered a hand to a passenger.

She stepped from the plane with all the boldness of the new birth experienced by a changed creature shaking off the cramped confines of its cocoon. She took the hand proffered and stepped onto the dock. She straightened and looked in the direction of

Tony and Jackal at the riverboat landing. Then, with a word to the pilot, she reached back through the door of the plane for a small, blue satchel and a medium-sized brown suitcase, turned, and carefully negotiated the length of the bobbing pier.

Once on land, the woman headed straight for the men on the landing. She exuded a forthright yet elegant bearing in her stride. Middle-aged, silver-haired, carefully groomed, she wore an olive green hunting shirt and pants, brown hiking boots, and a worn fisherman's hat. She stopped a dozen feet from the curious men and smiled confidently. "Might you be kind enough to tell me where I might find Ambassador William Fulgate?"

Fulgate stepped forward and bowed ever so slightly. It seemed the only appropriate form of greeting given her manner and the intensity about her. "I am Ambassador Fulgate, ma'am. How may I help you?"

"My name is Kay Wiggins," she said, voice strong and purposeful. "Can you help me find my husband?"

**D**ad's got a thing for smoked oysters," explained Tony Danson, checking the pack to make certain all four tins were accounted for. They were.

"I prefer *banganju* myself," said Jackal the elder, his scratchy voice full of merriment and optimism. He helped Tony, Kay, and the two officers load supplies into the police motor launch. "A pounded peanut paste, moistened with water, mixed with chopped greens. Cook 'til greens are tender, season with salt and red pepper. A spicy treat for happy, happy tongues!" The eyes far back in the old man's head shone with pleasure at the delicious recipe. "Sounds tasty," Kay said politely. "Have you tried a sprinkling of finely minced scallions?"

Ambassador Fulgate came toward them from the direction of the market, a lumpy sack of something slung over one shoulder. "*A* is for apple!" he merrily announced, stowing the sack. He let out an exhausted "Phew!" as if having just completed a difficult maneuver. "Negotiating for five pounds of apples in Epuluville is probably right up there with the skills needed to convince the Zairian police to stop extorting a street use tax from visiting Congolese citizens. Next thing you know, they'll be charging for the air we breathe!"

Tony was just happy to finally be moving in the right direction—upriver. The law enforcement officers of the People's Republic of the Congo were all studied efficiency. When they arrived at shore, they were crisp in fresh gray uniforms, a black stripe down each pantleg, bright yellow epaulets lending a jaunty military trim. One was tall and husky, burly as a fullback. The other was slender and elegantly fluid in his movement. Sunglasses and spit-shined black shoes gave the look of rising young cadets bucking for promotion. Throw in a couple of Smokey Bear hats, and Tony believed they could pass for state troopers back home.

They offered a sharp contrast to the two surly elephant poachers they dumped on shore, trussed up with leather thongs, wrists to ankles, like fowl for baking. These two were scrawny and filthy, clothes torn and stained, skin bleeding from several lacerations no doubt inflicted in the interest of good discipline. Barefoot, noses runny, eyes blazing contempt, they lay face down on the ground, cowed only by their predicament and the superior firepower of the police. Two ancient elephant guns, little more than blunderbusses, were flung clattering onto the rocks, little pieces of their antique stocks splintering on impact. The poachers winced at the ill treatment of their weapons, but their eyes kept returning to the AK-47 machine guns being carefully cleaned and replaced in their racks amidship.

The motor launch was as modern and spotless as the officers who commanded it, sparkling testimony that the People's Republic took law enforcement seriously. Officers George Akeley and Percival Katianda greeted Tony and Fulgate courteously but with a deliberate reserve befitting their positions.

"We must apologize for any delay that we have caused you, Mr. Ambassador, and you, Mr. Danson," said Officer Akeley politely, his English clipped and precise. "We were forced to track these two miscreants a half day's journey into the swamp before they would see things rationally. Hunting had gone poorly for them. We probably prevented their starvation, and don't you know how mixed are my feelings about wasting food on ones so miserable?" He sighed resignedly. "But the law is impartial, is it not, until the guilty are proven so?" He walked over, went down on his haunches, grabbed the head of one of the poachers, pulled back the man's lips, exposing his teeth. He spoke to the man, sarcasm in every word. "And then, with consciences clear, we may slaughter you for *your* ivory, yes Nyangwe?" With a snarl the prisoner tried to struggle free. Officer Akeley suddenly released his grip, and the man's nose and mouth ground into the dirt.

"Your heart has broken loose," Akeley spoke to the man in the dirt. "You have lost control of it, and it has made you a treacherous person!" The other prisoner spat on the mirror finish of Akeley's shoes, and for one awful moment, it looked as if the officer would kick the man's head from its shoulders. After a few seconds, Akeley grew calm and stepped back from the poachers. He looked at Officer Katianda and slowly nodded.

With the ease of a man carrying the groceries, the big policeman hoisted both men by their leather bonds and trotted off in the direction of the local commissioner's office.

A small smile played at the corners of Akeley's mouth. "The accused shall be stored there until the riverboat arrives and they can be taken to Brazzaville to stand trial. We'd try them here, but the government in its infinite wisdom does not believe they would receive a fair hearing. Can't imagine why, can you?" he spoke directly at Tony.

Tony started to reply, but Akeley wasn't finished. "Your father is not in the best of positions," he said. "Sangha Mission is in disarray. One of the pygmies of the compound was horribly attacked and bled to death in front of the entire village. Your father and the director of the mission, a Mr. Wiggins, departed almost immediately for hostile territory in search of a hidden people known as the Ologus. I'm afraid their reputation is nastier even than the animals your father is here to find. Personally, I believe the stories of a prehistoric remnant to be just that—good stories for the campfire, for those long stretches of the hunt when game chooses not to cooperate. The bush African loves a good story, for then he can speak from the bowels without the necessity for exactness of detail.

"As to whether it could have been the Ologus who murdered the pygmy from Sangha—ah, then I think you have a line of investigation worth pursuing. These tribal wars really are most annoying. Much of Africa is in a perpetual state of war over such squabbles. We need to put this one down before your father gets in over his head. Nasty way to spend a vacation. Safari in Kenya is the better choice."

Tony laughed despite his growing anxiety. "I don't think Dad knows the meaning of a vacation. But thank you for coming . . ."

"Yes, yes, thank you both for your willingness to turn right around and find Reg Danson," Fulgate interjected, his own misgivings on the rise. "The commissioner assured me you are the best on the force."

Akeley scoffed. "The commissioner is given to hyperbole, but we will do our utmost. When Officer Katianda has made our charges as comfortable as they deserve, we can be underway."

Kay Wiggins laid a warm and comforting hand on Tony's arm. "We *will* find them, Tony. We mustn't lose faith. I always warned Jigsy to keep his own counsel in times of extreme stress, but I want you to feel free to let me know when you're especially troubled. We'll help each other be brave, all right?"

He smiled appreciatively and nodded. Bravery was one piece of equipment they hadn't packed nearly enough of.

The chimpanzee sat hunched on the branch, looking pained and listless, its intestines harboring a knot of parasitic roundworms. Slowly, deliberately, the primate stripped leaves from the *Aspilia* plant and carefully swallowed them whole without a single chew. The highly toxic content of the leaves, a red oil known as thiarubrine-A, would safely bypass the acidic digestive fluids of the stomach. Not until the small intestine would the toxin be released in the exact location where the nematodes congregated. The invaders would be destroyed in short order.

The chimp's female offspring closely observed her mother's behavior, storing the information for the future. The child primate reached out and smoothed her mother's fur, patting and arranging the coat just so. The attention was welcome, the touch soothing.

Opening her hand, the mother let slip two *Aspilia* leaves. She stroked her baby with the empty hand and felt better.

The leaves fluttered and floated in a descending spiral to land near some fallen *Myrianthus arboreous* fruit. Highly prized by mountain gorillas, the fruit was also a favorite of the Ologus.

Suspended between dream and reality, thickly held in the last stages of an *iboga* stupor, Littleshot turned over in the dirt where he'd collapsed the night before. Enticed by the shadows, yet so afraid of the shadow-caster, he'd taken too much *iboga*. He had watched with grisly fascination the peeling of his own scalp like a banana skin. The operation was performed by another self that then lifted the top of the skull and sprinkled the contents with ants. The rest of the night had been spent feeling the insects burrowing and building egg chambers inside his head. Then his brain began bubbling and blistering, turning a liquid gray. Creatures with long necks swam in the soup of his mind and crawled out his ears and nostrils. When they tried to suck out his eyes, he turned over and looked.

She came toward him from two day's journey away. When the woman finally reached him, she stepped in the liquid inside his head and left gray footprints behind, receding a day's journey or two from sight.

Kimboki's mother glanced anxiously back at the sleeping clearing, no sign of life from the huts and only the one miserable hunter lying in the dirt. She was so frightened, so determined, so reckless for more of what she'd tasted a few hours before. Sweeter than the sweetest honey, more refreshing than the coolest rain, had been the taste of Truth. The captives had shown kindness to her and her son, and before she had been so certain that kindness had fled the forest.

The people had celebrated the night coming of the Strong One by consuming more *iboga,* but she was one of the few women who had not. Her abstinence hadn't kept the visions away, however. She knew flights of fancy every bit as fantastic as her drugged husband and neighbors, but hers were of true answers tall as palm trees, as sturdy as hard-shelled palm nuts. Now she hurried along, hoping to speak again with white Wiggins and white Danson, to somehow thank them for showing kindness to her and her boy. But if anyone saw her . . .

"Hey, hey, slow down!"

Reg'd said it softly, but she was startled nonetheless and nearly collided with the explorer. She possessed a proud, almost regal face, but what was most remarkable about her was how much the anguish and dread of the night had been replaced with composure and anticipation—as if she were expecting something good.

He smiled warmly and walked with her to where Jigs and the brothers were still snoring. Reg nudged Wiggins with the toe of his boot, and Jigs snorted awake. "What—what's the matter?"

"Come on, Wiggins, snap to. Kimboki's mother's back, and she seems anxious to tell us something."

Wiggins sat up, rubbing the sleep from his eyes and picking forest debris from his increasingly raggedy beard. He passed a ham hand subtly over his shirt pocket, almost as if brushing it smooth for the coming of company. But for the hundredth time, Reg caught the missionary's fingers doing a security check of that pocket. Reg had to know what was in there besides Blackhorn's Best.

Jigs spoke quietly with the woman. The eager voice was unmistakable. Reg marveled that she could show any enthusiasm after what she'd suffered under the rule of Ngomba. After a few minutes, Wiggins looked at Reg with brows furrowed into ravines of doubt.

"She says she has for so long felt pain all the way to her toes that she despaired of ever feeling human again. But last night with you and Kimboki, she experienced kindness in the midst of a mother's agony. Because we have shown her and her son sympathy, she felt a moment's hope and wishes to return the favor. She'd like us to follow her."

Jigs again spoke quietly to the woman, more earnestly than before. A set came to her jaw that Reg recognized as the international sign of feminine determination. He'd seen it in Barbara more than a few times. Reg looked hard at Wiggins who coughed uneasily.

"I don't think we should, Danson. We go off with this woman, and we put her in grave danger, not to mention ourselves. She says the camp won't awaken for some time yet, but you never know with *iboga*. One man's sleeping pill is another man's wake-up call."

"We should at least find out where she wants to take us, Wiggins. Tell her we won't come without knowing where we're going."

Jigs eyed Reg warily. "You're in over your head, Danson. It doesn't matter if she wants to take us to the Queen of Sheba. Common courtesy doesn't cut it here. We're dealing with a madman, and I say we don't budge."

Reg threw his hands up. "You know, Wiggins, you are one wimpy missionary! I think your past not only took the wind out of your sails, it took the spit from your eye. This woman and her son are the only light in this place near as I can tell, and if going with her makes her happy, then let's get going!"

Angrily, Wiggins spoke to the woman, motioning to Danson and himself, and back at the clearing. The name Ngomba surfaced a couple of times before she squared around and, short as she was, stopped Wiggins in his tracks with a look of pure defiance.

*Uh oh,* thought Reg. *Clash of the titans.*

Her response was swift and even more animated than Wiggins's speech. By the time she finished, it was clear that something she said had Wiggins stunned.

But instead of saying anything more, Jigs removed the infernal pipe from his shirt pocket and clamped it between his teeth, unlit, to signal an end to diplomacy.

"Come on, Wiggins, talk to me!" Reg was getting irritable.

"What she has to say is too fantastic to repeat. And knowing you, you'd buy it, and off you'd go, quite oblivious to any danger to this 'wimpy' missionary and his friends."

"Whoa, buddy. Sorry about the name calling, but let's don't start fighting amongst ourselves. We came this close to a face-to-face encounter with *Mokele-mbembe* last night, and this lady may be the only hope we have of finding out what really gives here. Let's cooperate."

Wiggins gave Reg a sickly smile. "Okay, Danson, you're the employer. Let's go." He spoke two words to the woman who grinned and set off at a brisk pace to the east of camp.

Reg caught up. "Whoa again, Wiggins! I want to know where we're going!"

Without breaking stride, Jigs said, "What does it matter? The lady's happy, isn't she? Besides, I wouldn't want to spoil the surprise."

They moved at an easy lope, ducking low beneath overhanging vegetation. The woman's bare feet "read" the faintest of trails and skimmed over the bumps and deadfalls that tripped up the men behind. Reg judged they'd gone two miles when the trail dropped down to the edge of the swamp. Kimboki's mother pointed, and the explorers sighted down a channel of water to the north, walled in on both sides by a tunnel of luxuriant green. Then she ran to a great, leafy thicket of vegetation and tugged on the end of a concealed pirogue.

The men helped her free the boat, and in they climbed. Danson and Wiggins manned the rough-carved paddles and dug deep into the dark, brackish depths.

Over and around them slid past the most incredible arboreal wonderland they'd ever seen. Orchids of intense, electric colors were visited by an orange and yellow snowstorm of butterflies as broad as a man's hand. Succulent fruit of staggering variety hung in golden apricot and tangerine profusion. Birds of bronze and jade and bottle-green joined others of sapphire, turquoise, and ruby red. Their melodic calls thrilled the ear; their feathered majesty confounded the eye.

They had entered a fairy mirage, a jewel box of exquisite craftsmanship from which Reg fervently hoped never to be delivered.

Their guide grew increasingly restive the further they went, and by the time the channel took a sharp turn back to the east, she was positively wide-eyed with agitation.

Wiggins gasped. Across the full width of the channel, thick wooden poles were driven into the swamp bed, forming a fence through which the canoe could not pass. Between the poles they could see glimpses of a beautiful palm-lined lagoon, another world.

Attached to each of the poles was an intricate string weaving done in a complex geometric pattern. Little feather bundles were tied to every third pole. Some of them looked as if they'd been dipped in blood.

The woman spoke rapidly to Wiggins, jabbing her arm at the barrier, standing and nearly diving overboard with excitement.

"I won't make you wait for this translation, Danson," Jigs said, making no attempt to conceal the awe he was feeling. "This is the most unbelievable moment of my life!"

"What do you mean?" Reg barely trusted his vocal chords. "What's going on?"

"I've heard of this place," Wiggins replied. "The strongest of pygmy traditions, the strongest of all African beliefs, is that there is one last place in the rain forest where man has never— hear me, Danson, *never*—set foot. It is the sacred place that for the ten thousand years since creation has been taboo to the forest people.

"This is it, Danson. *This is Eden!*"

*Whoosh!*

The poison arrow pierced the enchanted atmosphere as cleanly and surgically as a surgeon's scalpel, burying itself deep within the woman's breast. She fell against Danson. Quickly, he pushed her into the bottom of the canoe, cradling her back, shielding her body from further violence by the covering of his own. But there was no saving her. Life fluttered in her eyes for a last brief moment before surrendering. Kimboki's mother's blood bathed Reg's hands, and he felt an explosive rage.

Wiggins whipped the pistol from his waistband, pointed it at the orchids and the butterflies, and pulled the trigger.

The blast thundered obscenely through the garden, now made grotesque by man's sin. Creatures jumped and collided in their confusion. The colors of paradise ran together, a soupy mess of garish clown paint—so thin the canvas behind which murder waits.

Hot tears fell on the dead woman's peaceful face. How lovely she was, her countenance as one who had seen the door to heaven and found it almost reward enough.

Danson's heart was thick with dread. How could Ngomba deny these people access to the truth? He had the blessed Beginning in his own language. Genesis bore bold testimony to the Creation by One God, to the subjection of all creation to the lordship of man in obedience to the Lordship of Jehovah. Why was life so cheap in paradise?

"My God, my God! Has Ngomba no shame?!" Reg shouted to the trees. Wiggins translated as vehemently, but the only answer was the residual ringing in the ears from the gunshot, the fearful chatter of monkeys stunned from their daily chores.

And from beyond the wooden rampart, unnoticed, there was a mighty sucking and churning of still waters, a stream of oil-slick skin rising and falling away from the gunfire.

They waited, exposed, weak, for the next arrow to fly. It did not. The butterflies closed ranks on the bullet-torn leaves. Orchids flushed again with color and birds returned to the chorus, tentatively, like the church choir at the first rehearsal after summer break.

Reg looked at Jigs. Each nodded grimly at the other. The assassin was undoubtedly one of Ngomba's henchmen. But they knew what they had to do. The *griot* himself was an evil that must be eliminated if ever the Ologus were to be free to hear the truth.

Reg hoped three bullets would be enough.

# 13

**K**ay Wiggins kept the suitcase handle in her manicured grip the whole way to Sangha. Tony thought that strange. A woman new to the raw uncertainty of wilderness Africa might be expected to keep a closer watch on the smaller blue satchel where her passport and other items of personal security were more likely to reside. Why cling to a suitcase of clothes and cosmetics?

Not that Kay Wiggins needed to take her beauty from a bottle. She reminded him of Katherine Hepburn, as refined and elegant in shirt and jeans as the belle of the ball in gown and tiara. Even the floppy fisherman's hat gave her a certain jaunty air.

The powerful police motor launch knifed through the water at high speed, throwing a rooster tail of spray twenty yards off the stern. They sat back of the bow, searching every bend for signs of Sangha. The pulsing engines of progress communicated promise, vibrating through the boat's hull and up Tony's legs. Hope rode the waves despite a stiff breeze hitting them head-on, sweeping downriver like the hot breath of Hades.

"You must be immensely proud of your father," Kay said, her voice warm and strong. "He's made quite the stir in scientific circles with all his talk of 'cryptids' and other remarkable beasts of legend. After his success with Noah's Ark, I confess I've had to take another look at unicorns myself."

Tony, jaw set, met her eyes, ready to defend his dad from another scoffer. But what he saw were gentle brown eyes full of warmth and a hint of cavalier merriment.

He laughed. "Yeah, he's made a lot of believers out of former skeptics. Cryptozoology attracts its share of kooks. But more than half the international society of hunters of mystery animals are respected anthropologists, paleontologists, and zoologists from universities and museums in North America and Europe. Famed French zoologist Georges LaPierre thinks Dad's the best thing since *gigantopithecus*."

"Giganto-what-y-cus?" Kay laughed and made a face.

"*Gigantopithecus*—Bigfoot to the Yanks, Sasquatch to the Native Americans, Yeti to the Nepalese, Yahoo to the Australians. You know, the big guy in the hairy ape suit!"

"Ah, yes," said Kay, playing along. "I believe I dated him in college."

Tony hooted. He liked this lady. "Seriously, when Dad finishes up here, he'd better take a vacation. He deserves it! Especially since . . ." He trailed off and looked away from the kind woman.

She laid a gentle hand on his arm. "What is it, Tony?"

He hesitated before speaking. "My grandma died a few days ago, and Dad doesn't know it yet. They were real close. She got him interested in science and animals—you know, the chemistry set in the basement, the ant farm in the bedroom, a rabbit hutch in the backyard—the whole nine yards. He—he'll take her death pretty hard."

Kay Wiggins saw her own son before her. "I guess you and your grandmother were close too?"

Tony looked down between his knees at the flooring and a two-inch black beetle lumbering slowly along. The beetle stopped occasionally and pressed against the cooler metal hull as if for relief. "After my mom died, Grandma Carrie's was my hiding place. Grandpa Con died too, and it just seemed like Grandma and I filled in the blanks for each other. She had the neatest old house, so full of good smells, and a garden full of a million flowers. Sugar cookies and ice cream floats and stories of covered wagon days when she and her family came over the Oregon Trail . . ." He stopped, fighting back the tears.

"It's okay, Tony," Kay Wiggins said, her voice rich with a one hundred percent money-back guarantee just like his mother used to give whenever he fell or felt lonesome or threw up. He clung to it now. *God, help us, please . . .*

"Grandma's house was just the best place for me when I was hurting . . ." He stopped again and looked up into the hot wind. He smelled the putrid rot of death and quickly looked down. The beetle scuttled beneath the cesspool lid in his grandmother's backyard and the creatures within stirred again. Then they began to slide out and to creep up his legs toward his heart.

The motor launch sped past the river bar and the decaying remains of dead hippos.

Reg and Jigs fought the urge to ambush Ngomba.

"It must be done in full view of the village," said Wiggins grimly. "The people must see and experience that the spell is broken, that their *griot* no longer has power over them. You realize, we will have to assume command and take the Ologus back to Sangha with us? The government will help resettle them, but a few hotheads like Bigshot and Littleshot will likely have to spend some time in irons before they'll be broken. Three bullets is precious little with which to mount an insurrection."

Danson nodded, the crushing weight of oppressive heat and the depressing assignment before them making him dizzy. He prayed it wasn't the fever. The morning's tragedy weighed heavily upon him. If he'd just listened to Wiggins and stayed in camp, Kimboki's mother might still be alive.

"I think once they see their lives are no longer threatened by him, they will place bullies like Big and Little under house arrest," Wiggins finished.

They were barely a quarter of a mile from camp, having kept to the forest rather than expose themselves on the open trail. Nevertheless, they felt watched, as if at any moment an arrow would drill one of them or both, sinking deep inside, spreading its poison death to the core of their beings.

Wiggins hacked at the tough skin of the banana stem with his knife. He lapped at the thick, mucousy liquid inside. It tasted like swamp sludge, but it was water, and they were dehydrating. He gouged a slit in another stem and handed it to Danson.

"I just pray it doesn't backfire and their brains have been so badly warped that they decide we've done them no favor," Jigs said quietly.

Reg licked the slime from the stem and gagged. He fought to keep the moisture down. "There have to be others like Kimboki's mother, people who still feel in their heart of hearts that this is not right. I'm just so sorry we placed her in that kind of danger."

Jigs threw his palm frond angrily to the ground. His muscles bunched, and the serpent on his bicep squeezed the dagger more tightly. "She would have died soon anyway. She'd forget and hug her son or call him a pet name, and Ngomba would know. He'd have to kill her as an example to the others."

They both coaxed the last ounces of liquid from their palm fronds and tried not to remember the sight of the beautiful little woman lying on the ground, a three-foot arrow imbedded in her heart. They'd hidden her beneath the trees as best they could. They'd prayed, and wept, at the loss. Not able to abandon her without giving her a name, since neither had learned her real name, the men called her Edima, "precious thing."

Reg's feet ached, swollen from the forced march and the constant wet. He rubbed them now, resentful of the merciless forest. No one had to tell Reg that the forest was alive with things well able to make short order of a body so small.

They resumed their march parallel to the path, closing in on the camp. As they did so, the shrill sound of mourning rose and fell on the thick air in waves of human hysteria.

Reg broke into a run. "Kimboki!" he shouted. "Kimboki!"

He turned the last twist in the trail and saw the boy running toward him, the tiny bare legs pumping in a life and death race. The entire camp seemed to be running, dashing about the clearing in mass turmoil, the people wailing and flailing themselves with sticks until the blood ran.

Danson went down on one knee, arms outstretched to scoop little Kimboki up, just like naked little Tony Bear running from the tub into the big bath towel, warm from the dryer. Wrap him up, hoist him over a shoulder, and carry him to his mom so she could do "piggy went to market" on his wiggly toes.

Kimboki had no mom. If Danson touched him, Kimboki would die.

"No!!" Reg screamed, pulling back his arms, closing off the welcome, taking back the love. "Don't!!"

Kimboki stopped dead still. Around them raged the Ologus, an unknown sorrow tearing at their faces, hurling them to the ground in spasms of anguish. But for the explorer and the little boy, time was no more. The Ologus moved in slow motion, individual mouths muted by the collective roar of their bitterness.

The light of kindness and warmth spread so eagerly across Kimboki's face at the sound of the white God man calling his name held for a couple of seconds more, then flickered. A stony astonishment much too old for a child began to eat away the hope, leaving ugly lesions of dejection behind.

Reg sprang to his feet, whirled to face Wiggins, and wrenched the gun from the surprised missionary's hand. He ran to Kimboki who flew into his arms like a frightened bird seeking safety beneath its mother's protective wings. They hugged each other tight, and Reg kissed the little face, tasting the salt of tears. He brandished the pistol at the insane chaos before him, ready to shoot anyone wanting to pry the boy from his arms.

Barely aware, Danson saw Ndoki and Ndokanda rush past to bombard Jigs with their animated version of what was happening. Dimly, he knew the pandemonium held great significance, a clue perhaps to solving their dilemma, but it didn't matter. For a few blessed sweet minutes, nothing on earth mattered but the precious little boy who loved him, needed him, would undoubtedly die without him; here in the center of great danger, they were somehow safer than at any time since they'd met.

Then it passed. Another thought came crashing in, one wicked and destructive. By taking Kimboki into the shelter of his arms, Danson had poisoned the boy as surely as if he'd shot him full of pygmy arrows. Ngomba—or his henchmen—would slay the child. *Let them try.* Reg tightened his grip on the pistol. *Just let them try.*

At last it occurred to Danson how stupid he was. His faith was in a six-inch pistol and three lousy bullets when any time they wanted, pygmy marksmen could turn Reg into a human pin cushion . . . Some trust in chariots and some in horses . . . and some in guns . . .

"My heart is steadfast, O God, my heart is steadfast!" Kimboki sobbed against Danson's shirt. "I will sing and make music to you, my Redeemer!" Softly Reg began to hum in Kimboki's ear. "Come, they told me, pa-rum pum pum pum, a newborn King to see, pa-rum pum pum pum . . ."

"Danson! Danson! Snap out of it, man. Ngomba is dead! He took too much *iboga* and—Danson, can you hear me!?"

Reg felt the little boy relax and nestle closer to his friend.

" . . . Our finest gifts to bring, pa-rum pum pum pum, to lay before the King, pa-rum pum pum pum, rum pum pum pum, rum pum pum pum . . ."

"Danson! Give me the gun, man, we've got to see for ourselves. Do you know what this means? Danson!?"

Someone tore the pistol from Reg's hand, and he didn't try to stop him. " . . . So to honor Him, pa-rum pum pum pum, when we come . . ."

Ologus rushed past him in their grief, pounding themselves senseless, crying to the gods for their fallen chief.

Reg wrapped the boy tighter in his arms, and in the midst of the madness, Kimboki fell asleep.

# 14

She looked at her husband stretched out upon the butchering table and felt a stab of regret. His long, strong body, as beautiful and brawny in death as it had been in life, lay framed by the bloody spray of animals long since dismembered and the thick, sticky clots of the recent elephant kill. He looked only as if he slept, except there was no longer the familiar rise and fall of his mighty chest. How often she had listened to the powerful thudding from deep inside that chamber. His three other wives had listened too, and again she felt the hot shame of being only one of several who claimed his rough affections.

It was ghostly still in the hut of death where she had conceived his children and dreamed of freedom. Why did people enslave other people? She'd heard that the long ago fathers of Africa had been taken and tied to a land so far away you couldn't see it from the tallest *anjuafa* tree. She hadn't had to go so far away for her enslavement. In the time it took a man to make a quiver of arrows, she could be back to the place where her mother had wiped her dry of the birth fluids.

For a brief moment, she felt a perverse, defensive pride at nearly being sacrificed to the Strong One. Of all the wives, only she had retained some semblance of feminine appeal at the hands of Ngomba. The rest were haggard and witchly, made to forage further, lift heavier burdens, and work later into the night than she. Even in servitude, she'd had a small hold over him, more tender, more provocative, more mysterious than the rest put together. They were drudges. She was queenly. Ngomba had told her of a far-off place, a land of industry and regal bearing, of kings and queens and courts of gold. It had sounded too fantastic, but one look at his physical splendor, one insight into the cunning intelligence of his mind, and it seemed all too possible.

The wise, fine-looking *griot* giant had made her the envy of the camp until the food grew less and less, and Ngomba's wild demands grew more and more.

She'd given him seven children, five boys and two girls. Three boys and a girl died of spirit fevers, and another boy simply disappeared into the forest one day, undoubtedly eaten by a demon cat. The remaining boy once promised to be bold and strong like his father but had begun to waste away recently for lack of food. She begged Ngomba to share more of his food with his son, but Ngomba had glared and said that he dare not surrender a single morsel or the Strong One would overpower the Ologus and destroy the people. "Do you not think I am a god sent from the Far Place to protect you from the river beasts that live nearby, to make it possible for you to live in the kingdom of *Mokele-mbembe?*" he had asked.

Did he tell the other women of the Far Place? Little matter. He'd been harsh to her, displaying little regard for her humanity. She was useful for animal things, a receptacle for his frequent rage and ferocious passions. But that was the African way. Woman was made for fertility, to fetch water, to look after the dwelling and the squalling products of physical intimacy.

Had she been barren, she would have become like the shriveled old camp widow who now kept a young man on a leash. Forced to scavenge the leavings, she would find no acceptance even among the older women of honor who had borne many children.

But she was fertile, and it had gotten her into trouble. She should not have usurped her daughter's first conception by so soon allowing another of her own. But a tiny infant, even one she was not officially allowed to handle beyond suckling and washing, was one of the few joys left. Ngomba did not know that her sweetest caresses were reserved for her babies. She stole away in the middle of the night while he was deep in sleep. She could not have them die so young without first having tasted mother love. Nor had they been able to pry the dead ones from her embrace until a full sun and moon after their deaths. She would say her good-byes, or they must kill her too.

At the announcement of Ngomba's death, the other wives had probably gone to fling themselves into the river to drown or be eaten. It was a funeral rite of mourning she thought stupid and wasteful. Why die for one you never loved? If they survived the river, they were to live apart with special honors accorded the immortal wives of a king. Let them. She had other plans.

Rain began to beat hard upon the roof. It felt airless and sti-fling inside the *griot* hut. The chief had forbidden them to bury him for three days, should he die. The stink of him would infect the camp, but the elders would not act for fear of retribution from beyond the grave. Ngomba would have his way, alive or dead.

His thick, muscular calves hung over the sides of the table and the huge, chiseled feet nearly brushed the ground. His arms lay straight at his sides, fingers extended just as they were when he used to dance the Strong One to a stop so that the creature would not crush the camp.

She had never seen him so motionless. Even in slumber, his great muscles would sometimes twitch, and he would moan the details of his troubled dreams. Always about death . . . a mortal struggle and death. He would turn and reach for her, a terrifying grip that sometimes squeezed the breath from her body. He would awake then, look at the frightened, gasping bird in his hands, then release her with a groan.

Today Ngomba had ordered the death of the white captives, but he himself had died. The white captives had brought fire, saving the weakened Ologus from having to attack the Bwambati for theirs. The white God men knew High God and His Son. The white God men had been beaten and faced death, yet they showed love for Kimboki.

She would trust the white God men. The elders could do as they wished now that Ngomba's spell had been broken. She would listen to the new truth.

Fearfully, she reached a hesitant finger forward to touch the perfect gold ring glinting in the dead man's ear. So strong was the force of Ngomba's living presence that it had subsided little in death. The raw energy, the hard, unyielding muscle that had so long had its way with her still pulsed in that dwelling of frond and mud. She had put her faith in that energy; her survival had depended upon it. Now it was gone, yet its pull had diminished little. Perhaps she could never really be free of it in this life.

Her thin, bare shoulders slumped at the dismal thought. Then they straightened, and she did something she'd never done before, something forbidden when her husband had ruled the Ologus. She touched the gold ring, the only adorning part of Ngomba he had not been born with.

The dead man's head jerked almost imperceptibly to the right. At least, in the strained atmosphere of death, she thought it had. She let loose a nervous "huh!" in the stillness, chiding herself for letting the hardening of the dead scare her. It was just that he still looked so alive. Great men possessed great vitality, and it should not surprise her when it carried over to the grave.

She would seek out the captive white men and return with them to whatever world they'd come from. Would they take her? She'd lived all her life in the forest as had the generations before her, but that had been a very different forest, a simpler time when the struggle was seasoned with kindness and the playing of games.

She wished to know about the Son of High God, the rest of the story that the first white God men had not been able to tell before they died. She liked the thought of High God creating the earth and making woman from man's rib. Every time she had felt the contours of Ngomba's rib cage, she'd thought of the lovely story of the first man falling into a deep sleep and God doctor removing a bone to make of it a new creature not unlike man.

She smelled the white man before he reached her and turned to face him.

"Excuse me," Danson said, feeling awkward and intrusive. He was holding a tearful Kimboki by one hand and the pistol in the other. "I'm sorry your husband is dead. He—he was a very complex man. I would like to have known him better."

The woman stared uncomprehendingly but heard the sympathy in his voice. Reg looked helplessly at Wiggins to translate, and the missionary did so. He told her that the elders would meet with the people at sundown to decide what they should do now that they were leaderless.

But no one proposed further rites of death. It was as if all the dancing and ceremony, the wailing and gnashing, was now spent.

Jigs pointed to Kimboki and explained to the woman that the boy's mother was dead. Would Ngomba's widow comfort him?

Wiggins gave the boy a gentle shove forward. Bereft, dejected, he was a baby again and stood with one foot on the other before the woman, eyes at the ground, tears making little puffs in the dirt ahead of his toes. The woman went to her knees in the dirt, unsure how to approach this little boy, so long had it been since she'd petted her own little ones in secret.

She put out a hand and touched the boy's side, lightly feeling each small rib until the goose bumps showed. He grinned a little, then giggled aloud. She tickled the other side, then drew him close and let him nuzzle against her. How good and warm and alive she felt! She smiled at the two men; then, with one last look of regret at the still form on the butchering table, she rose and took Kimboki from the hut.

Reg moved to the table and looked down at Ngomba's lifeless body. He shook his head wonderingly. "We come charging back here ready to kill this guy, and God's already taken care of it—does the guy in with an overdose of his own medicine! Now, unless I miss my guess, we're probably going to walk out of here leading an entire tribe behind us who just a few short hours ago would just as soon have roasted us as look at us. I tell ya, Jigs, this serving God is a wildly, wonderfully, supernaturally rousing business!"

Wiggins did not respond. "Hey, Jigs, there's no more to be done for this guy," said Reg, anxious to be free of the hut. "He was his own worst enemy. Let's be glad for the Ologus, for us."

Wiggins nodded absentmindedly. He could not tear his eyes from Ngomba's body. He stared hard at the massive chest for the longest time, then drew near and bent over the face. He cocked his head and listened, then placed an ear just above the nose and mouth. Jigs went behind the corpse's head, crouched, and sighted back down the body at Reg.

Jigs lightly sniffed the air.

Without warning, Wiggins looked faint, his knees started to buckle, and he stumbled against the table. The body jiggled from the impact, and Reg hurried over to steady his friend. He threw one arm across the missionary's back and another around his chest. His fingers closed on the shirt pocket and the tobacco pouch within. "Jigs, are you okay?" he said, struggling to right the man.

Wiggins shot straight up, and Reg lost his grip on the pocket before he could tell what it contained beyond Blackhorn's Best. He'd felt something, though. *Little hard lumps . . . must be difficult to smoke those . . .*

Jigs shook off Danson's hold and leaned on the table a moment, again examining the deceased with all the clinical interest of a pathologist—or a coroner. "Yes, yes . . ." He reached out a hand.

Kimboki burst through the doorway of the hut and grabbed a thumb of each of the explorers and pulled and tugged with all his might. They smiled as he dug in his little heels and puffed out his cheeks in the titanic struggle to bring the men along. His tears were gone, smudges of their having been there now soft upon his eager face. They lifted him high into the air and swung him about until his delighted squeals grew piercing. "Re-edge!" he shouted, then "Je-eggs!"

Out the door they went, flinging their little friend about like a sack of potatoes, the three of them made exceedingly jolly by the feeling of weightlessness sweeping the camp. Even the adult Ologus had put away their clubs and sackcloth and were beginning to talk with mounting excitement of the future. The rain felt cooler now, refreshing, turning the little people a shiny bronze.

Tiny boys, barely able to walk, tottered about the clearing with their little infant bows and arrows, taking deadly aim at ants and seriously stalking butterflies. A little girl whisked along on crude stilts, moving deftly among her hunter brothers. Their hearts were light. The wicked witch was dead.

Only the elders held their grave expressions. They invited the explorers to their place of meeting where they expressed serious doubts about the tribe's survival now that their protector, healer, and dictator was dead.

"Apparently he did all their thinking for them as well," said Jigs out of the side of his mouth. An attempt by Bigshot to run for office died on the spot despite Littleshot's impassioned campaign speech on behalf of his most able candidate. The elders were not interested in a Ngomba clone, nor were they young enough to take the reins. Either the warriors tried for a coup, or the white God men took command.

"Your offer is too kind," Jigs hastened to say, "but the two of us put together could not begin to equal the forest wisdom of one Ologu. We can take you back to the outside world where you will be changed forever but will not starve. You have our word on it."

The two shots, Big and Little, looked in dire need of an antacid. "I guess they figured on an easy takeover," whispered Jigs, amused.

Before anything was settled, the camp erupted with the breathless news that another forest elephant had been spotted nearby. Apparently two elephants in as many days was a strikingly good omen.

The explorers came, the Nubian died, and the game returned. Reg figured it had all the signs of a revival meeting in the making.

The newly freed white captives and the pygmy brothers were swept along in a tide of Ologu hunters trotting in the direction of the elephant sighting. They hadn't made half a mile before a crash was heard. Around the next bend, an elephant's backside was making a hasty retreat down the trail.

Littleshot was the swiftest and sprinted ahead, his legs a blur. At first he chose the standard approach of trying to hamstring the pachyderm with a thrust of his spear. If even one leg were hobbled, the elephant could not move another step and would be finished off at the hunters' leisure. But this old bull was crafty, kicking its legs out behind and very nearly knocking Littleshot's teeth down his throat. Holding back, patiently waiting his opportunity, Littleshot lunged suddenly in the riskiest maneuver in his trick bag. He darted between the huge beast's legs and attempted to drive his spear upward into the great wide belly.

But he stumbled and fell, and the elephant's thundering hind legs knocked him flat. Before the others could stop it, the creature turned and gored the pygmy with four-foot tusks. A sharp fling of its great head, and the mammoth animal tossed Littleshot against a tree. Again and again it battered its attacker against the trees until little humanity was left in the man's features.

It all happened too fast. Reg remembered the pistol, but it was too small and might have only enraged the beast further. By this time, the younger boys caught up with the main hunters and were staring innocently at the recent carnage. Then, with an unexpected cry of rage and frustration, Bigshot grabbed Kimboki and raced for the river.

Two other boys were snatched from the ground before the rest scattered in terror. Off the two boys flew after Bigshot and the screaming Kimboki, each the prisoner of a strong Ologu hunter. Without thinking, Reg fired a shot in the air, but the hunters did not break stride.

Two bullets remained.

**W**hat's your favorite dinosaur extinction story?" Kay Wiggins asked, managing to pass melon slices all around while still keeping a firm grip on the suitcase. "No fair saying a universal flood wiped them out. That is much too preposterous for modern man to swallow." Though she was asking the question, Kay's thoughts struggled to be somewhere else. *Would Jigsy even want to see her again? Had she waited too long to come?*

Tony marveled at how sweetly she could deliver a load of sarcasm.

They were no more than thirty or forty minutes from Sangha Mission, and she wanted to ease the tense anticipation they were all feeling. A sweeping, drenching rain shower had done nothing to lighten the mood. They were all smelling hot and damp, painfully aware of one another's sweaty proximity in the cramped boat.

Tony raised his hand to answer. "My favorite's the one about how they overdosed themselves out of business," Tony chirped, feeling some better now that they'd dined on crackers, peanut butter, fish, and fruit. "Let's see. I believe it must have been in the Mesozoic Era when smart plants decided they were a vanishing species and had better start producing a few toxic drugs of their own like strychnine and such. Mr. Herbivore could not taste the bitter drugs as they had not yet decided to grow the proper tastebuds for drug detection. Needless to say, it wasn't long before the dinosaurs began to manifest the physiological stress of too much funny weed—thin egg shells, that sort of thing. Fossilized remains of dumb dinos by the droves have been found in the contorted positions of poisoning. But behold! The much smarter birds and mammals survived by learning to avoid those same plants, and they lived happily ever after."

Fulgate smiled forebearingly. "Ah, yes, Tony, that *is* a lovely story, but *my* favorite has got yours beat. It's the 'subway' theory of extinction. Just like New Yorkers stress out over their crowded underground transportation rat race, the dinosaurs found the garden filling up with—you guessed it—too many dinosaurs! The earth got warmer and the swamps got bigger, and as in all times of great prosperity, dinosaur couples had more and more babies. As the density of the swamp population grew, stress levels grew right along with them. And like cranky women everywhere, lady dinosaurs began to experience reduced levels of estrogen, leading to those thinner egg shells you talked about. The babes were easily crushed or subject to severe dehydration. They quite literally sweat themselves to death in the shell."

The two men eyed one another smugly, certain each had told the superior story, then turned to Kay for the verdict. "Ooh, gentlemen, you're both such fine liars! What I think really happened is that the male dinosaurs bored the females to death, and we all know that while you boys maybe can't live with us, you for sure can't live without us!" She popped another melon wedge into her mouth and smiled sweetly. "I win!"

Officers Akeley and Katianda did not join the laughter. They grabbed binoculars and scanned the distance. "Smoke!" Akeley said and pointed.

It appeared as if the colossal *baobab* tree of Sangha was belching thick, malignant smoke into the African sky. Nearer, they could see orange flame licking the sky, and nearer still, they saw that the main mission quarters were fully ablaze. The motor launch nosed into shore, and when the engines were shut down, mournful singing filled the clearing beneath the *baobab*.

The pygmies of Sangha, bodies smeared with white mud, stood in neat little rows, heads bowed, arms raised, two-stepping to the left, two-stepping to the right, and singing, "Je-sus! Je-sus! Je-sus!" repeatedly and without end.

Akeley approached Kakese, the three-tattoo woman, matriarch of Sangha. He touched her shoulder, and she turned upon him with abject sorrow. He asked a brief question. She answered him in detail.

Tony rose at Akeley's return, anxious to hear yet not wanting to know the worst. "What?" he demanded. "Please. What did the woman tell you?"

Akeley removed his sunglasses and peered sharply at the beginning of Likouala Swamp. He said nothing, just stood there probing the unseen places where living things could hide and never be found.

Kay Wiggins rose beside Tony and took hold of his arm for support. "Please, Officer Akeley. What did the woman tell you?"

Akeley looked at the fine lady from America and admired her strength. She would need it. "A spirit spoke to these people out of the grave of Sangono, the Christian recently killed by the creature of the swamp. It said that they should stop waiting and looking for the return of the missionary and the visitor from outside. They cannot return, for the jungle and the Ologus have swallowed them whole.

"They are burning the mission station because Mr. Wiggins will no longer have need of it."

Kay caught her breath. Tony put his arms around her as much to receive comfort as to give it. "Bu—but," he stammered, "they can't know that for sure!" The awful words of Gussie Jackson branded themselves upon his mind. *Your father . . . in grave danger . . . gone where he cannot go . . . to seek the dragon . . . stop him . . . the witch's lizard . . . will kill your father if you don't hold him . . .*

The flames cracked and popped. The Jesus chant rose and fell. Tony Danson and Kay Wiggins clung to one another for dear life.

# 16

Thick dread strangled Reg, cutting off precious oxygen. His heart felt coated in tar, unable to beat against the gooey elasticity that squeezed it ever tighter. Every step was a torture but he was scared to death of stopping.

*If anything happens to the children, to my Kimboki, I must die with them.*

The race to the river was a dash through hell. Bigshot tore through untracked jungle, trying to stop the white God men from following. Branches, stinging nettles, and vines slapped and stabbed and caught at Reg, but he did not care for himself. The blood ran from his cuts and his sight became blurred, but still he would not stop.

He didn't know—or care—if Wiggins or the brothers followed. He must save the little one who cared or die trying.

So suddenly did they burst from the jungle onto the riverbank that Reg stumbled and fell on his face in the shallows. The Ologus tore down the narrow sandy shore, their pounding feet triggering explosions of water and mud.

Bigshot reached into the tangle of bushes overhanging the water and wrenched a canoe from its leafy hangar. Only the strongest magic—innocent child sacrifice—could bring Ngomba back from the underworld. The Strong One would be pleased.

Kimboki screamed and punched with all his might but was slapped and flung hard into the canoe along with the two other crying boys. With a shove of his naked foot, Bigshot sent the canoe gliding swiftly to midstream.

The next few minutes for Reg collapsed into a swirl of horrifying images. The Ologu men fell to their knees on the sand, put their arms straight out in front of them like sleepwalkers, palms down, and threw their voices out over the sluggish waters, summoning whatever lived in the river to appear. The boys gripped the sides of the canoe in terror, their little hands draining of color, their little faces stricken in paralyzing fear, crying and shouting to be saved.

Reg dropped the pistol and was in the water, not seeming to move, feet trying to kick but as effective as if he wore cement shoes. Another man, black hair, brown body, went ahead, reached the canoe, and frantically tried to pull it ashore.

Everything seemed to stand still for five long seconds, then came apart in two.

The river beneath the canoe shot straight up like a torpedo blast, sucking the very water away from the shore. The canoe was lifted twenty feet into the air.

In the middle of the blast rose thirty feet of armor-plated muscle. Forty-five thousand pounds of thick flesh launched the canoe skyward, flinging the tiny passengers into the roiling waters. Sick at heart, Reg caught a nauseating vision of helpless pink grubs being dropped into a frying pan of hot oil.

Then he was in the maelstrom, grabbing for the soft assurance of Kimboki's wiry little body, dreading the hard, cold feel of reptilian hide.

Kimboki surfaced and with a deafening shriek wrapped himself desperately around Reg's neck.

Roaring its fury over the suddenly congested waters of its killing ground, the *Mokele-mbembe* unhinged its enormous, ragged jaws, and clamped onto the boat with steel spring force.

The log canoe snapped in two, as yielding as a floating twig. The beast spun in the water, wrenching the canoe apart as it would the pliant body of a young zebra. Danson frantically struggled for shore and literally threw Kimboki into Wiggins's waiting arms. He turned back to help Ndokanda, the brown streak that had reached the canoe first. The brave pygmy, neck still stiff from the bullet wound inflicted by Ngomba, struggled with a boy under each arm.

Ndokanda had to release one boy in order to propel the other into Reg's outstretched arms. When the pygmy turned back for the second boy, the creature surged toward them.

Ndokanda looked straight into the vertical slits of the giant reptile's pupils. He heaved his body about, bare back to the dinosaur's snout, shielding the boy from attack. With a cry of defiance, he shoved the boy into Danson's lunging grasp. Great jaws parted impossibly wide. Heavy, grinding teeth closed around Ndokanda's head and sank to the bone.

Reg fell sobbing to the sand, Kimboki and his chums shaking uncontrollably beneath the safety of the white God man's six-foot frame. From behind them came a brief, violent splashing, then silence as brave Ndokanda sank beneath the waters without a trace.

"Jigs? Jigs!?" Reg looked around to see where the missionary had gone and saw him at the far end of the sand herding the three Ologus into the water at gunpoint.

"Wiggins! NO!" Reg ran toward the three stoic pygmies and their executioner standing in the shallows. He halted when Wiggins brandished the gun in his direction.

"Get back!" he shouted. "They're stinking excuses for human beings. They wanted to sacrifice those kids to appease their gods. Mighty warriors, strong like lions! Ha! Don't make me laugh. As fearless as lion's dung, maybe. They lay all their trouble, their lack of food, their arrows that miss their marks, their dead chief, their poor miserable existence—all of it—at the feet of some idol so they don't have to take responsibility for themselves. Where've you heard that before, Danson? Savings and loan scandals? Government waste? Thieves, drug pushers, rapists? Well, if these people are victims of *their* environment, then I say we take them out of it right now!" He placed the barrel of the pistol in Bigshot's ear. He slowly began to squeeze the trigger.

"No! Jigs, you know we need to take these people back to Sangha and let the authorities deal with them. They've bought the lie, and we've got to show them a better way."

"That's not what you said about Ngomba," Wiggins said, face flushed beet red, looking as if about to sink his own teeth into the warriors. A splash sounded from the other side of the river. With a frightened whimper, the boys scrambled to their feet and ran back up the trail.

"He was an immediate threat to this people," yelled Reg, one eye on the trigger. "I was wrong to want to hunt him down and murder him. God is sovereign, and I can't become an assassin to kill an assassin. The boys are safe now. We'll take these guys back to the elders and let them deal with them. The bloodshed, the fear—it has to stop, Jigs."

The struggle was all too evident in Wiggins's face. At last, however, he lowered the gun and eased off the trigger. The three condemned men quickly left the water to stand on higher ground. On the trail appeared eight more Ologu males, two of them elders, and Kimboki. *Good, brave little Kimboki. Gutsy as a three hundred pound bungee jumper.*

With a wave of an elder's hand, two of the younger Ologus took charge of each of the three warriors and marched them up the trail toward camp.

"Sometimes takes more than a sanctified hymn to convince people," said Wiggins dejectedly. "Padded pew Christianity doesn't cut it in Africa, Danson. St. Paul said some get into heaven by having their tail feathers singed. If a gun—or a little dragon breath—speaks louder than the Apostles' Creed, then what's the harm?"

Danson forced himself to look at the river. Ndoki limped to the water's edge. He stood ramrod still, looking for his brother, leg streaming blood from a fall in a rotten stump hole. Reg put an arm around his shoulders and led him over to Wiggins. "The harm is that we put our faith in bullets rather than in the Holy Spirit of Mighty God. If we let our guns do the talking, pretty soon we'll be talking to ourselves."

Wiggins looked from Danson to the gun and out again at the now calm waters. He stuck the gun in his waistband. "I'm losing my brothers in Christ faster than I'm winning them, Danson. The ground is so hard won and so quickly lost."

Reg nodded somberly. He looked up at the lush canopy towering high above them, so bright green and rich in chloroform, so dark in spirit. He felt a malignancy in creation he'd never before experienced. "Sorceror's paradise," he mumbled.

The three men from Sangha placed their hands on one another's shoulders and prayed. They praised God for Ndokanda's faith in action. They asked Him to give Ndoki peace despite so great a loss. They thanked God for the beginning of the end of oppression. They asked Him to help them get the remaining Ologus to safety and for opportunity to tell them the rest of His story.

And silently, Reg said a prayer for Tony and Carrie Danson and Gussie Jackson, the strange little roommate at Powell Valley Convalescent Center. Her hair-raising reaction to the word *Congo* was making more sense by the minute.

# CHAPTER

## 17

Tony, Kay, and Fulgate prayed with the believers of Sangha before setting out for the Maya Maya. They were touched by the sincerity of concern expressed. There were actual tears in Kakese's eyes. She daubed each of them on the forehead with the sign of the cross in white mud. Then she performed a very moving solo in Bantu. In a cracked and quavering voice, she sang of an old rugged cross, sweet waters of everlasting life teeming with plenty of fish, and a new heaven where fresh meat and manioc were in abundant supply.

The people of Sangha were much encouraged that "Mrs. Happy Kay Wiggins" had joined the search. They gave her Jigs's broken Timex watch—its face was cracked but it worked—and a locket she had given him three decades before containing a faded photo of her and the kids. His Bantu translation of the Bible contained surprisingly intricate little sketches he'd made of pygmies walking through the Red Sea, pygmies strewing palm fronds before a pygmy Jesus, and the Last Supper with Christ and His twelve pygmy disciples. Apparently Jigs had taken another copy with him on the journey, for this was his personal study Bible, and Kay clutched it to her bosom for a long while, trying to absorb any trace of the man she had loved. These treasures were all the villagers had salvaged before the burning of Sangha Mission except the pheasants and a little sack of red jelly beans forgotten in the expedition's rush to be away. Kay Wiggins distributed the candies, laughing at the delighted children and the old men gumming the gooey sweets.

The rescue party motored slowly away from Sangha with a ration of what little food the villagers could spare. The police launch was well stocked with food supplies, but no one had the heart to refuse the kindnesses of so generous a people. Kay left four large sacks of vegetables with Kakese, and what passed between them at that moment was an understanding as between sisters. The exchange of food was like a hug—without the indignity of touching.

Leaving the wide Ubangi, Tony felt the oppressive closeness of every tree, every vine, and every leaf of the thickening swampland. He had the unnerving sensation they were sliding down an abandoned mine shaft into perpetual night and would never again see the surface. He opened his mouth to gulp the last of the open river air and fervently wished he could somehow stow the sun's light safely aboard.

The last pygmy child who had run after them waved, then was lost to a bend in the tributary. The three Americans felt a tightening in their throats. Officer Akeley maneuvered carefully around a water-logged snag jutting from the riverbed, then gunned the boat down a long, narrow channel. On the map, it was the entrance to the untracked Likouala wilderness. In their hearts, it was a rat hole leading into the unknown.

# CHAPTER

# 18

The Ologus did not protest when Reg via Jigs's translation told them they must not bury Ngomba. Men with authority from beyond the forest would want to investigate the strange life and death of the *griot* king, and the results might have a great deal to do with how the Ologus would be received in the outside world.

An around-the-clock guard would be posted at the main hut to keep animals from following the scent of death to its logical conclusion. Bigshot and his cronies would be kept under house arrest by four young men with bow and arrow, whose glowering expressions brooked no nonsense.

At first light, the rest—men, women, and children—would walk out to Sangha and radio Epuluville for help.

The elders ruled one more opportunity for the people to view the body of their fallen leader. For many so recently under the inescapable dominion of the mighty Ngomba, it was difficult to believe they were free. For all, to leave the jungle was in many ways a more frightening prospect than the Nubian's tyranny.

It was a solemn file that entered and exited the leaf dwelling of the man who had seized their individual identities and absorbed them into his own. If anything, the people looked more troubled when they came out than when they went in. Little children and some of the women entered quietly yet left crying as if a kindly uncle had passed on.

Danson played with Kimboki and his buddies, giving them piggyback rides, hugging and caressing them in their hunger to be acknowledged. He had expected at least the mothers and grandmothers to rush to the children, but instead they wandered aimlessly about as if they could not believe they could again show love without fear.

Or had they forgotten how?

The elders exited the hut like pale visitors to a haunted house where the goblins were all too real. They motioned Wiggins to join them in a tight huddle beyond the people's hearing. Reg stared in their direction, oblivious to the boy entwining his neck and the two wrapped around his legs, trying to hear, to catch a clue to what was going on.

The meeting broke up, and Wiggins feigned a casual indifference on his way back to Reg. He might even have pulled it off except for the fingers grasping the breast pocket of his shirt as if to shield the Blackhorn's Best from all comers.

*That must be one expensive blend!* Reg was surprised by the vehemence in that thought. He couldn't let the unknown go undetected. He hated secrecy between friends, even friends as uneasy as they'd been at times. "Hey, Jigs, I've been meaning to ask—"

"Save it!" snapped Wiggins. "Follow me."

Reg unwrapped the boys from his limbs and gave Kimboki a pat on the cheek. "Keem-bo-ki stay!" he said, ruffling the boy's tight, curly hair. He might have to adopt this one.

Jigs made a beeline for the *griot* hut. The last of the Ologus filed out, looking as troubled as the rest. Wiggins didn't even pause at the entrance.

Reg braced himself for the sight of a hardened corpse and the odors of death, but the atmosphere of the hut had not changed. The body lay as still and unaltered as before. *What have the people seen?* he wondered.

Wiggins again performed his curious autopsy, studying the body, cocking an ear over nose and mouth, sighting down the body from head to toe. He sniffed the air once, twice, a third time, the nose wrinkling as if tickled by the red beard beneath it.

He hesitated a moment, muscles tensing. Squaring his shoulders, he reached out a hand and placed it on the dead man's left breast.

He held it there for most of a minute, eyes staring off into the distance, looking for all the world like befuddled old Doc Wiggins on the end of a stethoscope, trying to separate little Billy's heartbeat from the ticking of his own watch.

Slowly, he removed the hand, and Reg saw that it shook.

Reg started to say something, but Jigs jerked an index finger straight up to his lips and scowled.

Wiggins felt for the carotid artery and when the hand came away at last, it shook more violently than before.

He jerked his head toward the entrance. Reg grabbed the elephant tranquilizer gun Ngomba had stolen from them. The palm frond doorway brushed against them on the way out. The dry rasping sounded like the rattle of old bones.

Jigs didn't speak until they were well beyond earshot of the camp. They stopped. The camp was as deathly quiet as the man in the hut. Reg's insides were shouting for information. *Why doesn't Wiggins come out with it?*

Jigs finally looked at him, pupils wide with fear. "Ngomba's alive."

Reg didn't trust his ears or his voice. He made a miserable little expression of protest, but Wiggins thrust out an angry, trembling hand to stop him.

"*Alive!*" he said again, frustration and disappointment fiercely denying any other possibility.

"It can't be! You're wrong!" Even as he said it, Danson heard the lack of conviction in the words.

"Open your eyes, Danson! We so badly *want* him dead we couldn't see what was right in front of our noses. Body, slack and supple. Skin, smooth and warm to the touch. Perspiration absent; no drugged struggle for life. No rictus of death. No smell of decay. A tiny, thin heart rhythm undetectable to the naked eye but there to the human touch. But who among the Ologus would dare touch a dead body? I've seen enough death to know a cadaver when I see one, and this guy doesn't qualify. He's alive, Danson! That wizard's in a catatonic state, but he's no more dead than you or I!"

Danson couldn't accept it. The events of the last twenty-four hours had seemed so divinely driven, the death of Ngomba so fitting an end for so cruel a despot. They could leave now and find freedom for the Ologus. How could the tables turn so quickly? Why, God, why? *Fearfulness and trembling have come upon me, and horror has overwhelmed me. So I said, "Oh, that I had wings like a dove! I would fly away and be at rest . . ."* The psalmist's words calmed him. Wiggins was saying something.

". . . could be induced by the ingestion of *iboga*. The symptoms are very like those of a hibernator . . . or maybe more that of an estivator. Estivation's the tropical counterpart to hibernation, you know. The torpor, the reduced heart rate, the lowered metabolism, the limited oxygen intake, the narcotic lack of even fine motor movement, such as flickering eyelids or twitching fingers and toes. Animal behavior's a passion of mine—helps pass the time and gives me a deeper appreciation for the place God's planted me."

Reg nodded abjectly. Wiggins grabbed his red beard as if to wrench it off but combed some of the twigs from it instead. They looked at each other. An unspoken thought passed between them. *The gun . . . two bullets remained . . .*

Reg looked away first, ashamed that he had again entertained a killer's thoughts.

Jigs cleared his throat to fill the awful silence. "The weed must have somehow triggered the pineal gland. It's just a speck of a thing buried deep in the brain. It secretes a tranquilizing hormone called melatonin. The way it usually works is about an hour after dark our pineal glands start pumping melatonin to slow us down and make us tired. Six, eight hours later, the melatonin starts to shut down so we're free to wake up any time. It's really the regulator of our daily cycle."

Wiggins fished out his pipe, tamped down some fresh tobacco, and lit it. "Evolutionists will tell you that as ancient man shed most of his body fur and walked more upright, he compensated by retreating to the cave and hibernating much of the frigid winter away. They point to a tribe of central Australian aborigines that to this day sleeps naked on the bare ground in winter temperatures often below freezing. They conserve body heat by somehow lowering their skin temperature to as low as fifty-three degrees Fahrenheit, well below anything you or I could stand. For that matter, the pygmies run around in the rain with no adverse effects. I've seen a nursing mother sit through a driving rainstorm without seeking shelter while her infant finished its meal. Neither seemed the worse for wear."

It helped Wiggins to talk on about the fine points of human resilience, but at last when he took another long drag on the pipe, he did not resume the discourse on mammalian metabolism. He stared at the ground, lost in thought.

Reg craved action. "That's all very interesting, but the fact remains the mice have got to act while the cat's napping. Let's get these people to safety, then worry about Ngomba."

They decided to bind Ngomba's wrists to his ankles as added precaution against any further trouble if and when he awoke. That would at least buy them some time to put distance between them and the *griot*. Reg didn't want to consider how slowly they might travel with women and children, many of them in a weakened state. Jigs double-checked the pistol in his waistband, and they headed for the main hut.

Ten yards from the entrance, Reg spotted a bare foot protruding from the dwelling. The pygmy guard was nowhere in sight. They began to run, Wiggins drawing the pistol from his belt. Scrambling into the hut, they found the pygmy sentinel dead on the hard earthen floor. Strangled.

Ngomba was gone.

# CHAPTER

# 19

The form sliced through the water, a deep dive, then back to the surface, turning effortlessly and plunging again for the bottom of the Maya Maya.

Pushing off the bottom, the body twisted like a corkscrew in its ascent toward the sun. Water streamed over angles and planes, lifting the body toward light, lending carefree buoyancy to leaden muscle.

The dark form descended again, swept along the river bottom, then darted into the cavern carved by ancient waters from the ninety degree bend called the Sombo-Sombo.

Surfacing in the great air chamber inside the earthen walls of the Sombo-Sombo, the form blew and snorted water from a flare of wide nostrils. Eyes like chips of coal widened, adjusted to the subterranean night, sensed rather than saw that the great chamber was unoccupied. It was quiet except for the gentle slapping of liquid against rock. Nothing filled the hollow, hidden void. Floating, resting, drawing the dank air of sunken earth and water, the long, silken physique drifted. Then, with a powerful kick, the form flipped over, shot out of the chamber, and made for shore.

In the shallows, the form slowed and glided to the bank, the feel of small stones and mud not unpleasant to its skin. Soft, waving blades of swamp grass stroked the thick, unyielding muscle of thigh and belly.

The form emerged onto dry land, shook, and stretched every fiber in the gossamer moonglow. Ten fingers strained toward the water. From deep within the tall form's throat rippled a primeval thrumming that increased in volume until it at last tore from the lips in a wild cry: "*Tombola! Tombola! Tombola!*"

One moment demanding, the next pleading, compelling, almost weeping, the voice filled the night with the urgent invitation: "Raise up! Raise up! Raise up!"

There was a mighty rushing and the river churned like a caldron. A heavy, plated head lifted serpentlike from the waters on the end of a slick, slender neck. Higher and higher it ascended until the head was fifteen feet above the supplicant on the shore.

The tall form with outstretched hands dropped to the sand on knees unused to humility. The thing bent its neck until the heavy-lidded eyes and plated head were inches from the one who had called. It parted lizard jaws and hissed in the face of the one who knelt.

The moist breath was hot and stank of bile and rotting vegetation.

The supplicant began a slow, rhythmic swaying to an ancient whirring from inside the powerful chest. The thing followed the supple torso in the sand, charmed by the flexing of muscle and sinew. Together, they moved as one in the dance.

Something passed between them. All movement, all sound, ceased. They froze in place, each having mesmerized the other. Slowly, the thing retracted its head, creating a slick, black loop in its neck. It blinked once but the one in the sand did not blink. Eyes locked open, paralyzed, the tall form was still as stone.

With a loud, gasping sigh, the thing blasted fire from its mouth and nostrils. The tall one fell over backward, face scorched and bubbling blisters.

The hard, plated head waited. When the figure in the sand did not move, the slick, black neck slid silently beneath the waters.

An hour before first light, a forest antelope wandered along the water's edge, its magnificent red coat "wrapped" in thin white lines. It lowered its muzzle to drink, twin antlers at the ready to spear any early morning enemies. Something in the sand ahead groaned and moved. The antelope snorted water from its nostrils, stamped forward once, decided better to be wary, and dove into the forest.

Great bats, ten thousand strong, swept from their holes in trees, caves, and from beneath drooping palm fronds to feed on the fruit ripening in the canopy above the Maya Maya. Three thousand clotted in the trees ringing the Sombo-Sombo, raining down rinds, pits, and juice on the form in the sand. He heard their loud slurping and smacking, sloppy but necessary feeding habits for creatures that hung upside-down when they fed and would otherwise drown in an excess of juice.

The sticky, splattered body sat up, went to its knees, then pitched forward into the Maya Maya. When it emerged five minutes later, dripping and gleaming in the last of the moonlight, it plunged back into the jungle from which it had come.

Little happened in the night, and that made it the longest in Danson's memory. Every nerve ending screamed for something—anything—to happen. He fought the demons of the night and prayed for angels. He and Wiggins and Ndoki alternated the watch. It was like guarding the ocean against a single shark attack. Though they kept their backs to a sturdy tree, none of the three experienced a moment's confidence; and when each took his turn at post, the other two lay wide-eyed and listening.

The jungle forest was as loud as a crowded gymnasium. Wild hogs grunting and the clack of a hornbill pulverizing a tough bit of fruit joined the scrabbling of the shrew, the shrill chatter of the cicada, and the crunch of a beetle's body in the mouth of a bearded chameleon. A serval noisily scavenged a dead gazelle. A startled elephant awakened to find its trunk invaded by a battalion of army ants. Snorting and trumpeting pitifully, it rammed headlong into trees and struck its trunk bloody to dislodge the voracious horde. But they clung and sliced off tiny bits of flesh and drove their immense host mad in the night.

Sometime in the hour before twilight, Ndoki climbed a tree and drained the water from the concave leaves into a skin bladder and all three men had a good and satisfying drink. The water was warm but sweet. "Full of mosquito larvae, but fit to drink," declared Wiggins. It was the adult mosquitoes that were dangerous, but Reg could have done without Jigs's smug pronouncements. *Hoist a flagon of yellow fever, me hearties! Down the hatch and not a bacterium wasted!* He'd give his birthright to know where the purifying drugs had disappeared to.

Reg hoped Kimboki would appear, but the boy had darted into a leafy abode, and that was the last he'd seen of him.

The minutes dragged by, the dark made darker by a craving for home and family. The Congo rain forest, all seven and a half million acres of it, became as claustrophobic as a locked closet. The old panic came back.

Once when Reg was six he'd crawled under the house to a spot beneath the neighboring duplex. There was a small vent hole to the outside where he could see the little girls next door having their backyard tea party without them seeing him. He called and growled and teased them mercilessly. Try as they might, they could not tell where the disembodied voice came from. At first their little heads swiveled back and forth, and they ran about the yard in confusion. They then became scared and ran into the house crying, their tea party ruined.

He had laughed hilariously, trying to cover his mouth with a grubby hand to keep the merriment from penetrating the floor above and exposing his whereabouts to the girls' mother. Spent at last and the objects of his cruel sport having fled, he'd turned to leave the crawl space. It was then he had discovered that he didn't know the way out. He had crawled into a web of spiders. Something dropped into his hair. The exposed pipes looked like skeleton bones. A cat darted from behind a cement support with a dead mouse in its mouth. He'd pushed up from the ground in fear and cracked his head on the flooring. Panic. He had wet his pants and yelled for help, beating both fists against the underside of the house, hot tears streaking his filthy cheeks.

The mother next door found him there and kept calling to him until he'd crawled to her and was pulled sobbing from the hole in the foundation. His elbows were torn and his pants damp and black with who knew what from the land beneath the house. But worst of all, he looked straight into the faces of the two girls he'd terrorized. They laughed right back in his face, and their mother said it served him right.

Now, the oppressive heat and lack of any breeze pressed down upon him as tight and confining as the crawl space beneath the duplex of his childhood. It was Ndoki's turn at the watch. Danson's foot was asleep even if the rest of him wasn't. He got up, stomped and hobbled about until feeling returned, then flopped back down, shifting Bascomb's Bible which doubled as a pillow. "Your word is a lamp unto my feet and a cushion unto my head," he mumbled appreciatively. Soon, though, he turned restlessly, punching the ground in frustration, trying to shove away the monsters of the mind.

The bush viper wound slowly nearer the creature thrashing about on the ground. The snake's skull bones were particularly sensitive to vibrations, and it made course corrections based on them. Its other major tracking device was the constantly flickering tongue. Sampling the air for microscopic scent particles, the tongue telegraphed them to the snake's sensors for instant analysis. The highly sophisticated chemoreceptor located internally on each side of the snout identified the odors as prey, mate, or other.

The viper paused. The night's hunt hadn't gone well. This highly agitated "other" demanded further investigation.

The viper summoned one hundred fifty vertebrae and ribs to attention, like a symphony conductor, resuming its forward glide as effortlessly as water on a slide. Taking advantage of every irregularity in the surface of the ground, it proceeded in lateral undulation until it was two feet from Reg Danson's right leg. It did not "think" about striking but sensed that it would. Its folding front fangs lay flat along the roof of the mouth ready to drop down and inject the deadly stream. Behind them were several reserve fangs ready to replace the main set which were periodically shed in battle or rough feeding.

One hundred fifty milligrams of complex toxin filled the venom glands of the bush viper. One hundred would be lethal to something this large.

The viper gathered into S-shaped coils. Danson stirred again, shifting his right leg, presenting a clear threat. He opened his eyes and saw the snake. The viper struck.

Instead of sinking its fangs into soft flesh, the viper's sensors locked on a closer, more immediate threat that in a split second had come between the snake and Reg Danson.

Snake jaws clamped around the stick at one end. A child's hands gripped the other. With a deft flick of the forearms, Kimboki flipped the snake and stick into the bush.

In place of a poisonous snakebite on his calf, Reg found a little boy scrambling madly up his leg, planting trembling arms around his neck. It wasn't the first time God had come in the form of a child.

"Four kids killed in Kenya last month," Wiggins mumbled sleepily. He coughed, snorted, combed something from his beard, and pillowed his head on rough arms. "They were fleeing bandits. Camped by a river. Three poisoned by cobras, the other crushed by a python. Dirty shame . . . dirty, dirty shame . . ." Wiggins concluded his report by snoring loudly.

Reg and the boy dozed together for a time, Danson at last able to relax around the bare bundle that was Kimboki. The youngster's even, peaceful breathing brought enormous comfort, like all ten pounds of Tony, the newborn, had on his first night at home.

When the clicking began was difficult to say. It was at first part of the cicadas digging deep for the bass notes. Then it separated and rose above the clearing. Kimboki went rigid at the sound, eyes flat with fear.

Reg, Jigs, and Ndoki bolted to their feet. The Ologus materialized from their huts in the twilight, spectral silhouettes bowed by the descending weight of the sound.

It had no discernable source. It grated, scraping the nerves raw, setting them on edge like nails on a chalkboard.

Danson slipped the Bible inside his shirt with the look of a drug enforcement agent donning a bulletproof vest.

The explorers rushed to the center of the clearing, whirling about, straining to spot the source, dreading its meaning.

"KKKKKEEEEKKKKK-KKK-KAAWWWW-KKKAA AKKKK . . ." It rained down from the trees, bounced up from the ground, tore the air with the bite of a ripsaw. The explorers stood braced, the tranquilizer gun in the missionary's grip, the pistol in Reg's, a bow taut and arrow at the ready in Ndoki's. Kimboki made little fists as if he too were ready for all comers.

But the people barely moved. They made no effort to arm themselves. They stood helpless, surrendered.

Ngomba appeared as if by magic on the wooden platform in the trees, one minute part of the trees, the next born of them. His face was a mask of white mud. He carried no visible weapon. He stood looking down at them, impossibly tall.

To Reg's astonishment, the Ologus—men, women, and children—went to their knees. They began to wail and throw dirt into the air. Many reached out to Ngomba, closing the distance between them and their *griot* by caressing the air in front of them.

Their chief had risen from the dead!

"White Danson, white Wiggins," Ngomba said, a smirk in every word. "You ought to be well pleased with events as they are."

"I don't follow you," Reg said, wondering if Wiggins could hit the man with the tranquilizer dart despite the distance, the shadows.

"Surely you've heard of the two men cooking fish by the river?" Ngomba did not wait for a reply. "One man tells the other, 'Please help yourself.' The other agrees and takes the larger fish. Some tense moments pass between them before the first man says, 'That wasn't really necessary. Had you given me first choice, I would have taken the smaller fish.' The second man replied, 'Then what are you complaining about; you have it, don't you?'"

"Your point?" Reg asked bluntly.

Ngomba grinned from ear to ear. "The point is that white God men prefer the lower estate, do they not? Once again you have it, so what are you complaining about?"

Jigs debated whether to shoot from there or to entice Ngomba to the ground. How? Invite him to a fireside chat?

"There's a vast difference between humility and ridicule," said Danson, measuring the words. "I would think that to be worthy of the title of *griot,* you would need to earn the people's respect, not terrorize them into it. What's to keep *you* from getting an arrow in the back?"

Ngomba roared with laughter. "*Debt,* you arrogant foreigner! Do you think they were better off *before* I came? The Strong One had reduced their numbers by half. Only someone with the authority and strength of Ngomba could reason with the Strong One.

"You think you have God's ear at all times, white Danson, and yet you know nothing of the devil in yourself. You and your puny faith! Even you owe my people a debt. Yes, it was the Nubians who preserved the sacred Ark of the Covenant passed to us by Menelik, son of King Solomon. We entrusted the chest with its Ten Commandments from High God to the black Jews of Ethiopia who kept it in a fortress on an island in Lake Tana, source of the Blue Nile. It is a gold-covered box, about this wide"—here he held his hands three or four feet apart—"and perhaps this high"—about two feet—"moved from place to place on long poles."

Reg started. "You don't mean you've *seen* it?"

Ngomba laughed again. "It is still there, I tell you, a relic like none other!"

Reg's eyes glowed at the thought. "Describe it for me. In detail. Please!"

"Danson!" shouted Jigs. "Don't be taken in by this charlatan!

"He's a conjurer and a thief. He led us to believe he knew only of the book of Genesis when, in fact, he probably knows it all. The man's a deceiver."

Reg fought the temptation. Wiggins was right. They had to stop Ngomba and stop him fast.

Quick as a bush pig, Kimboki charged into the open, picked up a stone, and threw it at the platform with all his five-year-old might. Physically, it fell far short. Symbolically, it struck Ngomba between the eyes.

With the agility of a jungle cat, the *griot* jumped from the platform and landed five feet from Kimboki, showering the boy in dirt and duff from the forest floor. Kimboki reached down, picked up another stone, and pitched it at Ngomba.

The rock bounced off the mighty chest like a pebble off a mountain. The white mud mask contorted into a devil's frown, and a giant hand closed around Kimboki's throat.

Lifted high into the air by his neck, Kimboki kicked and punched and fought as hard as he could, having all the success of a butterfly with its wings pinned together.

Reg fired, the bullet grazing Ngomba's left shoulder. The *griot* dropped the boy in surprise and turned on Wiggins.

"Save the last bullet!" yelled Jigs, taking quick aim with the elephant doper.

Ngomba stumbled forward at the same time that the dart struck his thigh. He grabbed the missionary by the front of the shirt and gave a mighty wrench. Jigs's shirt pocket gave way.

The pipe and the lighter fell at their feet but the contents of the pouch of Blackhorn's Best flew in every direction, a small wad of rich, black tobacco closely followed by an arc of glittering diamonds flashing brilliantly in the new dawn light.

With a shout and a rush, the people and Wiggins dove for the diamonds. Ngomba swayed and grabbed Wiggins by the hair, pulling him back from the melee. Every time a diamond was fished up from the ground, an Ologu held it aloft, exclaimed aloud, and promptly swallowed it.

Though Wiggins shouted for them to stop and threatened them with eternal punishment, the diamond feeding frenzy continued unabated until no more could be found and the Ologus collapsed in weary heaps.

With the crash of falling timber, Ngomba hit the ground.

Kimboki approached his Goliath cautiously, prodding the Nubian with one foot. Satisfied the man was unconscious, the boy hopped onto the sleeping man's chest and stood with hands on hips like the conquering hero.

Wiggins sobbed quietly, the empty tobacco pouch in his hand. Reg picked up the pipe and the lighter and set them in Jigs's lap. He put a hand comfortingly on his friend's shoulder and squeezed. "*Diamonds,* Jigs? Real, honest-to-goodness diamonds?"

Wiggins nodded miserably. "My ace in the hole. My one hedge against God's deciding I should die in the Congo alone. One more year and I was going to contact my Kay and ask her to take me back, see if maybe I couldn't find some acreage in some pretty little valley back in the Catskills where nobody'd find us and we'd salvage what we could of what might've been. Even if she wouldn't have me back—and who could blame her?—I'd give her the jewels as a small token of the king's ransom she was ready to give me once upon a time . . ." His voice caught.

Reg tried a different tack. "Why'd the people react like that, Jigs? Why'd they—why'd they *swallow* the diamonds?"

Wiggins laughed bitterly. "Pygmies are such romantics. They've never seen diamonds. When I showed one to Kakese back at Sangha, she lit up like a searchlight and told me it was a star that had fallen from the sky. These poor fools thought it was a celestial shower. Eat a star, rise up to heaven. They think they've dined on the divine!"

Kimboki jumped between the giant's legs, picked something from the ground, and took it to Jigs. He tugged on the missionary's pant leg and unfolded his little fist. The sun caught the pure, uncut diamond, and it flashed with the white light of a lightning strike. Wiggins brightened a moment and started to reach for the gem. He stopped and looked at the boy-who-grew-too-fast, whose eyes had seen too much and most of it sad. He grasped the boy's thin wrist in one hand and folded the fingers back around the diamond with the other.

"Kimboki's," he said, pressing the boy's fist against the bare little chest.

A violent harangue rained down upon them from the wooden platform. Bigshot was centerstage, strutting and yelling so fast the spittle flew. Unless Reg missed his guess, this one was bucking for promotion to *griot* first class.

"Who-wee!" exclaimed Jigs when Bigshot finally took a breath. "This guy says the gods brought their beloved Ngomba back from the underworld only to have him killed again by the white God men. To have killed a resurrected one is a first around here, but I wouldn't be surprised if it were punishable only by death. How long's Ngomba going to be under?"

Reg bit his lip. "I'm not sure. It only takes a fraction of an elephant dose to bring down a man, but I'm not sure how much was in the thing or at what strength. Let's just hope he won't be entertaining anytime soon."

"Hmmm," Wiggins said, pulling on his beard. "Well, then, I think I'll just see what I can get stirred up. Get away if you can."

He jumped to his feet, shoved Danson aside, and hurled his cap into the dirt. A stream of the hottest pygmy invective poured from his mouth, scorching the clearing in no uncertain terms. Wiggins hopped up and down like an infuriated leprechaun, then hoisted himself up a tree opposite the platform, finally settling into a roomy crotch between two gnarled, vine-choked branches. At that height, he resembled an Irish mountain gorilla, beating his chest and challenging the pretender to the throne on the opposite side of the clearing. Jigs flung his fists at Bigshot, denounced the braggart, and found it the biggest joke in the rain forest that his pygmy opponent should presume to know the fate of Ngomba.

"Ngomba is tired from his long journey back. We gave him a sleeping medication that will help him rest before again assuming all the many duties of governing the people. We have done Ngomba a favor, and this is the thanks we get? Come elders, bend your ears close to Ngomba's mouth and nose and feel his breath living hot upon your skin. A dead man does not breathe! This man, this big brave warrior up in the trees, is a liar! He wants nothing more than to rob your chief of his honor and his position while Ngomba sleeps!"

At that moment, the heavens split wide and rain such as Danson had never before seen fell in heavy, thunderous torrents. It was as if all the vast stores of precipitation above the earth were draining through a single hole right above them. Even the great, leafy aquifer of the rain forest could not handle the sudden release of an ocean of rain.

The jungle all but disappeared behind curtains of water. The heavy crash of the rain was deafening. The earth turned to mud and the humans became as sticks in the current. But no one sought shelter. Wiggins's foolhardy challenge to Bigshot rang in their ears. Bigshot himself seemed momentarily stunned at the effrontery. Then a deadly evil twisted his face, and he gave the order.

Six warriors advanced on the tree with its missionary, their drawn bows giving the command for Jigs to come down. Instead, he grinned like a lunatic, threw back his hoary head, and began to sing deep and raspy. "Wade in de wa-ter, wade in de water, chil-der-en; wade in de wa-a-ter, God's gonna trouble de wa-a-ter!"

*What's he doing singing Harriet Tubman's theme song?* Reg wondered. *Has he flipped his lid?*

The warriors with drawn bows looked confused. Would Ngomba be angry if what the missionary said was true and the *griot* merely slept? Should they take Bigshot captive?

Every eye in the clearing was riveted on the tree with its mad soloist shouting the Negro slave spiritual with all the gusto of a man about to step into a golden coach. Through the punishing rain they saw the faint outline of dripping beard and sodden torso. Those closest could see the serpent tattoo rising defiant opposite the torn shirt pocket. In moments, they were sure, the song would be silenced and the white God man would be face down in the swirling mud, the red of his blood consumed in a sea of brown.

Water cascading onto his head and pouring off his hairy chin, Wiggins gulped for air, tilted his face to the sky—eyes closed, a smile of pure joy on his lips—and threw arms wide as if performing Falstaff on a Paris stage.

Slick were the fingers that gripped the arrows. They awaited the command to kill, yet their minds were troubled.

Reg felt paralyzed. *Dear God, what should I do? Why is he doing this? What—*

" . . . follow the drinking gourd!" The blurry, uncertain thoughts in Reg's brain cleared in a sudden rush of understanding. Wiggins was singing to him in code.

The black slaves had followed the drinking gourd, the Dipper, to the north, to the Underground Railroad, to freedom. But abruptly Jigs switched back to "Wade in de wa-ter, wade in de wa-ter Reg-i-nald . . ."

Reg locked eyes with Wiggins. The man's eyes pleaded, then commanded, even the tenor of his voice besought him, implored him to take action. *He wants me to escape. Where? North? That's not the way we've come. No, he's not staying with that song. He keeps repeating the wading, wading, wading . . . I can't leave Wiggins and Kimboki here . . .* He looked desperately at Ndoki. The man jerked his head in the direction of the far fringes of camp, toward the river.

*I can divert their attention. They'll keep Wiggins and Kimboki as bait to get me back. Their attention will be split—divide and conquer. A miracle, please God . . .*

Danson backed slowly away from the flooding clearing and the fallen *griot,* unnoticed by the rest who took halting steps toward the tree, drawn irresistibly by the strange spectacle.

Danson turned and ran down the path that Kimboki's mother had taken. He must stay clear-headed, to capture the sense of Jigs's message. He left huge, deep tracks a blind man could follow. Trying to step only on the undergrowth, he slipped and fell on his face and sucked in a mouthful of gritty water. Rising again, heart pounding, he willed himself to remain still and to pray.

Wiggins, still singing with the abandon of an emancipated field hand, closed his eyes tightly and did the same.

The dark form watched the sodden, retreating figure through slitted eyes. Water sloshed over and about his body lying where it had fallen. He relaxed turgid muscles, reached down, removed the tranquilizer dart from the muscular thigh. He brought the leg to his mouth and sucked the drug from the point of entry and spat into the flood.

Any sorceror worthy of the name practiced the art. Indian fakirs were best at it, and one of them had taught him how to prevent sharp objects from penetrating the flesh beyond the superficial. Beds of nails were for the tourists. Real holy men could tense prior to impact and resist anything sharp and harmful. With his own eyes he'd witnessed knives thrown at a fakir bounce harmlessly off the man's rigid body. Stupid Danson did not know that the needle performed but a pinprick and little of the drug had been discharged.

He rose from the ground, rivers of brown mud washing down the steel-hard legs and over the ridges of powerful calf muscles. White Wiggins was on his knees in the crotch of the tree, swaying to the freedom song, hands clasped to his chest, face turned to God, oblivious to all else. Without a word, a warrior handed his bow and arrow to his twice risen chief.

Ngomba turned. The footprints were flooded and widening in the pounding rain but easily followed. The giant's mud mask cracked and ran. A cruel smile wreathed the black and white face. Kimboki saw it and started to run after his kind friend. Ngomba shot out a long arm and caught the boy by the hair. He lifted the child until he walked on tiptoes like a wooden marionette and was flung into the grip of the warrior. Wiggins, singing louder than ever as if to stay within Danson's hearing, did not hear Kimboki's cries.

The cruel smile broadened. Divide and conquer. First Danson, then Wiggins.

Some of the Ologus prostrated themselves in the mud and water, helpless before this god from a far place, this god that did not stay dead. Others, warriors, shouldered their quivers and picked up their bows, ready for pursuit.

Ngomba waved them off. He squared his shoulders and began the hunt alone.

# 21

The vast dome of the forest canopy formed a green and leafy lid to a world like none they'd ever seen. Kay and Tony, despite their anxious thoughts, craned their necks and exclaimed over the stunning array of life.

The day stank from the vapors that belched up from the swamp and crept about the motor launch. They were drenched to the skin by a recent rainstorm so powerful that all hands had been forced to bail. Now the steamy rankness of their clothing and bodies mingled with swamp bottom gases to create a stench which in its potency was quite unlike anything else they'd ever smelled.

But it mattered little. In fact, it transported them back in time to a primordial land where life was robust and took on the fantastic forms of massive beasts and enormous plants. Tony had little trouble imagining the four hundred species of dinosaurs that once roamed free and excitedly made certain none of the others had trouble imagining them either.

"Thigh bone ninety-five inches long! Reptiles four stories tall, the weight of a dozen elephants! Imagine *brachiosaurus* standing there in those reeds, reaching his neck up and shooing off a big old pterodactyl, a bird with no feathers. How could those incredible birds fly? Because there was probably twice the oxygen we've got now! Vapor canopy above, lush plant life below, atmospheric pressure at sea level maybe thirty-two pounds per square inch compared with not quite fifteen pounds per square inch today. That makes for 'heavy' air, and heavy air holds up flying dinosaurs with or without feathers, thanks all the same!"

Kay laughed at the young Danson's enthusiasm, which threatened to fill the boat as surely as the rain an hour before.

"And weren't the theropods delightful creatures?" said Fulgate, joining in the spirit of the thing, hoping to shake the gloom he had been feeling since Sangha. "The carnivores, not the least of which was *Rex* himself, weren't too neighborly. The skeleton of one *coelophysis,* a man-sized meat eater, was found with a baby of its own species inside its stomach cavity. Devouring your own kind, now *that's* unfriendly!"

Officer Akeley slipped the wheel over to the left, taking the launch on a smooth arc around a jagged rock outcrop that would have performed open-hull surgery on the craft had he not been paying attention. "Men have devoured one another for years," he interjected without looking at Fulgate. The hard set of his jaw, the inscrutable sunglasses, the military precision in every move, underscored Officer Akeley as a man of little comedy. He engaged in no banter.

"We are, of course, more sophisticated about it," continued Akeley humorlessly. "We dam the Mother Nile, the water backs up, and instead of washing away the filth of humans and animals as it did when it ran free, it collects the egg-bearing defecations, and our people drink parasitic plagues to their peril.

"Civil wars push people from border to border, people with no immunity to the diseases they find when herded into camps and crowded along the waterways. The black flies proliferate, and river blindness flows from their bites.

"Overgrazing and overcultivation are stripping away the fragile soil, and the great deserts are growing. The wildlife vanishes, and the 'enlightened' governments collect the displaced peoples into city slums where riots and disease may flourish unchecked. I would not worry about one infant dinosaur when millions of Africans perish in the name of progress."

"Such cheery news," Tony whispered in Kay's ear on his way to the middle of the boat where the bananas were stored in a metal cabinet. On the way back, he handed her one and spoke softly, "*Coleophysis* means 'hollow nature.' Part of their skeletal frame actually contained some hollow bones." He jerked his head in Akeley's direction and winked. "I'll bet you a dozen bacon double cheeseburgers this guy's bones are hollow. You on?"

Kay laughed and tucked an errant strand of silvery hair behind her ear. Her low, guarded reply took on a mock aristocratic tone. "Get away, you ruffian! You know I play the ponies exclusively." She reached out a carefully manicured hand and squeezed his arm.

Tony felt happy and sad all at once. She reminded him so much of his mother, beautiful Barbara Louise Danson who kidded and poked and took the top bunk at family camp when you were afraid of heights and the bottom bunk when you weren't. Barbara Danson, whose impersonation of Margaret Thatcher was perfect. Her Winston Churchill wasn't bad either, but her impression of Bob Hope doing Richard Nixon was priceless. This warm and generous lady beside him made him miss his dead mother. His grandma was gone, his dad missing . . . too much change. He wished his mother would call him over to the pencil markings on the wall by the refrigerator. He must have grown six inches since she saw him last, and a good two feet since "Tony Tiger, four feet high and rising" had been scribbled next to that thrilling milestone.

"Reptiles keep growing all their lives," he said aloud, attempting to jumpstart the conversation. "Hard to keep 'em in shoes!" He smiled crookedly.

An avenue of coarse ferns stretched before them, those on opposite banks almost touching midstream, forming a living archway above their passage. The air beneath the ferns was honeysuckle sweet, and an occasional growth of ugly orange protruded from the fronds. Akeley steered close to the bank, and Officer Katianda reached over the side and plucked the hideous pods. He proffered them to the other passengers. "While they are not much to look at, they contain a sweet disposition," he announced, much more agreeably than his partner might have. He tore the fruits apart and dispensed them to a delighted chorus of noisy sucking and lipsmacking *ahhs*.

"The Ologus' last known whereabouts is about a day's journey as the river flows," said Akeley, eyes locked on the spot where the next bend disappeared down the throat of the voracious jungle. "They've stopped traveling the river because they say *Mokele-mbembe* fills it." He smiled mirthlessly. "That is when superstition becomes the policeman's ally."

Three bends ahead, the river channel narrowed into a long, slender throat of a passage known as the Wamba-Goma. Reed-choked, in places the channel was navigable only by raising the propellers and poling through with long lengths of sapling.

Sweating, straining, calling good-natured insults to one another in encouragement, the rescuers pushed and prodded the sleek craft over and around the waving green and white vegetation that welled up from the bed of the sluggish Wamba-Goma.

A fantastic ceiling of matted growth, impossibly twisted together in a complicated weaving of forest artistry, pressed low above them. At one point, they were forced to lie almost prone in the boat. Progress was possible only when the two officers sank poles into the opposite banks and pried forward in unison at the same time Tony and Fulgate reached up and hand-over-hand literally pulled the ceiling past. Kay jokingly offered to go below and make tea.

It was not long before the stagnant, blistering air had them all perspiring like stevedores, dark stains turning the crisp, precise police uniforms sodden and limp. Muscles ached and hordes of insects fed upon white skin with itchy, stinging enthusiasm. The white victims slapped and groaned and willed the tiny monsters to die.

"Eat no bananas," ordered Akeley, not appearing bothered in the least by the flying hellions. "When you eat bananas, you sweat sweetly. That and your fair skin create mosquito paradise."

"*Now* he tells us," grumbled Tony, earning a look of mock rebuke from Kay.

Ahead, where the ceiling lifted and the Wamba-Goma ended in a widening of the Maya Maya, something stirred. In the fluid-filled canals of its brain, thin and delicate middle ear bones received the voices and the sloshings of approaching danger. It knew no enemies, only the occasional annoyance of a hippo or a crocodile. It had been some time since a boatload of the smaller, weaker mammals had ventured by.

The bones of six humans lay scattered among the roots and caught beneath the rocks that formed this portion of the Maya Maya. Thrown from their canoe by a titanic strength, they had drowned or been slaughtered by crocodiles and their bones cleaned of all flesh by fish and time.

It shifted, submerging beneath the waters like a descending submarine until only its cold, empty eyes and the flat top of its hard, leathery head showed. Like a mighty chain of pumping stations moving water from a mountain reservoir to the city, a system of eight hearts pushed thirty gallons of blood from the thick chest cavity to the brain through thirty-six feet of neck.

The brain made its decision.

The thing turned in the direction of the oncoming boat, sending a surging wave of water far up the bank into the forest beyond. It exhaled deeply, blasting water from its nostrils in a jet of milky foam. It settled again onto four heavy pylon legs and waited.

**B**igshot skirted the foot trail, preferring the protection and concealment of the untrod forest. The rain penetrated less in the close rank and file of tree trunks, stout vines, and rubbery undergrowth. His lean, lithe limbs barely grazed the ground as he ran, heart pumping madly, barely giving attention to the clumps and knots and tangles he maneuvered. He ran on instinct and hatred.

He held his weapon in a crushing grip, as if to squeeze it empty of fluid. The rough hide quiver scraped the muscled back and drove him on. It mattered not if white Danson or *griot* Ngomba came before him. He had poison enough for both.

He knew the trickery Ngomba was capable of, the smooth magic that fooled little children, doddering old men, tittering women, and impressionable youth. But an imitator, even a great one, couldn't fool another imitator. And Ngomba had made the mistake of turning Bigshot into an enemy by belittling him, ordering him about like a camp dog, forcing him to shrink in the towering shadow of the *griot's* deceit and cunning that rose higher even than the Nubian himself.

Only Littleshot had recognized the superiority in Bigshot, the toughness, the grit, the pure Efe blood that by all that was sacred above and below the earth gave him alone the right to rule the Ologus. As long as Littleshot was there to feed and stroke his older brother's ego, Bigshot had been content to bide his time and live off Ngomba's tyrannical favors. Now Littleshot was dead, and the only adoration Bigshot could expect was what he wrested from Ngomba's gigantic grasp.

The gods had sent the white men to entice Ngomba to his doom. So charmed was the giant by this outside challenge to his rule that he went blind to the greater threat at his right hand. Bigshot had dreamed often of slitting the stout throat and taking the ear with the gold ring as a trophy. Worn about his neck, it would serve as an emblem of strength and a constant reminder to the people that he now held their very lives in his hands—Efe hands, not the dirty hands of a Nubian.

Loud snorts warned of wild hogs nearby. Bigshot glanced defiantly in that direction but did not pause in his plunge toward greatness.

White Danson was a fool. The gods liked to use fools to accomplish their business. But he was a fool with a will and would have to die. White Wiggins might prove useful for raiding the villages beyond the forest. Bigshot's tastebuds craved the sweets and the meats of the river traders. The missionary knew the habits and the peculiarities of the river Africans. To keep him alive on manioc and monkey entrails would be a small price for the delicacies of the far places.

Ngomba, he knew, would play with his prey, keeping back, enjoying the stalk before pouncing. Bigshot would angle through the forest and intercept Danson quickly, kill him, and lie in ambush for the main quarry.

Overhead, low in the forked branches of the *anjuafa* tree, the shimmering patterns of light and dark shifted, and eight feet of dappled markings separated from the dance of sun and shade. The tawny yellow streak, dotted in spots of black, flowed silently from limb to limb, tracking the dark shape below, matching its pace.

Soon, Bigshot saw the muddy, disheveled figure of Reg Danson. Crouched low, Danson was making for the Maya Maya, fighting to keep a footing in the relentless rain. He kept glancing back over his shoulder, the weight of the Ologus bowing his back, the worry for his comrades haggard upon his features.

Bigshot stopped at the butt end of a recently fallen tree, thick and heavy with rot. He loaded the bow with a fresh arrow of glistening death. Twenty yards of unobstructed clearing lay carved by the fall of the tree. White Danson would cross it in less than ten breaths, and there the man and the arrow would meet.

When the man below raised the weapon and drew back the bowstring, something innate in the spotted creature above coiled and released. One hundred and fifty pounds of muscle and bone dropped from the sky and drove the pygmy hunter to the ground.

The leopard sank its teeth into the pygmy's throat, silencing him forever. Clawing and slashing the body to ribbons with powerful hind feet, it took the head in its mouth and gave it a sharp wrench. Bones cracked and the scalp came away from the skull.

Danson reached the gash of light in the forest canopy created by an immense fallen tree. He scrambled up onto its trunk and saw the sinuous flow of the Maya Maya beyond. He was exposed here, and the hammering of the rain made him pause but an instant. He looked back along the trunk to its base and saw a wild rustling in the bush. *Discovered?!* He didn't wait to find out. He jumped to the ground and plunged forward to the edge of the river. The words of Wiggins's song ringing in his mind, he waded into the shallows and immediately the telltale footprints were no more.

*Good old jungle boy! Hang on! God's got a plan to get us out of here; I've just got to figure out where He put it.* Reg prayed fiercely for protection for Kimboki and the dear old grouch of Sangha Mission. He'd kiss that grinch if he ever got another chance. "Please, God, another chance!" he said aloud.

The leopard's head jerked up, hot blood rimming its broad muzzle. A crimson coating dripped from the ends of white whiskers. More man scent drifted past his nostrils, and then it was gone. He'd be content with the kill he had. It was meatier than the hares, bushbucks, and scrawny dog pups stolen from the fringes of the man camp.

At last, having had its fill, the wiry cat grasped the carcass by the neck and gripped the bark of the standing tree with its strong claws. Another five minutes and the remainder of the leopard's food was safely stored in the crotch of the tree, out of reach of the greedy bushpigs and other ground-dwelling molestors.

The rains subsided, then shut off altogether with the turning of some meterological spigot. The leopard stretched itself full-length along a limb and began to clean and groom the soiled pads of its broad paws. The sun relit the scene, bathing the leopard in brilliant warmth. The cat yawned hugely and dozed, oblivious to the gathering flies.

The motors restarted with a well-tooled roar. The sleek white launch spit free of the dark green tunnel of the Wamba-Goma clean as a loose tooth. Kay and Tony whooped an enthusiastic "All right!" and inspected one another's hair and clothing for hitchhiking vermin. Tony flicked a two-inch beetle off her shoulder. It plopped into the water, righted itself, and with a husky buzzing, took angry flight.

Tony flexed his biceps and gave Kay an arrogant wink. "The Exterminator," he quipped boastfully. "Our muscle versus whatever bugs you!"

The bow rose with a sudden rush of engines and came down with a hollow thud as if striking a submerged log. With a sharp jolt, the bow flew skyward, nearly swamping the motors. Akeley fought the wheel, passengers and supplies hurled against each other in the stern.

Katianda wrenched the machine gun out of its holder, frantically trying to keep his footing. Akeley threw full power to the engines. At first, they gave a coughing growl, smoke and gasoline fumes pouring from them in protest. Then, with a whining howl and a surge of horsepower, the twin screws caught and chewed a hole in the Maya Maya.

The police launch flew up and over the obstruction. On the descent, the stern pointed to the sky, propellers flying free of the water. Passengers and debris slammed Akeley and Katianda flat against the steering cowl.

With a sickening *dang-chew-dang,* the spinning propeller blades bit deep into the obstruction like axes through a rotten log. A hideous bawling ripped the air, the inhuman wail reverberating through the hull and into the very marrow of their bones.

The stern began to descend and sky was replaced with the bloodied head and kinked neck of a mammoth reptile.

The hull of the launch smacked the surface of the Maya Maya with a loud clap.

The weapon lay dumb in Katianda's paralyzed hands.

With a mighty gurgling rattle, the thing inhaled as if sucking in the very wind. Blood spouting from its nose and ruined eye sockets, it stopped its intake with a crackling in its throat. It pulled back its head, jaws parted, and exhaled with the hiss of a thousand snakes.

A burst of yellow-orange flame shot twenty feet even as the slick, oily neck began its terminal slide beneath the waters. The mouth clamped shut before the flaming breath had dissipated and the terrible face was scorched a meaty red. The cold, vacant eyes glazed over, tendrils of mucus and blood trailed off its snout, and the creature swayed confusedly like a brain-shot elephant. It disappeared with a watery pant, swallowed whole by the Maya Maya.

The boat fled upriver as if it needed no guidance. Akeley's fingers locked rigid around the wheel. The others passed from shock and took a collective gasp, like the grab for air of a wailing infant. Officer Katianda let loose with a Bantu expletive, lifted the unused machine gun, and blasted the trees in a release of tension. Kay jumped and gave a startled cry, burying her face in Tony's chest. Fulgate looked stricken, his mouth moving, but no sound coming out.

Tony hugged Kay Wiggins tightly to his chest, as much to steady his own nerves as to calm hers. Pale blue eyes narrowed grimly, resurrecting the terrifying image of the unspeakable beast in the pool. He tightened his grip on the sobbing woman in his arms and felt again the searing heat of leviathan upon his cheek.

"Hang on, Dad," he whispered, jaw tight. *"Hang on!"*

Twenty-four hours, seemingly endless bends in the river, and a sleepless night were all that separated the rescue party from the terrors of the Wamba-Goma. Frightening images of an indescribable creature met them at every turn in the river—and in their thoughts. Their ears rang still with the hideous sounds of the mangled beast, and the pea-green water looked blood-red out of the corner of every furtive eye.

Even much of the steel in the stoic police of the People's Republic of the Congo seemed to have sunk beneath the unfathomable waters of the Maya Maya. "I thought we would have found them by now," Akeley announced dispiritedly, as if having to justify the delay to the others.

The most remarkable case of unwavering determination was Kay Wiggins's. She hugged her little suitcase all the tighter and kept an anxious but stalwart face turned upriver to the still unknown.

Tony admired the lady's fortitude and loyalty to a man she had not seen in a generation. They made the younger Danson love his dad all the more and want him back all the fiercer.

The river had become increasingly stagnated by luxuriant, waving stands of swamp grass and reeds. The going was slower, and the necessity of hand-poling past the worst congestion came more frequently. At least it kept them busy, forced them to do something besides remember the creature in the pool.

"*Apatosaurus*, from the Greek, meaning 'deceptive lizard,'" said Tony to no one in particular. "Deceptive, because it is often confused with other sauropods. But now . . . now I'd have to say it's deceptive because it's so unlike any sauropods we thought we knew. The head's all wrong, the *fire* . . ." He didn't finish, and no one expected him to.

Officer Akeley snorted in disgust, handed his pole to Katianda, and restarted the engines. "I am quite familiar with backward Western thoughts on all manner of things," he said dispiritedly. "Tell me why, if the African bushman is considered so primitive, your Western scientists believe in evolution and have pronounced what we've seen today with our own eyes as long since vanished from the earth? We've forever known that man's origins are the direct result of divine intervention.

"Yes, there's far more to life than meets the eye. You've heard of the Botswana study?"

Tony thought a moment. "Something to do with their disintegrating culture?"

Akeley looked at the young man approvingly. "It's good that you are learning something other than salvation through free market economics. The Botswana study of the Moshawent Tiokwa tribe shows conclusively that so-called 'civilized' man is headed for extinction because he's forgotten how to live off the land."

Tony nodded vigorously. "Yeah, I remember now. The village children were taught by whites and university-trained blacks that it was backward and savage to forage for fruit, wild grains, tree caterpillars, and other protein-rich insects in times of drought and barrenness. They taught them that civilized prepared foods were the mark of status. Canned peaches over local mangoes. Soon they lost the ability to identify, find, grow, or catch native plants and game. Once they adopted Western eating habits, they became much more susceptible to famine and physical maladies."

"Quite so," said Akeley, cutting the engines and automatically receiving the wooden pole back from Katianda. "While our social acceptability in the world order climbed a notch, our life expectancy took a strange turn for the worse. We need to return to the earth, young Danson, or pull it over us. Modern man is long on ingenuity and short on common sense." He jammed the pole into the bank and pushed with a sweaty grunt. Tony grabbed another pole and helped propel the boat forward through the weeds.

When they broke out again into unclogged waters, the channel widened, the surrounding terrain becoming decidedly less swampish and giving way to forest. Poles once again stowed, Tony gave Akeley an appreciative smile. "I think I could learn a lot from you, sir. I'm an American consumer, born and bred, but it wouldn't take much to send me back to nature. I like surviving by my wits."

Akeley looked him over appraisingly, two images of Tony reflected in the lenses of the policeman's sunglasses. "My guess, young Danson, is that you would outlast most of your white brothers in such a test." The officer turned back to the river, as stoic and detached as before. Tony flexed a bicep in Kay's direction, winked, then hooked both thumbs in his shirt boastfully.

"Even if you are prone to arrogance," concluded Akeley without glancing up from the river. The thin smile barely creasing his mouth was all that passed for amusement.

Kay had to laugh at that, and the tension eased a little. "Touché," she mouthed at Tony.

Whether the Ologu warriors were spotted before or after the arrow sank into Officer Akeley's thigh a hand breadth above the knee, no one remembered. With a shout of warning, Officer Katianda snatched up the machine gun and took a second arrow in the back of the thigh before getting off a wild shot. Both men collapsed to the floor, pulling Kay Wiggins down with them.

Tony lunged for the controls, ramming the throttle wide open. The launch shrieked forward, a hail of arrows clattering harmlessly against its stern as the craft sped out of range.

"No poison," gasped Akeley, visibly stunned by the sneak attack. "Meant only to scare us off. Find the bowmen, and you'll find your loved ones." He wrenched the projectile from his fellow officer's leg before taking a firm grip on the one in his own. Taking a deep breath, he pulled it out and promptly passed out.

Within seconds, Kay had the first-aid kit out, snipped open the trouser legs of both men with a pair of scissors, and was swabbing the seeping wounds with cotton gauze and antiseptic. She bathed their faces with water, pausing reflectively over Akeley's motionless form.

"This one," she said softly, laying the man's glasses aside, "is a whole lot of talk."

# CHAPTER

# 24

**R**eg Danson crouched in a little pocket of leather-thick fronds just off the trail, waiting for dusk. He'd spent a night there to make certain he'd not been followed and was now waiting again for the cover of darkness before moving out. The back of the hiding place was a dirt embankment, the front a screen of vegetation lit a startling emerald by the lowering sun. He was relatively dry now and had seen no one for several hours. He had begun to relax, his escape complete. He had to think clearly, seek God, find answers.

*Ah, the blessed martyrs! It was not the fire at their feet, but that in their hearts, that mattered most.* Jigs had said that when they'd passed up the chance to run for it back at the honey grove. It hadn't struck Reg as false bravado but as a simple statement of fact.

But that was before Ngomba, before the terrible fate of the Ologus, before life became a moment-by-moment proposition.

Reg wasn't built for martyrdom. Jigs Wiggins, maybe, with his dagger and serpent tattoo with its ironic command to *Kill or be killed.* He could see the bewhiskered red bush of a chin tilted upward in holy defiance of the infidels laying fuel at the missionary's feet. He could hear Jigs's last request that his hands be left untied in order that he might applaud the Almighty even as the flames leapt higher and higher. He could see the hoary head slump forward as the man's spirit left him, just before the flames consumed the stocky body.

He prayed it never came to that.

Reg followed the trail taken by Kimboki's mother, the trail that led to the magical channel that flowed through paradise, the channel that led to the wooden gate and the entrance to Eden.

More than anything, he wanted to become the first human ever to set foot in that place. His heart began to race. *Better than position, better than influence, better than reading about yourself on the front page is to be the first! To settle for last position is OK in Christian servanthood, but to be the first to find a cure, touch the moon, or break the sound barrier, that's the stuff of science. God, you who give me the hunger to solve mysteries, grant me this!*

An excitement and an awe gripped him. He'd encountered no one. Ngomba was drugged with elephant dope, and as long as he was under, so was the will of the pygmy people to go after white Danson. Jigs was a wily guerilla fighter who would keep the people mesmerized long enough for Reg to find what lay beyond the gate.

*Go, Jigsy, go!* Reg imagined how much spiritual hay Wiggins could make with a captive audience. He wouldn't be surprised to return and find an Ologu choir practice in full swing.

*Or he and Kimboki and Ndoki would all be dead.* Reg rejected the gnawing apprehension. What chance did they have with the Ologus? One of them had to get away, to find help, to find . . . *So, Reggie boy, how come you're not going for help? How come you're going back to the place that fascinates you most? How come finding* Mokele-mbembe *means more to you than*—

Reg jerked to his feet. Some things were bigger than the sum of the parts. Science would be utterly rent in two by the discovery of living dinosaurs. The evolutionists who thought they had all their fossils in a row would soon discover that the crypotozoologists they had dismissed as just so many loonies were right all along. The last dinosaurs had not gone extinct from constipation or a meteor strike at the end of the Mesozoic Era. Some had *survived,* along with their cousins the crocodiles and the tortoises. Oh, how all those smug, arrogant lab lizards deserved what was coming to them! Once the news was out, *they* might be the ones facing extinction!

Reg felt the smooth leatherette of Bascomb's Bible inside his shirt, flat against his belly.

He left the blind and waded back into the shallows of the Maya Maya that paralleled the river, careful to obliterate any sign of footprints. He waded in the water just the way Jigs had told him to in song. *Good old Jigsy, guiding me with your caterwauling. Thank you, my friend. Keep the porchlight on and I'll be back—just as soon as I catch me a you know what . . .*

Reg shook his head, willing the misgivings to be gone. It was just Satan trying to get him to abandon the mission, throw everything away . . . Jigs had bought him time. Jigs would want him to go on, to make the discovery a deluded world so desperately needed. He'd bet anything *Mokele-mbembe* lived there. The lagoon where no man had ever set foot was the perfect hideout for the great creatures. Unmolested by man, that little piece of prehistoric real estate was probably home and hearth to any number of exotic fauna from the past. He'd be careful to keep out of sight, observing their habits, marking their location in his mind for a return trip with reinforcements and cameras and . . .

*What about little Kimboki? He trusts you. When Ngomba comes to, Kimboki's life won't be worth . . .*

"And God created great *dragons,* and every living creature that moves . . ." Reg quoted Genesis 1:21 aloud, oblivious to being heard, forcing the voices of doubt to be silent. He deliberately used the word *dragons* instead of the more commonly translated *whales* or *sea creatures.* The translators, he knew, had never laid eyes on such animals, so they understandably substituted what they knew. But twenty-five places in the Bible referred to a creature called *tannin,* which can legitimately be translated *dragon.* In Jeremiah 14:6, these creatures were said to "snuff up the wind" and in Deuteronomy 32:33 were said to have poisonous fangs. In the latter instance, the translators assumed that the creatures were serpents.

"Look now at the behemoth, which I made along with you," Reg recited the words of Job 40, making his heart swell with excitement. The familiar magnet of the unknown pulled him along, filling him again with the wonder of God and the creativity of His hands. "Loins of strength, belly of power, bones of bronze, limbs of iron, 'first of the ways of God; only He who made him' can approach him . . ." *Dear God, grant me permission to approach behemoth this day.*

The banks of the Maya Maya were higher than his head here, then suddenly sloped sharply downward to a widening in the swampland where other waters met the river. The narrow, sketchy trail ended there, and Reg could just make out the flat spot on shore and the huge thicket from which Kimboki's mother had produced a canoe. He debated using the little craft now, then thought better of it. If the Ologus discovered it missing, they would know he had taken it and exactly where he was headed. If he left it, hopefully, they would incorrectly assume he was headed south in an attempt to retrace his way back to Sangha.

He peered down the narrow channel to the north, walled in so tightly by the jungle. In the final sprinkle of day's light, lovely orchid blossoms along the corridor shone like nightlights along a mansion hallway. He shifted in the shallows, the lure of the palm-lined lagoon at the end of the hall more than he could stand.

He hesitated. It was suicide to do what he was about to do. His mother would have had a fit, and wasn't he thumbing his nose at her prayers to even think of it? And what about the giant creature that had so recently dragged Ndokanda to his death? What about Reg's own horribly close encounter with the creature after the canoe flipped and he became entangled in the rope?

Danson's mind fought, and fought hard, to erase the monster's cold blank stare, to shout down the nagging voices. What about Daniel in the den? The lions did not touch him. What of Shadrach, Meshach, and Abednego in the furnace? No flame seared their flesh.

The forest was impenetrable between him and the lagoon. Without the canoe, there was simply no other way.

Reg went to shore and removed his clothes, folded them, and placed them on top of the pistol in the depression beneath a large, flat stone further back along the bank. On top of them, he placed Bascomb's Bible, caressing the cheap cover, thankful for the living Word, hating to leave it behind. He lowered the stone, arranged others randomly against it, and stepped back. The belongings were undetectable.

*But what if you die trying? What good will you be then to those you've left . . .*

Danson forced himself to look into the gloom beneath the trees where he and Jigs had buried Edima, Kimboki's mother, beneath a rude covering of forest matter. All that remained was a little patch of uneven ground scavenged by famished jungle cats.

He waded in to his waist, then struck for the middle of the narrow channel with a strong, easy stroke. The water was thick and warm and soothing against his skin; swimming in it was like bathing in unset gelatin. Reg reveled in the slick feel of it, the way it flowed between his legs and over sore muscles, the way it took the sting from his tormented skin.

Something sounded faintly at the rear of his mind, like the weak racheting of a spent alarm clock. In another place and another time, he might have investigated the source of the doubt, but in this enchanted grotto, making steadily for the forbidden lagoon, it had to wait.

His muscles eased, his limbs stretched, and he settled into the steady rhythm he used at the lap pool at the municipal aqua center back home. A slim Tony darted ahead of him, at thirteen agile as a muskrat. Reg switched to a backstroke, closing tired eyes and watching Tony slice for the bottom of the pool, brown as a Fiji pearl diver. Then he was belly-flat against the rough concrete, bubbles escaping in silver strings from the sides of his mouth. Tony's toes dug into his father's shoulder blades, positioning himself for the launch. Countdown to zero, and Reg pushed off the bottom of the shallow end, catapulting Tony into a shouting, laughing cannonball drop.

Danson smiled dreamily to himself, the green-black water surging over his shoulders and chest, slipping between the fingers with the feel of grape jelly. Tony playing baby beluga, submarining on his father's back, down, down, down . . .

His eyes snapped open. Reg twisted onto his chest, treading water, listening intently to the jungle night. The stream chuckled against the rough and leaf-crowded contours of the riverbed. There were few beasts abroad and a strange absence of insect sounds. Reg gave himself a little "Sheesh!" of derision.

He thought he had heard something, and while he waited, an overripe pod of fruit dislodged from a branch overhead and struck the water near him with a hollow *plook!* He gave himself a playful slap.

Reg swam energetically for the end of the tunnel of water, the scent of gardenia and jasmine wafting low over the river. An abundance of fallen petals, still sweet with aroma, parted to allow the breaststroking human to pass. Lovely, so perfect . . .

Something grazed his leg and with it rushed in a return of the old terror. He gasped, the pulse of fear pounding his forehead with sledgehammer blows. *My God, do not forsake me.* He held himself rigid, treading water woodenly, but the minutes passed and nothing more touched him but water and a faint breeze.

Twenty yards behind, a dark figure separated from the black jungle and slid silently into the water.

Reg floated on his back, resting, breathing deeply of ambrosia, pretending nothing would harm him in Shangri-la. He played the same game he'd played since childhood. He was Werner Janensch, curator of fossil reptiles at the Berlin Museum, and the year was 1909. Under his able command was an army of German paleontologists and hundreds of Africans. Their target: the reptile fossil beds at Tendaguru in what was now Tanzania, the richest bonanza of dinosaur bones in all of the Southern Hemisphere.

For the next four years, the Germans dug and the Africans carried out on their backs and their heads a thousand boxes, or two hundred fifty tons of bones, for shipment to Germany. The insects would have driven pack animals mad.

It was an enormous undertaking. Tendaguru was a four-day journey from the closest seaport, and it took more than 5,400 trips to clear most of the bones. Some of the gargantuan leg and backbones had to be hung on carrying poles slung between two men.

There was a disturbance and the water swirled beneath him. Suddenly, something clamped around Reg's ankle and yanked. He battled against it but it was too powerful. Thrashing and punching the water, Danson struggled to stay above water. It was no use. He was pulled under, managing a hurried lungful of air before the dark waters closed over him.

*The creature, the creature . . . No, God, no!* But with a shifting of fingers below, it was apparent a giant hand gripped him. *Ngomba!*

It was dark as pitch in the night soup of the Maya Maya. Danson fought the panic, chiding himself for being lulled into naked vulnerability by some stupid prehistoric romance. He kicked savagely and twisted his body hard, trying to loosen the vise grip on his ankle, feeling as effective as a mouse in a barrel of molasses. He entertained a brief but ridiculous image of himself stuffed and mounted over the entrance to Ngomba's hut.

The utter stupidity of it all enraged Reg. He lashed a vicious kick with his left foot, connecting solidly with something hard. The grip loosened long enough for him to kick free and scissor to the surface.

Madly, he swam for shore, stumbling to his feet in the unfamiliar shallows. In an explosive rush, his pursuer burst to the surface ahead and to his right in a tower of water like a monster reptile. Reg couldn't stop himself and collided with the dark figure. He threw his arms around the attacker's rib cage, drove his head into the breastbone, and bore him backward into the water.

It was like trying to contain a ton of dynamite once the powder's ignited. Muscles of coiled energy, hard as granite, resisted Danson's embrace. Gathering every ounce of strength he possessed, Reg squeezed. But instead of collapsing, the huge chest expanded, breaking Danson's grip in an instant. Snarling like a cornered tiger, Ngomba pinned Reg to the riverbed, pressing the air from his lungs with superior strength. A massive hand gripped Reg's hair and snapped his head back and down.

The water was no more than eight inches deep, but it closed over Reg's face, racing up his nose and into his lungs.

Ngomba's wild face was just above the surface, splitting and shattering in the distortion from the churning water, tiny blisters peeling off the last of the white paint in fragments of dead skin. Eyes of pure hatred bugged out of his head as he leaned close, all the better to watch the life go out of the man who threatened his paltry kingdom. Thick veins bunched across his forehead, saliva dripping from his crazed and contorted lips.

Then that image too came and vanished in a cloud of mud released by the struggle. Danson choked and thrashed, fighting to raise Ngomba and fling him forever from the earth. But Reg weakened, his lungs threatening to burst.

*Help me, God . . . Help me see your glory . . . help . . . see . . .*

Through the blackening haze of Reg's mind, a light flashed and his eyes followed it. The effort to focus was superhuman . . . a light . . . a point of light catching the incandescent sheen from a sliver of moon . . . a moon halted directly above the thin tear in the forest canopy that was the Maya Maya . . . a ring of gold in the night light . . . a hoop of precious metal hanging from a lobe of evil . . .

Reg threw up his arm and hooked the earring on his middle finger. He gave a savage jerk, felt the weight tip, and rose up at the same instant. His other hand closed on a fist-sized rock. He swung it around and caught the rising Ngomba on the bridge of the nose. The bone mashed dully and another roar stuck in the giant's throat, then died in a guttural choke. He fell back with a splash and was still.

Reg went to his knees, hugging himself, retching and spitting. All of his senses came thundering back at once, nearly knocking him out in their insistence to be heard. When he was thinking straight again, he pulled and wrestled Ngomba's upper body onto a little grassy ledge, propping the great head on a gnarled root. He wasn't going to drown an unconscious man, not even this one.

Another fit of coughing seized him. He doubled over, holding himself, until it passed.

With a deep breath, he returned to the Maya Maya, the wooden barrier looming just ahead. It seemed higher, broader, more impenetrable than before, like the thick, unyielding walls of a medieval fortress. The pygmy's feather bundles scratched against the wood in the faintest of breezes, hoarsely whispering their eerie rumors. The white weavings of string incantations, almost fluorescent in the pitch darkness, blurred into a single band of warning stretched across the barricade. "Do not enter! Go back!" it seemed to say, "Danger ahead!"

But Reg had become convinced that the worst danger in the rain forest was Ngomba himself. The *griot* lay behind, the prize ahead. Reg must press on. There was no time for second thoughts. The smooth wooden poles were as unyielding as before—no amount of pushing and prying budged them in the least. The indecipherable feather fetishes shifted uneasily at the intrusion.

Danson shivered despite the heat. "Probably some kind of symbols either locking evil inside the lagoon or offering dire warnings to would-be prowlers like myself," he said aloud, just to hear the sound of a friendly voice. He inspected the sides of the gate but found no footing in the sheer banks and slick vegetation.

He dove underwater, feeling his way to the river bottom, a stronger current flowing out of the lagoon than he'd at first thought. The stakes fit tightly and could not be weakened by any amount of exertion.

At the left side of the barrier, however, was a narrow gap through which the river rushed in a warm flow. Reg poked at the bank and was able to pull away a few good-sized chunks of dirt. He surfaced and looked about for a suitable tool for prying. A broken branch waved at him from the opposite bank, and he managed to snap it off. With another fill-up on oxygen, he went under and chipped away at the bank, gradually widening the gap.

After another five trips of furious digging, each shorter than the last, Danson felt he could slide sideways between the outside stake and the riverbank. He floated a few minutes to calm the jittery anticipation, looking furtively back down the corridor, trying but failing to discern Ngomba's inert body. Then, with a deep drag of air, he took the final plunge.

He wriggled into the enlarged passage, his back and buttocks scraping the excavated embankment, chest and belly kissing the bark of the wooden poles. Halfway through, the opening tightened and he stuck fast. He hadn't been able to reach far enough with the stick.

He pushed furiously against the poles and sucked in his gut as far as possible. With a mighty heave, and an even mightier petition to the God of drunks and brainless adventurers, he shot through the hole, scraping skin from his stomach.

He swam to the top and stared out at the night sky dusted with a billion white lights. It felt as if he'd been buried alive for years in the dungeon of the rain forest. Now he could see again, and what he saw put a lump in his throat.

The lagoon was an astonishment, as different from the world outside it as Manhattan from Yellowstone. Reg Danson felt like crying. Was he really the first man to see, touch, taste, hear, and feel it?

Tall, stately palms lined its shores and talked among themselves in confident murmurings. Water hyacinths bobbed fragrantly like goose bumps on the back of the oval bay, its glistening surface ruffling slightly in the gentle breeze. The shiny shells of turtles glinted brightly, each moonstruck in turn as he stroked quietly past their log rest stops.

Pristine and fresh, the air felt almost cool on Reg's face as if it rose from somewhere beneath the lake to soothe and settle. The tightness in his chest subsided.

Among the slender, naked palm trunks loomed what must be enormous boulders, big as townhouses back home. They appeared glassy smooth from a distance and as curious a find as anything in the lagoon.

He drifted in the timelessness of the bay, feeling safer than at anytime he could remember. Crossing the divide between the Maya Maya and the lagoon was like passing from a bloody Civil War battlefield onto the peace and security of an Amish farm. No one hated here, surely no one died. Everything seemed milk fresh, warm biscuit snug, eiderdown quilted.

*Am I the first—truly the first man in this Eden? . . . Any new animals for me to name?* Reg laughed at himself but could not help feeling lighter and newer somehow. To have literally nothing to his name, not even clothes, and not care, was a sensation without comparison. There was only God and His creation, and it was everything.

His stomach growled. He swam over and picked some fruit from shore, juicy warm and sugar sweet. He looked up at the boulder closest to him, curious about its oddly symmetrical shape and smooth surface, each so much like the others around it. *Where did they come from? Did they fall from the sky? There are no mountains within hundreds of miles . . .*

Reg turned back to the lagoon, enchanted by the play of moon on water. Sight was a controllable medium of perception.

One could look away from something, and for the moment at least, it was gone from sight. But sound was another matter. It crept up on you from behind and went to your heart through your ears without the slightest invitation. You could not listen away from sound.

A throaty snuffle rose from behind him, then the rasping wheeze of deflated bellows like the wind being driven from a fallen horse.

Reg was rooted to the spot. His neck prickled, every hair ramrod straight despite being wet. He did not want to turn— God knew he did not—but turn he must.

At first nothing appeared different from before.

Then a boulder moved.

Danson's blood turned to ice. A snuffle, a short, high-pitched whine abruptly cut off in the middle. A prolonged snuffling and the boulder shifted onto another plane.

It was alive. It was having a nightmare. It was *Mokele-mbembe.*

Reg Danson was swimming naked in a herd of dinosaurs. All the millennia of time since the Creation compressed into that single enduring moment of stunning realization. God had made leviathan. They had not vanished from the face of the earth but had been forced to retreat to the last great hiding place.

Three-quarters of a football field long, they wrapped their thirty-foot tails about themselves, tucked their thirty-foot long necks back along their bodies, and slept in herds, like cattle in an enormous show barn at the county fair.

A force other than his own drew Reg from the shimmering waters. He waded cautiously onto shore. The stark whiteness of his skin against the indigo night, backlit by the moon-fired sheen off the carbon black lagoon, created the sensation of being shipwrecked in a deserted Caribbean cove. He glanced back at the lagoon, half expecting to see the remains of a rough vessel with tattered sail jutting up from the ocean floor.

He didn't think to breathe. Everything else functioned in-dependently of his numbed mind. The sand and mud of the shal-lows felt foreign to the soles of his feet. He took a jerky half step or two and stopped, a child learning to walk. He wiped his eyes, sweating profusely. Sweat dripped off his brow and trickled down his armpits and chest. Muscles tightened in the grip of a primor-dial fear.

Reg stood next to the creature's back, its vast swarthy side expanding and contracting with the measured heaving of a pant-ing cow. But other than the occasional snuffling and an odd, high-pitched whine like a canine struggling through a bad dream, the creature seemed in no distress.

Danson's nostrils twitched from an acrid combination of sulphur and elephant bedding strong upon the night breeze.

*The more I know, the more does my faith approach that of the Breton pheasant.* Reg's first feeble, rational thought since stepping from the lagoon was that of Louis Pasteur, the brilliant scientist with the passion for true science. The more his revolutionary mind discovered, the humbler and more sincere Pasteur's faith in the God he could not confine to the laboratory.

Reg dropped to his knees and rubbed sweaty palms against bare thighs. He looked up at the black wall of skin and bone and flesh that loomed twenty feet above and swallowed. Every fiber of his being roaring in protest, Reg Danson reached out a shaky hand, hesitated, then touched *Mokele-mbembe.*

The skin felt tough and leathery like sun-baked cowhide. A tremor, hardly a ripple, passed beneath the skin as if the canine with the bad dream were involuntarily twitching. But these were soft puppy twitchings, and Danson was strangely moved.

He couldn't imagine killing one of these giants. In case of emergency, though, he knew the beast's special vulnerability was those same dread, cold-blooded eyes he'd stared into after the ca-noe dumping. Dragons had excellent night vision, so the theory went, endowed by the Creator with roomy skull cavities for the larger than normal optic lobes required. That meant the pathway from the eye to the brain was broad and unobstructed. Shoot them in the skull plate between the eyes and it would be as ineffective as firing on a tank with a .22. But shoot through the eye and it's lights out—provided you've brought a gun along at all.

He placed a palm flat against the creature's side and felt a deep, regular reverberation from within. Life—enormous, liquid, throbbing life—surged within the beast said to be extinct. *God, how like you to keep to your ways despite the puny protestations of man! Lord Jehovah, how great Thou art!* He spread his arms wide, flattened the other palm against the beast, and slowly, gingerly leaned in and laid his left ear and cheek against the hide.

It was all rough plane and chin bristle like his dad's face brushing against soft infant skin. Conway Danson had loved to launch a morning whisker attack upon his son, rubbing the tender little boy's skin pink with a man's stubble.

Reg could have embraced the monster forever. To touch, to feel, to "hold" behemoth was beyond exhilaration.

He heard the immense lungs swooshing oxygen to the tissues and vital organs within. He felt along the backbone and imagined the great train of fifteen vertebrae forming the mainframe upon which this thirty-ton colossus hung. He tried to comprehend the musculature, the neurology, the skeletal coordination demanded to hoist sixty thousand pounds off the ground and to propel it over land and through water with the agility of a fish.

The beast that had attacked him in the pool seemed far removed from the beast in repose.

Quietly, carefully, Danson stood and felt along to the narrowing of the big rump into the incredible tail "like a cedar." It wrapped out of sight around the animal's front. He knew that between the hip sockets, deep down where the pelvis attached to the vertebral column, was the afterbrain. In a massive swelling of nerve tissues at the end of the spinal cord existed a kind of second brain that, though it did not think, orchestrated the complex reflexes that moved hind legs and tail muscles so far removed from the first brain high in the cranial cavity. This powerful locomotion enabled the heavy creatures to lift, swing, and curl their tails and to even, upon occasion, rise up on their hind feet to reach the succulent growth in the tops of the trees.

Reg's heart thumped with the insistence of a jungle drum. Did he have the guts to go to the other side and inspect what his father would have called "the business end" of the creature? Even if he'd wanted to, he wouldn't—couldn't—stop now.

Feeling the way down the tail, he went twenty feet before being able to wrap arms around the appendage. Here, it draped up and over one hind leg. He placed a hand on it and hopped over the tail like a kid vaulting a low fence.

Danson found himself in a "pen" formed by the tail, the leg, and the rump, but he was too giddy with the improbability of his position to worry. The ground was in deep shadow on this side of the beast at rest between Reg and the moon's brilliant beam. He stumbled into the creature's foot in the darkness and experienced a slicing pain.

"Ow-ooh!" he exclaimed, the sound of it like a megaphone in church. Clapping one hand over his mouth, he shrank back against the dark protection of the beast's heaving side.

Leviathan shifted again, shooting its foot straight out as if it had gone numb, and tightening the curl of its tail. Reg slammed against the dinosaur's hip, turning in time to avoid losing a nose and some teeth but taking a ringing slap in the ear. He pressed hard against the reptile's thick skin, barely daring to look, but sensing the raising of the great neck like the boom on a derrick. His eyes went wide with awe.

The sight would be with him forever. The long, slender neck swished up through the moonlight in a fluid, sinewy motion like a mammoth nightcrawler feeling its way forward. Only the head at the end was a flat, angular wedge like the head on a rattlesnake. Its eyes lay deep-set in bony caverns, as empty of living emotion as a dead cat's. The head bobbed and weaved, and nostrils like bullet holes snuffled the air. It sought the source of the disturbance. It smelled for Reg.

Suddenly terror-stricken, Danson was torn between burrowing into the creature's joints and folds, or making himself as small as possible so as not to apply any telltale pressure on the thing's body. Before he decided, *Mokele-mbembe* opened its mouth.

A dazzling orange stream of fire blasted the air a dozen yards in front of the monster, illuminating the night and the surrounding bestiary with startling clarity. It issued forth with the sound of gas jets igniting and the stinging heat of it burned like the sun.

The air stank of sulphur and elephant bedding. Reg's eyes burned.

"God, please, no!" he yelled, throwing up his hands protectively. He braced for the stampede.

The monster herd did not move. The creature opened its mouth in a widening chasm, the jaws unhinging like a viper's. They snapped shut in less than a blink and the flame ceased as suddenly as it had appeared. The derrick lowered its boom and the terrible snout came to rest with a nasal nickering of contentment less than six yards from the quaking Danson. Its awful eyes were closed in peaceful slumber.

For several minutes, Reg didn't move, waiting for the beast to reawaken, waiting for his own heart to climb down from the trees. When his mind could again string more than two words together in logical sequence, he almost laughed at the relief the realization brought with it. *The thing yawned. That's all. Impressive, for sure, but just a casual "I'm too tired to check the locks, would you mind, dear?" kind of midnight yawn.*

"Sheesh!" said Danson under his breath. Both his legs felt as if they would give out any time.

When after a few more minutes nothing more dramatic than the usual nocturnal moanings had occurred, Reg vaulted back over the tail and put a good thirty feet between himself and the nearest sauropod.

Ten or fifteen minutes crept past before the old explorer's curiosity peeked around the corners of uncertainty. So did the pain in his leg. He looked down at a crimson smear seeping over his shin from a jagged wound three inches below the knee.

"How'd I ever . . ." he muttered. Wincing, he packed a handful of mossy grasses into the cut. "There's no broken beer bottles on *this* beach . . . how'd I . . ." It dawned on him then. When he'd tripped over the creature's foot, he must have caught the leg on a claw. He remembered the three sharp indentations in the sand at the end of each of the giant footprints that led away from the hippo kill. The thought both fascinated and made him anxious. To get nicked on a dinosaur's claw was a rare, even exhilarating, experience. To not know what diseases they might carry was disturbing. Cuts in the tropics became easily infected and sometimes failed to heal in the damp atmosphere. He would have to keep it clean.

Vowing next time to wear asbestos and a flak jacket—even just shoes would help, he thought wryly—Reg suddenly felt very tired himself. He laid down on a soft patch of sand, facing the mighty creatures. Scientists believed the brain of an apatosaurus— if that's what this was a cousin to—was no bigger than a human fist and that the average elephant was a good twenty times smarter. He wished those lab jockeys and armchair theoreticians could join him now. They wouldn't be able to revise fast enough.

At that pleasant thought, Reg Danson meditated on the twenty-third Psalm, drifting off to sleep around "Thou preparest a table before me in the presence of mine enemies . . ."

▼

It was somewhere in the predawn glow that Danson felt the earth move.

He was having a heated discussion with Andrew Carnegie about the wealthy man's hankering for a dinosaur skeleton "big as a barn" for the new wing of his Pittsburgh museum. Impossible, Danson told him, for one as big as Carnegie's ego simply did not exist. They finally settled on a fair-sized sauropod from Utah which Reg magnanimously named after Mrs. Carnegie—*Apatosaurus louisae*. After all, Carnegie could be a generous patron when the mood suited him, and erstwhile paleontologists did well to keep that firmly in mind.

A sharp, thudding vibration knocked Reg back into the present. He bolted up on his elbows, blinking away the sleep. There in the half light between moonset and sunrise towered three of the gigantic sauropods. A fourth rolled onto the pillars of its legs, rising hind legs first like a horse. Reg looked frantically about him and saw that he was lying in an open area that had been trampled flat, scores of huge footprints all about and beneath him. The vegetation was ragged and low-cropped for a quarter mile in any direction, having long since become food for the immense residents. He was a sitting duck.

The flames began to fly, and the mighty creatures turned in his direction. Reg flopped onto his belly and scrambled lizardlike toward the lagoon. He felt exposed in the coming day and a little foolish. "Nature boy!" he snorted derisively. He fervently hoped his lily whiteness didn't attract undue attention.

He slid into the water without a sound.

The rogue behemoth watched the white creature slither awkwardly into the lagoon. Unlike the others, the rogue hadn't grown complacent in the centuries its kind had spent unmolested in the region of the lagoon. Its tiny mind processed only three basic instincts: the need for food and water, the need to reproduce its own kind, and the necessity to keep its kingdom free of threat.

The first instinct was the one behemoth awoke to each day. At dawn, the herd moved out into the lush swampland, each sauropod in search of its daily requirement of one and a half tons of nutrient-rich vegetation, replenished by the rapid growth of the rain forest environment. Stomachs sated by nightfall, the monsters turned to one another to satisfy the second instinct before sleep overtook them. But so much energy was consumed in feeding that actual mating took place but once or twice in thirty days.

The third instinct for protection was little exercised among the great monsters who had, until now, no natural enemies, not even man. Three times the height of a giraffe and possessed of a strength greater than a dozen elephants, behemoth ruled Likoula Swamp. The pygmies were a minor distraction and easily killed. They now kept farther into the forest, back from the rivers and wetlands, their fear a scent easily followed if necessary. But behemoths rarely ventured into the deeper forest, dealing with the pygmy people mainly when they confused their fishing rights with the monsters' lordship of the waters.

Except for the rogue. It roamed wherever it pleased, erratic and irrational in its movements, as unpredictable to its own kind as to other beasts. Its minimal intelligence was further eroded by a cancerous growth on the sacral brain at the base of its tail. To rotate in any direction produced searing pain. To mate was agony.

It had attacked the only egg-ready female in the herd, crushing the young inside the mother. It had challenged a younger and smaller male to an underwater fight in the lagoon. The reluctant opponent drowned when the rogue simply sat on the younger beast until its lungs burst.

And now the rogue didn't like the white thing invading the lagoon. It looked like a man, but bigger and albino in appearance. Even its stink was different from pygmy stink. What had it been doing on the land near the herd?

The rogue watched the white creature swim toward the wooden gate, the skin of its back flashing white in the morning light like the belly of a fish. A primeval hunger rumbled deep within the cavern of its stomach. The rogue tossed its head side to side in anger and spit fire into the face of another having just lumbered to its feet from a bed of reeds. The second monster screeched in pained protest, swinging its tail in a reflex of self-defense. The tail thudded heavily against the rogue's legs, sending a jolt of pain through the spine into the diseased sacral brain. The rogue turned, unhinged its jaws, and clamped its mouth onto the throat of what instinct now declared to be an adversary.

From somewhere deep in its loins came a rush of virility and the rogue's jaws locked into place. The other sauropod's strength was no match for the crazed attacker and instead of fighting back, it attempted to twist free of the powerful bite that cut off its breathing. With a sharp snap, its neck broke and the heavy body crashed to earth.

Reg heard the concussion of the fall, paused, and looked back over his shoulder. The conquering rogue stamped on the head of the vanquished sauropod, then craned its neck skyward, sprayed the air with fire, and wailed in triumph. Breathing a prayer of gratitude that he wasn't still tiptoeing among the herd, Reg again made for the gate. Their tranquilizer gun was of questionable use against something that large. They'd have to encircle the herd and find a youngster with lesser bulk and thinner, more tender skin. He wondered if they behaved toward their young the way female grizzlies did theirs when threatened. If so, the Great Dinosaur Expedition would need the firepower of the Fifth Armored Division to make any headway at all.

The rogue wasn't satisfied with its kill. It had ended too quickly. The pain in its tail and the burning in its loins would not be silenced. With a screech of rage, the behemoth barged down the shore, covering the distance with the speed and alacrity of a starved crocodile.

Danson reached the gate just as the dragon plunged forward into the lagoon, not a scant hundred yards behind, creating a minor tidal wave like the launching of an ocean liner. Reg whirled around in time to see just the great humping back arc into a deep dive. He gulped a hasty breath and went under.

Arms and legs were leaden with fear. Where's the opening? Why's everything so murky? His eyes stung and his lungs held too little air.

Any second his flailing feet would be swallowed up by the creature, and he would feel himself sliding down the dragon's throat. He would die there, squeezed and suffocated by the contracting muscles forcing him down into a sea of acid.

Fingers groped at the widening between land and wood. Desperately he forced a way into the gap, lacerating skin on rough bark, ramming through.

*Mokele-mbembe* reached the gate, turned, and battered the barrier with its awesome bulk. Wooden stakes bowed outward, knocking against Danson's back, the thudding snap of timbers loud like underwater thunder.

The gate held.

Reg prayed for and received new strength. Shooting to the surface, he gobbled air and raced down the avenue of orchids, their beauty dimmed by danger. He reached the place where he'd fought the *griot,* but the unconscious body of Ngomba was gone, a few drops of dried blood on leaves and rocks the only sign of a struggle.

One thought alone drove all others from Danson's racing mind. *He's gone back to kill Jigs . . . little Kimboki . . . Ndoki. I'm so stupid . . . should have tied him up . . . should have gone back to camp and somehow convinced the others to surrender, that their griot had been vanquished. The gun!? I've got to get the gun . . . oh, Lord, don't let him find the gun . . .*

He scrambled onto shore, heart in his throat, sucking air. He slipped, banged his shins. *Nothing looks the same! Where's the rock!?* He saw it, fell upon it, wrenched the rock away.

It was there, all there, the gun, the Bible, the clothes. Reg felt sick relief, a sudden release of the strain inside. He sobbed, grateful, shoulders shaking weakly.

"Welcome, white Danson," said a deep voice behind.

Reg stood and turned, bringing the gun, grasped in both hands, to chest level, arms extended. Ngomba, tall and magnificent in stature, stood with bow drawn, arrow aimed straight at Reg's heart.

The big chief's face, nose broken and swollen, blood caked about the mouth and lips, was fixed in a morose scowl. The gold earring was tarnished with dried blood and the ear around it fat with infection.

"You have met the Strong One," said Ngomba, voice thickened by the ruined nose. "I think to kill you now would be more humane than to leave you to *Mokele-mbembe*—and so much more satisfying!" With an evil, lopsided grin, he released the arrow.

It struck Danson in the right shoulder muscle with searing force, knocking him to the ground. The gun flew from his hands and clattered among the stones.

*Poisoned, God? How shall I die? Why? I want to live!*

Ngomba laughed sourly at the stricken look in the explorer's eyes, the explorer who had entered his kingdom and ruined his rule. "That arrow will not kill you, white Danson. I did not dip it in the poison. But this one"—and here he strung another arrow and drew it taut—"carries damnation in its tip. In less than twenty heartbeats you will be no more."

From behind Ngomba came a cracking and wrenching of wood. Reg watched in horror the crazed rogue dragon breaking through the wooden barrier in a seething mass of foaming water and splintering timbers. On it came, spitting fire and wailing in fury, churning the corridor to paradise into a frothing maelstrom.

"Rise, white Danson, and face the Strong One! Feel the fiery breath of death on your face. The poison will stop your heart and the last sight you will take to your grave will be that of mighty Ngomba and the Strong One together, unquenchable, immortal, indestructible!"

Reg grabbed the shaft of the arrow imbedded in his flesh, squeezed his eyes shut, grit his teeth, and yanked the cursed object out. Ngomba laughed. Reg got to his feet, retrieved the gun, and straightened to face Ngomba and the charging monster at the *griot's* back. Ngomba laughed again maniacally. In answer, the creature's deranged wails filled the forest with the blare of insanity; its powerful, muscled torso forced the water from the channel and filled Reg's sight with the dread vision of raw, mindless slaughter.

And then, as if catching sight of Ngomba for the first time, the creature abruptly stopped its charge, the tidal wave preceding it onto shore, knocking waist-deep into the two men who braced themselves against it. The creature towered above them, gulping greedily like a boa constrictor swallowing a monkey by degrees, the throat throbbing and rippling with the sound of loud, wet sucking.

"MMMMMMM . . . MMMMMMM . . . MMMMMMM . . . MMMOOOO . . . KAAALAAAY . . . MMMMMMM . . . MMMBEMMM . . . BAAAY!" The awful, hypnotic summons originated in Ngomba's throat, then rained from the trees above and echoed from the rocks below. It seemed at first to placate the monster, supplanting the cold, vacant stare with an almost quizzical expression. The enormous serpent head lowered, bobbing and weaving to the rhythmic chant. A forked tongue slithered from the mouth, long, dark, and thick as an eel, testing the air, sorting with split second precision the dust from the fragrances, the animal scent from the humidity, the fear from the defiance. The glossy tongue wrapped around the creature's snout like a blackened slab of bad meat before disappearing into its mouth with a moist slurp.

The dragon tilted its head downward, seeking the source of the stupefying drone. Water dripped from its leathery hardness and the air escaped with the hollow roar of wind through a metal pipe. The jaws parted wide like a suitcase falling open. Down . . . down . . .

Ngomba's muscles tightened, fixing the tip of the arrow on a spot over Danson's left breast. He drew the bow back another two inches, stretched to the limit, lifting the mighty arms and shoulders in preparation for release.

Reg aimed the pistol, jaw locked in dread for what he must do. He only hoped a bullet traveled faster than a pygmy arrow.

The shot fired true. The monster's right eye burst on impact, the slug carving a lethal path to the brain. At the same instant, the suitcase snapped shut on Ngomba's head and neck, choking off the chant.

The powerful arms jerked skyward and with a vibrant *th-wang!* the arrow sliced sharply upwards, streaking for the treetops, silver droplets glistening in its wake.

Reg started forward and stopped, horrified. The *griot's* feet dangled off the ground, his strong torso disappearing by inches down the beast's expanding gullet. Soon the body ceased its jerking and went slack.

Danson grabbed his clothes and the Bible and ran blindly along the trail back toward the Ologu encampment. He felt through the pads of his pounding feet the moment mighty leviathan crashed to earth, dead on impact.

The female watched the man creature flee the Maya Maya. Every cell of her great bulk telegraphed the message to pursue. But without knowing why, she sensed danger from the tiny beast that walked on two feet. The white one was more intrusive, and certainly bolder, than the smaller brown ones. Was it a threat to the food supply?

The pockets of fat stored in her tail, thighs, and neck were becoming thinner. The herd would have to move soon in search of more plenteous habitat. Each day, they had to range farther than the one before.

Six-foot shoulder blades shifted, and the she-dragon moved from midstream, hauling out onto the bank where her fallen mate lay, a fountain of blood draining from the shattered eye. Lowering her armored muzzle, she sniffed the dead rogue without passion. The male had hurt her on numerous occasions and had eaten her eggs in fits of madness. Life would be less difficult now that the rogue's rage was ended.

But he'd still been her mate and instinct demanded that she not only find him but hunt and destroy that which had taken his life. The sauropod nuzzled the strange bulge caught in the rogue's throat, sniffed the sticky flow of congealing blood blackening beneath its load of flies, and turned in the direction the man creature had fled. For several minutes, its flat head weaved and bobbed, filtering the air through flaring nostrils, processing every scent and nuance of aroma.

Satisfied, it started forward to kill.

# 25

G ussie Jackson knew the cotton never would have gotten picked without a song. Hymns, hums, and hoot-a-longs separated the living and the dead in Hog Hump, Georgia, where she'd spun the dream cotton of her vivid fantasy life. Her mam was as much to blame as Gussie's imagination, however, having planted in her daughter the rich tales of the ruling Kongo kings and the haughty, self-assured queens of Africa.

"Uhm-m-m-m-m, yo-o-o-o" she murmured contentedly, fingers wielding the quilting needle with the swift, deliberate certainty of the conductor's baton. The quilt was new, a vict'ry cloth, maybe 300 or more hours of work, worth every stitch. They'd returned her needles. It was either that or let her screech. How could a voice in one so small carry like that? Gussie smiled. They'd never had to call someone home from the fields.

It had come to her in the night, kind of a release like the passing of a newborn from the womb, free at last. God gave her a peace, and she'd felt free enough to dance the possum ragged; and she had done it right there in the room at Western State Hospital for the mentally ill. With crazy Netta grinnin' from the next bed like some blame fool hound dog, Sweet Pone Jackson swayed and swirled, then stamped the beat on tiny feet, imagining little puffs of village dust rising from the cool linoleum. She sang, "*Jumbo, Danson, eoto mongo! Eoto mongo!* Hello, Danson, thank you! Thank you!"

The wicked witch and one of his lizards were dead.

She didn't know how she knew. Just that powerful knowing. You prayed for something like worrying a cranky root out of the ground. You pulled and you pushed and you grunted until your veins like to burst, and then when you was past thinking it could ever break loose, *whap!* the dirty thing snapped off and sent you thump on your rump. God never quite says he told you so at those times—too much the gentleman for that—but there's the pages of the Good Book rifflin' in the wind remindin' in print bold as a wart on the end of the nose that He alone is the rewarder of the faithful.

Then like manna in the mornin', some sass-mouth orderly had that day left her some of the prettiest swatches of tingly blue she'd ever laid eyes on. She'd whooped, squared her scrawny shoulders in the too-big robe, and commenced to forming the indigo bits into a center panel shaped like Mam's open Bible. The beast of the old quilt conquered by the Book of the new.

She stopped abruptly, as if to an unseen command. She glanced sharply about, her skin prickly, her stomach all odd-feeling. Then the feeling passed. Gas, she reckoned.

Hair uncombed, face unwashed, Gussie Jackson bent over the Book, humming. The hospital awakened around her, but she never knew if it came near. Nor cared.

# 26

**R**eg Danson made it halfway back to camp before the trembling overpowered him. He felt suddenly cold and old and sick. He pulled on clothes that didn't feel like his before sinking to the ground, clutching Richard Bascomb's plastic-bound Bible to his chest.

"My God, my God!" he sobbed. "Have I not first sought after your righteousness? Why has it come to *this?* Why?"

He rocked back and forth on aching knees, every muscle clenching and unclenching involuntarily from the strain of what he'd seen. His wounded shoulder throbbed. The jungle steamed and simmered, sunlight dripping like melted butter in rivulets of yellow condensation from leaf to leaf and finally to earth. Ngomba met a gruesome end, and Reg killed a legendary creature he'd come to prove and protect. It wasn't supposed to happen that way. He should have found and documented one of the natural wonders of the world. Instead, he'd found—and engaged in—wanton slaughter. A people dying at the hands of a bogus king; the most astounding animal ever created a mindless killer. Reg felt cheated, disgusted. Again, he'd chased after a mystery and stumbled over a mess.

". . . Do not under any circumstances kill or attempt to remove one of these beasts . . ." Bascomb's handwritten instructions had read. *Well, that's it, Bascomb. You can just get yourself another project coordinator. I'm going to go sell salt water taffy down at the seashore.*

He shouted his despair. "Bascomb, you knew this would happen! You promised me help and guidance and you gave me nothing I don't already have!" He squeezed the Bible viciously as if to wring it of its contents, ready to fling it from him. He rocked forward instead, banging his head softly against the book's smooth plastic cover, wetting it with a mix of sweat and tears.

" . . . all you'll need for a successful mission is contained in this package . . . That's what you said!" Could Bascomb have forgotten to include maps, directions, *answers?*

The explorer began to pant from the heat and a mounting panic that he'd blown this assignment, that God was finished with Reg Danson and Likouala Swamp would be his final resting place. What was one more set of bleached bones in a land laden with bones and fossils? Perhaps some future enigmatist or crypto-zoological weirdo would unearth the skeletal remains of *Reginus dansonia* and speculate about the abnormally small size of its cranial cavity. It didn't take a whole lot of brains to botch a job as royally as he'd done this one.

"The Lord gives and the Lord takes away, blessed be the . . ." *The Lord gives.* The thought made Reg stop rocking and stare at the Bible in his hands. "Sent from God," he mumbled, wonderingly, tearing the book open. *The bookmark!* He flipped to the place marked by a slender rectangle of plain card stock with a simple cross printed in black ink on both sides. A passage from the prophet Hosea, highlighted in brilliant neon yellow, leapt from the page: "There is no truth or mercy or knowledge of God in the land. By swearing and lying, killing and stealing and committing adultery; they break all restraint, with bloodshed upon bloodshed. *Therefore the land will mourn; and everyone who dwells there will waste away with the beasts of the field and the birds of the air; even the fish of the sea will be taken away.*"

Beside the highlighted passage was penned: "Habakkuk 3:17 & 18." With shaking hands, Reg fumbled the pages, then found the passage, also highlighted in yellow. "Though the fig tree may not blossom, nor fruit be on the vines; though the labor of the olive may fail, and the fields yield no food; though the flock may be from the fold, and there be no herd in the stalls—yet I will rejoice in the LORD, I will joy in the God of my salvation."

And all on its own, a third passage leapt to mind with startling clarity: "When I shut up the heaven and there is no rain, or command the locusts to devour the land, or send pestilence among My people, if My people who are called by My name, will humble themselves, and pray and seek My face, and turn from their wicked ways, *then I will hear from heaven, and will forgive their sin and heal their land.*"

"That's the key to the people's ruin," Danson shouted, leaping to his feet. "That's why they're starving, why the game remains scarce. They've bought a lie and lived a lie. They must overcome Ngomba's sorcery and turn back to God and their land will be healed!"

He charged up the embankment, unable to feel his legs and not caring, running like a condemned man just pardoned, away from the gallows and up into the light.

I want a miracle!" shouted Jigs Wiggins at the top of his lungs. "I'm sick of this stinking hole, this stinking lack of food, this stinking jungle. I want a miracle, do you hear me, a five-star, gold-encrusted, million carat, honest-to-goodness, shut-'em-up-in-Missouri miracle!"

Reg knew it was Jigs a hundred yards off. The tone was decidedly different from the spiritual-singing evangelical fervor of two days before, but it came from the same soloist.

They weren't at the old camp, having moved lock, stock, and barrel to a new location on the banks of the Maya Maya. Jigs had tactfully convinced them that should they require help, they had a better chance of being found if they weren't so isolated. But new huts weren't even up yet. The elders stood in a little huddle, thin and worn, watching white Wiggins rant at heaven. A listless Kimboki threw rocks at an ill-tempered parrot that kept just out of range, berating the little fellow for his bad aim.

"Thank God, they're safe," Reg whispered.

He peeked through the trees at the scene of utter dejection. The people looked pitifully emaciated and empty of spirit. They were leaderless, foodless, and joyless. No medicine man to make medicine. No will to fight on. No vision.

That, thought Danson with a prayer, was about to change.

He stepped from the trees. For the life of him, he couldn't think how to begin. "Hello," was all he said.

Kimboki broke into a dead run, slamming head-on into Reg's waiting arms. "Re-edge!" cried the little Ologu in delight. "Re-edge!"

Wiggins turned toward them haltingly like a man with a bad back. He'd been prepared to smile, but he'd lost it. Danson had returned alone.

"Where's help?" he asked huskily. "Why have you come back without help?"

The Ologus murmured among themselves, but their concern was plain. White Danson had come back and Ngomba had not. Had their king died a third time?

"Bigshot?" Reg asked.

"Gone." Wiggins threw the word out and away, wanting the answer to his question. "Animal kill."

"Then we're saved!" declared Reg with a wide grin. "I went back to the lagoon, Jigs. There's a whole herd. I touched the creature, even swam with one, although I wouldn't recommend it!"

Wiggins slid the unlit pipe between pursed lips like an angry sword swallower. "I've been knocking my brains out trying to placate these people and you're off swimming with dinosaurs? I could have been killed!"

"Not with your diamond personality," said Reg sheepishly.

Wiggins glared.

"Ngomba's dead." Reg took no pleasure in the pronouncement and the people stirred at the mention of the name.

Wiggins chewed the pipestem. "You kill him?"

"*Mokele-mbembe*," replied Reg. The Ologus visibly flinched.

"Where's the gun?" Wiggins pressed.

"I don't know. But the bullet—the last bullet brought the monster down."

Wiggins ripped the pipe from his mouth and flung it from him, storming forward and grabbing Danson by the lapels. "You *shot* and *killed* one of these things? Are you mad? Where? How far from here?"

"This end of the channel to the lagoon—"

"The bloody *gate* is down?"

"Well, yeah, the creature broke through—"

Reg did not finish before the earth began to thud. Concussions from a massive body in motion, each pulsation gaining in intensity, quaking up from the ground, coming their way. They heard a nearby *crack!* and then another.

"That," said Wiggins tightly, "would be the mate!"

"Mate?" asked Reg dumbly. Then it came rushing home that some reptiles, as if through a sixth sense, seek out their dead mates.

They ran for the far side of the camp just as the beast thundered into the clearing, saw the running, shouting people, and threw out its massive front legs to halt its forward momentum. Chunks of earth as big as Ologu huts flew up on impact and rained down, flattening a cooking table and burying a little girl who'd been playing with a string toy.

Instead of running, two women clawed frantically at the earth and dug the baby out. Reg wondered fleetingly at the new shoot of mother love in that one, desperate act.

The tall, loathsome creature towered thirty feet overhead, rippling along its entire length from the sudden stop. Its heavy, wedged head bobbed, fury in its bulging orangy eyes. The jaws parted with an almost metallic clank and twenty feet of flame roared from the mouth and outshone the sun. Charred leaves blew horizontally before falling as cinders into the people's hair.

The Ologus screamed and whimpered beneath the appalling gaze of behemoth.

The monster bent nearer the earth, its neck a switchback of cobra coils, and fixed on Reg Danson. The wet, probing tongue tasted the air, sensing the explorer's vital signs. "Get me the tranquilizer gun and syringe full of juice!" Reg commanded the missionary, not taking his eyes off the face of extinction.

The tail flicked, then swung in a lightning swift arc, scouring the camp of the people's poor belongings, catching a scraggly camp dog in its sweep. The yelping dog stumbled and fell, crushed flat beneath the tail as big as a tree.

A buzzing roar from behind them, downriver, grew louder by the second and muffled, as if shouted through a mattress, Reg heard Wiggins shout, "A boat! A police boat!"

Wiggins thrust the elephant gun into Reg's hands and looked frantically about for anything else in defense against the Strong One. The beast's head zoomed forward, filling Danson's vision with its hoary grotesqueness. When it seemed but an arm's length off, Reg lifted the rifle to his cheek and fired into the cavernous yellow maw that gaped before him.

The hideous mouth closed on the rifle barrel and tore it from Reg's hands as easily as a stick from an infant's. Tilting its head back, the creature swallowed the rifle whole.

And then it came for Reg Danson, jaws split wide, a terrible hissing and roaring enveloping him from ahead and behind.

"Hold on, but prepare to jump!" Tony Danson yelled to his passengers and steered straight for the bank and the looming, monstrous chest of leather and muscle.

"JUMP!" Four of the occupants of the boat dove over the side and a fifth was pushed. The emptied boat hit the shore full bore and became an airborne missile. Reg rolled clear just before the long, pointed prow pierced like a javelin, slicing cleanly through the monster's chest wall, deflating the lungs and severing the rope-thick arteries linking the chain of hearts.

The monster crumpled where it stood like a torn hot air balloon. The long, sinewy neck went slack as unravelled thread and the thick, plated head of leviathan slammed into the dust, leaking blood from its nostrils. The boat's prop blades chewed at the ground, then surrendered with a wrenching CLANG! A pall of acrid smoke seeped from the engine housings, wreathing the creature's neck in a funeral collar of sooty black.

*Mokele-mbembe* struggled onto its front legs without lifting its head, lurching forward a few feet like a crippled camel, digging a furrow in the ground with its hard snout. The hindquarters refused to cooperate and with a final heart-breaking bawl and a creak of useless limbs, the creature ceased to move.

For seconds that stretched into eternity, no one else moved. The only sound was the gurgle of blood spouting from the hole in the monster's chest cavity and the residual, haunting echo of the beast's last cry. Then all was pandemonium.

"DAD!" Tony grabbed Reg in a mighty bear hug, shocked at his father's haggard appearance and thin, scrawny feel.

"Tony?!" exclaimed Reg in amazement, certain he was in the enthusiastic grip of an apparition. "Where did you—how did you—"

Then he was being introduced to a grimy, sodden American diplomat while bloodied, limping officers of the People's Republic of the Congo herded the tattered, shell-shocked remnant of the Ologus into the center of the clearing.

Conspicuously absent from the excited greetings, shouts, and brisk commands was the loud, confident voice of the master of Sangha Mission. He too had seen a ghost.

"K—Kay?!" he stammered. The years had been very kind to her, the beauty of old lace and fine, lacquered wood in the sweet smile and the graceful, refined way in which she moved. She wore the locket she'd given him, and his old Timex watch was strapped to her dainty wrist. Even soaked to the skin, she looked as if she belonged on a giant screen, millions awaiting her every word and subtle expression. As always, despite the horrors around her, she exuded warmth and refuge to the man—the only man—she'd ever loved.

He felt at once elated and shabby. He had been able to give her nothing before, and he greeted her with nothing now. She shouldn't see him like this, a foolish steward whose talents lay largely buried among the twisted roots of the rain forest floor. He wanted to be able to give her so much. Instead, he stood before her without even a clean shirt to his name.

"Kay, sweet Kay," he said, choked with emotion. He sank to his knees, legs no longer able or willing to stand in the presence of Mrs. Wiggins. Tears coursed down the whiskery cheeks, losing themselves in the red tangle of beard.

Gentle, slender fingers caressed his head and pressed him close.

"Oh, Kay, you don't deserve this. How I wanted to give you diamonds, but all you ever got were rhinestones. I worked the mines; I took my pay in diamonds. For years, I stupidly hoarded a small pouch of them, waiting for a time when I would be worthy of you, a time that never came. Yesterday, God took those diamonds away . . ."

"Shhh," Kay murmured, ruffling his bushy head. "Edward Wiggins, you proud old goat, I *have* my diamond!" She extended her ring finger. The sun sparked off the modest stone he had given her a lifetime ago. Then, so young and ill-equipped, he'd slipped it on her hand in a burst of blind love. She'd teased about the size of the "phonograph needle" diamond and loved him back with all the tenderness and adoration any woman could have for a man. Against all odds, the ring had remained there through years of silence, years of uncertainty.

Except once. "After you left for Africa, I pawned it to pay the bills, then worked six months at two jobs to ransom it back!"

She cupped his face in her hands, and he saw that she was weeping too. "The kids love you, Jigs. They miss you. They're married now. You're a grandfather!"

She stooped and unsnapped the small, battered suitcase at her feet. Inside were crammed bundles of letters, some yellow with age, others more recently written, all soggy with the dark Maya Maya River. Jigs looked at her quizzically.

"Love letters to you. Thirty years worth," she said, running her fingers over them. "I never sent them, of course, not wanting to fill your bull head with any more confusion than it already contained. Until you could make peace with God and forgive yourself for the foolishness of youth, there was little I could do but pray for you. The letters were my way of talking with you, of saying how much I loved you, though you could not love yourself. I saved them so you could see you're still a big, big hit in Minnesota." She tried to smile. "I—I'm sorry they got wet . . ." She looked suddenly stricken, as if her now illegible love for him expressed in the saturated mess of letters was as irretrievable as Jigs's lost diamonds.

Jigs thought of his empty tobacco pouch and began to laugh, a deep, rumbling exclamation of sheer joy. He jumped to his feet, swept Kay into his arms, and planted a kiss on the same girlish lips he'd known a generation before. "The Swahili have a saying, my dear Mrs. Wiggins. 'The daughters of lions are lions too!' I'd say you have borne that out in spades!"

She eyed him ruefully. "I—I'm afraid the pygmies torched the mission mourning for you. Are you ready to rebuild, to start over?"

Jigs paled. Then his face turned a stormy red, and he rammed his hands into his pockets, pacing the clearing irritably. "Why bother? Who'd want to stay in a country this backward? There's only one doctor for every five thousand people. Even the tap water in the capital has to be boiled! One in ten die in infancy, a man can't expect to live beyond forty-six years, illiteracy's running thirty-seven percent . . ." He trailed off. She was looking at him in that suspicious have-you-got-a-better-idea way of hers that hadn't changed with time.

"What about our little place in the Catskills?" he finished lamely.

Her fists were on her hips the way he'd left her thirty years before. Her eyes were laughing at him. "Edward Wiggins, you'd be as miserable in the Catskills as a dog with nothing to scratch!"

Jigs smiled, ran a hand through his matted hair, and gave her a mischievous wink. "Ah Kay, sweet, sweet Kay, first lady of

Sangha Mission! Could you come to love these exasperating people?"

She nodded determinedly. "I learned to love you, didn't I?" She kissed his forehead lightly.

He believed her. "What are your thoughts about the nutritional content of caterpillars?"

She wrinkled her nose.

"Theoretically speaking, that is," he added, and they both laughed. He put an arm around her. "Come, dear, and meet the rest of the family!"

After introductions all around, including a solemn presentation of the newcomers before the elders, Kay and Jigs visited with the Ologu women and children, Kimboki serving as delighted interpreter. The entire entourage moved further downstream away from the carnage and enjoyed a meal of dried fish, fresh fruit, and vegetables supplied by the government.

"Are we safe from more of . . . more of *those?*" Tony asked, waving a hand in the direction of the huge dead reptile.

"Safe?" replied Reg with a doleful smile. "You're far more likely to be struck by lightning in the bathtub than to encounter one of these again. We'll document this one and a male I killed upriver, but my recommendation to Bascomb will be to let them have their Shangri-la. Two destroyed in a single encounter with the outside world—" He shook his head sadly. "Not good odds."

Tony couldn't believe his ears. "And *not study* them in their natural habitat? Dad, this is the most incredible living discovery of the modern age! It would be irresponsible, unprofessional, *criminal* not to do scientific observation on this species! We could build a blind, reinforce it with timbers, bring in high-powered stun guns if you're afraid of a stampede, but do *nothing?* I don't believe it; it's not like you!"

Reg admired his handsome son, so full of vinegar and passion and righteous indignation. How alike they were. "Maybe," he answered. "Guess I'm a little close to it right now—and to have spilt so much rare blood in so short a time . . . give me a while to sort it through, okay?"

Tony let the air out of his fervor and smiled apologetically. "Sorry. I get that way sometimes."

"All the best bone and fossil fellows do," said his dad, clapping Tony on the back. "Nothing to apologize for."

Tony used Wiggins's "secret recipe" salve to dress his father's cuts and shoulder wound. The two Dansons fairly stumbled over each other in their eagerness to catch up on the events of the past two weeks. Mostly, it felt good to be together and alive. Tony felt the cesspool lid of his childhood memories slide back into place, the demons once again sealed safely within.

"Hey, buddy, whattaya say when we get back home, we go swimming, just the two of us?" Reg smiled at Tony and smacked a smear of salve on the young man's sunburned cheeks. His son had never looked so good.

Tony gave a mock grimace but gratefully spread the soothing ointment over his burning skin. "Sure, Dad, but I'd think once you've swam with dragons, the city pool might not cut it."

Reg thought of a father and son tumbling carefree through chlorinated water, far from the terrors of an uncharted swamp. It sounded wonderful. "Yeah, well, I'd just like to swim again where I'm in no immediate danger of having my legs chewed off at the knees. I'm funny that way. How's school?"

"School's great. And this little unscheduled field trip ought to do wonders for my anthropology midterm. Will you write me a note?" He grinned, happy to find his dad in need of no more than a good, safe swim and a few hot meals. Then his handsome features clouded. He couldn't put it off any longer. "Dad, I've got some hard news to tell you."

"Mom?! Is she—"

"She couldn't hold out, Dad. She passed away peacefully, no struggle. I'm awful sorry." Tony's voice caught.

Reg squeezed his eyes tightly shut, seeing again the strawberry blonde wig, smelling the Emeraude cologne, listening to her tales of Al Einstein. *God bless the dear old warrior. If St. Peter plays pinochle, he'd better steer clear of Carrie Danson!*

Reg took a deep breath and hugged Tony. "It wasn't unexpected, son. I felt the power of her prayers over and over again on this mission. I have a feeling her influence isn't going to diminish much even in death. Let's ask God to keep her memory and her righteous vision sharp in our minds in the days ahead." Their arms around each other, Reg and Tony gave thanks for the power of God that'd been wrapped up in the neat little package that was Carrie Danson.

Tony prayed too for Gussie Jackson, the odd black woman in the beige robe who seemed to know more than she let on. "What'd you think of *her?*" asked Reg quietly, remembering the toothless quilter's hair-raising outburst in Room 218 of the Powell Valley Convalescent Center.

"A little scary, but she was quilting the likeness of *Mokele-mbembe*," said Tony soberly. "To a *T*. It was her warning that you'd die if I didn't come. I couldn't shake it." He shivered despite the heat, staring over his father's shoulder at the stiffening contours of the witch's lizard. "She believed in the interconnectedness of succeeding generations. She said, 'It's up to me to hold the hand of the generation before.' I figured your hand needed holding." He gave his father a lopsided grin, and they prayed some more.

As they praised God for deliverance from evil, Reg felt the excitement of discovery return. Their unlikely rescue coming on the heels of the revelations in Bascomb's Bible was surely divine provision. He had to proclaim the good news he'd been given.

"Jigs!" he shouted. "Gather the people. God has a message for them!"

When the weary and the wary were gathered, they made a ragtag collection of humanity. White Wiggins and white Danson stood before them, Tony, Kay with an adoring Kimboki, the police officers, Ambassador Fulgate and Ndoki to one side. With the conviction of a man forever set free by the truth, Reg spoke.

## THE LOST KINGDOM

"You have feared *Mokele-mbembe* more than you have feared the Most High God." The voice resonated strongly among them, its timbre rich and firm. He read to them from Holy Scripture what happens to a people who lose faith in the Creator, choosing instead to worship the designs of their own hearts and minds. To follow the wickedness of Ngomba, to shed blood and offer sacrifice to the beast, resulted in a revolt of the land and its creatures. No longer would the forest give up its fruit willingly or in sufficient quantity to sustain long, purposeful life for a faithless pygmy people. They'd taken the Most High God for granted and forfeited His benefits to follow the manmade lies of a false prophet.

Translator Wiggins matched Danson's ardor and persuasion but outdid his animation with elaborate gestures and facial expressions. The Ologus appreciated sincerity in critical matters of state. They recognized that what Danson spoke so forcefully of meant no less than tribal life and death.

Reg paused and took a deep breath. He'd wrestled with what he was about to say next but received no warning to hold back. It had to be said. He looked at Jigs, knowing that what followed might carry as much meaning for the missionary as for the Ologus. He sucked his teeth, glanced at Tony, and went on.

"You are a forest people, and yours are forest ways. We who live in the far-off places are concerned for the destruction of the rain forests, your home, and the variety of life that they contain, some of which we are only beginning to understand, and still more about which we know nothing.

"That is why I have traveled far to find your home and the existence of creatures of great power which in my home we know little of. I came to find *Mokele-mbembe* and to do what I could to save this great beast and its kind that once roamed the earth. What I found was a wild animal, unreconciled to man and therefore vicious in the face of a perceived threat from man.

"What I think I've learned is that these creatures must be left to their sanctuary to live unharmed, as long as God sees fit. For *Mokele-mbembe* is no more inherently evil than a bird or a flower. He is no god, for you can see for yourselves that he bleeds and dies like all animals and can be killed by man.

"All creation is caught up in earth's travail resulting from man's evil ways. Things kill; things die; things become extinct. But to ascribe to that struggle supernatural powers, to worship anything other than the Most High God, is spiritual suicide. In my home, too many of us have chosen to worship wealth, power, and pleasure. Our land has also suffered because of it, yet I believe that only the faithfulness of those who worship the true God has kept us from total destruction."

Danson looked at the faces about him, unable to gauge the impact of his words. At least everyone looked interested, especially Jigs.

"Far more important than the fate of the Strong One is your fate, the fate of every human soul that walks this earth. Jesus the Christ, the Son of the Most High God, gave up His life for the human soul. If you would receive God's favor, if you would turn to Him in your hour of need and repent of your past wickedness, then He promises to forgive you and heal your land. It is what I and my son, white Wiggins and his wife, Ndoki and his dead brother, and all who trust in God have had to do.

"That is the only hope for the Ologus, the only way to reverse the certain death that comes from disobedience to the Most High. Ngomba is dead, consumed by the Strong One. Ngomba will not return, but it is possible that the Strong One will. You can have life everlasting if this day you choose to love and serve the one true God. You can join the Christian family at Sangha Mission where you can learn more about this God Almighty and His love for you from His ordained servant, white Wiggins."

Reg's throat felt parched, his heart sore with the desire to convince the people before him to bend the knee. But it was by no force of his own oratory that they would choose to believe. He felt exceedingly weak and ineffective. Could untold centuries of contrived human thinking be undone in so short a span?

Six elders stepped forward, tufts of white hair dotting their chests and bare heads, and the chief among them motioned at the Bible in Reg's hand and spoke earnestly to Wiggins. "He says he'd like you to point to the words you've read," Jigs said quietly.

The elders formed a half circle and Reg stood in their midst, slowly reading again the old yet fresh truths and following along with an index finger. When Wiggins translated, he held the Bible and traced the approximate words reconstituted in Ologu idioms.

Silence at first followed the dual readings, then intense and animated discussion between the six elders. The chief turned at last to Wiggins and held out both hands, palms up. The missionary asked a brief question and the old man nodded dreamily, peacefully, eyes closed. Wiggins placed the open Bible in the chief's hands and stepped back. The chief visibly trembled, raising both arms and the Bible toward heaven. Reg dared not breathe. They stood there on that tiny plot of ground in the primitive Congo where one-fifth of all the tropical rain forest in the world remained. The old man held time in the palms of his hands. When he opened his eyes at last, it was with a beseeching look at the sky. He spoke reverently, in the Bantu tongue.

"MBOTE!" The single word sounded loud in the hush. Again he said, "Mbote!" And again. His face beamed, lighting the wisps of ancient hair that encircled the smiling mouth.

Wiggins grinned. "He's telling God hello!"

The elder spoke again and rubbed his belly with a satisfied smile. Wiggins laughed. "He says from this day forward the Ologus shall worship the Most High God who swallows all other gods and is made full!"

. . . *All you'll need for a successful mission is contained in this package* . . . Bascomb's long shot, for the most part, had paid off. No need to reinvent the wheel, just roll the one you've got.

But at what price to leviathan? Did subduing the earth mean destroying the greatest of beasts? Reg fought the infernal questions. Only man was made in God's image.

He held the Bible out, sweeping the entire clearing with his arm extended. "Praise the LORD from the earth, you great sea creatures," he read from Psalm 148, " . . . beasts and . . . creeping things and flying fowl; kings of the earth and all peoples . . . young men and maidens; old men and children. Let them praise the name of the LORD for his name alone is exalted; his glory is above the earth and heaven . . . Praise the LORD!"

Ndoki shouted exuberantly and began to dance about the assembly. Reg shot Jigs a wondering look and received a jovial shrug in return. "Beats me," he jested. "My guess is it's roughly the equivalent of 'Hallelujah, brother!'"

Ndoki then broke into a Swahili freedom song Jigs had taught him, his voice a surprisingly beautiful high tenor. No sooner had he sung a line, than Wiggins's raspy bass echoed the translation for the Ologus:

*"Tuna oomba moongoo atawah lay!"*

"We're praying that the Lord will reign!"

*"Tuna oomba moongo atawah lay!"*

"We're praying that the Lord will reign!"

The beat was infectious and soon all gathered took up the chant and prayed *bwana* (God), *jesu* (Jesus), *christo* (Christ), *roho* (peace), and *apendo* (Spirit) to reign. Curiously, stoic Officer Akeley was among the most zealous of singers.

The old command and confidence were back in Jigs's every move and it reminded Reg of the market in Epuluville when he'd first laid eyes on the Pied Piper of Sangha with a snake and dagger tattoo. Now the man's congregation—and staff—had doubled, and there was no doubting who their shepherd was.

"Hey, Reverend Wiggins, sir," interrupted Reg, Kimboki riding his shoulders and catching the missionary by a sleeve. Reg shouted to be heard. "Did you ever get that miracle you were after?"

Jigs Wiggins gazed at Kay, Tony, and Ndoki linked arm-in-arm, trying their hardest to follow the Ologu leaders in the worship dance. "You know," he said, crossing both arms contentedly, "I believe I have!"

He watched a moment more, turned, and clapped his hands heavenward.

## THE END

# About the Author

**Clint Kelly,** publications specialist for Seattle Pacific University, is also a happily married father of four and a prolific freelance writer whose articles have appeared in a wide variety of periodicals from *American History Illustrated* to *Writer's Digest.* Kelly's former occupations include teacher, forest ranger, and wilderness expedition leader. He is the author of *Me Parent, You Kid! Taming the Family Zoo.* His novel *The Landing Place* was the first in this series.